DENNIE WENDT

HOOPER'S REVOLUTION

A NOVEL

The Unnamed Press
P.O. Box 411272
Los Angeles, CA 90041

Published in North America by The Unnamed Press.

1 3 5 7 9 10 8 6 4 2

Copyright © 2017 by Dennie Wendt

ISBN: 978-1944700164

Library of Congress Control Number: 2017934027

This book is distributed by Publishers Group West

Cover Photograph of Trevor Hockey by PA Photos Limited, London
Cover design by Meagan Tuhy and Dennie Wendt
Typeset by Jaya Nicely

Dedicated to my family.

The author and publisher would like to extend grateful acknowledgment to the Hockey family of Keighley, England, for allowing the use of Trevor Hockey's likeness on the cover.

Some people believe football is a matter of life and death.
I am very disappointed with that attitude. I can assure you it
is much, much more important than that.

— **Bill Shankly, Liverpool Football Club manager, 1959–1974**

I hardly even know what a soccer ball looks like.

— **Dick Walsh, North American Soccer League commissioner, 1968**

PROLOGUE

The New York Giganticos professional soccer team played for friends and family in the early '70s, on a bumpy patch of grass in a high school football stadium on Long Island. By the summer of '76 they played in the biggest stadium in the city, a baseball stadium, on a smooth, lush green lawn. And even with their big, beloved, beautiful New York home, they were too big for any one city now, too big even for Gotham. By 1976, they had ditched their "New" and their "York" and had become only the Giganticos. Like a band.

The Giganticos, defending American All-Star Soccer Association champions, weren't just the most famous soccer team in the world in 1976—they were the most famous *men* in the world in 1976. Nine of the ten best players from the 1974 World Cup had been signed by the Giganticos of the eight-year-old AASSA, as were the best players from six countries who hadn't qualified. The Giganticos had signed Zaire's best player and the Haitian who had scored against Italy and Argentina. Their names, said together, formed a Portuguese-Dutch-Slavic-Spanish-French-Italian-Flemish-German epic poem to the heroic and creative potential of the game. Virtually everyone in the team's lineup was in the twilight of his career, finishing up his playing days while hanging out in the Manhattan club scene with fat paychecks, lithe European models, and minimal fitness expectations.

With their expensive, decadent, almost comical roster—a confabulation of conjurers only America could assemble—the Giganticos traversed the planet like benevolent gods, vanquishing their opponents—and what opponents: The Giganticos went to Munich and Milan and Madrid... and they won! They went to Mexico and the Middle East and Africa... and won! The Giganticos went to London... and won! In ninety-minute chunks they won in Liverpool and Leeds and Manchester and Glasgow and then...and *then*... they circled the pitch to adoring cheers from the defeated team's supporters. The fans stayed and sang and cheered just to be looked upon by the magicians from Brazil and Argentina and Italy and Uruguay and Holland, always Holland—how, how, *how*, the Russians wanted to know—and even the best from Germany, France, Belgium... and the Giganticos even had the best Liberians and Iranians who were magicians, sorcerers, geniuses too, but had never been able to prove it through their pitiable national teams. They flocked to them in the streets, surrounded their hotels, blocked their busses. They screamed for them, cried for them, clamored just to touch them, if they only could, if they only could.

The Giganticos were owned by a free-spending Manhattan media conglomerate whose European executives knew what few residents of the United States of America knew in the bicentennial year of the republic: that football—soccer—was the world's truest, most reliable, most incendiary, most tribal passion, and that the most beloved assemblage of humanity you could cobble together was a soccer team, a football squad—an entertaining, glamorous side that you'd love whether they were yours or not. The rich European men in Manhattan spent on the Giganticos. They spent and they spent.

In between AASSA matches against the likes of the Flamingos of Florida, the Colorado Cowhands, and the Rose City Revolution, the Giganticos hosted Europe's finest clubs at their big and beautiful New York stadium and they jetted off to Mexico, South America, and beyond for exhibitions attended by hundreds of thousands of adoring fans. The fans never rioted, they never fought. They came to watch.

Men wept. Women screamed.

The Giganticos' game was poetry, but it was engineering too. They built it right in front of you, assembled it for their audiences to appreciate moment by moment, minute by minute. Their goals weren't the sudden shock that they were in the pedestrian football world; they were flourishes at the conclusions of elaborate sequences of grandeur and beauty. The Giganticos were sublime.

When the Giganticos traveled they took their own airplane, purchased for them by the European executives of the media conglomerate, and they were delivered to their matches in airbrushed tour buses worthy of Fleetwood Mac. They stepped from their coach in a dazzling array of '70s menswear—bell-bottom trousers, the widest lapels the world had to offer, spectacular ties, scarves, cravats, ascots. Their colorful shirts bore patterns and collars you could wear only if you were the best in the world at something. Their Belgian goalkeeper wore a hat with a feather in it—and he was Belgian. They waved as they stepped off the bus to the local riffraff who had gathered to see if they were real—if it was possible that the Giganticos had really, really and truly, come to town from Montevideo perhaps, where they had just won a quarterfinal as a guest team in the South American championship, or from Cuba maybe, where they'd played at Castro's behest with a waiver from the State Department, or from Hawaii even, where they'd played an exhibition against the Japanese national team and won by five goals.

They made a mockery of the American All-Star Soccer Association. They won games 12–1, 9–0, and 8–5 (having played the second half without a goalkeeper). Americans filled stadiums to see the Giganticos thrash their home teams, even though the locals couldn't tell the difference between a corner kick or a goal kick or pronounce many of the players' names, and even though they didn't really know who any of them were. They knew they were good, they knew they were famous everywhere else in the world, but they didn't know who any of them were. Not really.

Except for one: the Pearl of Brazil. They knew who he was, and they loved him. Everyone loved him. On planet Earth, in 1976, if you did not know—and love—the Pearl, your tribe had not yet been discovered.

He had met the pope and the Queen of England. He had met the Beatles and Elvis, and he had visited the White House. Other athletes, men seemingly twice his size—boxers, basketball players, home-run hitters—clamored to meet him and bask in his glow. He had toured Africa—not as a footballer, but as a harbinger of good, a layer on of hands.

He had once been rumored to be dead, and millions had poured into the streets all over the world, wailing with grief. His country plunged into the deepest misery, but he had not been dead—just misplaced in Ethiopia on a goodwill mission (his handlers had all been imprisoned indefinitely upon return to Brazil). He was not big or strong, but he had a mystical connection with the ball and a supernatural sense of the game that gave him full awareness of everything that was happening on the field at all times. He was almost never dispossessed and he made the most miraculous passes, threading the ball into spaces that seemed not to be spaces at all, easing the ball to his teammates' feet with a mystical, gravity-defying lightness. And his goals! They were almost laughably acrobatic, wondrous creations that weren't just magic, but magic *tricks*. His fans (everyone) wondered how he pulled them off. And he worked his magic everywhere he went: in four World Cups, on tours to every imaginable locale, and now in America. He was as charismatic as a great president and he was as humble as a child. No one rooted against him.

To the footballers of the world in 1976, he was a deity, a benevolent being sent by even more benevolent gods for the betterment of football, and therefore for the benefit of the planet. He was their king. Describing him this way did not seem ridiculous; it seemed like an understatement.

But in 1976, the Pearl of Brazil announced his retirement. The season of the American Bicentennial would be his last. He had come to America to share his version of the game with the unwashed masses, to act as ambassador for the Beautiful Game. He would win one more championship, leave the game better than he found it, and walk away. The summer of 1976 would be quite a summer for the Giganticos, and anyone who wanted any part of the world's greatest footballer would have to get to him sometime that summer.

And a lot of people wanted to get to the Pearl of Brazil that summer.

ONE

Danny Hooper, of East Southwich Albion Association Football Club, of the English Third Division, was big and strong.

That's what they'd told him since he was a boy, and that's what people told him now. Over and over again they told him. "You're a big, strong lad, Danny. It's a blessing in this game, my boy. You're big and you're strong. We'll need you to play like it."

In the corner shop and at the chips stand by the Albion ground, they called him "big man." "Well done at the weekend, big man," they'd say, whether he'd done well or not. When he walked the gray and ancient streets of East Southwich, the old men nodded at him, the women smiled at him, and the kids just got out of his way. Today, on his way to the pub for a swifty with the only person he was talking to this week, the man in the coffee shop said, "Heyyyyyy, big man!" as he strolled by. Danny nodded, as big and strong men do.

In his youth, he'd enjoyed it—he was happy to have something that set him apart from the other boys. When you're young, you'll always get chosen for the team if you're big and strong. No one will expect anything from you but muscle, even if you'd like to show them your finesse, a bit of subtlety—but at least you'll always get picked. You'll always have a place. The thing was, at twenty-two, Danny wasn't so young anymore, and he was getting a little sick of being only and always the big, strong lad from gray and ancient East Southwich.

A few days before, at training, he had removed the ball from the foot of young Stevie Johnston, a flashy wisp of a young winger, and had kept possession as Johnston had caught back up to him to try to win it back. While Johnston made his hasty effort at the ball, Danny eased the soggy, leaden ball through poor Johnston's Eiffel Tower–ed legs with the casual insouciance of a Dutch or Brazilian prodigy. It was the third time Danny had nutmegged someone, anyone, in his entire life, and only the fourth time he'd tried it. It filled him with joy. For a moment.

East Southwich Albion's manager, a doughy and crusty World War II veteran named Aldershot Taylor, whose body had been infused through his feet with Third Division mud and through his face with third-division gin for decades, brought the session to an immediate halt.

"Danny, Danny, *Danny*," moaned Aldy Taylor, whose voice came only in the bruised shades of Shatteringly Loud and British Forlorn. At the moment, he was surprising the squad with the British version. The blue-tracksuited and orange-bibbed members of East Southwich Albion stopped and looked at forlorn Aldy Taylor. "Danny," Taylor said, "you're *paid* by this football club"—he motioned with his stumpy arms at the mud and the men and the faded glory of East Southwich Albion Association Football Club—"to be big and strong. Money changes hands, my boy. You must... stop... *that*. Stop... whatever *that* was, my boy. Please." *

The words hung gin-soaked in the dirty, damp English air while Taylor remembered why he'd said them, and then they

---

🎽 A NOTE ON DIRE VALE UNITED FOOTBALL CLUB: As of the 1975–76 season, the club held the remarkable distinction of being the only known footballing organization on the planet to have finished twelfth in every league competition they had ever entered. This had come to light all the way back in 1903, after the team finished twelfth in the Mid-Maidenfoot Alliance Second Division, despite a unique playoff system in which the teams were re-seeded after each match and the contests were scored by judges based on foot speed and playing style. In time, the club's management determined to build the squad based on a stated desire to finish in twelfth each year without ever being suspected of throwing a match; United's unique aims put them in the awkward position of paying exorbitant transfer fees for players of what the club deemed "exactly our kind of mediocrity."

hung waiting for the old man to free East Southwich Albion's Royal Blues to continue their preparation for godforsaken Dire Vale United in the FA Cup Fifth Round Proper. They hardly even belonged in the Fourth Division, Dire Vale United. Just up from non-League football, Dire Vale United was promoted on a series of technicalities after finishing their customary twelfth. A lucky draw for East Southwich Albion, Dire Vale United. One of the few sides in all the world that could make East Southwich Albion feel they'd gotten a lucky draw. East Southwich Albion would surely be moving on in the world's oldest cup competition, moving closer to that winner's medal that Danny wanted so badly, so badly, at the expense of Dire Vale United Football Club.

Then Aldy Taylor said, "All right then. Continue, lads."

If they don't want expression, Danny thought, *I won't bloody give them any. If they want big and strong, they can have that. And nothing more.* He determined that he would not speak until the FA Cup Fifth Round Proper match against Dire Vale United, and he did not.

Who on earth did Danny think he was? *Where* did he think he was? He could see it in their faces. Danny never imagined himself to have anything remotely *Brazilian* about his game, but he thought he measured up with a few of the Dutchmen. That didn't seem too far a reach. They were big and strong too, some of them. Huge. And they played in mud, the Dutch. No one told them to shut down their imaginations, at least as far as Danny could tell.

Danny had once told his father he'd like to win a championship someday. As far as hopes and dreams went, that was about it for Danny. He couldn't imagine a career without taking a trophy in his hands and kissing it just the once. Lifting it above his head and listening to the mighty, relieved *"Whoaaaaaaaaaaa,"* the exultant roar of men and boys and those few and brave women and girls who wanted nothing but to see that cup, whatever it was, held aloft in the springtime sun by its beribboned handles, ribbons the color of whatever shirt Danny was wearing at that very moment. Danny's father laughed a little and gave him an eloquent wink that said, *You'll do what you're told, Danny. If a championship comes from that, then fair play to you. Otherwise...*

Even the old man.

Everyone spoke to Danny in the gray, sodden language of the English weather. "You'll take what you're given, son." "You'll win if you win, Danny, but you probably won't, you likely won't, you won't you won't you won't..."

Danny walked through town every Monday to the shouts of "Big man!" and the nods of the old men and the smiles of the women and the scurrying of the children, to meet his dad down at the pub for a swifty. They called it a swifty, but it rarely turned out that way. They'd have a weekend's football to discuss, plus the goings-on in the First Division and the *Match of the Day* broadcast, and finally, after the two or three swifties had well and truly entered the bloodstream, a thorough consideration of the most recent East Southwich Albion fixture to write itself into the blur of East Southwich football history. Danny's father was a quiet man, opinionated in facial expression but, like his son, disinclined to make sounds. Danny had inherited this gene—except when his dad was around. When his dad was around, Danny opened up, rambled and jambled, said what was on his mind. Mr. Hooper listened—loved listening to his son address most any topic, but especially the Funny Old Game—and responded with a litany of eyebrow wrinkles, curled mouth corners, and even a few things that said plenty that he alone could do with his ears.

This Monday presented Danny with plenty to say and for his father to hear. Danny's East Southwich side, representatives of the only club either Hooper had ever supported, had conceded late and not scored at all in a depressing loss to Bloat County. "Bloat," Danny sneered, a light ale cream coating the underside of his mustache. "Bloody Bloat County, come to East Southwich and left happy. And why? Because we play pre-war football in these parts, Dad. It was a kicking contest Saturday. A kicking contest. Nothing more. How far and how high. And could you get stuck in, could you earn your right to play. Earn your right to play football? I'm bloody paid to play football, not foul gits from bloody Bloat County. But that's all they want, Dad, all they want."

He stopped, polished off another half pint, slammed the glass down on the table, looked at his father, and said, "Bloat. How they even stay up in this division I'll never know. All you'd have to do to nick the points off of Bloat County would be to keep the ball on the floor for a minute or two at a time. Pass the bloody thing, Dad, pass the bloody thing."

Danny slumped in his chair, leaned his head back to take in the dark brown ceiling of the Southwich Defeatist's Arms, and raspberried a frustrated, malty spray of alcohol into the close, warm tavern air and let the mist of disappointment settle back on his hairy face. "We can't take two points off of Bloat County at home," he said, and sat back up. "Not likely to win anything that way. Not likely to win anything at all."

Danny's father narrowed his eyes and wrinkled his nose. He locked his sons's eyes in his own gaze and held still, stiffening his shoulders. Danny said, "I know, I know. It's what I signed up for. It's what I wanted, to be a professional footballer, to play for the Royals, but I also wanted to win something, Dad. A cup, a medal, a little ribbon, something."

Mr. Hooper leaned forward, and Danny said, "I said I know."

Then Danny's father spoke. "Aldershot Taylor has the imagination of a horse. Since you lads were boys, I've seen his methods: his idea of a side is nine of the biggest boys he can find and two of the fastest."

Danny waited for his dad to finish, because he knew he wasn't finished.

"The nine of you graft and grind and kick the ball up to the fast ones. For decades, Danny, for decades..."

This was Mr. Hooper's version of a speech, and he was now most likely done speaking for a week. He took a drink from his third pint.

"I'll go play in Holland," Danny said. "It's not so far away. And it's real football. I could help some nice Dutch club win a trophy. I'll—"

Danny's father made an incredulous face.

"Why not?"

Mr. Hooper used his ear-twitch to say, *Seriously? You can't play in Holland.*

"I could do."

Mr. Hooper's crinkled chin said, *They wouldn't have you.*

"Well, I can't stay in this league forever."

Mr. Hooper raised an eyebrow.

"What?" Danny asked.

Danny's dad raised the other eyebrow, just to be perfectly clear.

"The mines?" Danny said. "No, Dad. Not the mines."

The elder Hooper surprised Danny and spoke out loud again: "Danny, your options are few. You play for this club because you're big and you're strong and you're from here. No one else is calling for you, are they? You lads can't even beat Bloat County. It's Albion until you're hurt, and then it's the mines for you, my son. Unless something happens that neither of us sees coming." *Now* he was done for the week.

Danny put his hand up in the air, which he did only to call for offsides or to get his hands on one more round.

TWO

The next Saturday afternoon, a late February Saturday afternoon, brought godforsaken Dire Vale United to the Auld Moors football ground for an FA Cup Fifth Round tie. As festive as a Fifth Round FA Cup tie might be, especially for a club like East Southwich Albion, the Auld Moors on a late February Saturday afternoon is still the Auld Moors on a late February Saturday afternoon, no matter the stakes: the creaky old ground, which was reaching an age of possibly preferring to be left alone, emitted the familiar odor of breaded fish, woolly perspiration, and Bovril—roughly the same odor as an East Southwich man of similar age let off on a Saturday afternoon. Danny inhaled the oil-saturated fish, the sweat of old men, the liquefied meat, and thought some version of what he always thought at two minutes to three o'clock on a Saturday afternoon: *I've been dipped in England.*

Despite its forever-midtable/lower-league grimness, the Auld Moors, festooned in bunting and ribbons and pennants

---

🎽 ON THE MATTER OF THE COCKEREL: East Southwich Albion's logo was a one-legged cockerel perched upon a ball and wearing a crown. The bird symbolized the Legend of the One-Legged Cockerel King who ruled the Greater East Southwich area during the Dark Ages. Legend had it that Edward XXVIII, of the Southwich line, had lost his leg while leading a swarm of cockerels into battle against a unified force of Gauls and Yorkshiremen who coveted East Southwich for its abundance of poultry. As the story goes, the enemy stood back and just let the swarm of fowl through, after which they cut off Edward's left leg, took the cockerels, and that was pretty much it. He was allowed to retain his throne because Yorkshiremen are generally nice people and Gauls have a complicated sense of humor, or the other way around.

and flowers, did seem to bring a little extra something this particular FA Cup Saturday. Elderly East Southwichmen wore blue rosettes and buttons and badges on their bulky coats and caps, testifying to their long and mostly dissatisfying relationship with the club. Ten or fifteen papier-mâché one-legged cockerels* of varying size and quality made their ways through the crowd, across the fingertips of eager supporters desperate to see the town's and the club's talisman brought to some measurable glory. Local women wore floppy blue hats and the mystified smiles of people who weren't entirely sure how to support a winner, if that was indeed what they were doing. A few real oldsters spun peculiar and irritating wooden noisemakers and filled the air with strange, archaic constructions along the lines of "Up the Albion," "On you Blues," and the difficult-to-say "Play up, East Southwich." The official capacity of the Moors was 11,500, but the day's official attendance would be listed at 16,579.

This was a special day, nothing like an average Third Division Saturday against Sadbridge United, Ffyddrhyrr Town, Scrumley Villa, or Bloat—not at all. Albion had only recently played a frigid, windblown early December match at Wolves & Wolves (recently merged)* in front of an announced crowd of

---

👕 A BRIEF HISTORY OF WWFC: Wolves United and the Wolfingstonesgreen-upon-Heath Wanderers merged in 1973 after United slipped into administration following a poorly funded and ill-conceived world tour during which they produced seven wins, against thirty-four defeats and eleven draws and four confirmed player deaths in forty countries over sixty days. When they returned, bedraggled and traumatized, for a preseason friendly in Wolfingstonesgreen, they learned that the Wanderers had lost three-quarters of their squad to a traveling cult/circus that had absconded to the Isle of Wight. The merger initially seemed not only logical but amicable, but it hit a snag when the new club's combined management could not determine whether to adopt United's colors of red and white or the Wanderers' white and red. In any event, United retroactively changed its colors to claret and sky blue, while the Wanderers posthumously reverted to their founding strip of green and white hoops. The new club, Wolves & Wolves, wore a halved jersey striped on one side in green and white and on the other in maroon and blue, occasioning Parliament to hastily pass an emergency act requiring W&W to play in all white for matches televised in color in the name of public safety. One snowy night in 1989, the team loaded its effects onto a boat off the Dennispool docks and traveled to America, where they became the Minnesota Timberwolves of the National Basketball Association.

487 that beggared the description of football as the "Beautiful Game."

This wasn't like that. Today was a joyful day, in a reluctant and nervous East Southwich way, of course, but the good people knew this might just be as good as it got, and so they tried: tried to be festive, tried to exult in being the home team and the favorite in a meaningful Cup tie. Today, the Royals' home stand, mostly shielded from the harsh acute-angle sunlight by its begabled corrugated steel roof, was awash in East Southwich Albion royal-blue-and-white scarves pulled taut by anxious supporters dying for a day, a memory, to call their own, a Cup tale they could pass along one day. "Ah, '76... I remember that one—'twas a cold, cold day, *right bloody cold* that day, when little Dire Vale United came to town. We were lucky in the draw—we had only to beat tiny Dire Vale..."

The truth of it was neither East Southwich Albion nor Dire Vale United had the slightest business in the Fifth Round of the FA Cup. But Albion had won on an own goal in the Third Round and had gotten a fortunate draw against another Third Division side who'd pulled an upset in the previous round to get out of the Fourth. And Dire Vale United had won in the Third after three replays and shocked a Second Division team, who had taken them lightly and had rested their first team for a meaningless midtable League encounter at the weekend and hadn't counted on Dire Vale waterlogging their pitch until it was a three-inch-deep swamp.

And now one of these two miserable football clubs—well, one was miserable, the other just not all that good—had a shot at a date with one of the real glamour clubs from London, Manchester, Liverpool, Leeds, which, no matter the result, would mean a sizable payday for the club and a chance for the players to show what they could do against real competition and maybe, just maybe, a shot at a First Division contract.

But that's not what Danny was thinking as he warmed up in the muck and the mire at the Auld Moors to play against Dire

Vale United in the Fourth Round of the Football Association Cup. Danny was thinking, *Enough of this shite.* Danny was thinking about his nutmeg of poor Stevie Johnston, and he was thinking he deserved a little more credit for undoing Johnston, whom the club would be looking to today for a goal or two. *Everyone loves a goal scorer,* Danny thought. A lazy forward, Johnston. *This shite ends today,* he thought, as he clapped his hands toward the main stand.

The East Southwich Albion faithful sang wildly and not at all well—never had so many of them been together, never had they filled the entire Frog's Bottom Stand, not like this, not shoulder to shoulder, not so you could get lifted off the ground and moved three or four chest-crushing, fleetingly terrifying feet, never so that your only hope of a piss was into the rolled-up newspaper in your own hand, never had they been so cautiously optimistic, never in quite such a First Division way had they all been together, together and this loud.

And never had the opposition been as boisterous either. The Dire Vale contingent was a disorganized but eager and enthusiastic rabble, reveling in a long, seemingly hopeless day out; they wriggled in their penned-in end like feral beasts, mocking the staid and nervous East Southwich faithful; they attempted rhymes of "wich" with a series of the most foul expressions; they frightened the home supporters, but they only motivated Danny and his teammates. Did Danny ever want to shut them up.

The sky was clear and an unusually clean blue, the sun white and low, determined in its customary disregard for this part of Britain to withhold its warmth. It would be dark soon. The pitch was green on the wings and brown down the middle, having borne too much trauma over the autumn and winter months, having been mercilessly trod upon by mostly graceless men, having been frozen and unfrozen too many times, flattened by too many cruel mechanical devices in an effort to keep it to the criminally low standard worthy of 1970s English League football. It was perfect.

The first few minutes of the match contained a spastic crackle missing from the weekly League struggle. Danny instantly broke into a ferocious sweat. Each of the twenty-two men on the pitch had fear to burn, a queasy awareness that an early fluke of a goal could be his fault, his own damn fault, a life of football culminated not in greatness and glory but in a horrific moment that would live in the hearts and livers of all these terrible, screaming, baying people; a hideous blunder that could change the course of the match and of his life, and of his club's and his town's history, could be the only goal of the day.

The best midfielder in each side made at least one awful pass (neither team completed more than two passes in a row in that opening flurry). A Dire Vale shot from distance spun wildly, struck the corner flag, and sat there in the mud (the crowd roared its derision). An East Southwich effort landed in the car park. Each side committed a foul that made absolutely no sense and brought admonition from the referee and "sod offs" and worse from all corners of the ground. A Dire Vale player was called for a foul throw. Even Danny laughed at that one. The Dire Vale end's singing had taken on a distinctly seaworthy tone, and you could sense the shame down in the Frog's Bottom end at having no decent response. East Southwich women shook their heads.

In the fourth minute, East Southwich Albion earned a corner, which floated directly and harmlessly into the arms of Dire Vale's goalkeeper. After the area cleared, the keeper rolled the ball to the edge of the eighteen-yard box, picked it back up, and launched a mighty punt into the chilled late afternoon. Danny positioned himself underneath it, right on the center line, easing a miniature forward out of his way as he did, and planted his feet, bent his knees, and headed the ball all the way back to Dire Vale's keeper. *Big and strong,* he thought. *Big and strong.* It had been his first touch, and it gave him the idea he could do whatever he wanted.

Danny drifted toward the touchline to his left. Dire Vale had a winger over there who looked an awful lot like the player Danny had nutmegged in practice, looked a *lot* like Stevie Johnston as a matter of fact. Danny knew that this poor Fourth Division Dire Vale winger, a waif of a lad, maybe eighteen years of age, maybe even younger, wasn't that wanker of a player, wasn't lazy Stevie Johnston, nor was he Aldy Taylor, or any of those old men, or anyone else who had crawled under Danny's skin, but that didn't matter one bit when the unfortunate youngster's left leg slipped out from underneath him on the slick and soft Auld Moors turf and he was left to reach for the ball with his right leg, outstretched, outstretched, until it was outstretched no more because Danny had seen that leg, exposed six inches above the ground, and Danny had decided to crush it to the ground with a mighty downward stomp of the sole of his boot—and pin it there. Danny felt and heard the boy's tibia break like a dry winter twig and he heard the boy scream, heard the whelp whimper, and Danny knew right then and there that he had done something very, very wrong.

He shouldn't have done it. Of course he knew that. But he was just being big and strong, everything he'd ever been told he could only and ever be. And he'd just proved them all right. Of course, of course—

Nothing Brazilian or Dutch about destroying a Welshman's leg and livelihood like that. Nothing at all.

The nearest Dire Vale player rushed him and slugged him in the face. A good one too. Right around the eye. Another Dire Vale man had taken a piggyback position upon Danny and was trying to pull him to the ground. Danny knew that this was how it had to play out—the melee, instinctive, inevitable, and grotesque as it was, was the correct reaction to what Danny had done. There would be general and malicious pushing and shoving and punching, and players yelling in Danny's face close enough for him to feel the warmth of their throats, the spatter of their spittle, and the sincerity of their anger. The Dire Vale players were doing the right thing by their teammate and by any recognizable understanding of the football code.

Danny went calm and let himself be punched again, let himself absorb his just deserts. He felt nothing. Dire Vale United's manager—a young one, in his thirties, and capable of doing real young-man harm—was trying to claw past his own players to land a blow to Danny's face, and the whole thing looked for all the world like it was happening in a dream, or on television.

The referee, a birdlike little man in a blousy, oversized black shirt with wide white collars, raced through the throng and stood before Danny—a full head taller—holding a red card* as high as he could, as if he were a child reaching for the top of the refrigerator. He rose to his tiptoes for a moment and, on landing back upon his heels, pointed to the changing room of the Auld Moors with a theatrical flourish—and Danny put his head down and started that long, lonely trudge. One more Dire Vale United player ran at him and landed an awkward slap to his beard, but that was it. Everyone seemed to back away after that and let the big man walk off in his quiet shame. As Danny passed the dugouts, a Dire Vale player, almost in tears, called him a "wanker," and Danny heard another one mumble something worse, much worse, but that one's tone was more despondent than pissed off. British Forlorn. Danny kept his head down, as you do.

Danny showered, got dressed, and was gone from the ground by halftime. It wasn't the right thing to do—you're sup-

---

👕 The sprite of a man was a pioneer of sorts. Having witnessed and taken solace in the introduction of yellow and red cards at the World Cup in 1970, he had been an early and keen advocate of their adoption by English football. As the FA had been reluctant to embrace the disciplinary revolution within the game, he had taken matters into his own hands and fashioned yellow and red cards of his own for moments just like this one. Sending off, a rarity in those days, had been a purely verbal business before 1970 (hence the introduction of cards for the World Cup to surpass the language barrier), and the League would not formally adopt the practice until the subsequent fall, but the gathering at the Auld Moors knew that Danny had to go and intuited that the man's red card was some new-fangled way of saying so. And so, as a footnote to a footnote, Danny Hooper received the first red card in English football history, and the last known to have been of the homemade variety.

posed to wait around for your mates—but he couldn't think of any other way to handle it. He lived near enough to walk home. The streets were empty; he could hear the stadium breathe—its oohs, its aahs, its screams and coughs of exaltation and dread. He could almost track the score by what he heard. Almost.

When he got to his destination, he got up on his bicycle, the only vehicle he owned or needed, and rode around for an hour, maybe more, reliving his mistake, trying to right his wrong on the streets of East Southwich, before finally returning home to his sad little flat, home to wonder what on earth might happen next.

THREE

Danny stayed in his flat all day Sunday. The phone rang four or five times. There were a few knocks at the door. A couple of the more aggressive local journos hollered at him. "Danny Hooper! I know you're in there. Just like a word, Danny! Someone has to tell your story, might's well be me! I'll do right by you, Danny!" But Danny managed to get through the day without speaking with anyone, not even his dad.

At 11:30 P.M., and with the lingerers no longer lingering at his door, he put on a drill top, gray sweatpants, and trainers and went out for another bike ride. He knew where to go so that no one would see him, and when he returned over an hour later, he took a short shower and went to bed hungry, nervous, embarrassed, and as tired as he could remember ever feeling.

On Monday, Danny made the short bicycle ride from his flat to the Auld Moors for his morning training session. He wasn't looking forward to it, and he timed his arrival to be as close to the beginning of the workout as possible to reduce non-footballing human interaction. To make matters worse, Dire Vale United had beaten the shorthanded Royals 2–1 on a goal in the waning minutes, something that almost certainly wouldn't have happened had the home side remained at full strength for the entire match. East Southwich Albion was now out of the FA Cup, and he was well aware that he was being singled out as the villain.

He saw the newspaper headline on his ride in: "Hooper Out of His Gourd, Royals Out of the Cup." The accompanying photograph, of Danny surrounded by aggrieved Dire Vale men, made Danny look like King Kong swatting at helicopters atop the Empire State Building, made him look like a criminally bonkers, maniacal brute. He shook his big head and mumbled something to himself even he didn't understand.

He felt he owed his teammates an apology, and they would get one today—first by example: no one would train harder this Monday morning, no one would show more dedication to the club and to the lads. And then afterward, as the men dressed to get on with their non–FA Cup lives, he would speak up— he dreaded having to do it, but he knew it was the right thing, the only thing—and say that while he knew he'd been in the wrong, and he would do anything in his power to make it up to the boys, what he had done he had done out of passion for his teammates, for the club's supporters, and for his deep desire to win something, anything. He was sorry, he would say, but the fact of the matter was he'd been dead determined not to let that little prick make his way down the left wing of East Southwich Albion's pitch ever again, and in the event, big, strong Danny Hooper had, indeed, not let the poor kid down that wing. *Sorry. I'm done talking now. All right?*

The team would nod and murmur. Someone would say something meaningless: "Unlucky," which would make no sense, but footballers say it all the time, or "Next time," which made *some* sense anyway... ; others, Danny knew, would remain silent, might never forgive him.

But when Danny arrived outside the ground, Aldy Taylor was waiting for him. Not what Danny wanted to see. Before Taylor could address him, Danny offered a contrite, "Hullo, Aldy."

"That's some black eye, Danny boy."

"What are you doing out here, boss?"

"Waiting for you, lad."

"Who's with the team?"

"Ol' Mumble's mumblin' at 'em," Aldy said, referring to Mumble McCray, a gray, unintelligible man who'd given his life to East Southwich Albion AFC, with the exception of the three years he'd given Her Majesty's Infantry during Her Valiant Defense of the Empire from Hitler's Hordes. McCray had led the Royals to their only trophy of any significance, the Amateur Midlands Shield, scoring the only goal against Birmingham Villa (which was neither Birmingham City nor Aston Villa, but was usually and conveniently referred to as "B'rmin'h'm" or "Villa" for storytelling enhancement purposes) in the third replay of that august entity's 1948 final. For this singular strike—which the real old-timers around the club would tell you was merely shinned in from a yard out, but he'd made a meal of it over the decades—he still had a job. No one could understand a word Mumble McCray said—not then (he'd had the nickname since he was nine), and not now—but as he was friendly enough, and otherwise unemployable, the club subsidized his meager existence in exchange for the odd service rendered. Danny said, "Well, they won't get much done then, will they?"

Aldy smiled and said, "He can roll the balls out well enough. That'll do for today." He put his arm around Danny and said, "Now come with us, lad."

Aldy guided Danny into the bowels of the Auld Moors Football and Sometime Rugby Ground. The euphemism "Auld" hardly did the thing justice: it was bloody *old*. It smelled of liniments and dirt, of tea and the drastic chemicals the women of East Southwich used to launder the club's grubby apparel; it smelled of all of it, and of leather and boot polish and cologne, and of alcohol and the middling jumble of the Third Division. The old man and the young man shuffled past the changing room, the boot room, the tea room, and the boardroom to the end of a hallway Danny had seen hundreds, maybe thousands of times—but in all these years since first joining the club as a schoolboy, Danny had never once made it all the way to the room at the end of the hallway. Aldy and Danny were now so deep in the stadium's interior that Danny had no idea where they were relative to the main stand, to the pitch.

The chairman of the board of East Southwich Albion AFC rose as Danny and Aldy entered his office. But he didn't come around from behind his desk, a monstrous dark slab of wood that very clearly separated His Eminence from the men—including Aldy—who muddied themselves on his behalf every Saturday and the occasional midweek. Danny had been in the club for over a decade and had never met the chairman face-to-face. Now he said, "Sit, men, sit." The man did not smile. Aldy sat, slowly and with a light, regretful grunt, as an old footballer might, and Danny sat too.

The chairman said, "Danny, you've been a loyal servant to this football club for a long time, and I would like to believe that we have been of some service to you, helped *raise* you, to some small degree, hmm?" Danny nodded. The man went on: "We take great pride in the formation of strong young Englishmen here, as I believe you are aware. We aren't a famous club or a rich club. We don't win many trophies. We aren't fancy or posh, but we do take care of our own, don't we, Aldy? And you are one of ours, Danny. I know your father. He's a good man. I knew your mum, may she rest." He paused and looked down, a great show of sincerity. "You're a good lad, Danny."

The chairman leaned back in his giant leather chair and breathed a long breath through his long nose. Then he lit a cigarette and breathed it in as if he needed it, as if he really *needed* it. The smoke rose through the dark room and caught the beams of white winter morning light slicing in through the narrow windows near the ceiling. The smoke swirled, dipped, and rose again and for a moment captivated Danny's attention before he remembered that he was in the chairman's office with Aldershot Taylor, and no one was smiling.

"Aldy," the chairman said, "would you please rise and face away from us?"

Aldy rose amid the mmms and ahhs of an aged and aggrieved body managing a terrific effort. He faced the wall like a resigned schoolboy accustomed to this sort of punishment.

The chairman sucked in a bit more smoke and gestured toward the back of Aldershot Taylor and said, "Danny, do you see what I see?"

Danny had a feeling that he did not see what the chairman saw. He didn't want to say so, however, so he looked back at the chairman in the silent big and strong stupor that big and strong young men learn to get away with as soon as they come to the full realization of what big and strong gets you in the world, and did not say anything.

"*Well?*" said the chairman.

Danny said, "Sir, I, um, I'm looking at the back of, um... Mr. Taylor?"

The chairman stubbed his cigarette into a well-populated ashtray, leaned over his desk, and eased a stream of smoke in Danny's direction before saying, "Ah, *close*, son. You're warrrrm, bloody warm, my boy, but I am quite afraid you are not warm e*nough*. Take a closer look. In the general area of Mr. Taylor's arse, if you please."

Aldy began to speak but the chairman cut him off. "*Quiet*, Aldy. Let the lad have a look. *Look*, Danny. What do you notice that's... *different* about Mr. Taylor's arse? Different to... *last week*, let's say."

Danny had no idea where the chairman was taking this. None. "I—"

"Don't know? Then I will bloody *tell* you what's different between the *arse* you are looking at right now to the last time you laid eyes upon it. It's *gone*. It's bloody *gone*, Danny, your manager's *arse*, which last you saw it thought it might one day see the Sixth Round of the bloody FA Cup, did that arse. But it has been chewed down to *nothing* by this town's miserable press, such as it is, by the despicable, dastardly, petty, and small people who run Dire Vale United Football Club, may they *rot* in *hell*, and by the fat bastards in bloody *London* who run the *bloody* Football Association it*self* who want a pound of flesh from little East Southwich Albion Association Football Club for what *you've* done, Danny. They've all chewed the *arse* right off of Aldershot Taylor, who fought in the goddamn war—you fought in the war, didn't you, Aldy?"

"Well, in a manner of speaking—"

"Who fought in the war *in a manner of speaking,* whatever *that* means, and there must be a good story to *that,* and who got this club promoted from the inky depths of non-League football to the Leeside Conference and through the *savagery* of the bloody Fourth Division and to within one reasonably well-played match of the Sixth Round of the greatest tournament football has ever known—and now this man... has... no... *arse.* It *was* there, but now it is *gone,* as you and I can plainly see. Or plainly *not* see. It. Is. *Gone.*" He paused. "All right then, Aldy. Sit. On that bum you no longer bloody have."

The chairman lit another cigarette, though he was so exercised he could hardly breathe. Danny, in his entire life, had seen few men as angry as the chairman was right now, and that included the Dire Vale men from Saturday.

Aldershot Taylor sat down on his former buttocks.

The chairman said, "Tell him, Aldy."

Aldy looked at Danny, and Danny thought, well, Danny didn't really think anything. After the chairman's outburst, he could scarcely imagine—

"Danny, it's been terrible. The press, the FA. The Dire Vale people. Even the poor lad's family. They've been merciless. Just merciless. And our supporters—they wanted this so badly, son. They were so sure we were through to the next round. They're furious. And the lads... they're gutted, Danny. Gutted. They just can't understand why you threw it all away like that. Why you lost your head." He put his hand on his brow and paused to collect himself. "There've been rumors of charging you with a crime. Grievous assault. They've asked for your head, Danny. Everyone has." He looked as if he might cry, if men who had fought in the war in a manner of speaking did that kind of thing.

The chairman said, "Aldy, tell the boy about the *money.*"

Aldy closed his eyes and breathed a long, resigned nasal breath.

"Danny," he said, though it was obvious he didn't want to, "the Fifth Round of the FA Cup is a real moneymaker, especially for a small club like ours. You cost us, son, you really did. Dire Vale United is on its way to Newcastle to play in the biggest stadium any of those players has ever seen. They'll lose eight–nil and it won't matter. The club will make a fortune. They'll be set for years. Us, we're stuck in the bottom half of the table—again—not close enough to the relegation zone to create any drama, and nowhere near even an insincere push at promotion. We're *nowhere*, Danny, adrift in between something and nothing—"

The chairman interrupted. "We could have paid off *years* of debt and replaced the South Stand, Danny. The whole rotting goddamn thing—" He inhaled, and the end of his cigarette ignited bright orange. "The club just can't bear under the weight of it, of what you've done. The Welsh lad's finished. Maybe forever. You broke his leg in two places. Clean through. And they had plans for him. He was a good little player—"

Danny had finally had enough. "He was not," he said.

The chairman sat himself up just a bit, annoyed and surprised at being contradicted on a football matter. "Oh, really, Hooper? He was not, was he? He was a Welsh under-21 international is what he was—"

"Exactly," Danny said. "Spot on. A Welsh under-21 international. He was bollocks."

The chairman's face reddened. "There were four clubs in Manchester alone bidding for his services, a good four more than have asked about you, Danny. The transfer fee could've got that miserable club to 1980 without taking another decent decision. And who on earth knows what the money would've meant to his family. Now he'll need a testimonial at nineteen..."

The chairman felt himself slipping, his anger getting the better of him, and he was disgusted with himself. He sputtered and waved his cigarette at Aldy, suggesting he handle the rest of this unfortunate business.

Aldy said, "Danny, I've known you since you were nine years of age. You've been..." And then he caught himself. He didn't want to go down this maudlin road with this kid. Not today. He was still cross with Danny, and Danny had brought this all upon himself. What had he been thinking with all that Continental nonsense about short passing and clever dribbling and resisting the obvious benefits of being so goddamn big and bloody strong? And why had all *that* led to *this*? If he'd wanted to change his reputation, then why... *What had he been thinking?*

"Danny," Aldy said, "you've been sold."

The word hung in the smoky, close air of the chairman's office. *Sold.*

So final, so past tense, so *done*—and such an obvious expression of what Danny Hooper and all the Danny Hoopers were to East Southwich Albion AFC and all the East Southwich Albion AFCs: commodities, bit and pieces, odds and sods.

Sold.

No longer East Southwich Albion material, Danny Hooper.

No longer good enough for this midtable Third Division club that couldn't knock little old Dire Vale United out of the FA Cup.

Sold.

"Danny," Aldy said, "Danny, you'll have been suspended for four matches, maybe more. London will throw the book at us, at you, if you stay. And we've naught to play for. We'll have to move Rigby to the middle and bring in Figg from the reserves to cover for him. And the supporters—look, Danny... your season in the League is as good as done anyway, lad, done. So we've sold you."

Danny looked at the chairman and then back at Aldy. "I—"

"Never a question of your commitment, son," Aldy went on, an avuncular sympathy taking over his voice. "No one's ever doubted your bottle, son. No one gets stuck in like you do—"

The chairman interrupted, belting out, *"SOLD!"* as if he had regretted giving the opportunity to say it over to Aldershot Taylor.

Danny sat back in his chair. He imagined the next headline: "Hooper Out of His Gourd, Royals Out of the Cup—Hooper Out of the Club." He thought that his torso was very nearly tinged blue from wearing East Southwich Albion's shirt for most of his young life; he thought that the Auld Moors wasn't just his home away from home—the Auld Moors *was* his home, it was all he had; and he thought there was no other team in the entire ninety-two-team Football League he could ever imagine ever caring about. He thought, *Who else would I play for?*

Danny said, "You couldn't have sent me out on loan until it blows over... ?"

"Ah," the chairman said. "A thinker is young Danny. Suddenly your *brain* enters into it, does it? Thought occurred to us, aye, it did, it did—but I'm afraid we need you off the books entirely, my son. And off the books you are."

So Danny cut to the chase and said, "Who?" which wasn't quite right for the situation and which confused the two old gray men.

The chairman sputtered, "W-well, *I'm* the boss around here, lad, and I made the decision. *I* did. Aldy—"

"No," Danny said. "That doesn't matter to me. You've sold me. It's done and dusted. Who *bought* me?" Danny braced himself for the worst. The only good news he could possibly imagine was that he'd been sold to a First Division club and would be soon staying in the finest hotels in London and Liverpool. But he knew just how unlikely that was—more likely he knew he was about to hear that he was off to Middlesby Town or Maidshead Tuesday or *Bloat*, or even more depressing, a non-League club, some club in a misty provincial conference that shared its ground with cricketers or greyhounds. "Just say it," Danny said. "Say the name. Whatever it is."

The chairman looked at Aldy and nodded Danny's way, as if to say, *Go on, man—tell the lad.*

Aldy turned to face Danny and said, "You remember Graham Broome, Danny?"

"*Graham Broome?* Broomsie-from-Cloppingshire-United Graham Broome? He's not in Cloppingshire anymore, is he?"

"Well, no. He is not in Cloppingshire. But where he is, he wants you. He always thought you could play, always liked your game. He's got a new team, a team he thinks can win a championship, and he needs a number five."

Aldy stopped, looked at Danny, looked over at the chairman, then back at Danny. "*He* called *us*, son. *After* he heard about what you did. We didn't call him."

Danny looked at the floor and then up at his former manager. "A *championship*?" Danny said.

"So he says."

"That sounds good, I reckon. But I have one more question, and I expect you'll know what it is."

The chairman blurted a bitter "I should think you'll have more than one, lad."

Danny said, "The championship of *what*?"

The chairman sucked at his cigarette.

Aldy sat back in his chair and squinted once and then twice, as if wishing himself away. Then he said, "America."

"*America?*"

"America, my son."

The chairman exhaled more smoke than Danny had imagined his rotund body could contain and cracked a tiny grin. He extended a large, reddened hand. Danny didn't—couldn't—move. "Go on, son," Aldy said to Danny. "Shake it." Danny remained still. "Shake it, Danny. You'll need to shake that hand, my son."

And Danny shook the chairman's hand.

FOUR

"There are a great many players of solid English pedigree in the American All-Star Soccer Association" is what Danny repeated to his dad over a swifty two hours later. "So said the chairman anyway."

"The American All-Star Soccer Association? A mouthful, innit?"

"I know how it sounds."

His father wrinkled his brow in hard thought as he worked it out. "The...*AASSA*? Of the USA?"

"That's it, Dad. The AASSA. It's the New York Giganti-cos' league. With the Brazilian and the Dutchman and all those World Cuppers they've signed up. A decent league, I'm told. McCoist, from that great Rangers team that won the League Cup in '72, plays in Toronto with a bunch of Serbians. Logan down at Southside Wanderers, he got his start somewhere in Texas. And Sweet Billy Robinson—Sweet Billy Robinson, no less, Dad—he's playing out his drunken career in Los Angeles."

Danny's dad's left ear twitched, indicating a desire for an-other round, so Danny ordered two more and then continued: "There's an entire team of Ukrainians in Chicago I think. Or Poles. The Butchers they're called. *Butchers.* You know what the chairman told me after telling me all this?"

His dad dipped his head. He had no idea what the chair-man had told him.

"'Go have a laugh, Danny. Have yourself a laugh.'"

Danny folded his arms over his big and strong body and looked at the wall behind the bar. There was an East Southwich Albion team photograph hung there, 1971–72. The blue-shirted Royals, in their post–"Let It Be" haircuts and Elvis sideburns, looked a grim bunch, not at all happy to have their picture taken that typically overcast day at the Auld Moors. Looking at it made Danny's heart tighten. That picture, of that barely-avoided-relegation-from-the-Third-Division version of East Southwich Albion AFC, had been the last team picture of the Royals not to contain one Danny Hooper. The next year's team would feature a young, tall, semi-bulky center back with limp hair that hung to his shoulders like a hood, toothy smile asymmetrical and eager. They called him a center half sometimes, but he was a back in every way a player could be a back. He hadn't grown all the way into his frame—and hadn't yet sorted that beard—but he'd made the squad on height and potential. He hadn't gotten in more than three or four matches that season—just didn't have the body for it yet—but it had been a glorious campaign as far as he was concerned, the culmination of his boyhood dreams (minus a trophy). He had become a *Royal*, a real one, had earned first-team privileges, had run out on the Auld Moors' lousy pitch before the club's true followers, had taken his halftime tea with men he'd watched for years. The people of East Southwich knew him now, and he knew them. He had not reached the mountaintop, had no medals, no cups, but he could see them from where he stood. East Southwich Albion was only a year or two from promotion to the Second Division, Danny could feel it—and once you're in the Second Division, things can happen, things can happen.

But not anymore.

His father wanted to know what team he'd be playing for in the American All-Star Soccer Association, and Danny said, "The Rose City Revolution they're called. In a place called Oregon. They've a decent following, says Aldy. Out on the West Coast."

His dad's eyes asked, *Now where in blazes is Oregon?*

Danny sat still for a moment, still looking at that old team photo. He said, "It's out by California. 'Rose City' is a nickname. Town's called Portland. Apparently, they've taken to football."

His father and Vic the bartender, who'd drifted down to listen, were now both wordlessly asking, *You're doing what?*

"Joining the great American Experiment, I guess."

Vic said, "I've seen photos of those games, Danny, in magazines and the papers. Unless the Giganticos are playing, nobody goes. Nobody's goes, me boy. Empty seats by the mile, 'orrible kits, them plastic pitches. It's a wasteland, Danny. A football wasteland."

The men of the East Southwich Hoopers looked at Vic as if his job was to pour the pints. Danny said, "That may be, Vic, old man, but I'll be making twice what I'm making now, and you know what the last thing out of Aldy's mouth was?"

Vic said he had no idea.

"Say hi to the Pearl of Brazil."

Nobody said a word after that, and Vic turned to pour another round.

Danny opened the door to his flat and walked to the kitchen. He grabbed an empty glass from a cupboard, filled it with water, leaned back against the counter, and tipped it back. He wasn't thirsty; he just couldn't think of anything better to do. He wasn't even sure what he was now. He was neither thirsty nor hungry, neither angry nor sad, neither East Southwich blue nor... anything else yet. Didn't even know what colors the Rose City Revolution wore. He felt purposeless without his club, empty without the validation of the rest of his back line, the mad blue mob behind the goal, the misguided but well-intentioned encouragement of Aldershot Taylor.

He had no mental picture of Oregon—was it named after a shape? What could an *oregon* be? He had no real sense of what the American All-Star Soccer Association was all about. He knew about the Giganticos—everyone knew about the Giganticos. But other than them, all he knew was that the league was a United Nations of football misfits, a circus of decaying oldsters seeking quick end-of-career paydays and free booze, young English League castoffs trying to prove Old Blighty wrong, one-eyed goalkeepers, hordes of Eastern Europeans and overrated Latin dribblers, random job-seekers from Haiti, Kenya, Korea, Australia, the odd plucky Yank. He'd seen those pictures Vic had been on about: garish uniforms and all those empty seats, acres of them. There were those pictures, and then there were the pics of a certain beloved Brazilian. Lots of those. No empty seats in those photos.

He had only ever wanted to win a championship, a trophy, a medal of some kind, any kind. Now he was out of the FA Cup, out of the English League. (Ninety-two teams, at least twenty men per team, probably more, that's... 1,840. Round that up to two thousand. Two thousand spots in the League, and not a one for Danny, no matter how big, no matter how strong.) And off to a league that already had its trophy spoken for by the Pearl and his Giganticos.

He was alone, still trophy-less, and confused as hell as he let his sore, bruised self drop down into one of two chairs in his kitchen. He closed his eyes.

When he opened his eyes, he was no longer alone.

"That is a *glorious* black eye, Mr. Hooper, if I may say so."

What the hell? Danny thought.

"Other than that small detail," the intruder carried on, "how *are* you this fine English day?"

A man sat across from Danny, right there in his kitchen. Where he had come from, Danny did not know. The man wore a black suit with a thin black tie. His suit was neither in style nor a good fit for his gaunt frame and paunchy middle. The intruder had spoken with the confidence of a fitter man in a better-fitting suit.

Well, Danny thought, *might just as well have a strange man in my flat. Why not?* But while his thoughts swirled, he was struck dumb.

The visitor went on, unruffled by Danny's silence: "It's all right, my boy. I am aware that you haven't been speaking much lately." He paused and took a cigarette pack from his breast pocket, dislodged one, lit it, inhaled, and kept talking, easing out a genteel cloud of smoke to swirl around his head. *"Talk, talk, talk,"* he said, describing a parabola in the air with his cigarette. "Everyone thinks everyone wants to hear them talk, don't they, Danny? Annoying, really. I try not to say more than I must... got it from my father. I think I heard the admiral utter approximately one nice clear thought a week. A reticent sort, and I quite admired him for it. Ah, but listen to me, Danny. *Me*, of all people. Going on and on. That's what happens when *you* don't talk, Mr. Hooper—*I* end up rattling and prattling, don't I?" He laughed and narrowed his eyes shrewdly at Danny: "It's a good trick you have there."

The man was maybe ten years older than Danny. Just early thirties, Danny thought. His face was the pasty color of the usual East Southwich sky—white with hints of blue and gray, like the exhaust from a car engine begging to die, or thin milk.

Danny thought, *Well, I could strike him. That would probably be the smart thing to do. Just punch him in the nose...*

And as Danny had the thought, some twitch or itch or inkling triggered something in the intruder's training or instinct or muscle memory, and the man in the suit said, "Oh, no, noooo—Danny. You don't want to do *that*." The man laughed a wheezy chuckle and said, "I should say, I definitely don't *want* you to do that. You're a far stronger specimen than I am, Danny, and such a terrific athlete. There's little chance I'd be able to fight back. I do have a few techniques I've been anxious to apply on an actual subject in the field, as it were, but still—I saw what you did to that poor lad from Dire Vale, and believe me, I have a full and deep understanding of just who qualifies as big and strong in this... well... *kitchen*." He looked around the space and said, "My gracious, man, do you never—"

"Who the hell are you?" Danny said in a burst of anxiety and panic and frustration.

The man laughed. "Ah, yes. How *rude* of me. I've been *terrible*." He shoved his hand across the table, and said, "Danny Hooper, late of East Southwich Albion Association Football Club, you may call me...Three."

Danny relaxed for a moment in the face of this preposterous announcement, relieved at the thought that he could either be dreaming or have been transported to some alternate reality that would soon cease to be, and he would soon be back on the training ground at the Auld Moors, rolling his eyes at something that had just escaped Aldy Taylor's mouth or trying to decipher an instruction from Mumble McCray.

"I see," Danny said. "Your name is... *Three*." Danny walked to the sink, refilled his water glass and took a sip from it. "Go on, then, *Three*. Explain."

Three attempted a smile, but it came unnaturally and only made Danny more certain that he was a weasely character, an untrustworthy annoyance. "I reckon you've opened your mind to the many reasons I may be here in your flat, and you have yet to demonstrate a commitment to physically attacking me. This is a relief for obvious reasons, but it also paves the way for us to come to an agreement upon the circumstances which will hold when I leave your residence, my dear man."

"Maybe I will attack you. If you keep on talking like that. I'm a dangerous and unstable person. I've proved that much, haven't I?"

"You may be all of that, but I don't believe you'll attack me. Not in my heart do I believe such a thing." He placed his hand across his breast.

"Explain yourself... now," Danny uttered, clenching his fists.

"Of course, of course. All business." Three waved his cigarette again. "Let us indeed cut the pleasantries just a bit short. I, Danny, am in possession of your plane ticket to America."

Danny winced as if *he'd* been hit. "*What?* Who the hell are you?"

"Yes, yes! *Now* I have you! Very good, Danny! Everyone comes around in time, in time. And you're a quick one! Well, I'm hardly surprised. Most of the athletes are quick, in one way or another. *Very* good. Now then, Danny, I have arrived at the point in the proceedings where I explain that I work for the Queen. The Queeeeeen, Danny. I do love saying it. Her Majesty. Her Royal Highness. The Crown. I work for *England*, laddie. Actually, I work for the *United Kingdom*—the whole bloody thing. Grrrrrrrreat Brrrrrrritain." He rolled his r's. "I am, in point of fact, here this very day on *your* behalf, to protect *you*, Danny, and those many millions like you."

"Listen—" Danny ventured, but found himself cut off.

"And here's where *you* come in, dear boy. *You* are going to help *us* protect the great British *we*—the greatest empire the world has ever known—from some genuinely bad doings. And the Americans too. You'll be protecting them as well. And the Western world, really."

It occurred to Danny that this man was mad. And then he really thought it through, and right at that moment, he realized that the fringe benefit of Three's bothersome presence and inability to shut his piehole was that Danny, for the first time in his post–East Southwich Albion existence, cared about something other than the reality of being an ex-member of East Southwich Albion. For this Danny was grateful. He leaned toward Three, put an elbow on the table, formed his hand into the obvious sign for *give me a cigarette*, and Three smiled. Soon, they were both smoking.

"Now," Three said, "football in America—*soccer*... I can barely even say the word—awful, awful word—is as foreign as passable curry and decent ska. Yes, all right, it has slight followings here and there, in the ethnic pockets, but mostly, Danny, people over there hate it. Simply hate it. They think it's a Commie sport. Collectivist, you know. All that *passing*. And all those short shorts and high stockings and strange names and no hands. The Americans, most of them anyway, just don't trust it. And draws... *tied games*... they just *hate* ties. They've banished them, actually, the Yanks have. Did you know that? Ah, but you'll see, you'll see. In any event, football—soccer—isn't at all American and they don't bloody like it."

Danny smoked and waited.

"Well, Danny, do you know what abhors a vacuum, other than nature, of course?"

Danny gave Three the same look he'd given that Dire Vale winger right before he probably ended his career.

Three said, "All right then, I'll tell you: Communism."

Communism? Danny thought. *This is about Communism? Communism abhors a vacuum? Since bloody when?*

"That's right, Danny. Communism. While almost all of America, including its government, the CIA, the FBI, and every home-on-the-plains sheriff with a nice big gun, has been ignoring the world's game, even as the world's game carries on right under their noses, would you like to hazard a guess who hasn't?"

Danny scarcely followed. "Who hasn't what?"

"Who *hasn't* been ignoring the American All-Star Soccer Association? The bloody Communists, Danny! The Red Menace! The whole league is a den of Marxist iniquity."

"All right then," Danny burst out. "That's it! That is bloody *it.*" Danny stood abruptly and reached for Three's collar. "Time to go back to whatever hospital you've escaped from."

Three ducked—calmly, as if he'd done this kind of thing many times before—and reached for a satchel on the floor by the table. "Calm yourself, lad." He removed a manila envelope inscribed with Danny's name and handed it over. "Inside you'll find your plane tickets, a Rose City Revolution match programme, and a little stipend."

Danny stood holding the envelope, still in a position to take a lunge at Three, and Three still looked at Danny as if an attack might be forthcoming. But Danny took a few breaths, reminded himself what happened last time he let rage guide his actions, and sat back down.

"The Russians are using the AASSA as a Cold War communication channel, my son," Three said as Danny reviewed the contents of the manila envelope. "They've loaded up all these teams with Hungarians, Bulgarians, Croats—the Chicago team used to be *called* the *Ukrainians*, for Christ's sake. *The Chicago Ukrainians.* There's a team called Red Star Toronto that's as Serbian as they sound, and the Colorado Cowhands are a front for a Romanian organization that pretends to be raising funds for orphanages—the rot really has set in, Danny. They pass if off as cultural exchange if anyone notices at all. *Red Star Toronto.* Honestly. It's like they're not even trying to conceal themselves. Of course that's Canada, but still and all. And don't even ask about the Cubans in Miami. *Cubans* in *Miami.* Do you know how much Cubans care about football?"

Danny had taken Three's question as rhetorical, but Three lingered for an answer. "Do you know?"

Danny had never heard of any Cuban footballing achievement or even of a Cuban league, so he ventured a timid, "Well, let me hazard a guess, Three. Not very much?"

"*Not very much?* How about not *at all*? Castro almost played for the New York bloody Yankees, Danny—all *he* cares about is baseball. I'd lay money your East Southwich boys could beat the Cuban national team nine times out of ten. But you run out a team of Gonzalezes, Garcias, and Hernandezes with 'Florida' on their kit and Americans think they're watching *Latin football.* The few that care, of course. Which isn't many. The Flamingos of Florida Professional Soccer Club is Havana's U.S. office, for Christ's sake, and no one's paying it any mind down there, Danny. No one."

Three took a deep drag on his cigarette, as if to calm himself down. "All right then," Danny said. "Let's say I'm following. I'm in no great hurry, mind, but cut to the punch."

"We've connected with a few of the smart ones over there, who you'll soon meet, dear boy, but you say 'football' to most Americans and they think you're talking about something else. You say 'soccer' and their eyes just go blank. They fall asleep at the very sound of the word. It's like an instinct. Pavlov's dog.

'Soccer': sleep. Remarkable phenomenon." He tapped the ash of his cigarette into Danny's water glass. Danny winced at the affront, but Three said, "These Communists are bloody brilliant. I'm impressed. We all are." He gave Danny a stern servant-of-the-people frown and said, "Danny, your country needs you. And, well, you need to get out of the country. So... to put a fine point on it... you're going over to, well, to fight Communism."

Danny got up, got himself another glass of water, returned to the table, pushed the ashy glass toward Three.

"From what I'm told, the Rose City Revolution is already full of Englishmen," Danny said. "What's this got to do with me? Just use one who's already there."

Three smiled, knowing he was making progress. He looked directly at Danny, sucked in hard on the shrinking butt of his cigarette, and said, "The Soviets are vicious, godless, barely human, and awfully frightening, but they're smart. Here's what they've worked out: football is the most important game in the world. It's the most important *anything* in the world. More people love football than love Jesus or Muhammad Ali or Buddha or the Rolling Stones, and a lot of the people who love all of those things love football more. If you want to send a message, and you want to reach the biggest possible audience, you send it through football."

Danny had never thought of this, but he knew it was true; he was surprised to find himself agreeing with Three.

"And if you want to plan something—something *big*—through football... or anything else," Three continued, "you plan for it to happen in America. That's the arithmetic."

This Danny thought was less obvious, and Three noticed.

"Come on, think about it: you can mix and match nationalities as you can nowhere else on Earth, you can humiliate the Yanks on their turf, and if you pull it off in *New York City*... the media of the *world* is right there, just waiting for a big story. And if they can pull off something big *enough*, the message will be that the Soviets are *winning*. That they can sneak anything they want right under the Americans' noses, that they can *do*... anything... they... *want*."

Danny shuddered. He hated thinking it, but he thought Three might be onto something.

"The message to the entire planet will be that the future is bloody Communist." He stubbed out his cigarette. Danny could tell that Three was proud of his little presentation, that it was well rehearsed and he'd done it just as he'd hoped.

"But what do they want to pull off, exactly?" Danny asked.

"That's what we'd like to know, lad. They're planning something in America. It's 1976. The bicentennial. They just can't get enough of celebrating being rid of us, you know. Still prattling on about it two hundred years later. Anyway, my boy, we believe Graham Broome may know what it is. We think he's one of them. Used to get away with calling himself Labour and getting worked up every time the coal miners went on strike. I'm not talking about 'Graham Broome hated Edwin Heath.' I'm talking about a serious mover and shaker in left-wing circles, anti–Vietnam War, the whole monty. We believe he's helping them somehow. Somehow you've got to help us work out."

"Everyone hated the Vietnam War," Danny said.

"You're not thick, Danny. You know what I'm on about. We have intelligence that Broome has helped pass information from a Bulgarian playing for the Seattle Smithereens to the Montreal Communards. That's what the team used to be *called*—the bloody *Communards*. Anyway, from there the trail goes cold. We're not even sure he knows he's doing it—they may have just found a sympathetic ear and they're using him, they're using poor Graham Broome. We need you there. We need to know their plan."

Danny stood up from the table. He towered over Three, and he could see he frightened the besuited bureaucrat. Danny said, "Why me? Two thousand players in the Football League. Why me?"

"We've been watching you, Danny. You're perfect. You're single. We need a single lad. We couldn't take a First Division player—too conspicuous. And we'd like someone whose game is distinctly English but who has an appreciation for the Continental and even Latin games—you're going to have to mingle with players from all over the world, players who don't think your English accent automatically makes you a world champion. Aldy Taylor tells us you're a sucker for that Dutch Total Football claptrap—you'll fit in over there. And you're smart. A clever lad. In a good way."

"And what if I say no?"

Three sighed. "If you stay in this country, you won't be happy with *how* you stay in this country. And now we know what you can do to another man in the space of a second or two. We may need that."

Danny didn't know which of the two sentences to respond to first, but before he decided, Three decided for him: "I've seen that look before, and that look is *Would you really?* and the answer, my dear boy, is I'm fighting international Communism. If making you pay for what you did to that little Welshman would help in even the slightest, smallest, most miniature way, then yes. Yes, yes, and yes."

"All right then," Danny said.

Three dropped his cigarette to the tile floor of Danny's flat and said, "*That's* what I came to hear." He reached across the table to shake Danny's hand. Danny reached back. The men shook.

"I will call you in your hotel then in your Portland flat whenever I need to speak with you. No matter what you hear, if it sounds like something—*anything*—to you, it will surely sound like something to us. Tell me everything. If you ever have anything to report that feels too sensitive to say over the telephone, you'll tell me your hamstring's shot. Should I hear that, I'll reel off a series of league scores that make up a number that you'll use to call me from a pay phone. Do you understand?"

Danny said nothing.

"Do you understand me?"

"I get it, I get it," he murmured.

"Now, listen. I can appreciate what we've done to your life. Two days ago you were stepping out on that pitch thinking you were about to help your boyhood club advance to the Fifth Round of the FA Cup, now... all of this. But your country really does need you—and besides, Communist Graham Broome thinks you're the missing piece for his side. He thinks with you there he can get the Revolution all the way to the Bonanza Bowl."

"The what?"

Three laughed. "Erm, yes, well—that's what they call their big final over there. The Bonanza Bowl. I know, I know. But the Americans do love a catchy name and a grand spectacle. It always gets a pretty good crowd of curiosity seekers. Scheduled for New York this year. The Giganticos will be there, of course." He sized Danny up and said, "Listen, son, go on over there, help us stop this sinister plot, whatever it is, and try to win yourself something. Get to the Bonanza Bowl. You'll be a hero times two by summer's end." Three looked at Danny and said, "For club and country, hmm, old boy?"

Danny raised an eyebrow and said, "For club and country."

Three turned, grabbed his satchel, and walked himself to the door. "Talk soon, Hooper. Travel well, my boy." He closed the door and left Danny in the half-dark silence of his flat.

Danny closed his eyes, shook his head, considered crying. His mind was both blank and overcrowded with everything that had been crammed into it over the last few days. The FA Cup. The chairman. Aldershot Taylor. America. Three. The Rose City Revolution. Oregon. The Russians. The Giganticos. The Pearl himself. Then he opened his eyes and stood up.

"The Bonanza Bowl," he muttered. "The *Bicentennial* Bonanza Bowl even. What a load of rubbish."

FIVE

Danny slept for most of the flight from London to New York.

He got off the plane in the United States of America to walk around the airport and get used to the idea of being somewhere not called England. It looked a lot like London, which surprised him—he'd expected something a little brighter and shinier, something that made a greater case for the inevitability of capitalism and the unstoppable progress of the West. But it was as grungy and unkempt as England, more or less the same as what he'd left, except for a handwritten sign in a cafeteria line that said IT IS NOT RUDE TO CUT IN FRONT OF SLOW CUSTOMERS. It was the most American thing Danny had ever seen. He had never considered the idea of rudeness being relative. Can you just make a sign that says something isn't rude, when it most surely is? If one made a sign declaring that separating the knee end of a young man's tibia from its foot end wasn't a foul, would the sign make the statement true? But Danny wasn't one to dwell on life's little puzzles for too long, and besides, he was living inside one of life's big puzzles now.

On the flight to Portland, Danny was drawn into a conversation with a man who assured Danny that he didn't know anything about soccer. "It's basically hockey, right? Without the ice or the skates I mean," said the man, laughing. Danny wanted to say no, it's nothing like hockey—Danny knew almost nothing about hockey—but he reconsidered and said, "Yes, it's a bit like hockey."

The man said, "Well, sure it is. Two goals, two teams, a point for every score. Nothing terribly exotic about *that*. Do you use sticks in soccer? No? Well, anyway, hockey's exciting as hell. I like hockey."

Danny nodded, sure that the first American he had ever met had a worse understanding of football than he had before they had met.

Then the man said, "Who do you play for?"

Danny had only had one answer for this question in his whole life, so he began to say, "East Southw—" but caught himself and said, "The Revolution City Roses. In Oregon. Wait a minute...that didn't sound quite right—"

The man said, "Revolution City? I don't think so. Portland's the Rose City. Rose City Revolution sounds more like it. That sounds like it could be the name of a soccer team. I've never heard of them, but it sounds like a soccer team."

Danny said, "Yes, yes—Rose City Revolution. That's right."

The man asked if the Rose City Revolution was in the same league as the Giganticos: "I just read about them in the *Sporting Times*. First soccer article I've ever read. I guess this Brazilian is supposed to be the best player in the world? Here to convert us all to soccer? I don't know, man—Americans don't go in too much for foreign stuff. I'm sorry, I'm sure it's a great game, and if this Brazilian character, whatever his name is, ever ends up on TV, I suppose I'll watch for a while, but how am I going to get excited if it's two to one and he only gets the ball for a few seconds at a time? And he's only, what, five-foot-six? How's a little man like that sup-posed to be the best athlete in the world? How's he going to com-pete with someone your size? You're *huge*. He doesn't sound like much of a *Gigantico* to me. You ever played against him?"

Danny had not played in the World Cup or in Brazil, so he said, "No."

The man humphed. "Well, are you going to now? Play against all those foreign stars I've never heard of? Is there going to be a big Revolution-Gigantico face-off?"

"We are in the same league, yes," Danny said. Danny told the man about the great German, Dutch, Argentinean, and Italian players who had migrated to the Giganticos, and he had the sudden realization that in one afternoon against the Giganticos he would accumulate the played-against CV of a man who'd qualified for two or three World Cups.

But Danny could see the man losing interest. Too many Jürgens, Johanns, and Diegos for his *Sporting Times*–infused brain, and the man finally just said, "Well, listen, Danny, that's just great. Real nice. Have a great time in our country. Try and catch a baseball game while you're here. Wonderful sport."

Danny almost told the man he was also here to help fight Communism, just to get his interest back, but he thought better of it and was instantly happy—and relieved—to have the conversation over and done with.

Danny looked out the window and saw a perfect white Alpine mountain cast against a sky of deep East Southwich blue. The snow-capped peak startled him. Entirely too close for his taste. No one else in the plane seemed much concerned about it at all, even as a sight to behold, but Danny couldn't take his eyes off it. He had the idea that he could leap right down upon it and ski to its base, if he knew anything about skiing. It was right *there*. Right bloody there—a good three times as high as anything in all of England.

"My sweet lord," Danny said to himself.

Soon the plane began its descent into a river valley of astonishing green. The place had a primeval, slightly overgrown quality about it. Danny could imagine thatched roofs appearing in what few clearings there were, surrounded by mythic beasts and humans wearing skins and furs. He pictured giants riding dragons, knights astride unicorns fully engaged in fierce swordplay—but he couldn't spot anything that might pass for urban America circa 1976. Rolling hills, trees, a thick and slow brown river—and yet the pilot announced that they were, indeed, descending into Portland International Airport. *International?* Danny thought. *What do they even mean by that around here?*

The closer they got, the more he got the idea that twenti-eth-century life might be happening in this mysterious land af-ter all. A congregation of houseboats appeared on the near shore; he made out fishermen in their small boats in the river's middle, a railroad line hugging its bank. Low buildings sprawled across vast parking lots. Every car he could make out from here ap-peared to be a pickup truck or a lorry of some kind. This wasn't one of those places where you lowered yourself from the sky into a city. This was one of those places you snuck into by hover-ing low over a deep wood. And then there it was, just like that, the airport. "Bloody 'ell," Danny said to himself.

The man next to him stirred in his seat and said, "What's that?"

I guess I didn't say that to myself, Danny thought, and then said, "Nothing. Nothing at all."

The man said, "Well, OK then. Welcome to Portland. Good luck with everything, kid."

"Bloody 'ell," Danny said again.

"That's what I thought you said."

A representative of the club met Danny at the airport, holding a sign that said DANNY HOOPER. Three had told Danny this would happen. He had imagined maybe a squat, swarthy man from Cloppingshire, some old drinking companion of Graham Broome's. But it wasn't a squat, swarthy man from Clopping-shire. Sent to greet Danny was a girl, *a woman,* maybe twen-ty-five years of age, possessed of a radiant hippie-disco quality that didn't exist in Greater East Southwich. Her hair was deli-cately feathered and carefully frosted, and she wore a blue plaid flannel shirt unbuttoned over a gray T-shirt that read PROPERTY OF ROSE CITY REVOLUTION PRO SOCCER.

Danny couldn't locate anything in her being that seemed even remotely English. Her fantastically blue denim widelegs had a black-and-white soccer ball patch just above her right knee, and she wore bright yellow trainers. If Danny had met her in a pub or a club, he wouldn't have known whether to ask her to dance or go camping, and Danny had never been camping. She was the most American sight he had ever beheld.

He wished he had some means to capture for posterity the fact that this female held, in her American hands, a piece of paper with the words "DANNY HOOPER" written upon it. She smiled in the most wonderful American way, and so Danny walked over to her and said, "Hello. I'm Hooper."

"Well, *of course* you are," she said. "*Wonderful* to meet you. We're *so* excited to have you here. I'm Molly Hart. I work for the Revolution. This is *great*. How was the flight? *Man*, you've been traveling for a long time. What a trip, huh? I mean, I've never been to England or Europe or anything like that, but I can only imagine. Is it tiring? Or do you just sleep the whole time? What do I know—maybe you're not tired at all. Like I said, I've never been on a long trip like that. And you with those long legs." She sized him up as if he were a statue in a museum. "You're *huge*. How did you fold yourself into those little seats? Maybe you get more space on an international flight. Longest trip I ever took was to Disneyland with my family. You *have* to go to Disneyland. I know, it's for little kids, but it's *so* much fun. We have a game in L.A. Maybe we'll go. Well, maybe. We'll see. Is that *all* you have?"

Danny had flipped his duffel bag over his shoulder and momentarily tuned Molly out—no easy task for a number of reasons—as he took in the sights, sounds, and colors of the airport in his new American hometown. "Oh, um, yeah, I mean—yes, this is all I have."

"In the *world*?" Molly said. "I mean, you do *live* here now. This is your home, Danny. That's *it*? Did you find someplace to store your other things back in England? Did you keep your old place?"

"Um, yes. I mean, no," Danny muttered back. He was groggy from the travel, and his head had been thoroughly discombobulated by Molly's babbly enthusiasm and questions and, if he was honest with himself, appearance. She was prettier than most girls, he allowed himself. She was like an English girl, but all smoothed out—wide confident shoulders, wide tanned cheeks, wide white teeth. She laughed and asked him what he meant by "yes, I mean, no." He apologized and said, "Yes, yes, this is all I have. And no, I didn't keep my place. It was a clean break, as they say"—Danny grinned a little at his first American joke—"but that's all behind me now."

He smiled to himself, then said, "Molly." It was worth a try, he thought. She smiled.

SIX

"So, listen, Danny, we're going straight to the stadium today," Molly said in the car. It was a long two-door Lincoln of some kind. Danny could've laid himself across the entire backseat.

"Last week was the first week of training camp and today's the first day with the press. I'm afraid you're going to meet the Portland media on the same day you'll meet your new teammates. We'll get there early enough to introduce you to Graham Broome and you can meet most of the guys. We'll give you a pair of shorts and one of these gray practice shirts, and you'll head out onto the field and answer some of the dumbest questions you'll ever hear. 'Do you ever just want to pick up the ball with your hands and run with it?' 'Do you think America would like soccer more if the goal was bigger?' Stuff like that. I'm sorry in advance. They're still learning the game... at least they care, huh? The good news is there's a lot of excitement about you. 'Our new center fullback straight out of England. Straight out of the FA Cup.' Most of the sportswriters in Portland don't know what that is, but it's what Graham's been telling them. 'Straight out of the FA Cup, the big lad,' he says."

Well, my whole team's straight out of the FA Cup because of me, Danny thought. *That's why I'm here, I guess. Or one of the reasons, anyway.*

"Our defense was *horrible* last year," Molly went on. "Gave up the most goals in the league. If you're everything they say you are, and you are most *definitely* big and strong, then you're going to cause quite a buzz around these parts, Danny. Are you one of the Clopshire Town boys? Most of the guys are. If you are, I suppose you'll know most of them—"

"Cloppingshire United," Danny said. "And no, I'm from another club. Don't know any of them lot. But they're not so different from us. Third Division grifters..." He trailed off, and Molly said, "Well, I don't really know what that means, but OK." She smiled and patted Danny's thigh. "Lighten up, big man, you're in America. It's summertime. Relax." She turned on the radio of the great vehicle. "Sister Golden Hair" by America was playing. She laughed. "Perfect. This is going to be great, Danny. I promise."

Molly and Danny had been traveling on a freeway—that's what Molly called it, a *freeway*—for ten or fifteen minutes. They passed a hospital, what appeared to be a shopping district with a few high-rise buildings. It was more or less unremarkable, other than a billboard featuring three footballers—*soccer players,* Danny told himself—in red-and-black-striped shirts in what appeared to be post-goal euphoria under the words "JOIN THE REVOLUTION." All of the O's were soccer balls. The other letters seemed to be vaguely Russian-inspired, blocky, Communistic. Danny shook the thought away. *Don't be paranoid.*

Molly veered to the right as the freeway met a river and what appeared to be an actual town, a city. "That's downtown," Molly said, picking up on Danny's expression. "On the other side of the river. It's no New York or L.A., but it ain't nuthin'." Portland's city center was crammed into a wedge of real estate between a boat-spotted river and a thick green heave in the land that had the look of a long wrinkle in a heavy blanket. The heave's soft, verdant forest looked to be a lonely urban wood—almost supernatural to Danny's industrial English eyes, like something that didn't belong in a city.

Danny asked what it was.

"You've never seen a forest, Danny?" Molly said.

"Not in the middle of a city I haven't. What's on the other side?"

"More people."

"Why don't they live in the forest? Wouldn't it be nice to live in a forest?"

"That's not what that forest is for," she said.

Danny thought that was the kind of answer that deserved to end a conversation. Danny saw another black-and-red soccer billboard. This one said "REV IT UP FOR THE BICENTENNIAL!!!"

Portland, Molly explained, was a city for people who weren't sure how to love a city; a Portlander's idea of a beautiful day was getting out of town: sneaking off into the woods, down to the river, or up into the mountains. Molly explained that it rained a lot, but it wasn't always the same rain: the autumn rain hung in the air and made you feel like your eyesight was going; the winter rain was a shroud of cold that made you feel as if you'd never be able to warm up; the spring rain cascaded through sheets of sunlight and cleaned the air; the summer rain was like the moisture that lingers after you've taken a long, hot shower. "Around here," she said, "the sun is mostly just a reaction to the rain."

In Portland, in those days, wood moldered, paint chipped, bricks decayed. The rain and the sun attacked the city in uneven rhythms, and the hippies, war veterans, fishermen, loggers, on-again, off-again longshoremen, and kindly descendants of immigrants mixed with Portland's earliest stock—the New Englanders who got there first and settled in their houses in the hills—and improvised a life thousands of miles away from American civilization and thousands of miles more than that from anywhere where soccer really and truly mattered.

Portland, Oregon, in the bicentennial year of the republic, was an outpost in a country that hadn't elected its president or won its last war. It hadn't figured out what to do about disco, Evel Knievel, or women in pants. Portland, Oregon, in the bicentennial year of the republic, was a counterculture refuge with the claim to fame that in its lawless early days, sailors had been drugged in its saloons and smuggled through underground tunnels onto ships bound for Asia—the origin of the singularly sneaky verb "to Shanghai."

Molly exited the freeway and wended her way through the tightly packed buildings of Danny's new city. She didn't seem to be near anywhere that might be called a football ground. They seemed to be circling flat buildings, old hotels, Chinese restaurants, a bar—it all felt like the inside of the airport in New York, dingy and drab, a little down on its luck maybe, but with fresher air—and then she drove through an open chain-link gate and down a narrow hill.

There, deep in a hole a good story or two below street level, was a giant, otherworldly football pitch. "We're here," Molly said, with her wonderful, giant white smile. Danny liked her wonderful, giant white smile, and he reminded himself everybody probably did too. All those wankers from bloody Cloppingshire United. They probably loved it.

Other than the strange configuration of the J-shaped grandstand hugging the areas along one touchline and one end line, something else seemed odd about the Rose City Revolution's home ground. Its pitch didn't look... *real*.

And upon inspection, it was not.

Molly drove down the long ramp behind what Danny reckoned was the south goal of the stadium. When she reached the ground level, she turned right, passed the corner flag, and, to Danny's shock and mystification, proceeded onto the playing surface before bringing the car to a stop sudden enough to leave a massive divot in any patch of grass. And yet none of the handful of players knocking balls around, nor any of the photographers watching them, flinched. Danny gasped. Molly said, "Are you OK?"

He said, "Well, erm, I, uh—everyone else is, so I guess I am."

Danny stepped out of the car and onto the alien surface of Portland, Oregon's Multnomah Stadium. He'd heard about these plastic pitches, but... He hopped up and down upon it two or three times and felt its strange little spring. It was like a rubber mat stretched taut on all four sides. He ogled a few players in their Revolution T-shirts launching star-spangled soccer balls at each other from thirty or forty yards and struggling with mighty bounces and slick spins on the slightly moistened turf. The balls pinged and ponged in entirely un-football-ish fashion, forcing the players to control them with un-football-ish maneuvers: a cushion with the back of a thigh, or a squeeze between the knee and the ground; a rounder man trapped a ball with his ass, then turned and had it at his feet.

Danny could hardly imagine a match taking place on the slippery substance at his feet. He was about to ask Molly if this synthetic trampoline had really truly hosted a football match when a stray red, white, and blue regulation AASSA soccer ball descended toward Molly's head.

Danny stepped in front of her, tensed his upper body, and headed the ball up into the concrete grandstand. It felt good— Danny hadn't touched a ball since heading that towering Dire Vale punt at the Auld Moors. His momentum carried him into his unsuspecting driver, and she held him up—just barely— with her version of a bear hug. As the two of them stabilized, she said, "Wow—thanks, man. That would've hurt like I don't know *what*."

He had no chance of responding before being set upon by a graying local photographer. The bearded, round man had raced over from the top of the penalty box, where he'd been casually snapping shots of players knocking the ball back and forth. He arrived a few steps in front of Danny, just ahead of an eager pair of reporters, and gasped an exhausted, "*Are you OK?*"

Danny said, "Excuse me?"

"Can you do that again?" he said. "Head-butt the ball like that? I mean, if it's safe to do that two or three times in a row— can you? For a picture?"

Danny looked at Molly, who gave him a shrug and a smile and nodded back to the photographer. Danny said, "I can do that, well, over and over again, really."

"I gotta get a shot of this," the photographer said, shaking his head in disbelief.

Danny made a face, leaned over to Molly, and murmured that he thought this was the *second* season of the Revolution. "How haven't these wankers seen a man head a ball yet?"

Molly stood on her tiptoes and whispered, "They all tried their very best to ignore us last summer. We're working a little harder at helping the locals understand the game this year."

He nodded. "All right then," he said to the photographer and the reporters, "throw something at my head. Anything. Give me your worst, lads."

What followed had the look of a dodgeball game, as the reporters and the photographer hurled starred balls at Danny and he steered them to safety with his giant forehead. They kept asking Danny if he was sure he was all right, and Danny kept saying, "Time of my life, gents." The reporters were in hysterics, and the photographer dropped his camera once.

Finally a voice interjected: "Leave my big man alone, you nuggets!"

A squat, bowlegged sixtyish man with wild, wiry gray hair, a peculiar wispy beard, and a black tracksuit was hurrying toward them.

"Danny *Hooper*!" he shouted toward Danny with an outstretched arm. "I'm Graham Broome. Put it there if it weighs a ton, my boy!" Danny reached toward the possible Communist's hand, thinking he had probably never shaken a Communist's hand before, and shook it. Broome looked at the photographer and reporters and said, "We had a solid club here last year, but *this*"—he used two arms to gesture to Danny's entire body, as if he were a model showing off a new Cadillac at a car expo—"is what we were missing. Men, *this* is Danny Hooper, a real number five, a big, strong center back in the truest and grandest tradition of English football. You may score on the Rose City Revolution in 1976, but you'll have to get by this great mountain of a man in order to do it."

He still held Danny's right hand in his and had eased in closer. He was now pressed up against Danny, facing the photographer and the two or three others who had scrambled over to meet and photograph Portland's newest professional athlete. Danny smiled his big bearded smile until Broome let go of his hand and pronounced, as if to the entire stadium, "Right! That's it. That's enough with the giant today. He's just got off the plane, he hardly knows where he is, and you'll get plenty of him this season. Off you go then," and he waved the motley Rose City media contingent away as if they were annoying schoolboys. "I've got to talk to the lads."

Graham Broome, now rid of Portland's slim soccer-focused press corps, gathered the team in the corner of the rubber pitch.

Danny had not been looking forward to this moment, but he knew it as a rite that had to play itself out. He'd been on the other side of it many times in his years at East Southwich Albion, as Aldershot Taylor and the chairman tinkered with the creaky machinery of the old club. As the new man stared at the ground, the manager/coach would say something to confirm the necessity of new blood by belittling the men whose toil had gotten the team into whatever straits they found themselves. "Boys, as you know, this club would like to be more competitive than it is at the moment. We need to put on a much better show for these people who inexplicably part with their money to see us week in and week out. And that is why I'd like you to make Colin/Ancil/Abdul/Jens/Mick feel at home today." At which moment Colin/Ancil/Abdul/Jens/Mick would offer a bland and abashed wave to his teammates' *you're not home yet* nods, and look back down at the ground. Then the manager/coach would utter a half-truth along the lines of "Anything that makes the team better makes us all better," or something like that.

So it played out this day in the cool late-spring Oregon drizzle. As Danny stood next to Graham Broome on Multnomah Stadium's prickly green rug, Broomsie said the usual things, ending with "he's a damn fine footballer and we're over the moon to have him."

At this, Danny offered his obligatory look up from the ground and saw, in full for the first time, the Rose City Revolution. Broomsie moved his arm around the semicircle. "This is Petie, Pete, John, Peter, and John. Pete's useless but don't tell him that, and Peter will nick the odd goal against bad teams. They all came with me from Cloppingshire. So did Trevor, Jimmy, Jimmy, and that Peter over there. That second Jimmy didn't play in England, but he's got an English accent and he's handy for banter so we brought him across for shits and giggles. Americans don't know the bloody difference, do they? By the way, Peter, how's the hammy? Good? Good. That's Peter Surley, Danny. Peter Surley, who has a dodgy hammy and can't push himself away from a table." All the players appeared to be in their early twenties, except for Surley, who looked a good forty-five and at least that many pounds over his playing weight. He was balding and unshaven, wore loose, old socks floppy about his ankles and his shirt untucked, and he could hardly have looked less like a professional footballer. He could hardly have looked less like a Sunday pub team footballer, for that matter.

"Yes, Danny, this is *the* Peter Surley, in the flesh, the very same Peter Surley who scored a hat trick for Nottingham Athletic in their famous '63 League Vase win over Southampton Orient. To this day, couldn't buy himself a beer in Nottingham if he tried. I bought him for Cloppingshire for two schoolboys and a bag of balls—sorry to say, Peter, but even after your three at Wembley, they didn't know your value, the miserable sods. Or maybe they'd just forgotten... it *was* 1963. Anyway, he's been with me ever since." Peter Surley reached out to shake Danny's hand, and Danny knew Peter Surley could see what Danny was thinking: *1963... 1963... nineteen sixty-three...*

But Broomsie just kept on: "Big Lou here is our goalkeeper and you can call him Big Lou. Played at Cloppingshire Town in the Mid-Central Council Conference with Petie, the other Jimmy, and that Trevor there before I rescued them. Here's Dave, Dave, and Kelvin, wingers all three of them. Three fastest men we have. Tons of pace, especially Kelvin there. Over there are the other Trevors. You need as many of those as you can round up, you know. This is Todd, Todd, and the other American, whose name is..." The other American identified himself as Dave. "*Dave*, that's right, but it gets confusing around here, so we call all the Americans Todd. Only one of them is any good. I'll not tell you who. And this is Juanito, Juan, and Carlos—two forwards and a backup goalkeeper. Juanito has been tearing up the local men's league the last couple years—he's on trial with us just now but I reckon we'll sign him up. Fast as hell. Going to be the biggest surprise in the league this season, eh, Juanito?"

"*Sure*, boss," Juanito said, though you could barely hear him.

"Boys, meet Danny Hooper. Danny, the boys."

The boys nodded. Not one spoke.

Danny looked back at Molly, standing by her car. She winked. A bird sang. He missed England for the first time.

Danny wandered off Portland's pitch in a haze. Still jet-lagged and thoroughly reality-lagged, he harbored a lingering feeling that maybe none of this was happening at all, that Dire Vale United was still coming to the Auld Moors, that maybe East Southwich Albion could still advance in the Cup, that Molly was an invention of his young English mind. Then he heard his name. "Hooper." Danny stopped. "*Hooper*. Turn around, lad."

It was Peter Surley, still sweating, walking toward Danny as slowly as an athlete could walk. Even the energy required of his pillowy form to shout Danny's name seemed to slow his momentum. When he got himself close enough to Danny for polite conversation, he said, "Fancy a pint?"

Danny would have liked to smile. He'd have liked to laugh. Of course he fancied a pint. But he knew better. He was too new. Couldn't yet show the weakness of a smile. That would come, but he still didn't know who was who or what was what, so he tightened his jaw and squinted into the Portland glare and said the obvious: "Yes, I would fancy a pint."

"Good enough then, big man."

"When will this be happening, Mr. Surley?"

"It'll be Peter from now on, son, and it will be happening now. Go on inside. Clean yourself up. I'll do the same. Then we'll cross the road."

Well, Danny thought, there might be a swifty with a softening old football man after all.

They crossed the road to a tavern nearly within sight of the old stadium's pitch. "Strangest town in the league is what you've found, Danny," said Peter from across a table and a pitcher and underneath a muted television showing a basketball game that Danny couldn't quite keep his eyes off of. "Other than them"—he motioned toward the screen— "the city isn't used to being in the spotlight. It's a frontier outpost, my boy, and in a frontier outpost, everyone's here for a reason. Everyone's looking for one last shot, or their parents were. Suspicious and polite people is what that breeds. No one asks too many questions, but everyone's wondering who's following you... and where they might be."

"Who's following you?"

"Oh, nice of you to ask, my boy. Just England, only England. The past. I've won this and I've won that back at home, played for every City and Town and County and United you could name—and they've always wanted more from me, always thought there was more to come. They just kept yelling, 'C'mon, Surley! C'mon, Surley!' as if there was always more I could give them. But there wasn't any more there really. I always gave what I could, and it was never enough for them. I swear to you, I *gave*. But I'm slow, slow and methodical, so they always thought I was holding back. One day I get a call from dear old Graham Broome, who's found himself a home in a town I've never heard of, and he says, 'Peter, come play for me, where the game is an amusement instead of a religion, where they don't even know the laws of the game. Bring your magic to a place that will love you for what you can do instead of regretting what you can't.' So I came. I'm running away, Danny, just like everyone else. But I've run to America, and they'll always give you credit for that. You're running too, ain't ye, lad?"

Danny looked about the tavern. In addition to a couple of flannel-clad loners and a pair of suspender-wearing workmen, whose beer glasses competed for space with dulled silver helmets on the table before them, were two men in the corner, looking entirely out of place, wearing suits and ties. To Danny's eyes, they looked a bit like Three, or at least like Three types, and they seemed to be staring right at Danny and Peter. Danny stared back at them, seeing if he could elicit a reaction, but they didn't budge. "Don't worry about them, kid," Peter said. "They're watching the basketball."

"Mmm, I suppose they are, I suppose they are." Danny inhaled half a glass of his watery beer, half believing Peter Surley, half wondering how much those men really cared about basketball. To distract himself, he asked Peter to explain Portland to him.

"They don't need much, the people here, and they don't expect much either. You go to the finest restaurants and you'll see jeans and sandals and jumpers and T-shirts. They believe what they believe, and they reckon you can believe what you believe too. Live and let live around here. To these folks, the teams that come and the players who play are as intriguing as the circus. To the good people of a distant western port town, men who can scarcely walk the streets in their native lands without being accosted by adoring fans are wonderfully exotic, not frighteningly foreign. We aren't any good, Danny, but these like don't know good football from bad. They're happy to give a strange new game a fighter's chance and they love us for bringing teams from L.A. and New York and Chicago to their strange old place, like these basket men up here on the telly. They were a little slow to catch on, but we brought the Pearl of Brazil to Portland, me boy. We brought the Pearl, but we've a loyal following, Hooper, and I'll tell you something—if we can win, Danny, if we can win..."

"So you like it here then?"

"Aye, Danny. I like it here. Paid vacation. I could score a hat trick of own goals against anyone but Seattle, and they'll have me back. And you know it's their bicentennial, Danny, 1976. Two hundred years. Two hundred years without us watching over them. They're making a jubilee of it. Everywhere we go, you'll see it. And you know they think we sound like Beatles when we talk. We'll be the Englishmen in the heart of their star-spangled summer."

"You didn't seem happy on the pitch."

Peter gave Danny a paternal look through the pint glass at his lips. "Look at me, Hooper. I'd have to lose one of myself to be at me playing weight. I'll *never* look happy on the pitch. It's not possible. But I am, lad, I am. No place I'd rather be." He set his glass back on the table. "Now tell me, Danny, who's following you?"

A small cheer went up in the room. The home team had just done something significant in the basketball game on the screen. Everyone cheered except for the men in the suits and ties.

GIGANTICOS

American Superthunder
super soccer team

RED STAR
toronto

ROSE ★ CITY REVOLUTION

American All★Star Soccer Association

1976 MEDIA GUIDE

WE ARE THE SEATTLE SMITHEREENS
PRO SOCCER TEAM

COLORADO COWHANDS
HANDS IN THE NAME   NOT IN THE GAME

DEMOLITION
DETROIT PRO SOCCER

LA Glitter
professional soccer

the flamingos
of Florida Pro Soccer

CHICAGO
Professional   Soccer
BUTCHERS
AASSA CHAMPS
1972 ★ 1973

SEATTLE SMITHEREENS

Last year's Bonanza Bowl runners-up have added Bulgaria's best player to an otherwise all-British starting lineup and they're ready to take another run at the mighty Giganticos!

ROSE CITY REVOLUTION

This plucky mix of Englishmen and young Americans had a rough go of it last summer, but they've added a tough new fullback and hopes are high out in Portland, Oregon.

COLORADO COWHANDS

The Rockies welcome a wandering retinue of Romanians to their remote rodeo ground for what promises to be a rollicking good time.

LOS ANGELES GLITTER

The Angelinos combine a Scottish defense with a Mexican midfield and a mercurial center forward into an intriguing and spicy, but potentialy lethal, brew.

AASSA

AMERICAN ALL-STAR SOCCER ASSOCIATION

RED STAR TORONTO

These Yugoslavians are possessed of refined skills and remarkable moustaches. They almost knocked off the mighty Giganticos last year–and they're ready for another try!

CHICAGO BUTCHERS

Some of Eastern Europe's finest players grace the friendly confines for a summer of outstanding soccer and quality bratwurst.

GIGANTICOS

Used to be called the New York Giganticos, but they belong to the world now. They may be the best team on earth, and they have the best player of all time. They occasionally play without a goal-keeper to keep them-selves interested.

FRONTIER CONFERENCE
LIBERTY CONFERENCE

DETROIT DEMOLITION

This vagabond franchise played in Milwaukee in '74 and Ft. Lauderdale the year before that. They arrived in the Motor City last summer and now they're really hoping to make Michigan their home. But they're not very good.

AMERICAN SUPERTHUNDER

An ambitious Bicentennial experi-ment in developing a Team USA that could win the World Cup as soon as the 1980s! Look out, World...here come the Yanks!

FLAMINGOS OF FLORIDA

The pink-clad Flamingos are comprised of Cubans who'd rather be playing baseball. Considered to be one of the best slide-tackling teams in the entire world, but they don't win very often.

1975 SEASON IN REVIEW

The American version of the game is exciting and unpredictable and exactly the kind of summer entertainment the U.S. sports fan craves. Last year's action brought more spectators out to see "The Game of the Future" than any season in league history, and they were rewarded with just the mix of rough-and-tumble thrills, spills and breathtaking skills that will keep bringing back a new generation of fans to the AASSA's stadiums and ballparks.

The season ended with the Giganticos outlasting Seattle in an exciting Bonanza Bowl in New York City, and both teams are ready to fight off challengers for their spots in the title game this year.

FRONTIER CONFERENCE

	W	L	GF	GA	Points
Seattle Smithereens	24	6	68	29	199
Los Angeles Glitter	20	10	54	34	172
Colorado Cowhands	17	13	75	66	163
St. Louis Apple Pie	14	16	61	56	132
Rose City Revolution	6	24	37	74	73
Dallas Debacle	1	29	11	123	19

LIBERTY CONFERENCE

	W	L	GF	GA	Points
Giganticos	27	3	114	22	233
Red Star Toronto	22	8	62	43	187
Chicago Butchers	17	13	75	68	165
Detroit Demolition	11	19	48	76	122
Flamingos of Florida	8	22	41	74	86
United States United	7	23	48	87	83

SEMI-FINALS: Each semi-final was a five-game total goals series played over three weeks. Seattle beat Los Angeles 19-14, the Giganticos beat Red Star Toronto 23-21.

BONANZA BOWL: Giganticos 3, Seattle Smithereens 2

Last summer brought the league to new cities, revived a few rivalries, and introduced the United States to some very old players. The league is more excited about soccer's prospects in the USA than ever before, and this Bicentennial campaign promises a memorable season of warm summer nights with America's hottest new game.

THE AMERICAN ALL-STAR SOCCER ASSOCIATION HOPES TO SEE YOU OUT THERE GETTING A KICK OUT OF SOCCER!

SEVEN

He awoke the next morning in the old-lumber-money comfort of the Benson Hotel in downtown Portland, Oregon, USA.

He was still jet-lagged and had suffered a restless sleep, but he had a job to do, and he put on his trainers, a pair of shorts, and a drill top over two or three layers of T-shirts. He went down to the lobby, had a cup of tea, and began his wait for Molly by picking up a copy of Portland's morning paper. And right there at the top of the Sports section was Danny's face smashed against a ball, bearing the facial expression of a man who might eat animals alive in the woods. "Heads Up!" said the headline. Big man, big beard—he even looked like he had big teeth.

Molly was right on time, waving her own copy of the paper. "Danny Hooper! You're a star!" She made a show of asking for his autograph. She asked the hotel's employees behind the front desk if they knew who their famous guest was.

One of them said, "A basketball player?"

By nine o'clock they were in Molly's car, heading uphill toward the forest that had captured Danny's curiosity on his way in from the airport.

Molly said, "Today the team runs. You ready for a run? How was your sleep?"

Danny said, "Horrible. I'm shattered, to be honest. Cream crackered. Haven't a clue what time it is, what country I'm in, what club I play for. Don't know that I'm up for much of a run, but I'll do what I can."

Molly reached over and up with her right hand and put it on Danny's shoulder as she drove. She squeezed a couple of times and said, "Ah, you'll be all right. This whole league is full of players who don't know exactly where they are or why they're here. And most of them can't run at all. Once you get body, mind, and spirit aligned, you'll feel fine. You have my word, Danny—you'll love it, and the folks here will love you right back."

Danny just wanted her to squeeze his shoulder again.

In what seemed like mere moments, Molly's car left a concrete cityscape and entered a forest. "Where *are* we?" asked Danny.

"Still in Portland."

He wondered at these trees that could so easily loose themselves from the soggy, saturated ground and crush four or five homes in one stormy, tumultuous moment. *But then, what's one more rainstorm? They're trees after all,* Danny reminded himself, *not impetuous center backs with chips on their shoulders... Why should they wish to end it all for the fun of crushing defenseless people who just happen to be in the wrong defenseless place at the wrong defenseless time? Why would a tree do something that cruel?* A chasm opened beneath them to his right—a steep ravine of impossibly deep green. Trees grew from trees, ferns grew from moss, ivy grew from whatever it could find and climbed whatever it wanted. He said, "So this is Portland, huh?"

Molly said, "This is Portland. Roll down your window. It'll be cold, but it'll feel good."

Danny did as Molly said and suffered the first blast of what was now, finally, March air, and it did feel good. East Southwich still smelled coal-heated and fish-fed—the local industry was the local smell, and you couldn't escape it with anything other than cigarettes and beer. Danny wasn't even sure what he smelled rising up out of that Rose City ravine, dripping from the green canopy above, streaming past his face, and now getting stuck in his beard as he hung his considerable head out the window of Molly's car. Was it a natural smell? He had no idea.

Molly turned and drove up a windy road, past numerous runners, walkers, bicyclists, dog-walkers, gravelly parking areas, and muddy trailheads, until Danny spotted a rocky shoulder in the distance filled with men in combinations of red, black, and gray football gear. The Rose City Revolution stretched, hopped, jogged, smoked, or stood in a loose orbit around Graham Broome, who looked not one bit like a man who could manage more than half a mile in these hills—though he was hardly the only one.

Molly pulled over, parked her car, and said, "Time to join the gang."

Danny stepped out of Molly's car and felt the stares of the twenty men he had silently met yesterday. Not one had offered him much more than a half-hearted handshake or a light nod of the head. Half of them—the fullbacks and the defensive midfielders—saw his arrival as a rebuke to their abilities and an open threat to their jobs, and the other half—the forwards, wings, midfielders, and goalkeepers—wondered how on earth someone of his astounding mass could possibly be agile enough to keep the league's strikers—mostly small, lightning-in-a-bottle Latin demons and sorcerous Slavic craftsmen—away from the besieged Revolution goal. Only Broomsie amongst them smiled as Danny crunched the pebbly grit beneath him on his approach to his new team.

"Danny!" Broomsie shouted. "Haven't seen you since I looked at the paper this very morn! Good to see you in the flesh, my boy! All right, lads, we're all here! Take a few minutes to stretch what ails ye, and you know what to do from there. Down that hill, take a left every time you can. It's four miles to the next car park. I will see you there."

No one said hello to Danny. And a few minutes later, Broomsie said, "Right then, let's go!"

And he turned his misshapen body down the hill behind him, disappeared along a trail, all bow-legged and jangly, and was followed in obedient silence by the Rose City Revolution: the Englishmen went first (except for Big Lou), then the Yanks, then Juanito and Juan, and finally the two goalkeepers. Danny watched it all, the men queuing at the top of the trailhead as if waiting for a beer or a toilet, giving the runner in front of him five or ten seconds before following (at first Danny thought this must have been out of a kind of forest-running etiquette, but he soon found that if you were any closer to the runner in front of you, your face would be caked in mud within your first twenty steps), and then plunging down the hill. Danny waited, taking his proper new-man place at the end of the line. When everyone else had gone, he went.

For a good quarter of a mile, Danny enjoyed himself. It was quiet in this forest, even with twenty-some other men. And Danny hadn't really moved his body in a meaningful way since crushing that Welsh boy's tibia at the Auld Moors. He could feel his pores reopen and gasp in delight at the clean, fresh air. He looked up and saw the mighty trees flicker by, the slivers of milky-white sky above them spitting down tiny capsules of un-soiled water onto his hairy face. He looked down and loved the mud beneath him on the trail. *Mud, yes, mud, yes,* he thought. He was cold, he was wet, and while he wasn't entirely content, he had his first hints of American happiness—

But that was only for a quarter of a mile.

At the trail's first curve, Danny slipped and nearly fell, just steadying himself with a deft left hand on the ground. It was muddier here, down the slope some; Danny could hear the sub-terranean *drip-drip-drip* of water rippling and settling into the hillside mud, something he'd never heard before. While Dan-ny placed his feet in careful, almost dainty increments, trying to place as much of his soles on the ground as possible, the other players navigated the sloppy path like native creatures of the wood, surprisingly sure-footed in the mud. His new teammates. By the second turn, Danny could feel them drifting away from him, and he worried he might end up lost in this deep American forest, thousands of miles from home. He supposed that Broome would make his way to the back of the pack in time, and Danny figured if he couldn't catch up to Broome, then he was a sorry excuse for an Englishman. But still he worried.

At the third bend in the trail, at a dead hollowed-out fir tree—*that's bloody huge,* Danny thought, *I've never...*—Danny felt a sharp pain in one of his calves. For the briefest instant, as he felt his legs give out and as he extended his arms to ease his eventual collision with the ground, he thought one of his Achilles tendons had ruptured—*just now, bloody just now, and here,* he thought, *bloody here.* The thwacking sound he'd heard seemed to have been the sound he'd heard before, usually in players in their declining years, the slow terror of the mid- to late thirties, when no one was even near them. They'd try to accelerate with the ball, a move they'd made thousands of times in their foot-balling lives, and *SNAP!,* like the full sound of cricket bat against ball. They'd scream, go down, you'd run over, and the look on their faces was more of grief than pain: *I'm done,* the look would say. *I've played this game since I could walk, I've scrounged a living out of it, built my identity around it, let it lead me around by the nose, and now here I am, on my back, in the mud, and one of my legs doesn't work and will never really truly professionally play again.* That was the sound Danny had heard as he plunged to the soft Portland ground, in this deep and wild American wood. *Do I really have the Achilles tendons of a thirty-seven-year-old man? Am I really about to be alone here in this forest with at least one destroyed Achilles?*

The answer to both of those questions was no.

Before he could turn his face to the sky, two men were upon him, wrestling him into the hollowed fir. One of them had a hammer... a bloody *hammer.* Danny screamed a generic *arghhh-hhh* and then a mighty *heyyyyyy,* calling the men a great variety of names; he swore mightily, threatened to kill them, even yelled for help—but the men remained silent until Danny was settled against the rough interior of the dead tree. Then one of them uttered a heavily accented, "We know why you are here, Mr. Hooper."

One of the men picked up Danny's left foot and held it aloft, creating a forty-five-degree angle out of Danny's leg and the ground. Danny thought it was a strange thing to do, but he was in no position to resist. Then the man who had spoken held the hammer up in the air. He said, "We are also knowing what you did to that Welsh player in the FA Cup." It had been difficult for the man to say "Welsh."

"I will maybe do that to you right now."

Danny said, "No, no. Don't." It was all he could come up with. He felt like an idiot, but his mind had been softened by the events of the last few days.

"Oh, and why not, Danny Hooooper?"

Danny thought that was a pretty good question. He said, "Well, first off, who would you be avenging exactly? I mean... you don't look like Dire Vale supporters to me, though they've got some frightening characters of their own...and I wouldn't guess you're much bothered about the future of the Welsh national team, such as it is. And here I am, trapped in these woods with the worst team in the American league, in a *bloody tree* with you two—I've been well punished so far, haven't I?" It was the most he had spoken at a stretch since meeting Three.

The man lowered his hammer—slowly, to his side. Danny continued: "And besides that, if you really know why I'm here, then you know nothing can happen to me."

Danny couldn't believe he had said this, because he couldn't believe he'd thought it. Maybe his mind had caught up to his body—both were in America now, totally engaged in a situation that was getting stranger with every move Danny made, or that was made upon him. *Yes,* he thought, *yes, Danny, you're goddamned right these probable Russians have to leave you alone... because if anything happened to you...* "Whoever it is that knows whatever they know and sent me here will know that you know what they know."

The men shot puzzled looks at each other and then back at Danny. "Say that another time please," said the one who hadn't said anything yet.

Danny said, "You know what I mean."

"Yes," said the man, suddenly pensive, and suddenly seeming like an entirely reasonable chap. "Yes, we do."

The men stood inside the tree for a confused moment. Then one of them, the more reasonable seeming of the two, said: "You are here to foil a plan that has been in place for many months, Hooooper. The American imperialists and their Western conspirators will fail. They cannot conquer the world without football, but we will not allow them to conquer the world with football."

Ah, for Christ's sake.

The other man took over: "America's ignorance of football will be its downfall. We will conquer from within. You may report all of this to your man in England. He will not stop us. This season, the bicentennial year of the great U.S. of A., we will use American soccer to make the greatest announcement ever— *ever!*—of Soviet power."

Danny looked for a means of escape. Inside a moldering former tree, with raindrops finding their way through the ferns and ivy and sundry fauna that occupied the space between ground cover and treetop in this greenhouse of a green space, Soviet agents were laying bare their intentions of using the 1976 AASSA season as a major milestone in Cold War brinksmanship.

"Yeah? Well, you can both sod off," said Danny inside that tree. He rose, and neither man could stop him. As he stood, he stumbled from the pain in his calf, but he still towered over each man. He pulled back a fist as if to punch the nastier of the two, who cowered, but Danny restrained himself. "You'll fail, I promise you that. You will fail. I never want to see either of you ever again, you got that?" Danny knew he'd see them again.

The men inside the tree were clearly scared of Danny's fist— but they weren't entirely intimidated.

"Danny Hooooper," one of them said, "you may go. But you will never be far from us. Remember, Danny—we know why you are here."

"I'm here to win a championship. That's it," Danny lied, though he sure wished he were telling the whole truth. "Now you can bloody well leave me alone." Danny ran out of the tree and down the hill, before realizing that he had no idea where he was going. So he ran back up the hill, past the tree, screaming terrible, terrible words in as intimidating a voice as he could summon, in the event the men were still there, which they most likely were. When he reached the car park, he considered waiting there for help, but thought that was too close to the Communists and probably useless, so he ran down the road—his calves hurt, oh, they hurt—thinking Molly, or Broomsie, or someone, would come along in time and rescue him.

It occurred to him to cry, and he did a little. Not tears of sadness or self-pity, but of confusion. He could hardly comprehend the madness that had overtaken his life since strolling out at the Auld Moors to the cheers of the good people of East Southwich, in the royal blue he loved so dearly, what, a few days... a week ago? Something like that. Since the first few moments of that match, since heading that goalkeeper's punt back up into the coal-choked East Southwich air, since scrambling for the ball with that whelp of a winger, almost nothing had made sense. He just wanted to be home, home in *England*, anywhere in England. Or on a football pitch, even here in America—a plastic one would do fine. He just wanted desperately, passionately, dreadfully, frantically to be somewhere he understood and as close to *now* as absolutely possible.

But he was on the side of a mountain road, on the side of a *mountain*, as far as he knew, in a distant and wild semi-metropolis, and he had no choice but to choke back tears and run and walk and run and walk until someone found him.

"Danny," Molly yelled out of her rolled-down window, "what are you doing here? I was just coming back to get the balls out of Graham's car..." She pulled over, got out, and put her arms around Danny, which felt good. "Oh my *god*," she said. "You look horrible. Get in the car." She guided Danny over to the passenger-side door and eased him into the seat. "You poor thing," she said. (*She really said that!* Danny thought.) She had a blanket in the back and she put it over him.

"Let's get you somewhere warm," she said. "Danny, what *happened*? Where have you been?"

Danny would have loved to tell Molly everything. But he knew how it would sound—he knew he would eventually have to say, "There were Communists in the tree"—and he knew he would have to find a decent place to start and he had no idea how he would do that, and he really just wanted to get into a nice long conversation with Molly about anything—*anything*—other than what had just happened. Instead, Danny just said, "I got lost. I'm new here, you know."

Molly blurted a spurt of air through her lips and said, "Yeah, right. The entire front of your body is covered in mud, you've scraped the side of your face that already has a black eye, it looks like maybe you've cut your lip—likely story, big man." She looked over at him with a dubious face that was nonetheless the most appealing sight Danny had seen in a good while, maybe even ever. Danny looked at her, held Molly's gaze until she looked back at the road, and said nothing.

"OK," she said. "That's fine. You got lost. I guess I'd be a little embarrassed too. Lost in the woods. Maybe attacked by a bear? Let's get you back to the hotel and get you cleaned up. You're off to one hell of a start!"

He kept his mouth shut, leaned his head against the window, and just watched the greenery go by as Molly drove him back downtown. He was anxious to speak with Three, a condition he had not anticipated.

After a shower, Danny sat on the bed in the hotel room and wondered if there even was a smart next thing to do. He wondered if he was just plain stuck—stuck here in Portland on this crap team that was unlikely to win a championship—and for his troubles he was doomed to be harassed by ninja woodsmen Communists whenever he let his guard down. He got out the manila envelope Three had given him in East Southwich, flipped through the Rose City Revolution match program. He read Graham Broome's bio. He took notice of the club's 1975 tagline—

THE REVOLUTION KNOWS WHAT'S GOOD FOR YOU—and thought it sounded fairly Soviet. And he read a history of the club that clearly had not an ounce of truth to it: "It was a simpler time. A time when roving Mexican revolutionaries could just stroll into Portland, Oregon, and get up a decent game with the first eleven guys they came across. And that's just what happened one summer day in 1959, when a lost band of Castro's men—separated from their regiment after the infamous Battle of San Berdoo— challenged a local guild of white-collar unionists known as the Stumptown Rosemen to a series of goodwill matches. The visitors defeated the Rosemen in game after game in stifling hundred-degree heat; eventually, the sympathetic Mexicans donated their uniforms to the Americans (who had played each game in full baseball flannels). In gracious response, the Rosemen renamed themselves in solidarity with the Mexican dissidents, and everyone adjourned to the Skyline Diner for a milkshake. In the years to come, the team fought bravely in local leagues, until one Sunday in 1965, when the Revolution got lost on its way to a game in Clackamas and, having lost the inspiration of their forebears and seven players (who were never seen again), just decided to stop off for a beer and forget the whole thing. But the 1970s herald a bold new era for Portland soccer, and the scent of fresh Revolution is in the air. The spirit and the club are reborn, determined to carry the legacy of rebellion, defeat, and frozen dairy products into a severely limited future."

"Is this true?" he would ask Molly. "Sounds rather fanciful. I thought the Revolution was a new creation."

"Oh, Danny, of course it's not true. But Broomsie thought the club needed some history, even if it's fictional. Says all English clubs live off the past. There was no Battle of San Berdoo. Who'd ever believe a load of BS like that? The Stumptown Rosemen... honestly, Danny."

Folded into the program was a sheet of paper with a list of phone numbers. First on the list said, *When you get to Portland, call this number.* Danny reached over to the phone, pulled it into his lap, and realized just how badly he wanted to tell someone about the Communists in the tree. He dialed the number.

"Hello?" said the voice on the other end. It was a sweet voice, a kind voice, it was—

"Molly?"

"Yes."

"Molly Hart?"

"Who's calling?"

"Molly Hart of the Rose City Revolution?"

"Maybe. Who's this?"

"Molly, it's—it's *me.* It's Danny. Danny Hooper."

"Oh, hi, Danny. I've been waiting for you to call."

"Excuse me?"

"How did you get the number?"

"I could ask you the same thing."

"That's not true, sweetheart. You called *me*, remember?"

"But that's because your number is on a piece of paper. This piece of paper in front of me here. This piece of paper I got from..."

"I know how you got it." She paused, then said, "You're not just here to help us win a championship, are you? Of course not." Her voice lost a little of its sweetness, and she said, "Wait forty-five minutes. Then walk downstairs to the front door of the hotel. Turn left. Go down a block. There's a Chinese restaurant. Go in, order, have a seat. Once you're settled I'll come in."

Danny didn't answer. He thought Molly sounded ridiculous. "Molly, this is crazy. You're talking like Three... like a—"

"Not on the phone. See you down the street." And she hung up.

Danny held the phone in his hand and looked into it as if it might let him in on the joke. But the phone was done talking, and finally Danny set it back on its handset. "Good Christ," he said out loud. He hung and shook his large head, rubbed the bridge of his nose with his thumb and forefinger, and let a great huff out of his big lungs. Then he got up and started getting himself ready for a walk to the Chinese restaurant a block down the street from the hotel.

EIGHT

One of the Russians had seen Brazil play the USSR in the 1958 World Cup and had been captivated. Captivated by all of them, by all of the Brazilians, but by one of them in particular.

The Pearl was only a teenager then, not yet the king of football, and he might not have been the best player on his team that day, but that Russian, then only ten years old, in his cramped Moscow apartment, had seen something in that young player—the way he had moved, suddenly yet gracefully, easily yet always effectively. The Soviets, who had seemed almost invincible in their previous two matches—a draw and a win in which they conceded no goals—now seemed too big, too strong, too stiff against the Brazilians and against the smallest amongst them. The Russian, Lev, loved football, and though he shared the name of a famous Russian goalkeeper, he found that he loved the attacking, Brazilian version more than he loved the Communist Soviet version that didn't just lack poetry, it discouraged it.

The Russian had watched the 1962 World Cup, hoping for more samba magic, but opponents hacked the Brazilians to bits that year. The Brazilians won the Cup, but only by surviving it. The Russian had gotten wrapped up in the dramatic '66 Cup in which the USSR advanced to the semifinals—but then the summer of 1970 happened.

The Kremlin could stifle its own rebels and iconoclasts, but it couldn't keep the planet's footballing championship from its people, and that meant that everyone got to see that the game could be as otherworldly and glamorous as anything else. For a nation deprived of the Summer of Love, those sixteen teams gamboling in the Mexican sun was its Woodstock, a bohemian discarding of decades of soccer science and custom. For that Russian, now a twenty-two-year-old named Lev, who had proven himself the best marksman in his military district during his compulsory service, it was the solidification of a worldview, a pilgrimage brought to him as if he'd ordered it at a restaurant. Lev hardly even thought of what he was watching as football at all: he experienced it as if it were a religion and he a recruit. The Brazilians seemed to be winking at the world, inviting everyone who understood what they were doing to come away with them to some distant island and create a new culture. Lev never doubted his own Russianness, never wavered in his patriotism, but he wondered why the nation that gave the world its best novels and ballets and architecture couldn't bring its abundant imagination to football. He wondered how the Soviet Union was ever going to spread its ideology to an eager planet if it couldn't show its superiority through the planet's favorite game.

When Lev was eleven, he and the boys from the neighborhood played football after school on the hard-packed dirt in between their apartment blocks. It had never crossed his mind to wonder where the two little rusted goals had come from, or whose ball it was that they used. The goals were just always there, leaned up against one of the buildings, and the ball—they had only ever used one, bouncy, rubber, a formerly white brown and getting browner—just appeared day in and day out, like a stray dog.

One year he saved a few rubles to buy a new ball for a friend's birthday. He bought the cheapest ball he could find, nothing special, but his friend was a gifted, clever player, the most Brazilian amongst them, and Lev had developed the idea that he, more than any of the other players, deserved his own ball. Lev never told the boy why he had bought him a football, but Lev had bought the boy a football because of what Lev had seen in 1958.

When Lev's parents found out that he had bought the ball, they were confused. Lev could tell that they were confused in an unhappy way:

"Why did you buy the ball?" Lev's father said at first.

"It's his birthday," Lev said. "And he likes football."

Lev's mother said, "Where does he play football? And when?"

Lev said, "Where we all play. Between the buildings. After school."

Lev's parents had looked at each other then, across the table, concerned. Now Lev understood the look. "It is a team game, is it not?" said Lev's father. "A collective game. How many footballs do you need? You need one. Now, thanks to you, you have two. And one is his. What good is that? To you, to him?"

Lev's mother said, "This will be strange for him. Now he is not normal. He has a ball now, Lev. Not you. Or any of the other boys."

Still, Lev gave the boy his ball. The boy kept it as his own, and for a time, Lev never saw it. The old ball grew slicker and browner with time, until one day it bounced on a piece of broken glass and popped. The boys stared at its shriveling carcass for a few moments, wondering if and when they'd ever play again, until Lev's friend sauntered over to his school bag and produced his ball, a nearly new beauty, which he rolled out amongst the group, and the game began again, and the ball was no longer, and never would again be, Lev's friend's ball. He didn't even take it home with him that day. He just set it next to the building with the ugly little misshapen goals, and that was that.

NINE

Danny entered the Chinese restaurant, which contained no patrons, and nodded at the man and the woman behind the counter. They each said, "Hello, sir," and he felt, for the first time, like a resident of the United States of America. He wasn't in an airport, he wasn't at a football ground, he wasn't in the woods—he was just an employee of an American organization, with American dollars in his pocket and nothing in his belly. He looked through the glass partitions between him and the food, looked at the strangely colored rice and the breaded mysteries before him, and he said, "I'll have that and... *that*."

The woman said, "That and *that*?"

Danny wondered if he'd made a disastrous pairing. "Well, uh, what is *that*?"

The woman was about to answer when Molly came up behind him and called the woman by name. The woman smiled, and Molly said, "Give him my regular, and give me one too." The woman discarded Danny's previous order and replaced it with noodles and vegetables. Then she prepared the same for Molly.

"I wouldn't have taken you for someone who'd order something he didn't understand," Molly said.

Danny said, "I've given up on understanding anything in my life just now. Especially my orders."

Molly laughed. "Fair enough, big man." She told Danny to put away his money, paid for the food and two Cokes, and motioned for Danny to pick them a table.

When they'd sat down, he said, "So... finally someone who can explain to me what's going on here."

"Well," Molly said, "I'll try. But I'm not sure I have as much information as you want me to have."

"But something's going on, right? Something big? I bloody well hope so by now, or I'm the butt of one of the biggest and sickest jokes of all time."

"Oh, something is very definitely going on, and you're a lot closer to the heart of it than you think you are. I think."

Danny sat back on the booth's orange particleboard bench seat, looked at the ceiling of the Chinese restaurant, and wished for the bleak northern sky over East Southwich. *What am I doing here,* he thought, and then he thought, *Why not say that out loud?* "What am I doing here?" he asked Molly. "And how might it be that *you* may know the answer to that question."

She didn't answer him, and he had a sudden wave of guilt at his self-pity and suggestion that Molly might be any less likely a component of this mystery than he was. "I'm sorry, Molly," he said. "I'm sorry. It's been a lot. A week ago, I thought I might be a hero in my own town. I was going to be one of the reasons my boyhood club was having the greatest moment in its long and mostly unpleasant history. Now... now I'm here. I probably couldn't find here on a map. I'm not in the English League, I'm in the All-American All-Star League. And worse, I'm in the middle of some frightening political intrigue that how the hell am I supposed to help solve it or fix it or I don't even know what I'm supposed to do?"

Molly said, "You got the name of the league wrong."

Danny pushed his food away. "I can't eat this."

Molly didn't answer him. Danny folded his arms. They stared at each other. She had a television quality about her, Danny thought—even as she sat across from him in a gloomy Chinese restaurant, she seemed like a girl from an American TV show, like she should be surfing in California or riding a horse in Texas. It wasn't that she was outrageously attractive—she was, actually, but that's not what overwhelmed Danny. Not exactly anyway. It was that she was devastatingly *American*. She could not have walked the streets of East Southwich or London or Stoke-on-Trent or Brighton or Bristol or Sunderland and have been taken for anything but an American, and it mystified Danny. She was probably descended from English people, or at least from Britain somewhere—her name was Molly, after all—but she seemed to have sprung directly from the New World's strange, lush soil, a different kind of being from any he had ever met. And in some strange way he did not quite have all the tools to manage or grasp just yet, she held some part of his future in her hands. "How much of all of this"—he waved his arms in a desperate circle—"are you going to explain?"

She smiled an overly confident, utterly comfortable American smile and said, "Oh, Danny, I can explain everything except for one part."

Hell, Danny thought. "What's that?" he said.

She said, "How it ends."

Danny sat back and said, "Does this place serve beer?" He ran his hands through his hair; a wave of exhaustion came over him. He felt like he'd been punched by an enraged Dire Valeman all over again.

When Danny had his ale, and one for his new friend, Molly explained: "Here's the thing: there really is no more land for the Soviets to conquer. Not really. Eastern Europe is theirs and they don't have to worry about China. They've got Cuba, a few chunks of land here and there in Africa, whatever's going on in North Korea—"

Danny interrupted. "I don't think this is actually beer, Molly."

"Oh, it totally is. Made right down the street."

"You can see right through it."

"Danny, I need you to focus. And get used to American beer. *That's* beer, OK?"

"Well, all right, but this isn't beer."

Molly leaned forward and squinted into his eyes. "Danny, I'm talking about the Soviet Union here. This is information you need. So enjoy your watery Portland beer and hear me out, OK?"

Danny sat back, took a mighty, sarcastic swig, and motioned for Molly to carry on. So she did: "So they're thinking, what are we gonna do next, take over Argentina? What good would *that* do? We beat them to the moon, broke their hearts two hundred thousand miles up in the sky—so now... what's the next great *something* in the Cold War, right here on planet Earth? That's the question. And wouldn't you like to know what it all has to do with you being here?"

"Well, yes, Molly, and if you have the answers, I'm listening." Danny motioned to the woman behind the counter to bring two more beers.

"That's what I thought, my friend." She smiled, though Danny still struggled to make out what she was so happy about. Then she offered an explanation of what just might happen next in the Cold War: "Basically, the rest of the world is waiting around while the USA and the USSR decide *what* to do. The English, the French, half the Germans—they work for *us*, for the Americans. All those other people I said before, they work for *them*. The Russians. But it's just boxers circling each other in the ring. We teach our schoolkids to hide under desks if the Russians bomb us. Did you know that? To hide under their desks. Do you know what good hiding under your desk will do in a nuclear strike?"

Danny was about to say, "No," but Molly said, "I'll bet you *do* know, Danny. Anyway, no one's bombing anyone, because if *any*one bombed *any*one, *every*one would bomb *every*one, and it would mean *no one* won *any*thing. You follow me?"

This time Danny decided on a twist: "Yes," he said.

"So what does that leave them with? Another dog in space? Come *on*. They're going to have to *win* something, and win something soon. Really soon." She laughed. Danny loved the nerve of it. Molly Hart, of frosted, feathered hair and surfer-girl smile, was *mocking* the USSR. He didn't know if it was the beer (couldn't be, could it?) or the girl or the circumstances, but he felt light-headed at all of it. She proceeded: "Are they going to win another proxy war somewhere? No, they have to prove to the entire world that they can ruin an American day—any day, whenever they want to. Unless the Cold War escalates, like *really* escalates, becomes... deadly on a massive scale, it's going to become psychological. Who can scare who and how bad."

"Are you talking about terrorism?" Danny asked. "Common... terror?"

"You say it like the Soviets are above it."

"But... but they have—"

"The bomb? Like I said: useless. It's like having all your money wrapped up in real estate. You can't buy lunch with a house, Danny."

"But—"

"Danny, we tried to slip Castro an exploding cigar. *Nothing's* below *anybody* or *anything* right now."

He was starting to see it, starting to see the logic of filling an American league with Eastern Europeans who rubbed shoulders week in and week out with some of the world's favorite people.

"They may be one of the biggest empires in the history of the world, Danny, but they're only the second biggest *right now*, and that's all that matters. They can't beat us... but they can scare us. And if they scare us bad enough... let us know that they're *there*, over our shoulder, in our blind spot, ready and willing to do some crazy stuff any time they want to, well, then... they're in the game." She put some noodles in her mouth. "You know what I mean, Danny?"

Danny finished off his beer and wondered whom Molly worked for and if she knew Three.

Molly wiped her mouth and smiled. "Guerrillas usually have an edge over their opponents, Danny. Kind of like home-field advantage. Except in this case, *we're* the home team. But there is a way they can come over here and take the advantage from us, Danny. Right out from under our noses. And we won't even notice it. Most of us won't anyway."

He said it out loud: "Football."

Molly smiled. "Yes. Football. Soccer." She sat back and looked at Danny with a nice big smile. "The Russians can't invade America, but they can invade American soccer."

"And?"

"Ah, *and*. Exactly. That's the smartest question I've heard since I've worked for the Revolution. Because who cares if the league fills up with Eastern Europeans? *Nobody.* Nobody raises an eyebrow. If there was a Slav in every 7-Eleven or if every dogcatcher was Latvian, don't you think people would notice? Of course they would. But fill up our league with Communists, and Americans are so accustomed to ignoring soccer already—except for the Giganticos—that nobody says boo. But guess what? All those people who think it's a Commie sport, they're right. But it's worse—it's a Commie *plot*. And it's going to be a *real* something, and it's going to be big. Something big and scary, something like Munich in '72, except that it will be in *America*, in *1976*. The bicentennial, Danny. And it will be something that makes the whole world look, believe me."

She put another scoop of chow mein in her mouth and looked at Danny expectantly, as if she'd just asked him to go skiing. Danny knew how to cover confusion with a center back's stone face, so he stared back at her as he would at a small Welsh winger.

"Do you know Three?" Danny asked.

"I know who he is."

"Does Three know you know who he is?"

"Not yet, but he will. Three thinks the Americans are all in the dark."

"Why does he think that?"

"Because most of us are. Do you know how hard it would be to hire four Yugoslavs straight from Belgrade to work in the deli across the street? No chance. But if you're the Chicago Butchers, and you want a back line from Kraków, somehow you have a back line from Kraków. First, Moscow saw how easy it was for someone with Red Army Football Club on his résumé to get a job in America, and then—finally, maybe even too late—someone in Washington noticed that our little league was filling up with these guys. And that someone, whoever he was, ran it up the flagpole and got enough salutes to place a few of us in a few key positions, and... well, we're going to stop it."

"Stop what?"

Molly's face changed, seemed to age by about ten years. The girlishness was gone: her face narrowed and tightened; her brow wrinkled. "We don't know."

"You don't know? But I'm going to stop it, am I?"

"You are. With our help."

"I'd think you might have a better plan than that. If you're really planning on winning this Cold War of yours."

"Cold War of *ours*."

By now Danny had waved the waitress over to their table and gotten himself a third beer. He finished it, set the bottle down on the table, looked at Molly, and said, "Who are you to the Revolution?"

"I'm the trainer. Or physio, you might say where you're from."

"You? You're our physio?"

"As far as any of you need to know, yes."

"So you'll be rubbing my thighs?"

Molly laughed. So did Danny, and he realized it had been a while. "Depends on how sore they get." The tension between them dissipated. A little.

"Now what?" Danny asked.

"Now you have to get over all... this." She waved her hands in his face, waved her arms at the window, at the street. "Your confusion, your hurt, your superiority to American soccer. No more walking around in your giant stupor wondering why you aren't still in the Third Division with East Southwich Albion." She said "Third Division" and "East Southwich Albion" with American dismissiveness, as if to say that if *she* and the people *she* knew didn't care what went on in the Third Division, then it really and truly didn't matter. "You're one of us now. You're in the Frontier Conference of the American All-Star Soccer Association, which the Revolution could win, by the way. Most of the team is happy you're here—we were a sieve in defense last year, people just slipped right through us. We must have given up four goals ten times. But we do have people who can score." Danny wondered why she was now talking about the Revolution. "We have an idea you may need to get the Revolution to the Bonanza Bowl. Don't know why yet, but we're working on a hunch."

"A hunch," Danny said. He laughed a bit.

"It's all we've got. Listen, Danny, keep that little smile on your face that I just saw, keep your eyes and ears open, tell me anything you see or hear, and we'll get to the bottom of this in time to do something about it. I'll tip you off to anything special you should be looking for game by game, but first, just show up at practice tomorrow ready to play hard. You can do that, right?"

"I can do that."

"Good, Danny. You might get your thigh rub after all."

TEN

The next day, Danny jogged the short distance to Multnomah Stadium. He had yet to acquire an American bicycle.

He entered through the same entrance Molly had used when she brought him from the airport, and he jogged down the ramp behind the goal. Halfway down he eased to a stop and leaned against the rusted chain-link fence overlooking the plastic pitch so that he might have a look at his new team before he joined it on a permanent basis. The Rose City Revolution was scattered in small groups around the field orbiting Graham Broome and Peter Surley in the center circle. Danny noticed the cliques, familiar enough to any footballer: the fullbacks in one corner launching thirty-yard lobs at each other, the forwards shooting on Big Lou and Carlos. The Todds—the Americans, the outsiders in their own country—passed amongst themselves in a small, lonely circle. A few of the speedy wingers were already running sprints—eighteen-yard bursts in the penalty box at the other end of the field. One player—there was always one—was running the stadium's stairs.

Danny determined to jog straight to Broome and Surley. As he ran, he remembered Molly's admonition—*let East Southwich go, let it go,* he told himself... *and smile*—and he tried to convince himself that this cavernous stadium so clearly built for other sports... *this* was his home and *these* lost souls were his family now—and the Bonanza Bowl was his FA Cup.

"Good morning, boss. Morning, Peter," he said with a nice big smile.

Danny shook Broome's hand and then he shook Surley's.

"Well," Broome said, "isn't this a treat! Is that a smile I see on big Danny Hooper's face? Peter, you may well have to assist me here—is that what I'm seeing here before me?"

Peter nodded and said, "He looks happy, old man. Happy to be here, are we, Danny?" Peter was smoking a cigarette.

Danny said, "I am, I am. Happy to be here in Portland, playing for the Revolution. Here to help however I can."

Broome laughed and said, "Well, it's convincing when you say it, Danny. And that, my boy, is the first step. Say good-bye to England, big man. For now, anyway," he added, reaching up to pat Danny on the back. "Say good-bye to the meat pies, the fish and chips, the warm, comforting beer. Say good-bye to the coach trips to small gray towns to play in small, drab grounds. Forget about the Queen, old Don Rogers, and the Goal of the Season. *Shoot, Match of the Day,* the League and the Cup, and the other Cup—let it all float up into the wide American sky, Danny. This"—he held his arms out before him, a grand gesture to the decidedly less-than-grand stadium, a thing of rusted beams, uneven bench seats, and chipped paint—"is football's frontier. The future of the game is here, Danny. You may believe it. No FA Cup for you, but we can get you a Bonanza Bowl. Your championship is not in England, son, but here, with me and Peter and these boys all around you."

Danny examined one of the stadium walls, a giant two-story billboard that ran the length of the ground opposite the main stand. It featured badly hand-painted advertisements for local banks, car dealerships, and Realtors. The most prominent image was a roast beef sandwich the size of two goals. A statue of a diving woman protruded from the corner, advertising swimsuits. It did not look like the future of the game.

Surley rolled his eyes and cast a puff of gray-brown smoke up into Broome's American sky. Broome whapped Surley on the shoulder with the back of his hand. "Don't you scoff at me, old man. Old Peter bloody Surley. This league is good enough for all those Giganticos, innit? Good enough for Sweet Billy Robinson down in L.A., it is. It's well and truly good enough for you and your belly and your smoky lungs. If it weren't for this league you'd be the darts champion of Tinklewick-on-Scribble and thoroughly pickled is what you'd be. Or *dead*. But here you are, you and your fat arse, rolling your eyes at your good fortune and making this young man feel less than welcome."

"Ach," said Surley, and he coughed. It was all he had.

"*Ach* yourself, Peter bloody Surley. We—those of us who care to give a shite—are going to the Bonanza Bowl, ain't we, Danny?"

Danny smiled—he thought of Molly and smiled—and he said, "I'm here to win a championship, boss. That's all."

"Aye, you are, Danny! Yes, you are!" He whacked Peter again and said, "The lad wants to go to the Bonanza Bowl, Peter! The lad's going to take *you* to the Bonanza Bowl, my old fat friend." He paused, looked down at the threadbare rug of a "field," took a great breath in through his nose, looked up at the milky sky, and raised his gruff Midlands voice and bellowed, "Lads! To the center!" and then went quiet as the Todds, the fullbacks, the forwards, Big Lou and Carlos, and the ghostly figure running the stadium steps coagulated around their possibly Communist coach and his overweight, over-nicotined, over-aged friend and the Rose City Revolution's new central defender.

"Boys," he said, "as you know, tomorrow we're off to Seattle for a little kickabout with the Smithereens. One last warm-up before the season proper, but preseason or no, they're still Seattle, so I'd like to hand them their Seattle arses. It don't count for naught other than that, but we've never beaten them, and we're expected to be at the bottom of the conference again and they're tipped to be at the top, so I'd like to give them some hint of what they're in for." He rubbed his hands, looked at Danny, winked, and went on: "So today we'll just divide up and play, Big Lou at one end, Carlos on the other. Let's knock it around a bit, get Hooper involved, show him our humble version of Total

Football, and then we'll head north in the morning. I'll mix in for a laugh, eh? Could use a sweat. Right? Right." He held a mesh bag full of bright yellow pinnies. "Whoever's with Peter takes a bib, the rest of ye with me down here."

Once the pinnies were on, he whacked a ball at Carlos, told him to get on with it, and just like that, Danny was moving his big, strong body toward the ball in his first Rose City Revolution scrimmage. He slammed into little Juanito, knocked him right to the ground, bent over to pick him up. He slide-tackled a Trevor—his first slide on the sandpapery pitch; he winced but knew very well he couldn't reveal just how bad it *bloody hurt*, then stood up, had the ball at his feet, played it to Peter Surley, fat Peter Surley, whose shirt strained against his beer-hardened belly, and who looked ten years older than the ten years too old he already was—Peter Surley, who pirouetted on his left foot, pointed the toe of his right toward the ground, put a delicate backspin on Danny's clumsy pass that allowed him to spin his defender and go in an instant from facing his own goal, Carlos's goal, to facing Big Lou's goal. Despite being marked by a Todd—a try-hard, harum-scarum Yank—Peter Surley had just bought himself a step, just a step, enough time to survey the field, look left, look right, then dig the outside of his left foot underneath the ball and send it bending into Kelvin's path on the left wing.

Danny hadn't moved since sloppily sliding the ball to Surley, and he stood with his considerable jaw slack and his eyes agog. Peter Surley was magic. Broome saw the look on Danny's face and yelled, "That's right, Hooper! We're going to the Bonanza Bowl, you big nugget! We're going to the Bonanza Bowl!"

The coach's gleeful twang entered Multnomah Stadium's ancient concrete semi-bowl on one end of its J and caromed around its metal struts and warped benches until it came out the other end as a merry bawl. "Yes, Danny! Yes, Peter! Yes, Trevor! *Sí*, Juan! *Sí*, Juanito!!! *Sí, sí, sí!* Yes, yes, yes!" Broome wailed and howled and roared, and by the end of a good hard hour, during which Danny had headed home twice, thumped three clearances up to the driveway behind the goal, stripped away most of the epidermis from his left calf, and rendered one of the Todds unavailable for the Seattle trip—nobody seemed to care—Broome was almost overcome.

"Come on in, lads," he huffed after Danny's last belt into the low Portland clouds. Broome breathed heavily as he walked through the next day's schedule, and then he told the team that he had just seen the Rose City Revolution at its very best. "Boys, boys, boys—if we had played like that just once last summer, we'd have made the playoffs." (Danny would soon discover that this was mathematically incorrect.) "You'd have *felt* it, *felt* what it was like to be that bloody good, and you'd have never turned back. I hope you'll not turn back now." The team nodded and grunted back, and Danny thought they might have even believed it.

It was mid–Third Division at best—but it was better than Danny had expected from what he'd been led to believe was one of the worst teams in the league, and Peter, who had hardly left a five-yard radius in the center of the action, was positively brilliant. Danny thought Peter had the finest touch he'd ever seen in person. He'd functioned purely as a hub—he could have smoked his cigarette during the scrimmage. The players had clearly been given a short menu of options: shoot, dribble, kick the ball as far as possible, or pass it to Peter. If they managed to get it to him, no matter how awkwardly, the old man could and would redirect the ball into whatever open space was begging for the ball at just that moment. It would be the right decision, and it would be the right ball. Without fail and every time. What happened to it from there was up to the skill, speed, and luck of whichever player was waiting for it, but the grizzled old grump would have provided that player with a step or two of freedom that he hadn't earned for himself.

Danny didn't know anything about the AASSA standard of play, but he thought he saw how this might work.

Danny was looking forward to playing in his first match since putting paid to the Cup hopes and dreams of generations of East Southwich football fans. Tomorrow, in Seattle. Might be a friendly, a little "kickabout," as Broome had called it, but it would be ninety minutes of football between teams that allegedly hated each other, and that was exactly what Danny needed. Broome said, "Hands in," and everyone put their hands together in the middle of the huddle and said, "Rose City!"

It seemed a little ridiculous, like playing football on a rug, like all these Todds scurrying about, like having to say "Bonanza Bowl," like the size of Peter Surley's gut, but Danny smiled.

ELEVEN

The road from Portland to Seattle, especially in a cool, damp early northwestern spring, possesses a stark grandeur, its blunt, two-dimensional vistas forcing the mind to wonder if it's even seeing in color: muted green-black hills set against solemn, menacing skies; desolate roadside towns murmuring loneliness at the passing traffic; every few miles a sprawl of freshly shorn log pyramids. From the highway, at seventy miles an hour, the first lot full of timber failed to alert Danny's mind to their majesty, but something about the second one—whether it was closer to the road, or the bus had slowed down, or because Danny could see the stripped hillside behind them whence they had come—helped him realize just how huge the trees were. He had a crushing sense of where he was and what this corner of the universe, so many miles and cultures and accents and kinds of thinking from where he belonged, was all about. These *were* European people after all (mostly anyway), people who had found the Old World unsatisfactory, people who had found what the first English misfits had created—*New* England—unsatisfactory too, and then had pushed through the first "West," and the next one, and the next one, until they had landed *here*, all the way over, pressed up against the last great coast of the last great "New World," and finally, having no choice, they had stopped, and they had just started cutting down trees and forcing this last chance to be their fertile, blessed home. They had fled *this far* into this seemingly (to them, anyway) primitive place and now here *he* was too, here he was, in a metal box almost full (mostly) of naturally born Englishmen, en route to a city named for an Indian chief (Danny had been told) to play an English game against other Englishmen (mostly), in the hopes that a segment of this new population of Americans of mostly European descent would find it more entertaining that any number of perfectly entertaining games the new Americans had invented for themselves and were damned good at besides.

If it weren't for the part about coming all the way out here for the general good of the Free World, Danny thought, this would all be entirely preposterous.

As the Rose City Revolution disembarked into a breezy, drizzled mist in the car park of Seattle's Municipal Stadium, Molly walked up alongside Danny and asked him about the soreness in his thighs. He turned, looked down at her, and said, "There's no soreness in my thighs."

She smiled and said, "Oh, yeah. That's right. I'll leave them alone then."

Danny laughed and relaxed, relieved to have made what seemed like a friend in his new life. Molly's look made it clear that she thought of Danny the same way, but then her face went serious.

"OK," she said with a conspiratorial hush. "Here's the thing with the Seattle Smithereens. They're as English as the Revolution—they were something Villa in England, but not the one you're thinking of. Anyway, they just packed up eleven men and sent them over. They all came on a plane two days before the first game last season and they made it all the way to the Bonanza Bowl. Lost to the Giganticos, of course, five–nothing, but they're good. Really good. And even better now because they've added their first non-English dude. Ivan Petrov, from Bulgaria. Scored three goals in the '74 World Cup. Helped FK Sofia win the Central European Trade Cup last year. Makes them even tougher to beat, but very suspicious. *Too* suspicious. From

FK Sofia to the Seattle Smithereens? Something stinks in Seattle, Ivan Petrov has something to do with it, and we gotta find out what it is."

Danny considered Molly's ominous declaration for a moment and considered the sharpening wind whipping through her feathered 'do, then said, "How do *you* know about FK Sofia? What do *you* know about the Central European Trade Cup? *I* don't know about the bloody Central European Trade Cup. That doesn't even sound real."

"You're good at your job. I'm good at mine. Is that so hard to believe?"

"I'm just impressed is all, Molly."

"You *should* be impressed, big man. You know what it takes to keep track of Bulgarian soccer from here? It's not easy, I'll tell you that." She reached up and patted him on the back. "But I'll complain about my job another time. Today, you have a job. Actually, two jobs. One: Make this team happy to have you. Show them what you can do. They need to want you around. I know this doesn't seem like the biggest game in the world to you, but play it like it is. None of that English looking down your nose today. Save it for later in the summer. You got it, Danny? Good. And here's the other thing: Keep an eye on Graham Broome. He knows Seattle's coach. He'll go over and shake his hand. When he does, you can go over too. Butt in. Use the English brotherhood. Bring up East Southwich Albion, the FA Cup, anything. They'll want to talk to you about it. While you're over there, see if Broomsie talks to Petrov. I think he will. No matter how meaningless it seems, get every word you can. Then tell me." And then she was off, asking one of the Todds about a dodgy ankle.

Danny took a look about. The stadium in which the biggest game in his world—today—was to take place was set in the shadow of a tall, thin monument that looked particularly needlelike today as its flying saucer top pierced a low fog that made the sky seem like an invading force. The stadium was surrounded by roller coasters, a Ferris Wheel, a merry-go-round, a monorail. Municipal Stadium itself looked serious enough, its two tall, modern concrete grandstands resembling something you might come upon in a lonely Yugoslavian plain to commemorate a partisan World War II triumph—but it was not a testament to a victory over Nazi hordes; it was just a joyless funhouse annex, and as Aldershot Taylor used to say, "You fly with the crows, you die with the crows." That was the phrase that came to Danny's mind anyway. He admitted to himself that it didn't quite fit, but clowns—there were clowns there, walking through the parking lot as if they'd just finished a lunch break—didn't fly. So crows would have to do.

As he neared the gate to the ground, round Peter Surley, who had once won the 1963 League Vase with Nottingham Athletic, eased up at his side and said, "You carrying an injury, new man?"

"No," Danny said. "Not just now, no."

"Mmm. Curious. You've spent a lot of time talking with young Molly for a lad without a nick or a knock."

A dash of blood zinged somewhere in Danny's brain and he wondered if it showed. "Well, she's been... hospitable," he said. "I don't really know anyone else."

"Yes, well, I've noticed is all." And old Peter Surley entered the empty stadium, passing a security guard who looked a lot more like a footballer than he did.

In a breeze-blocked, characterless changing room, under an exposed, sputtering light bulb, amongst the shuddering clank of ancient metal lockers and the sticky, sweet smell of athletic tape, magic spray, and unidentifiable goop and the groans of bodies about to embark on a long, painful summer—for each and every player, one of their last as paid athletes, and each of them knew that every ninety minutes brought them closer and closer... Danny Hooper put on a Rose City Revolution kit for his first time.

The team's jersey was striped red and black and featured heavy white canvas patches down each sleeve, roses on the left, stars on the right. Across the chest, a great white RCR, and on

the left breast, where the club's crest should have been, a nu-
meral. Danny's was 5, as it had been at East Southwich Albion.
The shirt's decorations were cumbersome and heavy and chafed
against his skin. He could hardly imagine what would happen
when the roses, stars, letters, and numbers got wet with sweat
or rain. Even his black shorts, short as they were, were similarly encumbered: striped with roses here and stars there; a giant,
unnecessary 5 well positioned to scratch against his right thigh.
Danny hadn't said "crikey" since arriving in America—he hardly said it in England—but he said it now.

Surley looked at him and said, "Yeah, well, at least you can
tuck your shirt in."

The pitch at Seattle Municipal Stadium was as mysterious as
Portland's, its yellow soccer lines overlaid with an American
football gridiron in white and sundry blue, red, and green lines
for what sport or sports Danny didn't know. The effect was of
electronic tessellation splayed over a vast low-tech circuit board,
and Danny could hardly imagine maintaining his concentration
with that kind of static underfoot. It was as plastic as Portland's
surface, but its strands were even more matted and worn, and
it had been patched here and there and not very well, seams
left exposed, edges wrinkled. Danny ran his hand across it and
found it sharp and rough; he thought they may as well have just
spray-painted the parking lot green and played there, and he
knew one of his greatest weapons—a good hard slide tackle—
was a last resort.

Even more curious, though not as hazardous, was the field's
crown—not the gentle slope as he had seen here and there
throughout the lower English leagues or in Portland, but a severe ridge that ran the middle of the pitch; less a crown than
topographical phenomenon. As Danny sat on the bench tying
his shoes, he could see players on the far touchline only from
the waist up. And he had yet to even notice that the field was a

good ten to fifteen yards narrower than a proper English playing surface. Twenty-two professional footballers were about to
be wedged onto two sides of a long, thin, slippery, wet hillock.
The sharply raked stands and the open ends would channel the
stiffening breeze (now more of a gale) and turn Municipal Stadium into a wind tunnel. Danny could scarcely visualize anything
football-like happening here, and he found himself simultaneously annoyed (he'd been looking forward to getting a decent
match under his belt) and intrigued (*How on earth?*).

During warm-ups, he tracked his new manager as Broome
made his way toward Seattle's bench to greet the Smithereens'
English coaching staff. Rivals or no, everyone smiled and shook
hands, laughed as if they'd known each other forever; he heard
them all call him "Broomsie." Danny would come to recognize it
as a form of immigrant bonhomie—no matter how much any of
the teams in the AASSA grew to despise playing each other, the
men in charge maintained a sporting can't-quite-believe-we're-
all-here bemusement. In Seattle, even the sounds were different:
the players squeaked as their feet moved along the damp turf,
the ball peeped and tweeted as it skittered and spun, the voices
echoed eerily in the concrete emptiness. Danny felt as if hadn't
just been sold to another team in another league in another
country—he felt as if he'd been sold to another *sport*.

His eyes traveled the vacant stands—today's match wasn't
for fans—and descended to field level. Danny saw Broomsie
deep in conversation with one Ivan Petrov, instantly recognizable Bulgarian World Cupper and late of FK Sofia, champions of
the 1975 Central European Trade Cup. They weren't smiling and
laughing the way Broomsie had been smiling and laughing with
the Englishmen; no, their heads were pressed nearly together,
their serious gazes pointed downward. Looked plenty conspiratorial to Danny, so over he went and said, "Boss, if I may... Ivan
Petrov? *Ivan Petrov* of FK Sofia?" He held out his hand. "Hooper. Danny Hooper. A great pleasure, Mr. Petrov. I respect what
you did in the World Cup, even if you didn't go through to the

knockout stage. Brave effort, and no shame in going out against the Dutch, no shame at all. And winning that Cup over the Austrians. Bravo, sir. It will be an honor to play against you today."

Petrov didn't look as if he'd understood much of what Danny had just said, but he offered a stunted, "Uh, thank you, Mr.... Hooooper." Danny pressed on, now aiming his barrage at Broome: "Say, boss, you didn't tell me you knew the great Ivan Petrov." He gave the Revolution's coach a sharper-than-required elbow to the ribs and said, "Don't keep any more secrets from me, boss," just to see what Broome's face would do, which wasn't much.

The Smithereens kicked off. They knocked the ball around a little, all short passes of five, seven yards as the Revolution offered nominal chase. Even in the awkward space of the constricted and peculiarly canted pitch, the Smithereens squeezed off their tiny passes with a surprising comfort and poise. They ran on their toes and danced about on the plastic, entirely unlike a mud-trained Briton who learned to drive his heel into the ground first for traction, traction being more important than grace. And yet they were Englishmen mostly—Englishmen like himself. He was impressed. He wondered if pitches like *this* made you play like *that*, and he thought maybe they were good for something after all.

A NOTE ON THE SEATTLE SMITHEREENS: What became Seattle's professional soccer team was founded in the early '70s as a psych/prog improv jazz-rock band called Puget Sound Bikini. Its cofounders, Nigel Smithers and Dean Fleens, were the band's only two regulars and only two Englishmen. The rest of the Bikini's rotating roster consisted of eight or ten session guys from the greater Seattle-Tacoma area, Smithers's and Fleens's expat community of drinking companions, and a few Seattle SuperSonics (who the band thought were members of the famed Tacoma garage band the Sonics and therefore expected to play for them someday). Since the band's inception, its leaders had gathered anyone they could roust on a late Saturday morning for a kick-around to sweat out the week's drinking and determine the roster for that night's show. The band had a pair of local cult hits in the early '70s, but when the Pacific Northwest's brief flirtation with psych/prog improv jazz-rock dissipated and gigs began to dry up, the Saturday soccer meet-up (which now attracted twenty to thirty people every

Petrov was the centerpiece of the whole thing, keeping the Smithereens calm and settled, forcing them to play a simple but canny, possession-oriented game, avoiding the customary over-the-top English approach. Danny grasped immediately that the Revolution was nowhere near the quality of 1975's Frontier Conference champions. The Smithereens were so much better even than the Dire Vales and the Hibbles and the Scrumleys, though no one back home would've believed it. An American team other than the Giganticos better than an English team? But the Smithereens were, they surely were—the combination of the Englishness and the Bulgarian and the odd Central American, and this pitch, the way they had to play just to keep the ball in-bounds... it added up to something you just weren't going to see in Staffordshire or Suffolk. And so the Revolution merely settled in, as if by instinct, to the space within forty yards of their goal in hopes of holding out for ninety minutes.

In time, Juanito and a Todd started chasing passes amongst the Smithereens' defenders just for something to do. This stretched the team out, and the Revolution's outside midfielders pressed forward a little bit—just a little—and more often than not got beaten by a Smithereens winger, who would then draw Trevor, the Revolution center midfielder who was not Peter Surley (who wasn't moving much at all) wide, and now Surley would

---

week) became the Bikini's primary activity—and grew into the foundation of the game in Seattle. In early 1974, when Smithers and Fleens got wind of pro soccer spreading itself across North America, they wrangled one last royalty check out of their beleaguered record label, sold what remained of the band's equipment, called New York, and said, "You'll have a team in Seattle next year, mate, and it will melt your face." New York agreed, on the condition that Puget Sound Bikini not be the team's name, and in the space of that phone call Smithers and Fleens landed on Seattle Smithereens. The first year's team was a combination of the band's pub friends and a few Sonics. This was a winless disaster, except that a six-foot-eight, 250-pound power forward from DePaul found out that he was a pretty good goalkeeper. The next season, Fleens joined the Doobie Brothers, Smithers imported an entire Second Division side from Muddleshire (except for its keeper—the power forward left basketball for good), and Seattle nearly won the league.

be alone in the middle, which meant that Petrov had the run of the place and was picking out his forwards—all three of them, sometimes even four (the Smithereens overloaded their front line knowing they could get by with less defenders against an inferior opponent on the narrow pitch). Danny saw within minutes that he was at the end of the funnel, and the Smithereens were going to be upon him for the entire match. One of Petrov's passes landed at the feet of a Seattle forward, who performed a nifty turn on the carpet, spinning the ball past one of the Trevors; Danny stepped toward the Seattle forward, who was clearly considering a shot, got there first, and launched the ball deep into the empty grandstand. Behind him he heard Big Lou saying, "Yes, Danny, *yes*," and he could hear Broome yelling, "Well done, Danny, well *done*."

The Smithereens threw the ball in, skimming it down the line toward the corner flag. One of the other Todds hadn't been paying attention and was beaten badly. Seattle crossed into the six-yard box and Danny headed it over for a corner, then headed the corner away, and when Seattle's center back thumped the ball back into the Revolution's box from thirty yards out, Danny headed that one away too. Danny mumbled an obscenity, and one of the Peters jogged by as the Revolution pushed forward and patted him on the back. "Welcome to America, Hooper," he said.

This went on for another twenty minutes, and then the rain came. And the wind. The stadium inhaled the weather like it was breathing. For the rest of the half, the Revolution had a wind at its back, which stifled a few Smithereens attacks but seemed to offer the Revolution no particular offensive advantage. Broome continued a chorus of *"Keep goings!" "Get stuck ins!"* and *"Unluckys"* as the Revolution somehow conspired to make its gusty tailwind look like a disadvantage, until a merciful halftime whistle allowed the red-and-black team to scuffle off the field, heads down, wet and cold, defeated.

When Broomsie got them in the locker room of Seattle's Municipal Stadium, and when the team was quiet, he said, "Peter Surley, fat Peter Surley, what's the score?"

Surley, obviously having been down this path with his dear old friend Graham Broome, groaned, "It's nil–nil, Broomsie."

"Ah, nil–nil, is it? Nil–nil. Against last year's conference champions. And who's winning, then? Eh, Peter? Who's winning?"

But Surley was wet and overweight and old and needed a smoke, and he hardly cared to participate in the motivational masquerade. He knew what everyone in the room was thinking: the first forty-five minutes of the Rose City Revolution of 1976, exhibition/preseason/friendly though it was, had revealed only one thing: the Rose City Revolution of 1976 was in for another long summer. The Rose City Revolution, forty-five minutes in, appeared to one and all to be what the Rose City Revolution had always and only ever been: Shite. Utter rubbish.

It was Broomsie's job to make the Rose City Revolution of 1976 believe otherwise, but Surley, still not quite believing he'd left his cigarettes on the bus and sick to death of watching what Ivan Petrov and the Seattle Smithereens were doing to this summer's version of the Revolution, just didn't have it in him just then in this cold, drafty, aromatic Municipal Stadium locker room to be Graham Broome's partner in Graham Broome's little theatrical production. And so he remained silent.

But the silence didn't linger. The old coach knew what he was doing, or what he wanted to do, and so he said, "Hooper. New man. Who's ahead out there? Who's *winning* this football match?"

Danny looked, took a deep breath, thought, *OK, why the hell not,* and said, in a low big-and-strong-man kind of way, "No one is, boss. No one."

"Not Seattle, then, Danny? Not the dreaded Smithereeeeeens?"

"No, boss," Danny said. "Not by my count."

"Really? *Reeeeally?* I'd be under the impression, from looking at you lot, that the Seattle Smithereens must be in the lead in this little *soccer* game"—he feigned an American accent on the last two words, putting special emphasis on soccer's r. "But unless all of you know something about how this game works that

I don't know... Todd. Yes, *you*. Let's ask an American, shall we, lads? Todd, does zero–zero mean something in this country that I don't know about?"

The Todd answered with a fresh, American, "No, sir! Zero–zero means zero–zero, sir. The game is tied."

"Ah, thank you, lad. And you are correct, even if you aren't very good. It *is* tied, drawn, *even*. Square. All knotted up. We are forty-five minutes in, and *we* haven't scored and *they* haven't scored. I'd happily take a draw today in this godforsaken place, wouldn't you all? For England's sake, boys, let's do it again. Forty-five minutes of *that*. I'll bloody *take* it." He paused, took a breath, gave a long look at the room to see if maybe anyone believed what he was saying, and said, "Go. Get back out there. Same eleven." Nobody moved. "Bloody *go*," he said, "and don't let those bastards score. Please." By the time he said "please," his voice was a whispery rasp, nearly vanquished even before the season had really begun. The team walked out the door, as downcast as it had walked in.

The Rose City Revolution took the field for the second half of their only preseason match in the face of a horizontal rain that entered Memorial Stadium from the open end behind the Smithereens' goal and slashed its way directly into Danny's wide face. They weren't up against wind and rain. They were up against a storm. Danny, who had not a shred of belief in his big, strong body that the Revolution could survive the next three-quarters of an hour without conceding five or six to Ivan Petrov and his merry band of villans, thought, *Well, forty-five minutes was pretty good.*

The second half was the same damn thing: the Smithereens comfortable on the ball, despite the weather, rotating calmly and precisely around the magisterial Bulgarian; they could pass five, six, seven times in a row without any real trouble, and when anything went wrong it was usually their own fault—the Revolution seemed entirely powerless to interrupt their impressive flow. And they *were* right bastards too. Chippy as hell. Shoulders and feet left in as they ran past, every tackle a bit worse than it needed to be, everything—bloody everything—followed with nasty banter. The Revolution accomplished almost nothing, maintained almost no possession, and mounted no threats upon the Seattle Smithereens' goal. But the fiftieth minute became the fifty-fifth minute, and Seattle's breakthroughs on the Revolution's goal led to a badly missed shot from close range, a skimmer off the crossbar, a pair of astonishing Big Lou saves, and one of the Todds saving off the line without knowing much about it. What he had been doing there, clueless Todd, Danny didn't know and couldn't have guessed at, but he was there, and he'd kept the score line level, and Danny was starting to think, *Well, maybe.* Then Danny saved one off the line too. That was in the sixtieth minute. Danny could see Broome screaming on the touchline, but the wind whisked the old man's words up into the menacing Seattle sky.

Then Petrov's icy Eastern cool disappeared, and his team followed his lead, coming just a little undone with each missed trap or poorly hit through ball. Petrov's frustration grew, until Danny could see his mental acumen easing its way out of Seattle's Municipal Stadium, joining Broome's screams in the clouds. Petrov barked in his native language, gesticulated as if to make it perfectly clear that it was the fault of no Bulgarian that the Seattle Smithereens were unable, by the seventieth minute, to take a lead against a team of the Rose City Revolution's minimal quality. The Englishmen wagged their fingers at the Bulgarian, then at each other, until both teams were forced to stew in Petrov's foul mood.

But then—in one last flurry of blind hope—a young Seattle winger broke through the congested midfield and wound up to shoot from twenty-five yards; he drew his right leg back, rooted his left to the hard ground, and—Danny took him out. Popped him off his left-leg anchor like flicking the head off a dandelion.

The youthful Smithereen sprawled across the artificial turf, his neck slamming the back of his head against the firm surface.

A sound came out of his cranium like a knock on a door and a whisper puffed itself out of his mouth like the exhalation of a gas tank. The referee blew his whistle, booked number 5 of the Rose City Revolution without saying much about it—he seemed frightened of Danny—the obligatory pushing and shoving ensued, Petrov missed the free kick badly, almost hitting the roller coaster, and...

...and the Revolution realized they were but ten bitter minutes from a full-time draw with the Seattle bloody Smithereens, 1975 Bonanza Bowl runners-up, second only to the Giganticos and their magical menagerie. It *was* preseason, yes, and no one was there to see it, but forget about all that: the Smithereens were *good*—*really good,* and for all of Danny's built-in English superiority, he knew they were better than East Southwich Albion and maybe better than anyone in the entire Third Division and maybe as good as some Second Division sides—

And on that day, in Seattle's empty Municipal Stadium, in a rain-soaked, wind-blown match that did not count, the Smithereens did not defeat the Revolution.

As the Revolution filed onto the bus for the drive home, Broome stood at the door to shake each man's hand. Danny could not recall seeing a manager so happy after a scrimmage in an empty stadium that his team didn't even win. When he shook Big Lou's hand, he patted his face too. When Surley approached, he grabbed the back of his head and pressed Peter's forehead to his own. "*Yes,* mate," he growled to his ancient, rotund friend. "*Brilliant,* old man," he murmured, and then shooed the oval figure into the bus. Danny was happy too—he knew he'd played well and shown his new teammates what he could do—but he was hardly heartened to see his new boss so giddy after a match in which the Rose City Revolution had failed to take a single shot on goal.

When Danny arrived at the door, Broome showed him in, then climbed the steps after him and announced to the full bus, "Lads, your man of the match, big Danny Hooper!"

A small, tired round of applause arose—the group wasn't wildly ecstatic at the new man getting the shiny-penny treatment, Danny detected that, but there was an air of *we didn't lose* lightness in the bus, and Danny recognized that the squad knew what he had done, and that the squad was happy that the Revolution would not have to travel four hours through the mystic darkness of a foreign land mulling yet another Revolution defeat.

Broome leaned toward Danny and mumbled, "Sit with me, Danny. Let's talk, my boy."

Danny was in no mood—he was just so bloody tired—but he realized he might be able to sort a few things out over the next 175 miles if he let his coach do most of the talking. He was so happy, the old man—who knew what gems might tumble forth from dear old Graham Broome if Danny just kept nodding and smiling.

Danny caught Molly's eye, and she nodded back with a wink and that American smile.

"Danny, Danny, Danny—that was impressive what you did out there today. No one has ever really done that before in a Revolution shirt. I have only one question for you: Can you do that again? Keep those bastards, and bastards like them, to a clean sheet?"

Danny thought that was a fair question, and he thought it deserved a fair answer. "No," he said. "I should think not. I doubt it anyway."

Broome laughed and patted Danny's shoulder. "Ha. Of course, of course. We benefitted from some rather extraordinary luck today, yes, yes, that's true, my boy. How they didn't put one past us is beyond me. But you were a giant out there. I haven't seen a central defender control a match quite the way you did today since Der Kaiser in the World Cup. And he doesn't have your *strength*." He pressed the tips of his fingers against one another, and he smiled as if he'd just won at the dogs. "Seattle's a good side, lad. You shut them down. The goals will come—they always do..." Danny doubted the goals would come for the Revolution: Kelvin had shown some promise as a speedy winger on the right, and Juanito up front had flashed some skill and industry in his few opportunities to engage in the proceedings, but mostly the team just wasn't that good... but he kept his mouth shut. ". . . and when they do... *imagine*, Danny, as out of sorts as the Smithereens were today at nil–nil. We get them down a goal knowing they have to get through *you*, lad. They'll crumble like dried meat pie, and so will L.A. and Colorado and even Chicago, even *Chicago*..." Broome laughed—cackled—and rubbed his hands together. "The Giganticos are a different story, of course, but the rest of the league..."

"But the goals..." Danny ventured.

"Ah, the goals. Right, right, the goals. But here's the thing: league games don't end in draws. If it's level at full time, we settle it."

"Penalties?" Danny responded. As much as he contained a natural footballer's disdain for the crapshoot finish of spot kicks to settle up ninety minutes' hard work, he'd been impressed with Big Lou's game in goal; the idea of dragging the Revolution's game to penalty kicks seemed like a way to sneak a few cheap wins.

"Ah, well, uh, no. It's not quite that simple, I'm afraid. A shootout here in America is a little different to what you may be accustomed to." He paused as if he was about to get into something more complicated than he wished to explain, as if about to break bad news. "Over here, you see, every fifth corner results in a free kick from the center spot. No one between you and the goal. A Sniper Shot, it's called. Sounds simple, but it's a surprisingly complicated little task for most, I must tell you, especially with the state of the pitches in our league. But Peter Surley, bless him, can make them with his eyes closed, and often does just for his own entertainment. One of the few advantages we have over other teams. Soooo, if you're tied up after the ninety, it's three of those each. They call it a Super Soccer Showdown."

Danny stared at his coach.

"I know, I know, but the fans do love it. Eat it up with a spoon. We didn't bother today because there weren't any fans and frankly it's a little silly. But during the season, a win's a win, innit? Even if you come by it a little, well... on the cheap."

Danny thought for a moment and then figured he'd seen and heard plenty stranger than that in his short time in America. "Two points is two points, I reckon," he said.

"Ah, yes, yes, Danny, and about that..." Broome paused as if what he was about to do would take considerable effort, which turned out to be the case. "You see, Danny, your 'two points for a win, one for draw' is English thinking. Over here, if you win in regular time—no Super Showdown now, win it on the pitch, in regular time—you get four points—"

"*Four* points?" Danny said.

"Well, not just. You also get points for every goal, up to four."

Danny made a face as if he'd gotten a bite of greased newspaper with his fish and chips. "So four–nil is... *eight points*?"

Broomsie looked up at the bus's ceiling and mouthed the numbers: "...six, seven, eight—yes. Eight. Well, actually nine. You get a point for a clean sheet as well."

At this stage in the conversation, and in his life, Danny would've believed anything. "A point for the defense as well? Well, that's nice. Get anything for having the best kit? We'd have taken that one today, wouldn't we?"

"I suppose we would've done, yes. Nice of you to say so. I designed it myself."

Danny was getting into the spirit. "And what about the losing side then? Say you lose four–two. Get anything for your troubles?"

"Yes indeed. Two points. Loser gets their goals up to three."

"Not four?"

"Just the three. Don't know why."

"And if you win on... Sniper Shots? A Sexy Soccer Show-down?"

The gaffer laughed. "Good one, son. Sexy indeed. You get four points for that. Full stop. No matter how many you score. They had to make it more than losing. But just. And if you lose a Super Soccer Showdown, you still get a point for each goal up to three. Does that make sense?"

"Are you sure you're right?"

"I think so."

"Well *you* ought to get a point for that, boss."

"Aye, lad." Broome chuckled again. "Aye."

"So if you win a Super Soccer Showdown after a three–three draw, you get four and the other guys get three. But if you win four–three in regular time, you get eight and the other side... still gets... *three*?"

"There you go. It's a tall order to keep track—I was never much at maths—and last summer it didn't much matter. We were well out of the running by mid-July. You don't have to count your points quite as carefully when you're down at the bottom, I'm afraid. But hopes are higher in this bus now, my boy."

In his fatigue, and in Broomsie's warm welcome and hearty congratulations, Danny felt more relaxed and comfortable than he had since he'd been in the United States. The bus was big and warm and comfortable, and he had an inkling, but just an inkling, that maybe things were looking up for the Rose City Revolution. And then he remembered why he was in the big, warm, comfortable bus: "How do you know Ivan Petrov?"

"Oh, yes. Petrov. Good man. Tremendous player, as you've just seen. Different class. I knew his father. When I was a younger man, I was with Slovenly Rangers in the old Second and a Half Division Northwest—early fifties, I suppose it was—and we toured the Balkans one summer. Coast of Croatia, just beautiful, up through Serbia and Romania, and we finished off playing in the Planned Economy Cup in Bulgaria against three teams named Dinamo. Went out for a friendly toast after the final, ended up being eight or nine friendly toasts and a long conversation with Stefan Petrov, became fast friends, and there you go. When I got my own team, I took them down there every summer to get away from gray old England and train against some of the best passers in the world. Bumped us up two divisions in three years learning the Balkan game. You'd think it would've translated here in America, but the only Cloppingshire sods I managed to bring over were the lads who couldn't get into the first team. Anyway, we'll get there, Danny, we'll get there. Just need a few more results like this one, and the boys will believe. But yes, yes... Ivan. It was my idea to get him to come to America—Bulgaria's pretty to look at, Danny, but that's not where you want to make your life. I used to think it was; I used to think Communism was the future, Danny. Can you believe that?" He laughed, as if considering a girl he used to love but couldn't remember why. "All for one, one for all, all that. It's not such a reach when you put it like that, you know? But that's not how it works, you know. It's just not. Like I always say, I'd be a Communist if only the Communists would be. Long story short, I couldn't get the Revolution to pay for Ivan's services so I got him on at Seattle as a favor to his old man. Bittersweet—I've known him since he was a boy and I love him like a son. But I'd rather make Seattle a better team than leave him behind the Iron Curtain. Funny, yes, yes, indeed. And I still have a plan."

And so Broomsie rested, having said his strange and convoluted peace. Danny knew Molly, just three rows back and on the other side of the bus, would have done just about anything to have heard all of that. And channeling her helped him ask the logical follow-up question:

"A plan?"

Broome brightened. "Oh, yes. Ivan will wear the red and black someday. This summer, I hope. I don't know how yet, but we'll get him, and when we do, it shall be the Bonanza Bowl for the Revolution. Mark my words—we're one great Bulgarian away from the Bonanza Bowl." He gazed out the window and into the dark, and Danny could see him ponder a Revolutionary Bonanza Bowl.

"Now get some rest. You looked right knackered, and you should too. Close it down, Danny. We open the season at home against Toronto in a week, and they're as good as the Smithereens. Serbs, or almost all Serbs. You have no idea."

Danny closed his eyes, let the Pacific Northwest dark embrace him through the windows of the bus, and he thought. He thought hard.

Graham Broome seemed like an honest man, a good and trustworthy football man, but: there *had* been Communists in the trees—and so *some*one knew *some*thing about why he was here. And Danny knew that if those men in those trees had anything to do with Broome, anything at all, then this was exactly the conversation Broome would have had with Danny: a convincing cover story of a onetime Communist fling and a thorough, utterly believable explanation for his relationship with Ivan Petrov.

Still, Danny had felt the lilt of Broomsie's voice—the lads all called him Broomsie—and sensed the debilitating tension of his desire to win, and Danny thought, *This man's soul contains only football. This man may be a leftist of some kind,* Danny's knackered brain went on, *but he is no threat to the Free World. This man just wants to win the Bonanza Bowl with all these poor Cloppingshire lads he's dragooned into moving to Portland, Oregon, USA, to wear red-and-black-striped shirts with roses and stars sewn into the sleeves.*

Before Danny fell asleep, he was looking forward to picking up the phone and hearing Three's voice on the other end.

When the team walked off the bus and into the Portland night, Molly eased up next to Danny and said, "Good game today. You must be sore."

"Dead on my feet. My first two days on the plastic, and four hours folded into that bus. I can hardly walk, to be honest."

"I'll bet," Molly said. "I can help. And we should talk."

TWELVE

Danny's residence for the summer was to be a place called the Grand Douglas Apartments. Molly had explained to him that the entire team lived there—made things easy when they'd first brought the Cloppingshire players across.

The road to the Grand Douglas felt like a road to a secret lair—Molly drove through trees and tunnels, around bends, over hillocks, and beneath underpasses of elaborate masonry.

"Still in Portland?" he intoned, still gazing out the window at the passing greenery.

"Still in Portland," Molly hummed back, and pointed at a deer.

And then, as if Molly knew a secret, she angled the car down a steep drive and into a clearing that featured a sizable parking lot and a modern wooden structure. A low, seemingly hand-carved sign identified the camp-like, welcoming locale as the Grand Douglas Apartments.

"Welcome home, Danny," Molly said.

As remote as the location seemed, it had only been fifteen minutes since Molly had picked Danny up at the hotel; Danny was still baffled that such a secluded sylvan sanctuary could be so near to Portland's downtown, but here it was, dripping with the remnants of a spring rain and bathed in the green glow of a coniferous canopy that just about concealed any evidence of sky.

The entry of the Grand Douglas featured a spacious common area filled with numerous small tables surrounded by small chairs and overstuffed couches and a pool table, all in various shades of brown. It felt like a modernized hunting lodge, as if there should be trophy heads of great bears and elk on the walls, but there were only oil paintings of woodland scenes: a river making its way through a forest, a snow-peaked mountain rising above a vista of evergreen, a waterfall. And a television—a low and long console TV—and gathered around it were the men of the Revolution, each sipping a beer.

The players stared at the screen; not a one of them had flinched at Danny and Molly's arrival. Molly made a show of clearing her voice, to no effect; she finally just raised her voice—just a little—and said, "Excuse me, gentlemen! We have a new resident." Only one man responded—it was one of the Todds, who was on the outer ring of the television audience; he turned to Molly and Danny and said, "The Giganticos are on TV."

Danny dropped his duffel bag—everything he owned—right where he stood and went to stand by Todd. He fixed his eyes upon the screen. "Who are they playing?"

Todd told him they were playing a team from Italy, though Todd didn't know which. Danny could see right away that the game was in New York—the dirt cutout of the baseball diamond befouled the Giganticos' otherwise pristine home pitch. The stadium seemed to be close to full, and the game had the cheerful atmosphere of an Olympic opening ceremony or a daredevil jump.

Watching the game was difficult; the camera seemed to follow only the Brazilian, seldom offering any full-field views that might provide some sense of the game or a feel for the other team. But Danny did get a sense of the way the great man moved as he eased in and out of the camera's tight square, his tightly packed little body rotating with a strange combination of slow unpredictability on the gyroscope of his spring-loaded hips. The Italians looked giant and clumsy as they tried to track his languid movements; they surrounded him when he didn't have possession, and yet when the ball found its way to his feet, he kept it for as many touches as he needed, progressing toward their goal in ten- and fifteen-yard chunks, then laying it off at the last possible split second before ghosting in behind the Italians and appearing free once again to receive a nice and easy touch back from a teammate... and then moving another ten or fifteen yards to wherever he wanted to be.

The Revolution gasped at the screen and hummed short and dark oaths amongst themselves. Danny knew what the other Englishmen all knew: that their upbringing had been a comforting, nationalistic lie, or at least a patriotic untruth; that football may have been an English invention, but it was most definitely not an English game. It was this man's game.

The ball went for a goal kick and the game went to a commercial. Danny saw an opening and said, "Just let him try that at Multnomah Stadium."

The Rose City Revolution turned to look at Danny, stared at him for a moment, and then turned back to face the TV. He'd been in this situation before: a quick outburst followed by no real plan. But he'd never been new; Danny had never been new anywhere. So he tried the only thing he could think of that he guessed everyone in the room might want to hear: "Anyone up for a few pints? First round's on me." He thought it was worth a try, and judging by the faces in the room, he'd been right. "Your place, Peter?" Danny said to the round man, knowing of no other place. "Down by the park?" Surley nodded. The men went off, Molly too, and the Revolution joined the flannel-clad crew at Surley's local for a proper baptism of the bicentennial soccer summer of 1976.

The next morning, Danny awoke with the sun. His head was a little cottony, but the feeling wasn't too bad. His big frame could handle a few rounds, and he'd managed his intake on his first night out with the lads. His body felt heavy, as if something were pressing it into the bed, but it was a good feeling, a good *football* feeling. Just the post-match aches, the kind that made you feel like an athlete, the kind that felt well earned. There were now

more men in the world who believed in his footballing power than had believed in him twenty-four hours ago. That felt
good. That felt bloody *great*.

But he hadn't tried to move yet.

He tried, tried from his stomach. *Just shift the core a little
bit*, he told himself. *Mmm. Mmmmmm.* He grunted as he did,
grunted as if he might even vomit, as he tried to twist the middle of his body to the edge of the bed. But the grunt was the
most noteworthy thing his body could accomplish. *No, that's
not going to work.* Then he thought, *I'll use my legs,* and he tried
to swing his right leg up over his left and roll his big, strong
self out of the bed and onto the floor, deal with it from there,
crawl maybe—he'd done it before—but that didn't work either. It wasn't even really pain that he felt. He just felt *heavy*,
pressed into the mattress. His leg just didn't... move.

"Just stay here, Danny," Molly said. "You don't have to be
anywhere until the afternoon."

She was on her side, faced away from Danny, her legs ex-
tending from beneath her carefully placed covers and tapering
toward her ankles like the handles of an ax. "I am," she said.
"Hope that's OK, Danny," she murmured.

"That's a good word for it. But"—he wasn't quite sure
how to say what he had to say—"maybe a little... fast? A little
soon?"

"What?" she said. "It's still the fifties where you're from?"

He laughed. Felt the muscles in his gut. "Yeah," he said. "It
is, I mean it's not—"

"It's all right, Danny. I know what you're thinking. I know...
does this happen often? With the other guys. And the answer
is no."

"No?"

"No—and you want to know why? Because you're the
first player on this team that I've brought over."

"But this is my room." Danny was utterly confused, and
his gut muscles tightened again.

She rolled her eyes and sat up and Danny took it in. Her shoulders were so nice. He liked her shoulders, and that surprised him. "Not like that," Molly said. "I've been monitoring your progress."

"You? Brought me over? You've *known* me?" Even as he said it all, Danny wasn't quite sure what it all meant.

"We've had our eye on a few of you over there, Danny. We needed someone. And I've always known you were the right one. Then you took out that kid from Dire Vale. Once that happened, it was time to get you over here. Pretty good timing, actually. If you were still in the FA Cup, I don't know that we could've gotten you here."

"So—"

"So this isn't as fast as you think."

"So—"

"So we're a team, Danny. We have to be. We aren't alone. There are more of us throughout the league, but for now, in Portland, it's just us, you and me, and we have to figure out some pretty important whats and wheres and whens, and fast."

"Three's going to call me today," Danny said, feeling like he was doing his part. "He'll want to know what I know so far."

"Tell him they want the Pearl."

"Excuse me?"

"That's right, Danny. That's all we know so far. They want to take out the Pearl. At the Bonanza Bowl most likely. It will be his last game. The whole world will be watching. The whole world, Danny. Watching an American soccer game. And if we want to stop it, we'll need someone there." Molly was up now, wearing a bathrobe, sitting in a chair on the other side of the room. "And that someone had better be you."

"Me?"

"You, Danny."

Danny forced himself to sit up, groaning and wheezing as he did. Some combination of bone and gristle in his hip made a popping sound. He lifted his right knee and it crackled like crumpling a piece of paper. "I'll not be there with this side, Molly. The Revolution is a shambles. Horrible squad. We'll need new players. Let's get bloody Petrov for starters, if he's such good friends with Graham Broome. Meantime, we find those Communists from the trees. They know—they *know* what's going to happen. I tell Three the Russians know about me, the Americans know about the plot, whatever it is, and we need players."

"Not as simple as all that, Danny, but I like how you're thinking."

"Molly, they're not going to... kill the Pearl, the Pearl of Brazil. They can't."

The Molly who looked across the room from the chair wasn't the Molly from the bed, even if one of those shoulders was peeking out of her bathrobe. This Molly was a spy, and her look said that they could. Then she just said it: "They could, Danny, and they will. It's the bicentennial. The opportunity will just be too great. They won't be able to help themselves."

He was out of breath. He looked at Molly with the look of a man who'd just run a hard ninety minutes, and she said, "You'll have to stop it. And by the way, you're going to need a cortisone shot." Molly breathed in, held it, and breathed out. "Tell Three whatever you want. Then tell me what you told him. We'll go from there." She paused. She closed her eyes. She shook her head. "I'm just glad you're finally here, Danny."

Danny looked at Molly and almost didn't say (but he did): "I'm glad I'm here too." Then he said, "How are you going to get out of here? People are going to see you."

"Jesus," she said. "I'm a spy. You don't have to worry about me."

The phone rang, and Danny picked it up. "'Ello," he said.

"Hooper?"

"Yes, Three," Danny said. "It's me."

"And you're alone. We can talk?"

"Three, yes, we can talk." Danny was impatient and a little nervous. He had a feeling that lying to someone like Three probably had consequences. Some kind of crime against the Crown or something like that. Misrepresenting the facts to a magistrate of London. And he remembered that he didn't really like or trust Three. But he also knew that if he hemmed and hawed now—

"Three, two Russians pulled me into a tree and made it quite clear that they know why I'm here. I rather wonder how well you keep your secrets over there if the cat's already out of the bag in America about superspy Danny Hooper."

Three sputtered, trapped between excitement over confirmation that something Soviet was indeed afoot in the AASSA and embarrassment about the Russians in the tree. "Th-they pulled you into a tree, my boy? A *tree*, you say, Danny. Well, that's rather stunning—"

"Stunning, is it, Three? 'Rather'? I'd damn well say so. I suppose I'm glad you agree, Three—"

"So it's on then, is it? That's what we know. They *are* up to something, the clever bastards, the clever bastards. Ah, yes, good, good, Danny—gooood. Well, Hooper, here's where we go from here—"

"No, Three," Danny said, gaining courage from his annoyance with the number on the other end of the phone. "*I'll* tell *you* where we go from here. Not only do the Russians know, but the Americans do too. At least some of them do. So right now I'm considering the possibility that the Crown, or however you describe what you are, may very well be the least educated outfit in this entire little drama. But here's the good news: you were right about Graham Broome."

Danny could hear Three's outlook brighten right through the telephone. *"We were?"* He sounded a little too surprised, and he caught himself. "I mean, we were? That's good to hear, Danny. How, um, how exactly do you come to have this intelligence?"

"Well," Danny said, "I come to have this intelligence because he told me."

"Told you what exactly?"

"Told me that he's a Communist sympathizer."

"Excuse me. He just... he just *told* you this? I'm not sure I quite follow why he would have wanted to do that."

"Well, Three, I leave it to you and the crack secret-keeping team over there in your secret-keeping lair to work that one out. But I suspect the reason he told me is because he trusts me, which is why I think I can get even more information out of him."

Again it happened—Danny wasn't at all certain how, but he could feel Three's mood improve. "Well, yes, Three," Danny went on. "He'll talk, but it will cost."

"I'm sorry?"

"I said 'He'll talk, but—'"

"I know what you said, Danny. You expect me to give this man *money*? And why on earth would a true believer give us information in exchange for mere cash?"

"I should have known you'd be a sharp one, Three. Good questions, good questions. The answer to your first question is that he's a Communist, or was, and by our present definition, he's inherently untrustworthy. So there's that. But more importantly, Three—here's the fact you can take to your superiors: the Revolution needs to make it to the Bonanza Bowl."

Three laughed. "That may be beyond our powers, my boy. I mean, the Revolution is shocking. The Revolution is horrible, Danny."

"They want the Pearl, Three."

The line went silent. Five seconds, ten seconds. Danny wasn't in any hurry, so he waited. He knew that Three was piecing it together on his end: the Bonanza Bowl, in New York City, the Pearl's last game, the worldwide television audience, an assassination unlike any other assassination.

Then Danny said, "You there, Three?"

"How do you know all of this, Danny? So soon, my boy?"

"I may be a little better at this than you'd thought."

"Mmm. Danny. If you're right... if your sources are—"

"We can stop it, Three, but we'll need to be there. I'll need to be on the pitch. At the Bonanza Bowl. And the Revolution aren't built for that, not right now." Danny was feeling his advantage. "To win, we'll need players, and to get players, we'll need money—"

"I don't like giving Commies our money, Danny. The Russians *or* Graham Broome. Doesn't feel right, not at all. But I'll think on it. I must say you've produced rather exciting results in your short time over there, even if the plan is truly, truly shocking. The Pearl. Beggars belief anyone would hurt the Pearl of Brazil, even for political gain. They're diabolical. Savages." He paused. "We have heard about your performance in Seattle, Danny. We have heard."

"Thank you, I guess," Danny said.

"Well done, lad. And if you want back in a real Football League, keep up your work on the pitch. I'll make sure the right people notice."

And he hung up.

Danny hung up too and realized he was going to play for a championship at the end of the summer. Even if he couldn't imagine how.

THIRTEEN

The Rose City Revolution's first home game took place on a murky Wednesday night. The field had been marked in goopy white chalk that got tracked around by the players and the ball as the teams warmed up, quickly making the field look as if it had received spotty summer snowfall.

The playing surface's crown was positioned down the center of the narrow American football gridiron and not the much wider soccer field, so that an unnatural portion of the action was drawn over to the near touchline. Just outside the center circle on the side farthest from the grandstand was a ten-square-yard concave, sinkhole-ish hollow where the ground had given way once upon a time and had simply not been restored. It abutted a giant, recently painted-on silhouette of a nutria in what Danny would come to understand was center field and where the ball skittered an extra skitter on the slick paint; and just for variety, the pitch featured four giant muddy squares—the baseball infield—where the artificial turf was replaced with clay.

The topographical variety of the massive pitch—it was almost a square—gave a player the impression he was playing in a separate game from some of his teammates. They were just so far away, and Danny could see them only from the knees up. And to contribute to the strangeness, some of them, despite plying their trade on an inorganic surface, were splotched with mud.

Multnomah Stadium was also a sound chamber unlike anything Danny had experienced. Its covered J may have been ideal for a capacity crowd, Danny imagined, but for sparse gatherings like the one he saw this chilly midweek evening, the shivering voices of the scattered few hundred who thought, *What the hell, maybe the Revolution doesn't suck as much as they did last year,* rattled about in the wooden rafters like marbles in a tin can. Danny could hear them talking—"Look at the fat dude," "I'm cold," "This sucks, man"—and whenever the referee blew his whistle, at least one *"You're blind, asshole,"* no matter what the referee had called. Danny liked hearing that, thought it sounded about the same in any dialect. Other than the accents of Broome and his Cloppingshire cronies, it was the only familiar thing he'd heard since arriving in America.

The opening night opponent was Red Star Toronto, a team made up almost entirely of Serbians, though it did include "What's-His-Whatzit" McCoist from the Rangers, who won the League Cup in '72. They were endowed to a man with remarkable mustaches (including McCoist, who now had himself a set of downright Serbian whiskers) and dressed in the red and white stripes, white shorts, and white socks of Belgrade's de facto government team. Broome had known a few of them, had shaken their hands during the warm-up, even exchanged what seemed to be a greeting in their native tongue. Danny had run over by where Molly was massaging Surley's thighs and given her a look. She said, "Bulgarian's not that different from Serbian."

Before kickoff, Surley escorted an elderly woman out onto the field in what was now a full Portland drizzle to kick out a ceremonial first ball. Danny would later learn that she was a city councilwoman who had been instrumental in luring an AASSA franchise to Portland, and she would kick out a ceremonial first ball before every game.

Red Star looked like the real deal: their shirts tucked in, their socks betasseled, their uniforms devoid of bizarre flourishes, outlandish colors, extraneous stars, or excessive decor. Molly told Danny that they had lost a brutal five-game series to the Giganticos in last season's Liberty Conference championship and were widely considered to be one of the best squads in the league. Before kickoff, Broome told the team to "give the home crowd something to sing about." Danny could tell there would be no singing. There wasn't even really a crowd. *These people don't sing,* he thought. *They don't even sit together.*

High up in the seats near the roof, at the scoop of the grandstand's baseball-purposed J, behind the north goal, a gaggle of hippies huddled beneath a billow of smoke that never ceased for the entire match—for the entire season. It smelled sweet and wet and sticky, and Danny learned to instruct Surley to request that the Revolution defend that goal if he won the coin toss as it could inflict a contact high on the opposition's forwards—the Revolution would grow immune to it—that would usually hold until the end of the game.

But this night: Red Star Toronto.

Multnomah Stadium's vast pitch suited the Stojanovićes, Savićevićes, Prpićes down to the ground. They had all the room they could ever want, and they entertained themselves by exchanging short, sharp passes that were far more precise than anything the former Cloppingshire United had ever had to contend with in England. In the lower rungs of English football, all you really had to do in the rain was wait for the mud to make great players worse; here, the plastic amplified the difference between men whose feet knew how to massage a waterlogged football and common plodders whose waterlogged bodies would soon need a massage.

And so Red Star passed, and the Revolution chased. Danny felt like a spectator: from his vantage just in front of Big Lou he could only watch as Toronto eased the ball around the perimeter of the Rose City midfield. Every few minutes a Serbian winger would grow impatient and lob in a cross; either Danny would head it away to safety or Big Lou would come and collect it, prompting Multnomah Stadium's chatty PA man to intone, "Say Looooooooooooou," and the scattered crowd would let loose with a wet *"Loooooooooooou"* that would carom around underneath the stadium's cover.

Either way, the ball would soon be back at the feet of a confident, comfortable Red Star defender and the whole thing would begin again. If Surley were any younger, all the passing would have eventually drawn him out of position, but he was too old and overweight to be bothered, and every time Toronto made an effort to run their attack through the middle, Peter would be there, and lacking the mobility or grace to win the ball back, he would commit the foul that would allow his team to reset itself, and Red Star would use the free kick to start its attack over again... and the game of keep-away would be on again.

After the sixth or seventh Red Star pass, the PA man would boom out some inanity, like "Let's make some noise!" or "Get *loud*, Portland!" which would be followed by a burst of enthusiasm... that would die out as quickly as it had arisen. Or music would come from the loudspeaker—something by the Bee Gees, which Danny rather liked, thought it put a bounce in his step, or "Rhinestone Cowboy," which Danny just thought was weird. What Danny also thought was weird was that Red Star had yet to take a shot. The scoreboard counted down instead of up in the AASSA, so Danny tried to ignore it—just too confusing—but what he could figure quite plainly was that it was in the twenties. The Revolution had made it approximately a quarter of the way into their home opener with something like 5 percent of the possession—but Toronto had yet to seriously threaten Big Loooooooooooou. Danny was starting to get the feeling he'd gotten in Seattle.

Kelvin, over on the right wing, near the benches and the grandstand, lurched at a Red Star defender who'd gotten a little too comfortable on the ball, and for a fleeting moment Kelvin had it at his feet. It was his first opportunity of the match, and he tried to take it—he made a sudden burst to the defender's right, in an effort to get down the wing, and he got a step on the giant Serbian left back. He was still forty yards from the goal, but the

Toronto defender stuck out a toe and poked the ball away, sent it skidding down the touchline toward the corner flag. On any natural surface it would have held up, but here it just kept gliding along the chalky plastic and water, slipping and sliding its way toward the Revolution's first corner kick of the regular season.

Surley went to take it, and it must have been a good minute or two before he finally got it off, so unfamiliar was the Revolution with how to handle such a thing. Toronto engaged in the long-standing but pointless tactic of positioning a man eight or ten yards from Surley—maybe to force him to loft the ball, which he would want to do anyway—so Peter wallied his corner kick off the player's shins for another corner. Then he did it again. When Peter tried to earn the Revolution a fourth corner, the Red Star player bailed out and Surley's low kick was easily collected by Toronto's rangy Croatian goalkeeper. But Danny understood what had just happened: Surley had just brought his team 60 percent of the way to a Sniper Shot. If the Revolution could somehow, in the next hour, earn two more corner kicks, Peter would convert a Sniper Shot from the center spot. And if... somehow, some way... the Rose City Revolution could keep Toronto from scoring more than one... the two teams would settle it with a Super Soccer Showdown. And then...

Toronto's goalkeeper launched a mighty boot into the Portland rain. Danny rose to meet it and headed the ball on a parabola back toward the Red Star goal. The Croatian took it again and punted it again. Again Danny headed it back. As it settled into the keeper's hands, Danny glanced at the clock. Since Kelvin had stolen the ball and Surley had conspired to make one corner into three and Danny had twice headed the ball, a full six minutes had passed. Broome clapped his hands and shouted, "Yes, Danny, yes. Stay stuck in boys. Brilliant, *brilliant*." Danny even heard a shout from Molly. "Come on, Danny," she yelled, and then, as if to cover herself, "Go Todd, go Peter," which took care of most of the team. Even the hippies seemed to have the idea that the Revolution had a chance. The disseminated hundreds sang along with "Time in a Bottle" over the PA system, a choice Danny promised himself he would request was retired after this match.

And then the clock read 00:00. A buzzer went off. Frightened Danny terribly. He'd never heard such a thing. He almost threw himself to the ground. But it was good news: halftime. The Revolution smiled to one another as they left the field. Three halves against good teams, three halves of almost zero sustained possession... three halves of zeros on the scoreboard. Peter shook Danny's hand. Danny clapped Kelvin on his back and told one of the Todds to keep it up. Big Lou ran up behind Danny and said, "Let's beat these wankers, Danny. We can, man, we *can*." Broomsie barked at his charges as they jogged off the pitch, offering a string of enthusiastic platitudes: "Well done," "We've got them where we want them," "They bloody hate playing us, don't they, lads?" Danny admitted to himself that he thought the Revolution could win. He caught Molly's eye—she winked at him—and then he looked over at Red Star Toronto. He was sorry to see they looked quite comfortable and scarcely fatigued as they strolled off the field. The Croatian goalkeeper was struggling to light a cigarette through his mustache in the rain.

The second half was just like the first, except that a noticeable portion of the Revolution's fans had gone home. Danny thought there were no more than five hundred people remaining when Toronto kicked off and commenced their patient passing drill. Broome had commanded his team to stay in its shell—he even commanded Juanito and the Todd up front to stop trying to steal the ball from Red Star's defenders. "We can't get stretched, lads. Can't let them find any spaces behind us. If they're fifty yards from the goal, they're fifty yards from the bloody goal," he'd said at the half, "and they're *not winning this match*." And he was right. They weren't.

As in the first half, sooner or later a Red Star player would weary of the wall of red and black in front of him and try something from distance, giving Big Loooooooooooou the opportunity to collect the ball and launch it into their defensive third—his punts were the best Danny had ever seen. On one occasion, a Big Lou boot descended with a wind-caused wobble and Toronto's big Bosnian central defender misjudged his header—it skimmed the back of his head and ran out for another Rose City corner. This time Surley failed to convert one into two, but precious time ticked off the clock and the 0–0 score line carried with it the anomaly of zero corner kicks for Toronto to four for the Revolution. Danny looked to the sideline, where Broomsie was screaming himself hoarse and Molly was leaned back on the bench with a sly smile. The scoreboard clock said twenty-seven minutes. An inch of rain sloshed about on the pitch, mixing with the white chalk to make a gluey, gloppy substance that was making Red Star Toronto's life just a little more complicated.

Still, the visitors controlled the match, and their crosses were no longer speculative lobs from thirty-five yards up the wing but low darts from deep in the corners. And they were getting on the ends of them too. A header from inside the six-yard box skipped by the far post. Big Lou produced two mighty saves, and Danny got away with a slide tackle that he knew should have been a penalty. The PA boomed out something by the Doobie Brothers, the hippies started hurling insults Danny knew the Serbians couldn't understand, the sugary smoke mixed in with the rain, and Danny felt like he was in a football match, a real football match—not an American sideshow, but a pitched battle between Englishmen and Serbs, and he thought, *If we can hold on, we'll have played two games with no losses—we'll be unbeaten in the league—and these hippies will leave happy and these Serbs will leave sad, and... maybe maybe maybe.*

But then Red Star scored.

It wasn't much of a goal, but it was the kind you give up when you've been defending for too long. One of the Peters had cleared a Toronto cross only as far as McCoist at the top of the box, who had a chance to wind up a longish shot while an exhausted Surley just watched. The shot wasn't anything special, but its slick passage along the viscous film atop the pitch sped it into a thicket of legs, and who knows whose it even hit but the deflection wrong-footed Big Lou entirely and the ball skidded into the netting of the side Big Lou was not on, and it was 1–0 Red Star Toronto with eleven minutes to play.

The Revolution hung their heads. Danny got his up sooner than any of the others, which he knew for a fact because all he saw was ten downcast men who looked like they were done for. The hippies got up to leave. The rain came harder, and Broome essayed a hoarse yell that Danny couldn't even understand. Danny jogged over to Peter and told him to get the kickoff from Juanito and knock it back. Peter was too exhausted to answer, but he nodded.

Juanito touched the ball to Peter and Peter passed it back to Danny, who leaned back and lobbed the ball just behind Toronto's right back. The mammoth Kosovar turned to watch it slip along the turf and out for a Red Star goal kick—but that's not what happened. It did accelerate as it hit the ground, but Danny's trajectory had been just right: the ball met the mud that surrounded baseball's home plate, which today encircled the corner flag—and it stuck in the mire. Juanito had detected Danny's plan and was upon Red Star's defender as he reached the ball. A third of the ball was concealed in the home-plate mud, and both players hacked at it in a vain effort to dislodge it. Another Toronto player arrived on the scene, but Danny and Peter (now aware of the plan) waved the Revolution's players off, knowing that more Toronto legs and less Rose City legs improved the odds.

Juanito finally got enough of his toe under the ball that it sprung up against the defender's shins and slopped over the end line for a Revolution corner kick—its fifth of the match. *A Sniper Shot.* The referee pointed to the center spot and waved Toronto's goalkeeper out of the way. Toronto's two muddied defenders stood ankle-deep in the baseball sludge, hands on hips, faces drenched in rain, shock, and confusion at a North American rule that tore at their senses of football justice; the two of them made a nice photograph in the next day's Portland Sports page. Portland's deep-voiced PA announcer bellowed over the tinny sound system that the Revolution had just earned a "SNIP-ER SHOT! A free shot at the goal! Let's make some noise, Portland!"

The referee walked the ball from the corner and set it on a tiny mound of white chalk on the center spot. Surley stood over it, hands on his knees, breathing heavily through his mouth, heaving as if at the point of nausea. Danny waded over to see if Peter thought he could manage the fifty-five-yard lob it would require to get the ball over the puddles and ponds of standing water that pockmarked the pitch and into Red Star's goal. Broomsie was yelling something from the bench, but neither man could understand him. Danny said, "You got this, Peter?"

Peter looked up, red-faced, and said, "No, lad, I bloody well do not." He huffed and he puffed, and not in a good way. "You take it," he gurgled, and waddled away through the slurry until only Danny was left to take the kick.

And then the referee blew his whistle.

There Danny was, alone, in the rain, with the ball. To his right, nine mustachioed Red Star Serbs (and one Englishman); behind him, his new teammates. Toronto's keeper stood next to a post, outside the goal, and endeavored to stare a hole in Danny's forehead. He sensed relief amongst the Slavs—a giant central defender having been sent to replace the surgical but spent first choice to take the Sniper Shot. There Danny was, bigger and stronger than most, the game upon his shoulders. And yet it was more than a game: it was his standing in his new club, his hard-earned-in-Seattle standing. With an opportunity to level the score and put his team in position to win, could Danny keep his head, could Danny deliver—or was Danny only good with a head of steam, in the heat of a moment... was Danny only good for crushing bones and sending smaller men sprawling across the field?

Danny thought, *I ain't scared of nobody,* and took the Sniper Shot himself.

"You're brilliant, lads, bloody brilliant," Broome said in the locker room. The lads, the bloody brilliant lads, leaned on their lockers, sprawled on their benches, hung their heads between their knees in stark, spent exhaustion. But they were victors. Unbeaten. Danny had made his Sniper Shot, the match had finished level, and the Super Soccer Showdown had gone the Revolution's way.

Juanito and Peter had converted their Sniper Shots in the Showdown, and one of Red Star's had clanged off the post. The big and strong newcomer from East Southwich had converted the winner in front of a couple hundred hardy souls and British expats, and the Revolution was undefeated in the league. Danny was his team's leading scorer—that had never happened before—and while he hadn't learned anything about the encroaching Red Menace, he had learned a little something about himself: he could score goals.

Meanwhile, that same night, in front of sixty thousand New Yorkers, the Giganticos staged an exhibition against the reigning German champions and destroyed them 7–2. The Pearl had been credited with an assist on his own third goal after playing the ball off the crossbar and back to himself for a volley into the upper corner. The Germans had applauded.

FOURTEEN

The second game of the Rose City Revolution's 1976 season was scheduled for the following Saturday on the road against the Colorado Cowhands.

The Cowhands were in their second season in the league. They had played the '75 season as a mostly native-born American side in Denver's cavernous football stadium, regularly drawing four-digit gatherings to the sixty-thousand-seater, with the exception of one particularly chilly April evening, when only 531 hearty souls allegedly paid to see the Cowhands concede seven to a local college team that had been paid in beer to wear T-shirts emblazoned with the Flamingos of Florida's mostly pink logo, the Miami team having decided that the trip wasn't worth the money or the trouble after hearing from Chicago's management that the Cowhands could be beaten with any eleven men who knew the rules of the game.

After a summer of failing to capture Denver's attention with their earnest Americans, the team had vacated the Mile High City and settled in the frontier town of North Beef, Colorado,

---

👕 This was not the AASSA's first experiment with less-than-traditional venues. In 1971, the league placed a team in Las Vegas. Seemed like a nice idea at the time, until the Irish business concern that had made the investment learned that an average summer day in Vegas was hotter than any recorded moment in the entire history of the British Isles. The team settled on playing indoors; the Snake Eyes' home was the casino with the highest ceiling they could reserve before a match. Before games, a crew of valets, bellmen, and busboys would scramble around the room, setting up a few rows of maroon-padded gold metal chairs. A boxing announcer did the PA in a tux, rumbling along in guttural, barely audible tones and giving each player's weight and measure-

enticed by local boosters who had plied the Cowhands' ownership with a summer full of free dates at the local rodeo arena*
and a set of thirty western shirts with pearlized buttons and the
team's logo, a cowboy lassoing a soccer ball, embroidered on
the front.

When the Revolution's bus arrived in the parking lot of
North Beef's 7-Eleven, a little over an hour's drive from Denver,
it was met by the mayor, a gaggle of civic-minded locals, and
what appeared to be the Cowhands, looking a little ashamed of
themselves (and vaguely Romanian, which they turned out to
be, mostly) in bright blue satin jackets and pants bejeweled in a
manner befitting country music superstars. The North Beef High
School Marchin' Varmints, in star-spangled red, white, and blue
costumery, arrayed themselves in loose formation, fiddling with
their instruments to a patriotic American march. A small squad
of jesters in face paint and cowboy attire—Danny would soon
learn that they were something called "rodeo clowns"—goofed
around with soccer balls in the parking lot, while the band eased
out of its Yankee tune and settled into a riff on "I Want to Hold
Your Hand" in acknowledgment of the coach full of Englishmen
that had just arrived.

Broomsie walked off the bus. Danny saw him shake hands
with North Beef's dignitaries, including an older man in a cowboy hat and a blue satin Cowhands jacket of his own. The man
seemed to be a team official of some kind. Broomsie nodded with
the vigor and feigned happiness of a man who was done being
surprised by American soccer. "The pioneers get the arrows,"

---

ments, while walking around the room with a gold-colored handheld mike taking drink orders. The Snake Eyes signed two actual soccer players—a pair of
over-the-hill Irishmen who claimed some non-League background; everyone
else was on the bell staff at whatever hotel the team called home that night.
The Irishmen and one of their Irish businessmen would show up with a pocket-
ful of fifty-dollar bills and do whatever they could to round up a side. The team
claimed attendance of about sixty-five people total for the two or three home
games before moving to San Francisco for the balance of the season and then
quietly declaring bankruptcy.

Broomsie had once told the team in an apparent effort to show what he'd learned in America. No one followed him off the bus.

Once Broomsie's handshakes were done, he waved for the Revolution to come on out and receive its Colorado welcome. When the team had—with some reluctance—assembled itself in the parking lot, the mayor spoke. "We don't do anything small around these parts, especially not with the bicentennial and all," he said, opening his arms as if to give the visitors a hug. "I don't much understand this game you play, and you all talk funny, but we are just *tha-rilled* to have you here in town. Now this is a pretty big to-do around here—we've never really had anything like pro sports happen in these parts, other than the rodeo of course, so what we're gonna go ahead and do is have us a parade. We got the band, we got a fire truck and a few police cars, the rodeo clowns here, some Cadillacs, and a nice big tractor. Both teams will march, of course. It'll be a *ta-reat* for the folks here in town. You boys bring along a few soccer balls and do your thing, pop 'em on your head a few times, if you think that's safe, kick the ball to each other, whatever you want to do. It'll be just great, just great." He smiled a wide smile, and he slapped Broomsie on the back a little harder than he was used to being slapped. Broomsie hopped forward a full step and looked as if he might choke, but he recovered himself and thanked the mayor, who said, "Well, all right. Tell you what, Coach, the Cowhands here are all ready to go, so how about you boys get dressed and meet us behind the 7-Eleven here and we'll get this parade rolling?"

Molly glanced down the row at Danny and mouthed "Romanians" as if Danny needed the tip-off.

Meanwhile, Broomsie looked a little surprised and said, "What—*now*?"

The mayor looked at his watch and said, "Oh, yes, Coach, now. The game's in a couple hours and we gotta get this parade on through."

The coach looked at his lads and gave the now-familiar (even to Danny) *Well, we're in America, so I guess this is going to happen* look. The team spelunked twenty duffel bags out from below the bus, went around back of the 7-Eleven, and donned its spangled and flowered costumes. Soon, both teams and the Marchin' Varmints were assembled, and the motor vehicles stretched down a small road back into North Beef from the rear of the 7-Eleven.

A large man wearing a bolo tie and a baseball hat that said IF YOU'RE GONNA BE SUCH A TURD, WHY DON'T YOU GO LAY IN THE GRASS made a speech about how everyone in that part of Colorado had always believed that North Beef was a big-time town that should have had its own big-time team a long time ago. "I never thought it would be a team full of Romanians playing a sport where you can only use your feet with the words 'hands' in its name." He paused and waited for a laugh, didn't get one, and moved on. "But hey," he said, and shrugged, "we'll take it. You boys look big-enough-time to me." Danny thought that was a nice thing for the man to say. He did think the Romanians looked big time. They didn't look that different from Red Star Toronto. They had mustaches.

After the large man spoke, the man in the cowboy hat barked orders at the players. He followed each of his statements with "Can everybody understand me? Everybody here understand English?" Danny nodded to him each time, figuring he was the biggest body there and that if the man saw him nod he'd figure all the Rose City players knew what to do. It seemed to work. The Romanians looked baffled but capable of following along.

Once the man was satisfied he had the teams and the band where he wanted them, he yelled, "OK, boys! Roll the fleet!" and down the little road came a red Thunderbird, an old Mustang, a Corvair covered with primer, and an open-topped Nash Metropolitan, every one of them with an American flag draped across its hood. The man turned to Danny, pointed to the Nash, and said, "You're the biggest boy here. If we could get you into the smallest car, that would be a hoot and a holler." Danny was about to say yes—he didn't see why not, and he'd never knowingly contributed to a hoot before—when Graham stopped him. "You'll pull a muscle just trying to get in."

Danny looked back at the man, nodded at his coach, and said, "Thanks, but the boss says no." Still, he liked being singled out and he'd never been invited to be in a parade. He caught eye contact with Molly. She smiled back.

The man who had summoned the cars started shouting, "OK! OK! OK! Everybody! Everybody! Here's how this is gonna go," and he explained the order of the parade: first the "public safety vehicles," then the fancy cars, then the marching, then the teams, home team first. "Oh, and the horses," he yelled. "Where are the horses? The goddamn horses, people!" And then there were horses. Danny wasn't sure where they'd come from, except that they weren't there and then they were. "The horses go before the teams!" the man yelled, which Danny thought was too bad.

When the teams came out from behind the 7-Eleven, Danny saw some bunting, some hand-made signs—REMEMBER, 'HANDS— NO HANDS!!!; KICK 'EM, 'HANDS!; and the motto that was right there in the team's logo, HANDS IN THE NAME, NOT IN THE GAME, affixed to street signs and parked cars along the route. A festive enough atmosphere, Danny thought. But not very many people. Broomsie sidled over next to Danny and said, "Everyone loves a parade, eh, Danny my boy?"

"Well—" Danny began, but the coach cut him off: "It's no open-top bus, lad, but this isn't exactly London either, is it? Or Cloppingshire or South Eastwich, or wherever you come from. But this is our life now, Danny, this is where the football gods have decided the likes of you and I belong. Soak it up, lad. It ain't so bad."

Danny thought maybe Broomsie was right. He thought maybe he should've been pretty sore about this fool's errand in this strange part of the world, but then he thought of Molly, he thought about his conversation with Three—could he really be the key to foiling something of worldwide importance? Would that be as good as a championship? Would that *be* his champion-ship? *You could do worse,* he thought, *you could do worse. Couldn't do that from East Southwich, save the bloody world from the bloody Russians.* He thought of the game in Seattle, beating Toronto; he thought of the smile on Broomsie's face in the cement desolation of Seattle Municipal Stadium, in the locker room after the Red Star game; and he thought, *Hey, it's a parade. For us. Maybe some-thing nice could happen for this team. You grow up dreaming that the best thing that could ever happen to you is you find a semiregular spot in a midtable Third Division club, but now here I am... in America... in Colorado—sounded a lot more exotic than Portland, Oregon, and now there may be a parade down the main street of this nice sunny town with Beef right there in its name. Maybe... maybe this could work out after all.*

One of the cars had a giant dead-looking wreath laid at-tached to its grille. Broomsie said, "What's that for?" The man organizing the parade said, "Well, we had a big Christmas pa-rade a few years back." Broomsie looked at Peter Surley and then back at the man. No one said anything. Then the man said, "Go!" and the parade started.

When the parade finally got to town, Danny saw a corner barbershop with maybe ten old guys out in front, sitting in lawn chairs, smoking and talking, a couple of them playing cards. Danny could see a guy inside getting his hair cut. The men all waved at the Revolution and the Cowhands as they went by. Kelvin flicked a ball off the wall of the barbershop, smack be-tween the heads of two of the old men, and settled it gently be-tween his shoulder blades on its return. One of the men barked out an obscenity, but the rest gave Kelvin a boisterous round of applause. The barber stopped what he was doing, came to the door, and broadcast a big, bright, mystified smile to the for-eigners parading through the streets of his odd little town. Dan-ny smiled back, in spite of himself, and it crossed his mind that maybe he was where he was supposed to be, on the team that needed him the most just now.

Danny's career reeled itself before him: the trip up to Bumfleet for the Boys Shield semifinal in 1968, when he'd positioned himself in front of the home side's wall on a free kick just outside of the box and had his pants pulled to his ankles by a mischievous Bumfleet Wanderer striker. First time he'd made the front page of anyone's newspaper. The worst own-goal he had ever scored, the result of a miscommunication with Franny Mother, the Royals' goalkeeper of so many years, who had come out to deal with a speculative floater from thirty or forty yards screaming, "Franny's ball!" but Danny stumbled as he tried to make way and plowed into poor Franny, collapsing both of his lungs—they'd had to carry the old man off on a stretcher—and somehow, some way, Danny had made cranial contact with the ball and it rolled into the East Southwich goal, causing a 1–0 defeat for his side. And a defeat somewhere so far north he could hardly believe it wasn't Scotland in howling wind and more-than-ankle-deep mud, after which the locals had chased the Royals back to their transport and tried to tip the coach over. The driver kept yelling, "Everyone on *that* side now!" as he eased out of the car park, desperate to stay upright and not to have the death of some severely intoxicated, nearly Scottish hooligan on his conscience. And then Danny looked up at the Colorado sun, the few well-wishers on the parade route, and thought, *Well, could be worse. Could be Bumfleet, and Bumfleet's bicentennial was seven hundred years ago.*

Danny walked over to his old bow-legged manager and said, "You know what, Broomsie—this is going to be great."

Broome grinned a wide gate of a grin and said, "Yes it is, son. I imagine you're really going to love it here. And you know what, I think if we can squeeze one more season out of old Peter Surley, and Juanito and speedy Kelvin find the bloody goal every now and again, and with you in the back, we can make it all the way to the Bonanza Bowl. I really believe it."

Danny laughed and said, "Eh, boss, I wasn't thinking quite that big—I was just talking about the parade." This made Broomsie smile again, and Danny *was* thinking that big.

Then the man leading the parade yelled out, "Well, I hope you liked it!"

Danny looked from the man to his new coach. His new coach looked from Danny to the man.

"Excuse me?" Broomsie hollered.

The man laughed. "That's it. That was the parade. Small town. Short notice. The fellas down at the barbershop were about all we could round up." The parade had gone past the barbershop three or four times, though no one had really seemed to notice.

The horses, the cars, the fire truck—they all quietly dispersed back to where they came from. The parade organizer yelled out his thanks to everyone for making the time and asked one and all to come to the rodeo grounds for the big game. "Starts in an hour!" he yelled.

An hour, Danny thought. *An hour? We're going to play in an hour?*

The Romanian Cowhands, not at all bothered, walked back the 7-Eleven, where their duffel bags were stashed in a storage room, and grabbed their things and began the short walk to the rodeo ground. Danny and his teammates climbed into their bus and tried to adopt a proper pregame mentality. Within moments, they were in sight of the bunting-bedecked North Beef Stampede Days Arena, a humble but handsome structure fronted by a magnificent sculpture of a cowboy barely holding himself to a bucking horse. The bus stopped, and the door opened.

The man in the satin jacket boarded the bus and offered an explanation of how the events of the day were "gonna go down," which concluded with "wait until the rodeo clowns clear the manure before you come on out of the bucking chutes."

"The bucking chutes?" Broomsie said.

Surley asked about the manure, and no one even mentioned the clowns.

The man said, "Well, now, before you boys play your game, we're staging a little bit of a rodeo for the kids here in town. Was the only way we could imagine getting folks to come out to your kickball game. So anyway, they're inside there havin' a high ol' time right now, and we're gonna try and keep the energy cracklin' after the barrel races by havin' you all come out from the chutes down there under the grandstand. About the same time, the Cowhands will come out the time chutes down at the other end and we'll just go ahead and play ball." Danny wondered if the life of the world's greatest footballer was worth running out of a bucking chute, whatever that might be.

"Just *'play ball'*?" Broomsie queried, an eyebrow raised.

"You got it, champ. There will be a ball right there in the middle, and, well, you boys will, uh, get to playin' with it however you do. Pretty simple."

Broomsie looked at Surley, and Surley looked at the Todd who was sitting next to him who just looked back at Surley. Surley looked at Broomsie. Amongst them, there was not one facial expression. From the back of the bus, however, there was one question: Juanito, who seldom spoke, piped up with the astonishingly relevant, "Where are the goals?"

"The *goals*, of course, the goals. Who asked that question? Give that boy a star. We got you covered. We're used to moving stuff around the grounds—once you and the Cowhands bust out of those chutes to get to that ball, we'll just roll 'em on out. They'll be there by the time anyone gets to shootin'."

Graham said, "Listen, mate, just get us in there so we can have a look at the ground. Then we'll hide in whatever chutes you want us to hide in."

"Well, all right, chief. Will do. Come with me. Bring the whole darn team." So the Rose City Revolution followed the man in the cowboy hat and the satin jacket toward a rear entrance to the North Beef Stampede Days Arena. It was a rickety structure down beneath the grandstand, a decades-old latticework of wood infused with a pungent barnyard aroma and decorated with hay and feedbags and all manner of wrangler paraphernalia. What had from the outside looked like a semi-viable, if down-home, sporting arena seemed less and less like a place where two teams stocked primarily with European footballers might put on a soccer game. When the Revolution climbed a few steps back into the sun and looked out upon the playing surface, they were even less convinced that the match was even going to happen.

Before the man in the cowboy hat and satin jacket could say anything, Broomsie said, "Oh, dear me."

The "ground" was devoid of grass, and not in the English Third Division way—there was not a single blade to be seen. And the available playing surface, which was a pool of brown-black dirt, sprinkled here and there with sawdust, was about two-thirds the size of a proper football pitch. It was unlined. Nothing about it said football, soccer, or anything that could be done with a ball. Horses trod upon it as Graham Broome's charges gazed in disbelief.

Broomsie said, "I have a squad of paid professionals, men who've played in the FA Cup, men who have represented their nations. Well, Trevor played for the Isle of Man in a testimonial once—isn't that right, Trevor? Yes, yes, right. Peter Surley, right here, this pillar of a man, scored for Nottingham Athletic in the '63 League Vase. The *League Vase!* You cannot ask these *men*, these *footballers*... you... you simply cannot be serious."

The man said, "Hey, Graham, you seem like a nice guy. I like this team of yours. I like the way you say 'vahhz,' and 'foot-baller' is a funny word. But I sure don't know what in blazes you're talking about. FA *this*, Notting-ham *that*. Everything you just said... whoosh!" He laughed. "In one ear and right out the other!" He pointed down to the muddy enclosure. "In thirty minutes, you play right down there. Now I gotta get a move on. You boys get yourselves dressed right here under the stands, all right? We'll send the referee on over to talk you through how this is gonna work." He looked down at the horses prancing around on the muck, patted Broomsie on the back, and said, "My god, ain't that one right there a beaut? Look at that animal, Mr. Broome. Mmm-*mmm. A specimen!* Well, good luck, all right?

OK!" and he ambled off down the planked wooden concourse, waving at just about everyone.

Broomsie looked as if he might throw up. Danny felt for him—he knew he had nothing to do with the farcical situation that presented itself to the Rose City Revolution at the moment, but the coach did seem at least partially responsible. He wasn't the reason the Colorado Cowhands had moved from Denver's football stadium to the North Beef Stampede Days Arena, but he was the reason Cloppingshire United and associated hangers-on were now the Rose City Revolution of the Frontier Conference of the American All-Star Soccer Association, and Graham Broome looked like he missed Cloppingshire very much indeed just now.

Still, he collected himself and uttered a nervous, "Let's get dressed, boys. Believe it or not, I can think of a way this can get worse, and that's leaving this travesty upon the game of football in defeat. Someone's going to win today down in that mudhole, and I for one would like it to be us."

Even Surley nodded, and the team followed his lead. "Come on lads," Peter said, though he didn't seem at all happy about it. "Let's get bloody dressed."

As the Revolution prepared to play—not in a locker room, but in an open area underneath the bleachers—a man dressed in the black and white stripes and the long black pants of a basketball referee approached Broomsie and said, "OK, sir, I assume you came to this country to have a unique experience—broaden your horizons, as it were. You could've stayed back home in England if you were into tradition, right? If you were concerned with the proper way to do things." This last part he said in a head-bobbing Beatlesque accent meant, it seemed, to mock all of Britannia. "Well, this is America. We do things a little different over here, which is to say we do things however we want. Today you and your team are going to have one of those experiences, and so am I. Are you familiar with ground rules? Kind of a baseball concept—every ballpark's a little different, so we make allowances in the laws of the game for the shape of this fence or the location of that flagpole, et cetera, et cetera. Gather your boys around and I'll explain what the next ninety minutes in that rodeo arena are going to be like." He waited for the team to come over and then he said, "First off, boys, there's no way we're fitting twenty-two full-grown men in there. So it's seven against seven today—"

"Hold on," Broomsie said. "Seven on seven? We're here to play football. Football is eleven on eleven. That's all there is to it. I can't make tactical adjustments for four less players in the side."

The man in the referee uniform said, "Like I said, Coach, we're broadening our horizons, aren't we? And it's the same for both teams. Hell, the other guys don't even speak English, so they aren't gonna get the same talking-to as you boys. Now, you all are going out there seven against seven, like it or not. There is no out of bounds. The ball hits the fence around the arena, we play it. The ball goes into the stands, we wait for someone to throw it back down, and we play it. It's soccer, but different—"

Graham Broome's face was so jammed up with confusion, anger, and frustration that nothing came out.

The referee said, "All right then. Get your team ready. This thing's about to go down. When I blow this whistle, send seven of your men through that gate right on over there. The rest go through that one over yonder. It'll take you to your bench. Got it? OK. Good. Have a great game," he concluded, and he jogged off.

Broomsie placed his hands on his hips and looked down at the uneven surface below him, a surface that had plainly been trod by horses and cows as recently as that morning. He shook his head, and he knew that when he brought it back up and looked into the eyes of the Cloppingshire United men amongst the Rose City Revolution, they'd be blaming him. They'd be blaming him for yanking them out of the oldest and most re-vered football league in the world, a league that allowed every club and every player—no matter their place in the rigidly stratified pecking order—a legitimate shot at national glory. A match of the week, a goal of the week, a promotion run, a heroic cup moment. And some of them would yet have those opportunities again, but for now they were stuck here, underneath the grandstand at a rodeo arena, in a place called North Beef, about to play before people who thought this—*football*, the Beautiful Game, the *World's* Game—was the sideshow to chute dogging and mutton busting.

The Cloppingshire players and the rest of the Revolution looked at their coach, and their coach said, "Boys, I'm a practical man. I worry about what I can control." Then he rattled off seven names and said, "When that twat blows his whistle, you lot run out like it's the bloody World Cup final. Any who don't, any who are too big for it, are done for the day." He wanted to threaten them with being off the team, but he knew that right now some of them would've happily traded their red and black stripes for a ticket to Heathrow. "The only thing that will feel worse than this place smells is a trip back to Portland with a loss around our necks." The whistle went. "Now bloody go," he barked.

Danny and six of his teammates ran up a shaky wooden ramp and into the bright sunshine of the rodeo ground. For a moment, his eyes were useless—blinded by the sun—and his ears filled with country music from the PA. When he adjusted, he saw that it was a nice enough little stadium: beautiful white-painted grandstands sheltered by a quaint, barnlike cover. Wasn't all that much different from the sheds Danny had seen throughout the depths of English football. The problem, however, was beneath Danny's feet: the fourteen players were herded into an enclosure that could hardly have been less fit for football had it been designed to specifically to humiliate the players. And yet...

...Juanito sprinted after the ball as if he'd been born for rodeo soccer, and while most of the other thirteen players on the "pitch" were adjusting their eyes to the sun and their ears to the blare of cowboy music and the rest of their bodies to their surroundings, he took two bounding dribbles, found himself within ten yards of the goal-like structure—a little smaller than a proper football goal, a little bigger than a Volkswagen—at the Cowhand end and rocketed a shot past the shocked Romanian goalkeeper, and before Danny even had his bearings the Revolution had their first goal of the season from open play, and their first real lead of 1976.

The referee motioned for Colorado's disoriented keeper to restart from there. The field was too small to bother with a standard kickoff, so the Cowhand keeper rolled the ball to one of his fellow Romanians, who still looked as if he'd rather be behind the Iron Curtain than in this sham. Juanito scurried over to him, scooped the ball off his bewildered feet, turned back toward the goal, and slotted another one home. *Two–bloody nil.*

This time Colorado's keeper catapulted an angry punt from his goalmouth. It nearly exited the ground, just dipping underneath the arena's gabled roof and into the amused crowd. The PA announcer was hollering along with the activity, and when he yelled, "Now throw it back, folks!" someone did, and he yelled, "Hey, that was great! Now let's hear some noiiiiise, North Beef!" and the crowd whooped and shrieked, and the ball bounced around on the clodded dirt while the players tried to settle into some semblance of soccer, and the loudspeakers filled the arena with music Danny had never heard before and the occasional exhortation for the crowd to cheer on the leather-fringed home team.

In time, the game came to look a little something like soccer. The Romanians were clearly skilled passers of the ball, and Danny was certain they were the superior team and would play keep-away with the Revolution on the giant flat field in Portland. But here they just seemed despondent, coming to terms with the summer that lay ahead, trying to demonstrate their footballing superiority in front of these people who would rather be watching men tie helpless goats into tidy little pretzels.

Juanito never let up. Broomsie cycled his entire six-teen-man roster in and out of the game, including Carlos the back-up goalkeeper, but never took Juanito out and Juanito never stopped scoring. The Revolution's new hero finished with six. The Cowhands had their moments too, but they never quite recovered from conceding those early goals and the Revolution ran out of the North Beef Stampede Days Arena with a 10–7 victory and no catastrophic injuries. Broomsie was elated, and the team showered its congratulations upon its double hat trick man, but the Revolution boarded its bus quietly, a little ashamed of having just performed as an anthropological exhibit in a foreign country, an Old World amusement on a former colony's frontier. They had been the two-headed barnyard animal at the fair.

The Rose City Revolution made their way to the far-off Denver airport in a near-catatonic state. The post-rodeo/victory euphoria had dissipated into the vast Colorado sky, and the team was left with the feeling that they'd flown all the way out here and hadn't even played a football match. Danny suspected they'd been part of something worse: an insult to the game they all took as their rationale for existence. None of them acknowledged—even to themselves—that they were evangelists for something inherently English (even Juanito and Juan and Carlos), but they knew it in their footballing marrow—and they knew they were less English now than before they had slopped about in the dirt like cows and sheep. They knew, in fact, that if cows and sheep, or wolves and coyotes, or aardvarks had been released into the North Beef Stampede Days Arena for the amusement of the North Beef Stampede Days patrons, the Revolution and the Cowhands would have carried on gamely and grimly, trying to maneuver the ball through and around the varied animalia en route to an ever-higher, ever more grotesque score line that was more embarrassing than exciting. And Danny could feel the shame in the team in the bus, in the walk through the airport, and on the plane.

He had not sensed in the Romanians anything conspiratorial: no desire to play a part in a hideous assassination, as if he knew what that sense might be, and he had confirmed with Molly that she hadn't either. Something awful was happening to the great game of football in Colorado that summer of '76, but there didn't appear to be any real threat to the American Experiment out there in cowboy country. The Romanians had too much to deal with in North Beef to be part of any Cold War intrigue, Danny thought. Though Molly and Danny agreed: That's a lot of Romanians in one place—and vowed to keep an eye on the Cowhands.

Danny leaned his giant head against the airplane's window and felt the weight of his big eyelids descend over his big eyes, and he thought, *If people can't beat us, maybe we don't need new players.*

And he fell asleep.

A couple thousand miles away in New York, the Pearl of Brazil, gorgeously attired in an all-white suit and platform boots, gave a spoken-word and poetically Portuguese-infused rendition of "The Star-Spangled Banner" while smoking a cigarette before that night's game against the American SuperThunder. After his performance, he removed the suit, right there on the field, revealing his green number 10 kit. He scored a hat trick in the first twenty-five minutes and played the second half in goal, wearing his white suit jacket as his goalkeeper jersey.

FIFTEEN

Graham Broome gathered the team around him on the Multnomah Stadium carpet the following Monday morning and
described the upcoming week. "Light workout today, lads. Re-
introduce ourselves to the game of football after that farce in
Colorado. Tomorrow, we run in the woods. Wednesday's off.
You can all watch your shows and play your pool up at the
Grand Douglas. Thursday we're back here for a little match prep
and then we're off to Chicago to play the Butchers." *

Danny thought: *The woods. And Chicago. The Poles and Ukrainians. The Butchers.*

👕 A NOTE UPON THE CHICAGO BUTCHERS: The team was something of
an anomaly in the American All-Star Soccer Association—they were neither the
pet project of an eccentric American businessman fascinated with the "Sport of
the Future" (the "Permanent Sport of the Future," as one prominent national
sportswriter had derisively put it) or the creation of a moneyed expat bent on
spreading the Good Word of the Beautiful Game. The Butchers were, in fact,
an established team with a deep and complicated history, a football club and
social organization formed by immigrants between the wars. They had variously
been known as the Chicago Ukrainians, Polish-Ukrainians FK, Polish White Ea-
gles, Pipefitters Local 521, the Chicago Americans (for a couple of years in the
late '50s), Polish-Ukrainians (again), before landing in the AASSA and finding
themselves in need of a marketable, merchandisable moniker.

They had been a dominant force in the ethnic Chicago leagues during the
1950s and '60s, when a weekend slate of games at a vacant baseball park could
draw 20,000 Slavs of one kind or another and receive absolutely zero notice in the
local non-immigrant press. They had won three American Open Cups, back when
that was a thing, in the '40s, had taken a smattering of obscure national amateur
championships, had toured Mexico five or six times and had represented Poland

"But before we get to that, I've a little announcement to make." Broomsie smiled wider than Danny had ever seen him smile. He seemed to levitate an inch off the ground. "For the first time in our club's short history, we're going to be on the television. Lads, we're going to be on the telly. And what's even better, *they're* paying *us*. They know we're in first place, and they think we're a good bet to stay in the hunt. The city's laying a wager on us, my boys. And more money, more exposure, more fans, I should think. This is a great day for the Revolution, a great day indeed. It's a first for the team, and I bloody well want to win this one." He stopped and looked around the group, anxious to bask in the glow of admiration the Rose City Revolution owed him on the occasion of this announcement. But Danny saw the looks. The looks said: *They're going to watch us play... in Chicago? Who'd want to watch* that? Graham Broome felt the tension: "Come on, lads—TV. Television. It's good news, right good news." Cloppingshire United, et cetera, only recently having played in manure, stared back at Broomsie, who knew what he'd done and just forged on, now with an added edge. No one like his good

---

(without Poland's knowledge) at the 1962 Chicago Transnational Challenge Cup where they tied the US Olympic team and beat Bermuda 4-1.

When the American All-Star Soccer Association had run itself from twenty-two teams in 1971 to just four solvent clubs ready to compete for the '72 championship, the league made a desperation call to the Polish-Ukrainians and begged them to play a season just to keep the AASSA alive. The Association waived its expansion fee on the stipulation that the team rename itself in keeping with US sports fans' expectations and soccer's desire to Americanize itself—and thus was both the Chicago Butchers Pro Soccer Team (and an ad campaign: "Witness the Slaughter").The Butchers did slaughter what remained of the league that summer. Over a shortened schedule, they made easy work of the laughable Dallas Debacle, the over-American Apple Pie of St. Louis, a not-yet-star-studded version of the New York Giganticos, and the Rochester Foreign Stars. The Butchers, decked out in frightening dried-blood maroon, were declared 1972 American All-Star Soccer Association champions without a Bonanza Bowl as the second- and third-place teams had no money left for travel and no desire to line up against the Butchers one last time. The team won the championship in '73 too.

news? Fine, thought Broome. "All right then. Last time I try and do something for you sorry lot. You half over there. Grab pinnies. The rest of you over there. Let's go. Let's bloody have it. I want someone to get hurt."

Danny had heard most of what had happened last year in Chicago: the Revolution had been throttled by a score no one on the team would even repeat. The lads feared the Butchers even more than they feared the Giganticos. Danny could feel it. The name—the name itself was a competitive advantage. Danny thought more English teams should name themselves like this. United, City, Town, Wanderers, Rovers, Rangers... these weren't intimidating names, not in the least. Wolves, maybe, but *Butchers. My god—Birmingham Butchers. Terrifying. Southampton Slaughter. Manchester Maulers. Those were names*, Danny thought. *Who'd want to play the Manchester Maulers?*

The *Chicago Butchers*, though—Danny could see what the combination of those words did to his teammates. The Revolution did not want to go to Chicago. Danny had asked some of his teammates about the Butchers and he could see, even in Peter's apathetic eyes, that Chicago's entry in the AASSA had left Rose City's Revolutionaries in an existential void, wondering if they were even footballers at all.

"What *happened* out there?" Danny asked Peter.

Peter said, "Danny, it's better you don't know, mate."

The next morning, Danny stayed back as the team began its jog through the woods. The slower Todd, just in front of him, asked Danny if he was doing all right, and Danny said, "Bumps and bruises, Todd. Takin' it easy today—don't worry about me. I'll keep you in my sights." And the Todd eased away. Danny didn't pause. He just went straight to the tree and waited, with Molly well hidden nearby in case anything got hairy.

Sure enough, the Communists soon joined Danny in the tree.

"So," one of them said, "we have been expecting you."

"No," Danny said. "I've been expecting you."

"I do not think so," the Russian said. "We have been waiting here in the forest and now here you are with us."

"Maybe it works different in Russian," Danny said, "but I was here—"

One of the Communists took the hammer out of his pocket—the same hammer with which he'd threatened to ruin Danny's career prospects at their last meeting—and said, "Stop talking, Danny Hooooper. We can do with you what we wish. There are two of us in this tree and only one of you. We do not wish to argue the English language with you at this time."

Danny said, "You've lost the element of surprise, boys. It is no longer two against one."

"Oh, is that so, Danny Hooooper?" said the Russian who had yet to speak. "You have brought the girl? Very well then. We know this Molly. She has courage and she is smart girl. Nice shoulders. You are a clever boy to hide her behind some nearby tree? That is very well, Danny. But"—and he raised the hammer again—"she cannot stop this hammer."

Danny knew that the man was right, but he maintained his bravado and said, "Boys, just tell me what you want to tell me. And if you want to hit me, just get on with it."

The Russians gave each other a surprised look and withdrew the half inch or so that the tree's interior allowed. Then one of them said, "Danny Hooooper, you are indeed a worthy foe in the battle between our ways of life. We see that now. But you will lose, and we wish to prove it to you."

"That so?" Danny said.

"It is so."

"Fine then. How do you plan on proving this to me?"

"The Rose City Revolution will win in Chicago. We will see to it."

"I don't know, boys. From what I hear the Butchers have the Revolution's number. I don't reckon the team's bringing loads of confidence on this trip—"

"You will win, Danny Hooooper," said one Russian.

The other nodded and said, "It is already certain."

Danny did like the sound of three wins against no defeats. Danny opened his mouth but the first Communist said, "Now run. Catch up with your team. We will speak with you in Chicago. And I can assure you that we will regain the element of surprise."

The other said, "Say hello to Molly. She is very pretty. Now go. Run, Danny Hooooper."

"Wait," Danny said. "You'll speak with me in *Chicago*?"

One of the men said, "Stop talking. Run."

So he left the tree and ran. Hard. His thoughts ran as hard as his legs, and he caught up with slow Graham after only a couple of minutes.

Meanwhile, the other Russian, the Russian who preferred hockey to football and who was not named Lev, who thought that Russian novels were baroque and bourgeois when simplicity and economy would have done just fine and held a belief in Communism that was not intellectual but religious, could see, as could anyone, that the Pearl of Brazil was a player of rare skill, but he also saw him as the football equivalent of all those authors' fictional finery. The other Russian didn't enjoy watching Brazil play. He liked Russian football and Russian hockey: players made the pass you expected them to make—the right pass—dribbled when dribbling was called for, shot when shooting was called for. The work the men were in America to do was as clear, simple, and necessary to him as the Revolution itself.

When the team arrived in the Chicago hotel lobby, two men sitting in large leather chairs behind dramatically unfurled newspapers by a fireplace caught Danny's eye. Danny saw each of them peek over his paper as the Revolution stood about waiting for Molly to get the team checked in. He didn't acknowledge them, nor did he let on how they made him feel. In fact, he supposed it was possible that they weren't even the Russians. He couldn't see their faces, but...

...he knew. They had followed him to Chicago.

The Revolution took the field for pregame warm-ups before the Butchers did. Danny liked their little home so far. It was tight quarters for sure—he couldn't quite picture how a baseball game could take place in there, but he wasn't quite sure how baseball worked anyway. The fans, more on one side than another, were right near the field. They'd been near the players in Colorado too, but that hadn't felt at all like football. This place, even with its odd dimensions, was more like a proper football ground, and the early arrivals bustled about in the stands like proper football fans, taunting the Revolution, basking in the sun, roasting all manner of Eastern European–smelling comestibles. A loose cloud hung over the field, a low dome the smell of an exotic kitchen.

The park's notable feature hung just behind one of the goals, nestled right up against an already crowded grandstand of maroon-clad Butcher rooters: a cow, skinned and rotating on a spit. It was attended by the Butchers' butcher mascot, a man in a red-and-black flannel shirt and white blood-spattered smock who wielded a pair of elongated butcher knives as he riled up the crowd. As the cow cooked over simmering coals and released a sticky, fleshy smell, the butcher tossed his knives high into the air and caught them with marvelous, juggling flourishes that made the crowd murmur and hum. Danny had never seen a cow on a spit before, and he had never warmed up for a football match in the startlingly close proximity of flying butcher knives, and he had never smelled most of what he was smelling right now. But he'd had the *feeling* he was feeling: the Chicago crowd smelled blood, and it wasn't cow's blood. That was a feeling he knew plenty well.

Danny jogged over to the team's bench and sat next to Molly. He took off his right boot and said, "Pretend you're wrapping my ankle."

Molly knelt in front of him and started to apply a loose Ace bandage. "This place is a charnel house, Molly," he said. "I'm happy to play on grass... mostly"—he waved his hands at the vast swaths of infield dirt that made up half of one end; there was even the small hill of a pitcher's mound left in—"and it's nice to play in front of people who know the game, but it smells like blood and onions in here. Like wearing a kidney pie around your neck—"

"You're going to win today."

"Don't think so, sweetheart." The Butchers had taken the field, and Danny reckoned they looked downright frightening in their blood-maroon sweat suits and bushy mustaches. "Look at them. They're horrifying. Sinister, is what they are."

"It's not what you see. It's what you don't see."

"Excuse me?"

"Four of them are gone. At least four."

"Gone?"

"Gone. Their best three are gone for sure. Maybe even their goalkeeper. One of the missing players played for Poland in the World Cup. Real players. Can't be a coincidence."

"What do you mean *gone*?"

"Danny, I'm not trying to make this complicated."

"OK, then—how do you know? I mean, so soon—how do you know which players?" She kept wrapping and unwrapping and rewrapping Danny's ankle. Danny said, "Maybe they just haven't come out yet."

"A man told me in the lobby yesterday," Molly said.

The men in the tree were the men in the lobby. Of course they were.

"Let's just call it a good news/bad news situation. The good news is they want us to win this game. The bad news is they're sending us a message. And it can't be a good one."

She unwrapped Danny's ankle for a final time and told him to get his shoe and sock on.

"Go win the game. We'll worry about where those Poles are later."

The Chicago Butchers staged an elaborate pregame show featuring flares and smoke in the stand above the cow and a small fireworks display emanating from just behind the cow-end goal. The butcher produced a branding iron the size of a manhole cover and applied it to the poor thing's flank. The resulting haze choked the penalty area of the Rose City goal.

And then the Butchers, even with their depleted roster, scored first.

Before the game was a minute old, a mustachioed right winger lobbed a ball toward Danny and Big Lou and a charging Butcher. The ball disappeared for a moment in the greasy cloud, and the Chicago forward initiated a mighty collision, leaving Danny, Big Lou, and the Butcher on the ground and the referee pointing to the spot. Danny had no idea who had run into whom, but he knew he'd been going for the ball and he know Big Lou had been trying to catch it. Danny screamed at the referee, bellowed in his face the most foul, awful things. The referee was instantly surrounded by Revolutionaries demanding an answer. As soon as the referee attempted to give them one, and as soon as the Revolutionaries realized it was in a some as-yet-unidentified Slavic language, the Englishmen filled the Slavic air with a chorus of oaths intended to indicate their disgust at both the call and the obvious pointlessness of engaging with this particular referee. One Ukrainian penalty kick later, Chicago had a lead.

The crowd boomed a thunderous, guttural roar, which Danny actually liked—Chicago's bloodthirsty horde was what a football crowd was supposed to sound like. They weren't English, but they were European, and Danny could tell they knew the difference between soccer and the rodeo and he felt a kinship with them for that at least.

But then something happened that Danny did not relate to: just behind him, no more than fifteen or twenty yards away, the butcher went to work, and the roar turned truly savage. The butcher manipulated his knives in a series of flips and jabs, and their brightness reflected glinty shards of Chicago sunlight. The crowd's sound deepened and coarsened, and the butcher finally plunged one of his knives sidelong into the flank and began to carve. The roar carried on in ever more animalistic waves as the butcher cut away at the meat until he had freed a giant fleshy slice and held it aloft with two hands. The fans screamed their approval as the butcher held the beef aloft. Then the butcher turned to face the rest of the stadium, and the rest of the Butcher fans cheered too. Danny wondered if there was anywhere in the AASSA where barnyard animals weren't part of the show.

It was a startling display—not the kind of thing that filled you with the belief that you were just going to fight your way back into the match, even the score line, and eventually take the points (or most of them). Not at all. It was the kind of thing that seeded in your subconscious the idea that you might not fight your way out of the stadium.

But as play restarted, the Revolution found themselves with space to move the ball. The Butchers gave Surley more freedom than he'd had against Toronto and far more than he'd ever had in North Beef. He received the ball in comfort, turned, looked around, gave the ball to whomever he saw, and the Butchers continued to lay off. Danny eased toward the sideline and shouted at Broomsie, "Who are they missing?" By now the coach had been briefed by Molly and had also sussed the situation out for himself. "Mankowski and Willimoski at least," Broomsie yelled back, and waved Danny over closer so he could complete his thought. "Danny, that's the center of their midfield. They're a right doughnut without them. Peter can do whatever he wants. They're ahead one–nil and missing their midfield—and they think we're last year's Revolution. They think they've got it won.

Don't score yet. It'll only wake them up. Don't score until the break."

Danny ran back toward the middle and drifted toward Peter. "Knock it around 'til half, Peter. No goals. Gaffer says." Peter looked at Danny as if Danny had insulted the Queen. Danny said, "He's got it all sorted, mate—we'll talk inside. We're going to win this one, Peter!" The ball whizzed just over each of their heads, and Danny took off after it and put it into touch within close smelling distance of the cow.

Peter took Danny's relayed message to heart. Each time the ball arrived at his feet, he lobbed it toward a Chicago corner with a mechanical delicacy that backspun the ball to a stop within five yards of the flag. The poor Butcher wingbacks were regularly in the position of chasing the ball down with one of the Todds or Kelvin or Juanito right up his back. By the time the whistle went for the interval, the Poles and Ukrainians had mishit just enough awkward clearances to put the Revolution on four corner kicks. Surley had enjoyed his time in the middle of Chicago's cozy little park that the Revolution's one-goal deficit felt like a lead as the Portlanders jogged off the baseball field and down through the labyrinth of dugout/clubhouse/mysterious anteroom designed for a sport as foreign to most of the Revolutionaries as soccer was to America.

One of the younger Peters even got lost. He took a left where the rest of the team had taken a right and got himself tangled up in the black netting of what turned out to be a batting cage. Molly had to use a pair of scissors to get him out. For a few minutes, as he sat in a large storage area the Butchers had provided the Revolution as a changing room, listening to Broomsie explain how the Revolution (minus a Peter) was going to win this match, Danny thought maybe the Communists had abducted him too. But then Peter walked into the room, looking slightly traumatized and as if he'd just gotten out of bed.

"I don't know where their men are," Broomsie said. "The boys who played in the World Cup aren't here, lads, and without them, they're nothing. Nothing. They're lost out there. Lucky to be up and now they're hoping you can't score because last year you couldn't, and they're thinking you'll be frightened by the full stadium and that poor cow and the git with the knives and the smell of the place, but you won't, you won't be frightened. That's last year's Revolution, my boys. This year, we find a way. They won't score again. If they even try, they'll run into Danny, and if they get through him they'll have to deal with Big Lou. Run the ball through Peter, he'll take of everything. Understood?"

The team grunted and nodded.

"When we get one, and we will," Broomsie went on, "they'll wake up, but just for a few minutes. When that happens, put the bastards under. Give them no time. Frighten them. Foul them. Run through them. Once they realize what they're up against, they'll withdraw and hope they can win a Super Soccer Showdown at the cow end. Then finish them off. No Super Soccer Showdown. Not today. Bury them with two late ones and that'll be that, lads. Bob's your uncle."

As a Todd kicked off to Juanito to open the second half, there wasn't more than three or four Chicago Butchers within twenty-five yards of the halfway line—but the maroon jerseys in Chicago's penalty area were about close enough to hold hands, the bus well and truly parked. But Juanito knocked the ball back to Surley, who took a couple casual touches before lofting it toward the right wing to a speedy Kelvin, who drew a defender his way, took him on, got to the corner flag, lofted a cross toward the Butcher goal, and... nothing. Chicago's goalkeeper got under it without an ounce of trouble, surrounded by four or five giant teammates and not a Revolutionary within troubling distance. He rolled the ball to his left, dribbled it toward the edge of the box, and picked it back up again. Dribbled it two or three times, rolled it out to one of his giant defenders, who put his foot on it, looked upfield, didn't see anything he liked, and passed it back to the keeper. The Butchers had used the first ninety seconds of the half to place their cards on the table: *You can come and get us, Englishmen.*

At long last, Chicago's goalkeeper finally punted the ball into the hot, savory late-afternoon sausage-and-onion vapor. Danny got under it—he didn't even have to leap to win the ball from the solitary Chicago forward who knew better from his own training sessions than to try to win a header from a man that size. Danny headed the ball wide, knowing that the Revolution's way forward was around and not through, and knowing that Kelvin had the better of his man. Kelvin welcomed the service and attacked again, beat his man again, but this time his cross was headed out by a Chicago defender... and now the game was on.

Danny could feel it from the Butchers, could feel it from their followers, could feel it even from the butcher himself: Chicago might not win this game. Chicago was scared.

The ball settled at Surley's feet, and the Revolution proceeded to move it around a perimeter thirty-five yards from the Butcher goal without any great trouble. It was the most sustained possession they'd had all season. They never quite looked like scoring, and Danny was a little curious to see how his teammates might break through the home team's cynical but effective strategy, but it was nice to see the lads playing something that resembled real football. The eleven they had on the pitch just now—Big Lou in goal; Danny and a Jimmy in a holding, defensive midfield spot; a Trevor at left back and another one on the right (the other Trevor, the one on the right, was the next best defender on the team, Danny thought, a golden retriever of a kid... you could beat him once, even twice, but he'd just chase you down, over and over again, tongue dangling just slightly out of his permanently smiling mouth); Kelvin at right midfield; Surley in the middle; Jimmy on the left; Juanito and two Todds up front—this group could play, really play. Danny had seen the team fight in Seattle and at home against Toronto, and he'd seen glimpses of what some of them could do in Colorado, but here in

Chicago, with its seasoned smell and opponent and a full house, he saw the team share the ball with each other, resist panic, embrace the idea that victory—against legitimate (if less than full strength) competition, in a hostile environment—was a genuine possibility.

Danny himself felt his first inklings of American footballing confidence, manning the middle with size and strength but also with something else: an uprightness and intelligence on the ball that felt downright Dutch as it climbed through his ankles, into his shins, through his knees, and upward toward the rest of his body. He dribbled and pointed, moving his teammates around as Surley never quite managed to do, drawing Jimmy on the one wing toward him and sending Kelvin on the other wing away. He drew Juanito his way to receive the ball at his feet, got it back, and eased it over to Surley, who chipped into the box for an onrushing Todd—but that one was scooped up by Chicago's time-killing goalkeeper.

As the hands-on Butcher goalie whiled away another sixty seconds bouncing and rolling (and massaging and examining and considering) the ball, Danny eyeballed the ancient Surley, shirt hung distressed out over his belly longer than his shorts, socks down and floppy around his ankles, no shin guards. At every break in play, his hands were on his knees, and he gasped for breaths he couldn't quite catch. The score was only one–nil for Chicago, and the Butchers hadn't crossed halfway since the first half, but Danny knew it was eleven on ten now, and that Broomsie didn't have it in him—or in his bench, really—to remove Surley, who had led Nottingham Athletic to the 1963 League Vase.

Danny eased himself five yards, then ten yards upfield, unilaterally, converting the Revolution from a 4-3-3 to a 3-4-3, and became, for the first time in his life, an offensive player. He won a loose ball, turned, and found himself just thirty yards from the goal. It was intoxicating. *I could shoot from here*, he thought. The blood burgundy of the Butchers' uniforms whizzed by him like cars in an intersection; he slipped the outside of his foot along the ball and forced one of them to keep whizzing by; he sensed another one somewhere in the back right of his peripheral vision and finessed—*finessed!*—the ball over with his instep and had a light, easy sense of convergence: *I can do this,* he thought. *I can do this.* He played a nice, easy square pass to Kelvin to his right—just enough backspin on it to make Kelvin's trap as easy as catching the ball with his hands. Kelvin took his first touch facing Danny, then slapped at the ball with the outside of his right foot and dashed down the wing—it was the burst of speed that had made Kelvin Cloppingshire United's 1973 joint-four top goal scorer, which Kelvin had demonstrated only often enough to make him an overall disappointment in the English League, but here he was dominating a left defender who had come on as a substitute for Poland at the World Cup, and just as Kelvin was about to get his cross in from the end line, a barrel-chested Butcher defender slid in with his studs high, sent Kelvin flying into the ballpark's brick home-run wall, which he hit the way a bird hits a window: full speed and awkward, as if his body thought he'd just keep flying. That would be it for Kelvin for a good two weeks. Now the ball was out for a corner kick.

Bad news for Kelvin, but there was good news in it for the Revolution: it was their fifth corner of the match.

Surley was still on the field, but there was never any question of him taking the Sniper Shot. He didn't look like he could've kicked a soccer ball from the penalty spot to the goal, much less from the center spot. So the team stood about, waited for the referee to finish logging the barrel-chested Butcher in his little book and walk the ball to the center of the pitch. The crowd was irate at seeing one of its players disciplined—despite the act's attempted-murder quotient, which had been high—and was filling the already satiated air with a general, angry roar, which Danny suddenly realized...

...he loved.

This isn't America, he thought. *This is bloody football. This is* better *than East Southwich. This is well better than Downcast Borough* or *Glumditch Town. This is a big stadium in a big city full of big smells and big people who know the difference between good football and bad.*

Broome pointed at Danny, and Danny didn't mind. Not at all. He looked over at the cow on the spit, up at the maroon-clad minions, and into the low-slung Slavic smoke. He thought that the Communists from the tree were probably in the crowd, mixed in there somewhere with the immigrants who wanted Hooper to fail. And Danny, confidently, assuredly, took the kick: 1–1.

The Butchers didn't even have a backbone to break. With their core hidden away somewhere by the Communists from the tree, the 1972 and 1973 champions of the league just withered, withered into nothing, and Danny ran around Chicago's beloved baseball diamond as free as a child. He believed he was playing the best game of his life, matching the defensive abilities he'd had since he was a boy with the offensive game he'd always known was in there somewhere. He roamed from touchline to touchline, opening himself up for passes from the men on the wings, turning gracefully to switch the ball and force the entire Chicago defense to shift itself, which opened up little gaps that made entry passes to Juanito's feet as easy as a warm-up kickabout. The Butcher defense flagged in the heat, humidity, and hovering tang of quality sausage, and Juanito finished with a late brace. Even Todd scored one, and the Revolution ran out 4–1 victors against a team that had shredded them 9–1 the season before. Evening fell, the Slavs drifted

---

👕 The displaced Butchers were rescued in the small Idaho panhandle town of Sandpoint by the local high school's Spanish teacher, a Paraguayan who hoped to form one of the state's first high school soccer teams from a handful of basketball players and members of the track team. The Paraguayan promised the Poles he would get them back to Chicago if they would coach his players for a couple of days in a clearing in the woods, outside of the townspeople's prying eyes. The Paraguayan asked his high-schoolers to tell their families they were going for a long run, but Sandpoint's football coaches got suspicious, tracked the

away, the Butchers' butcher wheeled the cow quietly, grimly under the stand.

Broome couldn't contain himself. He ran onto the field at the final whistle, hugging anyone who would hug him back. He knocked Juanito to the ground; he patted Danny on the face and said, "You marvelous big, strong beast of a man!" Molly made her way to where Surley was sitting and gave him some water. He looked as if he might disintegrate into the meaty ether.

The hotel's lobby was empty except for two men by the fireplace. Danny broke off from the team as they dragged their bodies toward the elevators with a "Good night, lads. Brilliant, brilliant, just going to say hello to some old friends," and he walked over the hearth, sat in front of the fire, and looked at the Communists.

"You were good today," one of them said.

"Very good," said the other. "You might have even won without our help."

The first Communist looked from Danny to his comrade and said, "No, no. Do not talk crazy. The Butchers are good team. Better than Revolution sure."

The other man answered in Russian, and it looked like an argument. Danny said, "Wait—*wait*. Stop. Where are the players? *Where are they?* Did you... *kill* them?"The men laughed. "*Kill* them?" one of them said. "Kill them? No, Danny. That would be foolish. Too much attention. There are newspapers in Poland covering Chicago matches. Those men are heroes. We kill

---

clandestine company, and broke up the secret soccer by firing over their heads (but not by much) from their own duck blinds. Local police determined not to press charges because the gunfire had been provoked by "severe maltreatment of basketballs, an important symbol of America," and because no one had actually gotten shot. "You just can't kick basketballs," Sandpoint's mayor said in the town's first-ever news conference. In any event, the Polish players were sent back to Chicago at taxpayer expense and the Paraguayan went with them and finished the summer with the Butchers.

them, too many people know we are here. No, no, better than kill them—"

Now they were both laughing. "Let me tell," the other one said.

"Yes, yes. You tell."

"Two nights ago, Danny, we took them out for some drinking. Them drinking, us not drinking. Then we took their money and wallets and put them on a train to... *Idaho*." They were slapping each other's knees. Danny had never seen such happy Communists. "What, Danny, you think we are having no humor?"

Danny said, "Where's Idaho?"

"Far, Danny. Far. Far from everything. They will wake up in place that hates Communists even more than most places hate Communists, with nothing but their accents and no U.S. dollars! I do not know how they will get back. See, that is funny. We are funny."

Danny did think sending the players to Idaho was funny, but he did not think these men were funny. "Why did you send them to Idaho?" Danny said. "Why did you want us to win this game?"

"Two reasons."

Neither man was laughing anymore.

"We needed you to be serious about us."

"Yes, to take us seriously."

His comrade turned to him and said, "Is that how you say it? Take us seriously?"

"That is how, yes." And the other man took it from there: "That is what we need. You need to know that we can do things like that with anyone we want."

His colleague said: "Anyone."

Danny paused for a moment and asked himself if he believed these men. Was he even scared at their threat? They seemed comical even when they were threatening him with a hammer in a hollowed-out tree; now, here they were slapping each other's knees in a Chicago hotel lobby, laughing it up through their pungent sweat. But the Revolution had just dealt the mighty Butchers a 4–1 defeat, right there in Chicago, right in front of that dead cow, and Danny knew these men had helped.

Danny said, "All right then, what's the other reason?"

The Russians looked at each other and then at Danny. The first one said, "Because we want the Revolution in the Bonanza Bowl."

That night in New York, the Giganticos beat the Flamingos of Florida 6–0 in front of forty-five thousand people.

The Pearl of Brazil scored three, including one on a bicycle kick. The other three were scored by World Cup veterans, including one by their famous Dutchman, who had dribbled through the entire Flamingos team after receiving the second half kickoff, finishing the move with a backheel and a wink.

SIXTEEN

The Los Angeles Glitter was the pet project of a Scottish pop singer named Tartan Ron. Tartan Ron had had a string of early-'70s hits that blended bagpipes, disco, and his willingness to wear a kilt at all times. Ron's irrepressible funkiness, architecturally surprising hair, and penchant for newsworthy, alcohol-fueled antics frequently thrust him into the press on both sides of the Atlantic and had made him a global superstar.

In addition to his music, his kilt, his behavior, and his hair, he had managed to become one of the most prominent proponents of soccer in his adopted Californian home, regularly appearing in concert and on television in a remarkably tight-fitting green-and-black-striped jersey of the Highlands club he supported (and had briefly represented as a schoolboy), St. Mungo Caledonian Thistle of the Scottish Second Division. He launched soccer balls into the crowd at his shows and palled around Los Angeles with some of the game's biggest international stars.

Tartan Ron was one of the richest soccer fans in America.

So when the nascent American All-Star Soccer Association determined that it needed a Southern California franchise to cement its big-league delusions, Tartan Ron was a prime target as a potential owner/investor. The league's first conversation with Tartan Ron reached its desired result after a solitary pint. "I'm in," Ron had told the league's delighted and somewhat surprised commissioner. "Where do I fackin' sign?"

Within a week, Ron had had a silver sequined jersey made with a pink-and-blue L.A. GLITTER surrounding a bejeweled soccer ball over the left breast. He wore it everywhere in place of his old St. Mungo shirt; he got himself photographed in the new jersey with the nice people who happened to be awake at three A.M. on Hollywood Boulevard, and the photos ran everywhere. Ron and whomever he was with—actors, musicians, models, basketball players—usually looked worse than usual for late-night wear, but the stunt worked. In the space of a week in the spring of 1974, the Los Angeles Glitter, a team which had never played a game, had no players and no stadium and only one jersey, went from being a beer-sodden half-thought in Tartan Ron's beer-sodden brain to being one of the most well-known teams in American soccer history.

When the time came to actually build a squad, Tartan Ron called an old drinking compatriot from Muddledeen (his and Mungo Caley's hometown), gave him a healthy budget, and told him to round up fifteen of the finest Scottish footballers he could find forthwith and get them all on a plane. Hugh McBelfry arrived in Los Angeles three days later with Thistle's reserve back line and goalkeeper and a Mexican phone number of dubious provenance in his pocket.

"You taking the piss, Hugh? Five players from a Second Division reserve side and a *fackin'* telephone number? This is the most glamorous city on the face of the *fackin'* earth, Mc*Bel*fry. If you think I'm going to use my good name to persuade the most beautiful people known to mankind to associate themselves with the Los Angeles Glitter football club so they can see five men with the grace of a misshapen giraffe, you must be off the rocker your mother told you wasn't even your *fackin'* rocker, Hugh *fackin'* McBelfry." He wiped the spit from his cheeks and from Hugh's. "This is the promised land, Hugh. This is not bloody Aberdeen. The people of California have to choose between us, bloody surfing in water that may as well have come from the bath tap, and sexual congress with waitresses who would be the most desirable women in every county on the British Isles, *Hugh.* Between us, laying in the *fackin'* sun, and actually *getting laid*, do you hear me? They'll nae pay to see these Mungo rejects *fack* a *fackin' goat*."

Hugh calmed his old friend down and said, "Ronny, mate, this phone number will get us all four Hugos from the Mexican national team, laddie. All of them. There's your midfield right there. Put them in front of five violent Scotsmen and you're a center forward away from being difficult to beat anywhere, much less this wee cheese shop of a football league they're runnin' over 'ere."

Hugh McBelfry was the only person Tartan Ron listened to—and in this case that was a good thing for the future of the AASSA's Los Angeles franchise. "You best be right, Hugh, you *twat*. You best be right." And then, with the benefit of a rare pause for thought: "A center forward, Hugh McBelfry... aye, a true striker, a poacher, a fox in the box—yes, yesssss, Hugh. That's where we spend our duckets." He thought for another moment, and then he said it: "*Billy*—yes, Hugh, we must get Sweet Billy to come to America. Sweet... Billy... Robinson."

Sweet Billy Robinson, like Tartan Ron, had resisted the urge to put his profession above alcohol and a good time, and while this inflated his legend and occasionally his waistline, it was just now, after a mostly glorious career pockmarked with the odd spectacular failure (showing up blotto for a World Cup qualifier in Finland, not showing up at all for a Cup tie in Spain, an entirely unexplainable month-long adventure in Thailand during which he had appeared in two Thai league matches for two different teams and scored seven times), that it all seemed to be catching up with him. No one in Britain wanted him anymore. The Scottish national team was desperately trying to move on without him, despite fans' clamoring for his return with each successive Scottish defeat. He could still score, he could still dribble himself out of almost any situation, but he was catastrophically pissed most of the time and a pain in the arse (and seldom wore a shirt) all of the time, and had not been known to pass the ball since 1971. "Last I saw him," Ron said to Hugh, "he was on the front page of the *Sun,* and he looked right crap. Bloated like a drowned pig. Shirtless as always. He's out of contract, Hugh—no one over there rates him worth the headache. Let's get him—now." Hugh nodded at Ron.

Ron looked at Hugh.

Hugh looked at Ron.

Ron raised his eyebrows.

Hugh raised his eyebrows.

Ron barked, "No, Hugh—not *Scottish* now, *American* now. Get ye to a phone. We've got to get him while he's down. Get us Sweet Billy Robinson, or you're sacked."

Hugh got him. Hugh got Sweet Billy Robinson for the Los Angeles Glitter for a song. Tartan Ron still sacked Hugh McBelfry—then rehired him, sacked him, and rehired him again. This happened at least once a week.

Thus it came to pass that the Los Angeles Glitter of the AAS-SA had a Scottish Second Division reserve back line, a Mexican midfield named Hugo, and the greatest dribbler that Britain had ever known installed as its only real forward.

The team's first season, the spring and summer of 1974, went according to plan. The stark Southern California summer sun seemed to detoxify Sweet Billy Robinson. He kept drinking, but the weight fell off him. He acquired a rather dignified Hollywood tan, and he played with a casual, besmirked comfort and scored at will. Once put in five in front of 435 people in Dallas. Once put in a penalty off both posts on a dare. Once played a half in Miami bare from the waist up. The British tabloids ran every photo of Sweet Billy and Tartan Ron they could get, especially if they were in the comfort of American starlets or the sloppy embrace of some touring English rocker; the photos usually appeared with some small description of just how many goals Billy was piling up in the American league and how great this team of Tartan Ron's was getting on. Ancient gray men murmured on the BBC about the tragic wasted talent of Sweet Billy Robinson, how if only he'd had half the mind of Britain's noblest footballers Scotland might have had a shot, dare they even think it, much less say it, at a World Cup. "And not just qualifying and advancing, but..." the ancient gray men would say. "Instead he's pottering around in the American sunshine, making a mockery of what God gave him and the game God gave us all... It's not right, not British."

The Glitter advanced to the '74 Frontier Conference Championship, where they played to a 9–9 draw against the Atlanta Astronauts (the match having been played over almost four hours in crushing Georgia humidity with the oversized goals of a local carpenter's making and with an Atlanta timekeeper's insistence on stopping the clock at every dead ball). Sweet Billy scored three in a spectacular first half before having to be removed in the late going, red-faced, furious, and drenched in high-alcohol-content sweat. He threw his shirt in McBelfry's face, to the delight of everyone except McBelfry. The Glitter lost an eleven-round Super Soccer Showdown to the unloved Astronauts, who immediately disbanded (to be reconstituted the next season under new ownership and featuring an entirely new roster), but Tartan Ron had gotten his taste of success and vowed to give Billy and the Hugos all the help they needed to get the Glitter another conference championship and maybe even the Bonanza Bowl.

The next summer, even in Sweet Billy's addled Californian condition, even after all the celebrity-strewn late nights and the drowsy beachy days utterly devoid of training, he tore up the American league again and the Glitter seldom lost, and the team reached the Frontier Conference championship...

...but Sweet Billy wasn't really championship material, and there was nothing anyone could do about it, neither gray men at the BBC nor rich Scottish singers in the USA nor desperate old Hugh McBelfry, and Sweet Billy failed to show up, and the Glitter lost to the Smithereens in Seattle.

But the Mexicans loved playing with Sweet Billy. After the Hugos had taught the hulking, artless St. Mungo defenders to actually *pass* them the ball once they'd dispossessed some terrified Dallas or St. Louis or Rochester forward instead of launching it in the general direction of the other team's goalkeeper, or putting into touch to "reorganize," the Hugos got into the habit of doing everything within their considerable capabilities to get the ball to Billy's feet. Not out in front of him or plopped into the space behind the opposing defense, but right at his supernaturally supple feet. Then the Hugos would watch the show.

Once in possession of the ball, Billy's complaints to the referee would begin. "He's gonna kick me," he'd say, having not been fouled, and then, "See? Did you see that? He kicked me. But I'm all right, sir. I'm all right," then, "Referee, sir! He did it again! Are ye gonna do anything, anything at all?" But Sweet Billy would still have the ball, and the referee would indicate Sweet Billy's advantage with outstretched arms, and Sweet Billy would swerve this way and then that and pull the ball back a few times in unrepeatable ways, and then he'd be in the box, and then he'd beat a man, and then he'd wait for the man to come back so he could beat him again, and then he'd score, and the whole way back he'd be arguing with the referee, who'd be saying, "But you scored." And Sweet Billy would say, "Aye, no thanks to you, refereeeee. No fackin' thanks to you, sir."

On top of the Sweet Billy Robinson show, a game in Los Angeles was a social event. Ron would persuade as many of Tinseltown's beautiful people as he could to come out and see his team, and he knew they required an extravaganza over and above twenty-two (mostly) foreigners in a wide variety of physical conditions huffing and puffing about on a bumpy gridiron in soccer-like uniforms. A Glitter game featured bikini-clad cheerleaders who chased down balls that left play, a ten-minute national anthem by a man with a cigarette and a tuxedo (for example), mimes, magicians, a strongman in a leopard-skin tunic, and whatever other manner of circus-like performers Ron could round up that day. For a man who loved football, Ron knew the American audience was not yet ready for ninety minutes of the game on its own—and he knew that if they ever saw any football of genuine quality on TV or in person when European teams visited America for half-hearted summertime exhibitions, they would wonder what exactly it was that the AASSA was trying to sell them. Ron wanted the answer to that question to be "A bloody good time." So in addition to the carnival atmosphere, Ron himself performed at halftime. And not a little two- or three-song performance either—he assembled his entire band on a shimmering wheeled stage and powered through one hit after another for his patrons, sometimes performing for upward of an hour while the players tried to keep their bodies warm in the catacombs of the vastly oversized Los Angeles bowl. Word spread throughout the league that Sweet Billy employed a traditional Scottish method of keeping his decaying but still brilliant body warm during Ron's shows, and visiting teams grew to expect a greatly diminished force in the second half.

The day the Rose City Revolution arrived at the Glitter's enormous stadium to play Tartan Ron's team, Sweet Billy wasn't even there. Broome and McBelfry chatted on the sidelines as the teams warmed up—they had known each other when Broomsie had played a couple years in Scotland to facilitate a divorce and hide some money. Danny jogged by—as he usually did just to see what old men like that talked about before a game, and to listen for Communist chatter—and he heard McBelfry complaining about Sweet Billy: "I've nae seen him for days. The shite of it is if he shows his mug Ronnie'll make me use his blootered arse. Billy'll be soused and he'll curse like an Irishman and he won't bloody move. Your big man here'll be pissed just stood next to him, but he'll be in nae danger of bein' scored upon. Nae danger at oll. Aye and it's a right good thing the Hugos cannae understand a word of what he's got to say or they'd be well done with him. He's a right goon, Graham, a right goon, but ah when he's on he is on I must say. But he'll nae be on today."

Danny stopped to introduce himself to McBelfry. "I saw you play when I was a boy, sir. Caley was down to play Albion in the

North Sea Cup—your Scots showed the Royals a thing or two that day, they did, sir. Best football I'd seen with me own eyes it was. The year Thistle won the Scottish League too, if memory serves, Mr. McBelfry."

McBelfry blushed through his boozy sunburn. "Well, Hooper, I'll admit I've heard your name too, but I'm afraid it was in the same sentence as the name of a young Welshman. But you do seem a nice lad. Hey, Brooooooomsie, I propose a trade: you give me young Hooper and you can fackin' take Sweet Billy fackin' Robinson with you in a fackin' hearse."

At this Tartan Ron approached. "'Ello, lads. Danny Hooper? *You're* Danny Hooper? You're a terrifying boy, Hooper. Don't ye fackin' kick *me*." He laughed at his little joke. "But less talk, more rock, eh? Am I right? I'm nae payin' ye to flap on aboot nuthin'. I'm dead ready for some football. Hugh, where's your Sweet Billy?"

McBelfry took on a serious face and addressed his kilt-wearing boss in as serious a voice as he could muster. "Ron, there is no Billy. Not here, not today. No Sweet Billy Robinson. Sorry, sir."

"*Sorry?*" Ron spat back. "Soooorryy? Do ye see the people of Los Angeleeez settin' in the sun here before ye? They have paid good moooney, Hugh, paid it to *me*, Tartan Ron, to see the great Sweet Billy Robinson, his dribbldyness, in the flesh. No Sweet Billy, no happy. Where in *fffffack* is he, Hugh?"

"I'd bloody like to know, boss. Where *is* me star player, Ronnie?"

"That's *yours* to know, Hugh," Ron hit back, with particular disdain laid on the word "Hugh": "Hyuuuugh"—he dragged it out as if it disgusted him to speak it—"*find* him."

And with that, Ron spun to face the sun-drenched crowd, pulled a microphone out of a fold deep in his kilt, and screamed, "Are ye ready for some rock and roll, Los Angeleeez?"

The crowd was a fair crowd, close to twenty thousand, more than could've fit into the Auld Moors, though it looked sparse spattered against one side of the gently canted bowl. The stadium was built for one hundred thousand, and though forty thousand eyeballs was a mighty sum for anywhere in the AASSA other than New York and maybe Chicago on a Polish holiday, it didn't feel like a crowd here. So the loose gathering of semi-interested Californians sprinkled through the stands like picnickers on a lawn offered Ron a half-hearted "Yeah" in response, to which he shouted back, "That wasn't very gooood, Los Angeleeez. I said, are you ready for some rock... and... rolllllllll?"

This time Ron didn't wait for a response, and he just started crooning a song that rhymed "Glitter" with "winner" and rasped something about getting his kicks in.

The fans' enthusiasm grew somewhat with Ron's singing, but only in a laid-back can-almost-smell-the-ocean-from-here way. The crowd's energy did pick up some when the Glitter, their bejeweled shirts throwing off bright fragments of light in the afternoon sun, made their way through a gauntlet of equally bejeweled cheerleaders and out onto the pitch—minus Sweet Billy Robinson.

Danny, who until approximately five minutes ago had been a Tartan Ron fan, decided then and there that Sweet Billy or no Sweet Billy, the Rose City Revolution was going to beat the L.A. Glitter that day in sunny Los Angeles, California. Danny was disappointed, however, to find his team down two–nil after half an hour.

While Danny and his teammates were unfamiliar with the hardpan underlying the field's clumpy grass, the Hugos of L.A.'s midfield controlled the wildly bouncing red, white, and blue AASSA ball as if they were corralling a misbehaved puppy that for all its mischief still aimed to please. As for the Revolution, they were still Cloppingshire United after all—accustomed to English mud (and Portland's wet artificial turf) and waterlogged balls. The ball bounced a little higher and rolled a little faster than any of the Revolutionaries expected. For the first time in the summer of 1976, Danny thought he was having a good look at the version of his team that finished bottom in '75. The Revolution failed to string more than a pass or two together before turning the ball over to the nearest Glitter player in what might have been taken for a series of kindly acts of sportsmanship. L.A.'s St. Mungo defenders—and Rose City's Juanito—hardly broke a sweat as the Revolution stayed away from the Glitter goal for the entire forty-five. Danny and Big Lou played well enough, keeping the Glitter from adding to the score line, but at the interval the Revolution was still down two, and Ron was singing his heart out along the sidelines, and Broome was at a loss for a fix that might bring his side back into the match.

Little did he know that his fix had just stumbled into the Glitter's locker room, shirtless, pissed as a sailor, and in the company of three of the most beautiful actresses in that summer's slew of Hollywood blockbusters. "'Allo, dobbers," Sweet Billy said to his teammates and to McBelfry. Sweet Billy pointed to the center forward he knew had filled in for him in the first half. "You," he said, "take off yer kit. Yer done today, and I forgot mine. Hugh, change yer plans, old man. I'm goinnn' in."

McBelfry told Sweet Billy to forget it. "It's two–nil, Billy. We done what we came to do. Ye can only hurt the cause now. Take the day off, lad." But Hugh said it with no conviction. He knew he was wasting his time trying to keep Sweet Billy out of the match, putting up his desperate front just for the rest of the team out of professional obligation. "No, Billy—" he repeated, as if waiting for Billy to say—

"*Fack* you, fackin' *Hugh*." Billy was unplayably drunk, but everyone in the room, with the possible exception of the three girls he'd brought in with him, knew he was going to play the second half. What they didn't know was: "And *she's* going in at left back." He pointed to the prettiest of the three, who wasn't so pretty now that a horrified look had come across her face. Sweet Billy shouted at the Glitter's trainer to produce an extra kit and told the team's smallest player to take off his shoes—"You'll nae play anyway, you ponce"—and give them to the girl. "Now then," said Sweet Billy, "let's go finish these boyyys oofff."

The girl played the rest of the match at left back, and Billy, hardly a footballer at this point, bellowed and swore and cursed at his teammates for not getting him the ball. He drifted into the midfield to bring his displeasure closer to the Hugos, then wandered all the way back to defense to give the poor left defender a sloppy kiss and an unseemly grope. With fifteen minutes remaining, his shirt was off and he was wearing only one boot. The referee, who hadn't understood enough of the invective thus far to care, finally cautioned Billy, after which Billy called him something that most of the nearly twenty thousand people in attendance heard and understood just fine (those with children got up to leave).

Juanito had taken up residence on the right wing in Kelvin's absence—and opposite the starlet Sweet Billy had installed there—and was growing comfortable enough to be unstoppable. By the time of Billy's caution, he had scored once and McBelfry had attempted to substitute for the poor young lady. This just raised Billy's ire—he ran to the sideline and spat pure alcohol into Hugh's face with his objection that "she's doing fine, *Hyuuuuugh*. She stays or I go." McBelfry paused for thought and looked over to his bench, from which Ron was observing the proceedings. Ron raised an eyebrow. "All right then," Hugh said, "we'll move her up front with you then."

Billy was delighted with this proposition, and he spent the rest of the match at her side. A picture ran in the papers the next morning of Billy with a tongue in her ear and a hand on one of her breasts.

By now, the Glitter's concentration was more than shot. Danny, realizing that neither of L.A.'s center forwards had a prayer of scoring, eased himself into the midfield again. The four Mexicans had grown bored with Sweet Billy's antics and allowed Danny and Surley full control of the balance of the game. With three minutes remaining, Jimmy got himself free on the wing and crossed the ball toward a waiting Todd, who would never have had the skill to propel a shot on goal, but it didn't matter: one of the St. Mungo giants did exactly what Broome had been waiting for one of them to do for the last eighty-seven minutes if the Revolution could just get the ball in the air in the box. He took Todd down with a bear hug around the waist, as if he were a rugby player. The referee had no choice but to call for a penalty.

Tartan Ron, Sweet Billy Robinson, even Hugh McBelfry ran to the referee and joined the five St. Mungo brutes in a circle of the least reasoned profanity—it didn't even sound like human utterance but like a wild boar inside a dying car engine—but the referee stood there, basking in the shower of abuse and the sunshine as referees do, pointing to the spot. He made no effort to clear the enraged Scotsmen—he just waited them out, and they did indeed lose steam, drifting back to their rightful places one by one, exhausted from the pointlessness of their assault. Surley, knackered in the heat but rested enough after the Glitter's game delay, buried the penalty. The match's final three minutes drifted away amid the Glitter's attempts to hit the referee with the ball and the Revolution's effort to avoid an embarrassing late mistake that might erase their continued good fortune.

This meant another Super Soccer Showdown for the points. Ron took to his microphone again, trying to get the baked Los Angeles fans to simulate the momentum his superstar had drained from the home side with some "good old-fashioned American nooooiiiiissse," but he didn't get much; the day had fizzled with Sweet Billy's antics, the blown lead, and the barbarous St. Mungo defending.

And yet Sweet Billy was not done.

Juanito scored the Revolution's first. Danny scored his in between two of the Hugos, who lobbed theirs in without much effort or concern. Then came Surley, who looked like "shite," as Sweet Billy reminded him with a shout from the sideline, but who calmly placed his Sniper Shot into the Los Angeles net.

The Super Soccer Showdown stood at 3–2 for the Revolution, with one Glitter shot remaining, when a shoving match in front of the L.A. bench became a scuffle and finally a full-blown brawl. The Revolution's players watched it dispassionately; to a man, they knew exactly what was going on and how it would finish: Hugh and Sweet Billy were arguing over who would take the Glitter's final Sniper Shot, and, of course, Billy emerged from the melee—now in only his shorts. He grabbed a ball and wandered unevenly toward the center of the pitch.

The twenty thousand was now more like ten, but they arose from their sun-drenched stupor with the realization that their soccer afternoon of rock and roll, cheerleaders, celebrity ogling, foxy left backs, and shirtless men chasing a ball likely had just one more kick left in it. The man in the shorts, the obviously incapacitated man with the hairy chest and flowing locks, the man who had brought the beautiful left defender onto the field to represent the home team, the man with a reputation as a world-class footballer, the man who might have been a World Cup champion by now if he'd been born a few miles to the south of Muddledeen, needed only to put the ball in the goal, without a goalkeeper, from fiftyish yards away to keep the Los Angeles Glitter from suffering an ignominious defeat to the lowly visitors from humble Portland, Oregon.

The Great Hope of Scotland stepped to the ball some five thousand miles from home with ten thousand Californians clapping as if they really cared, but they really didn't—not that much, anyway, not anywhere near as much as the people of East Southwich Albion wished they could move up a division, or get into the Fifth Round of the FA Cup, not like that, not like that at all—and the ball spun off Billy's foot and veered to the right as Billy fell to the ground, passed out cold, and the referee blew his whistle, and that was it. The game was over. The tanned, beautiful people got up to leave, Ron tucked his microphone back into his kilt and told God himself to sod off, and the day was done.

The Revolution was unbeaten, on its way back to Portland for its first regular-season matchup with the dreaded Seattle Smithereens. Danny thought, *Well... never thought I'd see that.*

But no sign of Communists down here.

That week, the Giganticos had played a home-and-home with Red Star Toronto, winning a hard-fought 3–1 battle in Canada and taking an easy 8–1 cruise in front of forty thousand at home. The Pearl scored twice in the first ten minutes in the away leg and removed himself from the game to the adulation of the Toronto crowd; he was forced to circle the field twice to receive their adulation. He scored the first and last goals in the New York match, one of which he headed in after juggling the ball five times on what appeared to be a casual jog in from the eighteen-yard line.

SEVENTEEN

Danny sat in the corner of the Grand Douglas lobby, nursing a bottle of the abundant free Henry Weinhard's the brewery left for the team each Friday, listening to Three prattle on about the Revolution's run of good form. "Congratulations, Danny," Three said over the phone. "Well *done* to you and the boys. Four on the trot. The mighty Rose City Revolution has won more times with you than all of last season. You're unbeatable, laddie. On your way to the Bonanza Bowl without any help, aren't you then?"

"Walk in the park, Three. Easy peasy." He paused. "Strange doings over here, Three. And saying we're getting it done without any help is a bit generous, I'm afraid."

"I don't know, my boy, the results just keep coming—"

"Cut it with the clever, Three. If you don't see what's going on, I'm not entirely sure I can believe you are who you say you are. There are Russians, Three, chasing me about in the woods. They followed me to Chicago. They fixed the match. They put the best Butchers on a train to the Wild West. There's no bloody way the Rose City Revolution can beat the Chicago bloody Butchers, Three. No way Cloppingshire United can compete with the Polish national B team. Then in L.A. somehow Sweet Billy Robinson shows up at halftime drunk as a lord. Are you daft, Three? Off your nut? You really believed we earned those points? The Communists *want* us in the Bonanza Bowl, just like *you* want us, just like *I* want us, just like *everybody* wants the bloody Rose City Revolution—just last year the worst team in the conference, this year the toast of the town—in the *bloody Bonanza Bowl*, Three. It's nigh upon common knowledge amongst people who have their lives threatened by Communists in Portland trees, Three."

"Danny—"

"Three, they told me they want the Rose City Revolution in the Bonanza Bowl. They told me in Chicago. They *want* us there. And so do you. So I'm asking myself, if it's so bloody important, Three, why haven't you sent us any better players than Cloppingshire bloody United?"

The line went silent. Danny could hear Three breathing. Three had nothing clever to say.

"Well, Three?

"Well, Three?

"*Well*, Three?"

"This is serious, Danny. I mean, not that Sweet Billy Robinson was drunk—not sure that means much—but the rest of it. Serious indeed."

"What do you mean, 'this is serious'? Of *course* this is bloody serious, Three. I've got Russian men following me around the country, fixing football matches. They're going to kill the Pearl, and we're bloody in their *bloody* plan, Three."

Three responded with silence again. Just breathing.

"Why, Three?

"Why, Three?

"*Why*, Three?"

Three said, "We'll find that out, Danny. Good-bye." And he hung up.

Danny called Molly. "Can you meet me in the lobby? The lobby of the Grand Douglas."

In fifteen minutes, she was there.

"Just got off the phone with Three," he said.

"What did he tell you?"

"He doesn't know any more than anyone else as far as I can tell. But I don't trust him."

She humphed and looked down, disappointed.

He said, "But, Molly, what do *you* know?"

"No more than you."

"That's not possible," he said. "You're a spy."

"Danny, they're *feeding* you information. The only problem is that at this rate it doesn't look like you'll get the ending—which is all we really care about—until the end. That's a pretty serious problem."

Danny said, "Yes, it is. It is indeed."

"So, Danny," she said, "let's talk about *exactly* what they told you in Chicago."

"I already told you everything. They told me they wanted the Revolution in the Bonanza Bowl."

"So that's not so bad. *You* want the Revolution in the Bonanza Bowl too."

He lifted a bottle of the abundant free Henry's the brewery left in the refrigerator of the Grand Douglas lobby and looked past Molly to the woods behind the apartments, to the dreary, wet Portland night. He imagined the forest crawling with Russian agents and smarmy English spies. "Why? Why do they want us in that game?"

Molly didn't answer.

"Why would Moscow manipulate the fortunes of a soccer team in Portland, Oregon, so they could assassinate the Pearl of Brazil?"

"That's what we have to find out."

Danny grunted. He didn't think this was a particularly insightful remark for someone in the espionage game. *No kidding,* he thought, and he felt like an American for thinking it. *No bloody kidding.* That was more like it, but he kept it to himself.

"Relax," she said. "We're going to work this out."

"Work this out?"

"We'll work it out, Danny. Our side usually wins."

She didn't sound at all convincing, and he wasn't convinced.

The unbeaten Revolution represented hope for a city unaccustomed to winners. The televised Chicago game had caught the city's attention—all that ripped cow flesh, the full baseball stadium, the Rose City comeback. Then the win in L.A.—any win for a Portland team over a Los Angeles team was a rare treat. The reporters and photographers who used to panic and giggle over players striking soccer balls with their heads now spoke with some knowledge about the Revolution's "stout defense," "nifty wingers," and "fighting spirit." Hardly an article failed to mention the players' accents—the Rose City press was especially intrigued by Peter Surley's low, vowel-rich murmur, and everything the paper had to say about the team referred to them as imports, as if they were a shipped commodity. But coverage was coverage, and the team realized what it meant as they passed the Sports page amongst themselves over breakfast in the Grand Douglas lobby: Portland *cared*.

Peter, mouth full of toast, said, "This isn't good."

A Todd contradicted him. "This is great, Peter! We have fans, man. Fans! What's your problem?"

Peter said, "I've played for people who care. Leads to trouble is what it does." He shook his head and hummed something into his toast about how this was supposed to be a paid vacation.

Big Lou made a face at Todd, assuring him that any further exploration down this route would be a waste of time. "Well, I'm getting excited about the Seattle game, and you can't stop me."

Danny agreed with all three men.

Dreaded Seattle: basketball, hockey, baseball, rock and roll—anything beginning with "Seattle" wedged itself right into the heart of Portland's inferiority complex. It hardly mattered that the Smithereens had stumbled to a 1-3 start or that the game was in Portland—the newspaper coverage reeked of little brother hoping against hope to knock off the bigger, badder older sibling.

Danny read it all and despised it. He had already lived inside the pessimistic lowliness of a humble town and club convinced by the crush of decades that its factories, its people, its ground, and its team were all Third Division to the core.

Portland was new to Danny—its green still astonished him and the rest of the Englishmen, nearly neon in the spring terrarium of the city's spooky mix of dark drizzle and bright sun shot through thick clouds. But despite its earthy fertility and the general friendliness of its inhabitants, Portland seemed to hope for so little, and to the (small but growing) extent it hoped for anything at all to do with the Rose City Revolution, it certainly didn't waste any time hoping for a victory over the Seattle Smithereens.

But the citizens came out for a Sunday afternoon at Multnomah Stadium to see another chapter in the Portland-Seattle saga. To Danny's surprise, the lonesome few thousand who had braved a weeknight rain to see the Toronto game had each grabbed a few friends, and now the old place had the proper thrum and heave of a real (lower-division) derby—there was even a green sliver of Seattle fans pressed into a narrow, isolated section in a top corner. Danny had the sense of two cities that just didn't like each other very much, and he relished it. The Chicago fans had been great, but they didn't care about the Rose City Revolution; they were only there for their team and their food and to commingle with the odors and faces that recalled the life they'd left behind. These people, the people in Multnomah Stadium today, whether they wore red and black or green, didn't understand this game—they just wanted northwestern blood.

The place was hung with hand-painted banners: SMASH THEM TO SMITHEREENS, "ROSE" TO THE OCCASION, PORTLAND'S "REVOLTING"!— all horrible, Danny thought, really awful, but he liked the spirit: these Portland fans wanted Seattle to lose as much as they wanted the Revolution to win. The hatred of the familiar. Danny smiled and wondered to himself what gift he should expect from the strange Russian men today.

Before the match, Molly gave each player a rose and told him what she'd been told to tell him: to go up into the stadium and give one to a fan, a female. Danny and Peter Surley caught each other's eye, and Danny could see that Peter would rather slide one of his rose's thorns into his eye than climb into the benighted Portland soccer public and offer a flower to a Rose City maiden, but Danny smiled at him and nodded up to the grandstand as if to say, *Could be worse,* which Danny knew very well it could be. The team drifted up into the stadium's rows with its flowers and made fans for life. Or at least that's how it seemed: Danny had seldom felt so many pats on the back, so much good-hearted encouragement, such genuine support. He knew why, of course: the Rose City Revolution had never let any of these people down. The previous year's team had been a disaster, but no one had hoped for anything different, no one had really even cared. There was no history of misery, there was no past clotted with disappointment. Now, though, *now,* having never asked for anything from the good people of Portland, Oregon, the Rose City Revolution, the only soccer team Portland had ever known, and in only its second season, was 4-0, sitting right up there in first place above the exotic likes of Los Angeles and Chicago, and if they could just get one more point ("Is that what they call it, a point?" the fans asked each other) today, this day of all days, one more than Seattle, than the Smithereens—what a stupid name—just today, then Portland, dear old Portland, would be... could be...

When the Revolution returned to their bench and Broome gathered them for a final word, he said, "Men, the Clopping-shire ground couldn't hold this many. None of you, not one, has ever played in front of this many people who *actually want you to win.* Now I know they don't want you to win like they do back home, not like that, and they're not even completely sure what it is that you do, but you're playing for their city against the city they like the least, the least of all, and if you win today, they'll be back, they'll be back." He paused, used the back of his hand to wipe the spit from his mouth, and said, "If you don't, if you commit the sin of beating Toronto, Colorado, Chicago, and Los Angeles and not Seattle, they will sod off and never be back." He stopped, thought for a moment, and said, "They will right sod off and go to a baseball game, they will, and you'll have lost more than a football match."

Danny knew he was right. The rubbery field may have been crisscrossed with a labyrinth of mystery lines, and the stadium may have had a strange baseball shape that Danny still couldn't really understand, and the supporters didn't sing—a little singing would've been nice—but there was enough malice in the air to take him back to the vividness of English loathing... *Yes, yes,* he thought. *I've felt this before...*

And he knew the Revolution would win.

He was just a little surprised as each team took the field to see Ivan Petrov, Seattle's imperious Bulgarian. *Hmm,* he thought, *might've expected the Russians to take care of that one,* but his concerns over Petrov and the Russians were soon replaced by his concerns about the entire Seattle team.

The Smithereens kicked off and immediately established the same dominance they'd maintained during the preseason draw at their place. *Oh... maybe we won't win,* flashed through Danny's brain. The Smithereens moved the ball around Multnomah Stadium's massive pitch with astonishing ease—their passes were the kind that would have clanked off most of the Revolution's players' inelegant feet; Rose City players were constantly leaping at Smithereens as they received the ball, expecting it to bounce off their feet... but it never did, and the Revolution's overenthusiastic attacks left them vulnerable to deft Seattle moves that availed the Smithereens of acres of space and left Rose City defenders lunging into the warm Portland air.

The crowd felt it, and though they didn't sing, they did murmur. The majority of the gathering had no real idea what was going on, but they grasped one thing: Portland, at least for the first ten minutes, had the second best team on the field. Still, they dutifully filled the space above the players with their oohs and aahs, cheering mighty kicks and gasping at headers. In the third minute the Revolution and the Smithereens produced four headers in a row and the crowd whooped and laughed as if they were at a circus. In the fourth minute, the Smithereens produced eight short passes in a row, lulling the crowd into a stupor close enough to silence that the player could hear a spectator yell out, "Just kick the damn ball!"

Danny's heart marinated in his belly. He hadn't had this feeling for weeks, the feeling that the Revolution was about to humiliate itself. The first halves in Chicago and Los Angeles had been frustrating, but he knew that even if they'd lost those games no one who really mattered was there. And while the Colorado misadventure had been an existential shaming, nothing would compare to this: The team had today, and today alone, to convince the residents of this perfectly nice city that the Revolution deserved their love. Blow this one against Seattle, and the town would determine that, to paraphrase one of the Todds' explanation for just about everything, Portland "didn't need this crap."

Seattle procured its first corner kick and, smelling blood, brought seven men into the box to await Petrov's cross. Danny knew exactly how perfect Petrov's cross would be, and so he yelled at Juanito to come back and help defend. Juanito, some forty yards away, put a hand to his chest as if to say, *Me? Help on a corner? I don't think so.* But Danny kept yelling, and finally Juanito came.

Danny positioned Juanito in the semicircle on top of the Revolution's box and said, "Get ready to run, man." Petrov's corner went right to where each of his corners in Seattle had gone—right to the penalty spot—and Danny was easily the first one there. He nodded it down just to the right of where Juanito was standing, just as he had planned to do, leading the speedy forward into the open space along the wing closest to the stadium's main stand. Juanito was off at a full sprint, past Seattle's bench and then in front of Portland's, and the crowd rose in a wave as he passed. A Todd had run out with his teammate, so that when the ball eased out of Juanito's control Todd leapt in, pointed Juanito to where he wanted him to be, and flicked a pass in behind the surprised Smithereens that put Juanito in on the

Seattle goal. A jolt of panic shot up Juanito's spine. Danny saw it, saw Juanito straighten for an instant, a little hitch in his run. Danny knew that Juanito had heard the crowd, had heard Todd yelling, *screaming* at him, had heard the *slap-slap* of the defender's feet on the turf just inches behind him, and Danny knew that Juanito was afraid, afraid of ruining this moment... but when Juanito looked up, he saw that Seattle's goalkeeper had hesitated—just half a second, maybe less—before coming off his line, and now Juanito relaxed, took one last slowed step, looked down at the ball to secure a clean strike, and eased it into the side netting, just inside the post, and...

... down at the river, and up in the hills, and downtown where people shopped, they heard it. A roar Portland hadn't heard in years, a roar that had been reserved for home runs hit by flannel-clad postwar men, or for touchdowns scored by leatherheads in leather helmets for fedora-wearing patrons—all times and games and moments that Hooper and Broomsie and all the Cloppingshire men from England and Juanito, whose parents had come from Mexico, knew nothing about and would never know—but a roar that those ancient Oregonians fishing in the river, hiking in the hills, and shopping in the shops knew and they smiled, alone in the river and the hills and the shops, and the home team was ahead one–nil.

The goal activated a situation Danny knew well: less-talented home side gone ahead against the run of play. Though he'd never really thought it through, the if-then chart in his caveman football mind—and the collective mind of his teammates—forecast the next step as clearly as red-light-stop: *Now cause chaos. Don't let the Smithereens get comfortable again.* Seattle would try to recapture the momentum through superior football, would try to break the Revolution back down by spreading them out, employing greater player-by-player skill to pin the Portlanders up against their own goal and just wait, wait, wait for the heartbreaking equalizer to come... and then take it from there. The mistake that lesser teams made was to try to match quality football with quality football, to try to prise possession from the Smithereens and keep it—and Danny knew it. And Danny knew this wasn't going to work, that the Revolution didn't have the goods to play keep-away from the Seattle Smithereens. What he also knew, what his protean soccer brain knew—even if he couldn't explain it, he knew it—was that if the Revolution spent the next ten minutes pressuring every pass, every trap, every *thought* their opponents tried to make, every single one—they could force the game into a desperate, frenzied state, simultaneously frustrating the Smithereens and stoking the crowd's fury.

It worked. Of course it worked. Even Surley gave chase when Seattle players entered his cramped mobility radius. Todd dropped back into the midfield too and ran like only Americans run. The Revolution committed two fouls forty yards from the goal that had Seattle beside themselves—Petrov waved his arms at the referee like a child learning kung fu and screamed things no one within a thousand miles could understand—but the free kicks were too far away to cause any harm, and the crowd cheered each foul, each disruption, each mindless mighty clearance from the Rose City defense. The Smithereens moved a little faster, a little more aggressively, and committed a few fouls of their own, and the crowd got louder, and Danny thought, *This is working, this is working, this is bloody working...*

But he knew the next step of the flowchart too: the Revolution would fade before the interval. The test now was for them to fade close enough to halftime so that they could spend the last few minutes of the half making certain no actual football took place, just a series of throw-ins and goal kicks until both teams trudged to the stadium's dungeons to plan forty-five more minutes in front of the world's newest soccer fans.

The Revolution passed this test. The whistle went, the crowd whooped and cawed, and that sweet, smoky smell emerged from the scoop end of the stadium's J, and Danny Hooper looked up at the thousands and thought, *This place is all right.*

The ancient woman who had kicked out the first ball before the Toronto match was there as the team left the field, slapping each player's hand as he passed. "You can do it, boys. You can do it," she barked. "Portland's behind you!"

Danny could imagine Aldershot Taylor's words at a time like this—a one–nil lead at home over a better team: "Stay back, don't try anything, kick it to the corner flags." That is what passed for conventional wisdom in the English Third Division, and Danny wondered what he would hear from Broomsie in the Rose City Revolution locker room.

"I should tell you to stay back," Broomsie said. "I should tell you to avoid all risk, to keep the ball away from our goal at all costs—but I've a feeling, lads. I don't know whether to trust it or not, but it's deep within me, a feeling that we're destined to win this match and win it playing *real football*. These points are ours, boys, not theirs—let's *take* them, not *hope* for them. Let's push our luck. Let's give the people their money's worth, shall we? Let's well and truly *have* it," he said, sweating in the humid nether reaches of old, sweaty Multnomah Stadium. "We're a long way from home, boys. No reason to be here at all if we're not going to bloody *have it*." Danny couldn't believe his ears. Up one–nil, one–nil in a derby, and his English coach wanted the team to *play*, to play *football*, to *entertain*.

Danny loved the sound of it, and the second half, encouraged by Multnomah Stadium's screaming Portlanders—Portlanders who cheered at odd times, buzzing at the sight of a long throw-in, howling with joy at every lengthy Rose City clearance—started at a blistering pace. Seattle tried slowing things down, tried to establish themselves as the eventual, inevitable victors, but the Revolution pursued each and every loose ball like pups, egged on by the neophytes in the stands who loved what they were seeing, who were finding out for the first time that scoring alone isn't what made a sport interesting, who knew that Juanito's strike could stand up if the home team kept up the fight. And they liked it.

The Smithereens' goalkeeper liked nothing more than to roll the ball out to one of his wing backs, and from there Seattle's preference was to ease the ball through its midfield, forcing the opponent into a fruitless pursuit of their passes until bit by bit, line by line, they'd broken down the opposition physically and mentally, and pretty soon they'd gone from seventy yards to fifty yards to thirty yards from goal and you'd have hardly even noticed their progress. But you could only do that against a team that was pacing itself, that was happy to lay back, keep you in front, and protect its advantage. The Revolution wasn't that team— not this day, and not in front of these fans.

Broomsie had asked his men to stand back whenever Seattle's keeper had the ball. "Invite him to roll it out," he had said. "Then pounce. And don't let them pass it back to him either. Get to the inside, we'll pinch them on the outside, and good things will happen, lads. Good things will happen." And so they did. Teams like Seattle—well built, proud of being called "organized," proud of "keeping their shape"—are slow to come off their tactics, and the Smithereens were slow to recognize that the Revolution wasn't going to let them off their back foot. The keeper kept rolling it out, the Revolution kept forcing passes into the middle of the park where Danny would win the ball as if it were his to win all along, and Danny would pass it to Surley, and Surley would find a Todd (usually) who would lose it (always), and the whole thing would play itself out all over again as time passed and the Smithereens grew more and more frustrated—especially the great Petrov, who seemed consumed with near-paralyzing disbelief at his team's inability to break down their mediocre opponent—and the Revolution ran and ran, chased and chased, tackled and tackled, believed and believed.

With twenty minutes remaining, after Danny had won another ball in the midfield and laid it off once again for Surley, Petrov's frustration boiled over, and he gave Surley's bare shins a vicious scrape, drawing blood, enough blood to leave a conspicuous burgundy blot on the Multnomah Stadium rug, and the crowd grew louder, grew meaner. But Surley stayed in, and Surley took the free kick, and Surley lobbed it into the goal-mouth with the battered but unbowed aplomb of a man who'd once done it at Wembley with a League Vase in the balance, and Danny, thousands of miles from home, thousands of miles from the Auld Moors, rose in front of the Portland thousands who didn't know his name—not many of them anyway, not yet, not like they did in East Southwich, where they knew him and his family and his past and his prospects and what he could do and what he couldn't do—Danny rose into the Portland twilight, and he headed the bloody ball into the bloody goal, the *Seattle* goal, the *Smithereens'* goal.

Danny ran around behind the goal, chased by the red-and-black blur of his ecstatic teammates, ran around in front of the concentrated masses of Portlanders, Portlandites, Portlandians, and Danny screamed a scream of relief and confusion and desperation, an eyes-closed, big-and-strong-man *arghhhh* that actually struck fear into some of the Revolution's new fans, fans who had no idea that a soccer player could be a giant Anglo-Saxon of Beowulf proportions. But of course they loved it—they loved having a winner, they loved sticking it to Seattle, and they now loved their new East Southwichman.

The Smithereens fought back, and the Revolution lost their discipline here and there, and the Smithereens scored and probably should have scored more, but they didn't, and the Revolution saw them off 2–1 and somehow, someway, they were undefeated, undefeated and in first place in the Frontier Conference of the American All-Star Soccer Association.

They shook the Smithereens' hands and gathered in the center circle, as had become their habit during their string of victories. Surley gave his standard, subdued "Well done, lads," but this time he added something at the end: "Like to say something to the boys, Danny?"

Danny knew he was a major reason the Revolution was succeeding, but he'd never been acknowledged as a leader before, never been considered anything but the beast in the back, the overgrown curiosity who could head the ball farther than most men could kick it.

"Me?" he said.

"You," Peter said. The Revolution looked at Danny.

"Well, boys," Danny said. "Seems we're unbeaten." The team murmured its agreement. "Work left to be done but... I came here to win a championship. And right now I reckon... maybe we can."

"To the Revolution," Surley said.

"To the Revolution," said everyone else, and as the team dispersed, prepared for a nice, slow walk to the locker room, they saw something they had never seen: the crowd was still there. *Still there,* the Rose City Revolution's fans, in each corner of the stadium, newly enthralled with its team and with its foreign game. And now that the players had left their huddle, the fans started to cheer, first slowly, but then it picked up. The Todds realized what these people wanted: they wanted an acknowledgment that they had helped beat Seattle, that a relationship had started here, today. It was the Todds who led the team on a victory lap, the Todds who showed downtrodden Cloppingshire United what love American-style felt like.

The team finished its lap behind the goal where Danny had scored, where the sweet smell had gushed out toward the field at halftime and where it still gushed, along with the affection of the loudest of the Revolution's new fans. The fans cheered, the team cheered back, but Danny sensed an awkwardness, a suspicion that no one quite knew what to do, and fearing that the moment might pass, Danny—for the first time since he'd been a ten- or eleven-year-old in the Blue Shed End at the Auld Moors—sang. It just popped right out of him: "We are the Revs, we are the Revs, we are, we are, we are the Revs." He sang as loud as he could sing, and the Cloppingshire boys picked up on it. "WE ARE THE REVS, WE ARE THE REVS, WE ARE, WE ARE, WE ARE THE REVS." Danny saw Peter Surley singing—

Peter winked at Danny, smiling a boy's smile. "WE ARE THE REVS, WE ARE THE REVS, WE ARE, WE ARE, WE ARE THE REVS." And then the crowd picked up on it, not beautifully at first—there was something distinctly British about it that the good people of Portland weren't quite getting—but the team kept singing until their followers were singing with them, and then the fishermen in the river, the hikers in the hills, the shoppers downtown, they all heard it, and they knew Portland had won. Everyone knew that Portland had won.

Danny sat in front of the locker that bore his name. He was happy to have won a derby, but he hurt. Really hurt. Sitting down felt fine, but the in-between, the transmission from brain to all those joints, all those joints that had pounded away all that time against that godless turf... it made him wince just to think of it. He stared at the old concrete floor beneath him, considered that that very concrete had been right there underneath the thin layer of turf and foam out there on the Multnomah Stadium's pitch, and traced one if its cracks with his exhausted eyes as if it could answer one of the many questions in his exhausted mind. The Communists? The championship? Molly?

The *future*? He wasn't so old for his body to feel like this, to be this far from the Football League, to be out of East Southwich Albion's plans. He wasn't so old—was he?—for the American All-Star Soccer Association to be his last best option. *Was he?*

He was the last player in the Revolution's locker room; the team had gone, and the crack in the concrete floor held no answers for his half-formed questions. He knew it was time, it was time to stand, oh god, it was time to bloody stand.

He was the last player, but he was not alone.

"Danny, lad," said Broomsie, just emerging from his office. "Didn't know you were still here."

"Couldn't bring myself to stand up, boss."

"You all right, son?"

"I'll be fine, I'll be fine." Danny was up now and dragging his body toward the changing room's door.

"You were brilliant today, son. Brilliant."

Danny didn't answer right away, just observed the silence and then offered a feeble "thanks" to fill the gap. The two men left the changing room. The coach locked it behind them.

Broomsie said, "For a lad who just sang for the public, you don't speak much, do you, Danny?"

Danny smiled to himself—he preferred this judgment, that he was a quiet man who minded his own business and took care of his business on the pitch. So he grunted a "No, sir" and Broomsie said, "No, didn't think so."

Then Graham Broome said, "In fact, you're quite a mystery, Danny. Not so long ago, the phone rings, the chairman of East Southwich Albion is on the other end. I don't know the chairman of East Southwich Albion. Never met him. I don't know the chairmen of any Third Division clubs, as a matter of fact. But he wants to sell me a big, strong defender who has a great many fine things to recommend him but the chairman of East Southwich Albion has to tell me—because he knows I'll find out—that this big, strong defender is the reason the club hasn't advanced in the FA Cup and he's the reason a youngster from Cardiff will not be representing Wales in World Cup qualifying. May never play again, some say, the young Welshman, a boy really, a mere strip of a thing. Everything to play for one day, and then... nothing to play for. Nothing at all, the poor lad."

Danny didn't say anything.

"I tell him no. I know all my boys. Don't need any strangers. Don't need the trouble."

Danny stuttered in his step at the last word of Broomsie's story, and Broomsie said, "I said no. I've known these Cloppingshire men for years, and the Americans on the team come well enough recommended. I found Juanito myself. Love him like a son. Then there's you. You, who I told the chairman of East Southwich Albion I didn't need."

Danny's instinct, an instinct correctly sussed by his new manager, was not to answer. He didn't have to answer. Didn't owe Graham Broome anything if he kept helping him win games. But he fought the instinct and said, "So what am I doing here?"

"The man didn't even say who he was. But he wasn't the chairman of East Southwich Albion, I can tell you that. He told me quite clearly that I'd be buying you, would most certainly be buying big and strong *you*. Told me a few other things too, but I'll keep those to myself. For now."

"And?"

"And I bought myself a number five. You."

Danny and his boss walked out from under the stand and stood on the drive behind the stadium's south goal. Graham Broome stopped and said, "Danny, here's what I want to know: What *are* you doing here?"

Danny felt a rush of blood to his face, thought he might tell Broomsie that he was here because the Rose City Revolution's physio was more than just the Rose City Revolution's physio, and that she wanted him here and so did some other people, people he didn't really know or like or understand, and he was here to save the greatest player in the world, one of the most famous men in the world, from the Russians, from the Soviets, the bad guys. But it was dark, and he knew that Broomsie couldn't tell he was flushed, and he knew he didn't owe the old man this information, not now anyway, and he didn't trust him just yet, so big and strong Danny Hooper decided to go with his big and his strong: "What am I doing here, boss? What does it look like I'm doing here? Trying to win a championship is all, boss."

Broomsie looked like he wanted to believe what Danny had told him. "Just all seems a little strange, doesn't it?"

"Wanting a championship?"

"No, that's not what I mean, son. I mean last year we were an embarrassment. Almost didn't come back for another season.

Nearly out of money. And terrible. Abominable. Now we've got you, an expendable Third Division number five, and now... we can't be beat."

"Juanito is new."

"Noooooo—this isn't about young Juanito. This is about *you*. You seem to have turned us into a mighty force. I just think it's a bit strange is all—"

"Dunno, boss. So far we've played in a rodeo ground against a team of Romanians, we've played in front of a skinned cow, against a shirtless Scottish international. We've won two Sniper Shoot-Offs or whatever they're called, and suddenly the city of Portland is singing for us. That's *all* strange, if you ask me. I'm a bloke who needed a lifeline out of East Southwich and I ended up in America. Compared to what I've seen in this league so far, boss, I have to ask you: Does that really strike you as strange? I mean, compared to everything?"

Broomsie considered that line of reasoning and raised an eyebrow. He knew Danny had a point, but he wasn't satisfied. "Danny, let me tell you something: the Rose City Revolution is not a good football club."

"We're five wins and no losses, boss. We might be good."

"Twelve months ago, we lost six–nil in *this* very stadium to *that* very side, and we were lucky to keep it that close. We didn't take a single shot in a hundred and eighty minutes of football in Los Angeles last summer, Danny. And believe you me, lad, that poor cow in Chicago got cut up right good when we went out there. Right good. But now we're unbeatable. *Unbeatable.* And the luck seems to be going our way too. Can't understand it."

He stopped, looked at the ground. Danny waited. Then the coach said, "Funny enough, that, but stranger still, people are throwing *money* at us, Danny. They put us on the telly. *Us* on the bloody *telly*, Danny Hooper. Does that make sense to you, big man?"

"With respect, chief, almost nothing about this place makes any sense to me."

"Convenient, Danny, convenient. You've even got the girl, haven't you? You and Molly. I've seen it."

Hooper looked at Broomsie. Broomsie looked at Hooper.

The coach said, "There's more here than meets the eye, isn't there, Danny?"

Danny knew that the answer was yes, but he didn't know any more than that, so he said, "Maybe, old man, maybe. But here's what I do know: I'm here to win a championship. We've got five wins running and we've just won a derby. Most teams that do that can win things. Let's win something, boss, and we'll worry about the details later."

Broomsie squinted his eyes and looked deep into Danny's face. "You get to be my age, Danny, with a team like this, you know better than to think you can *win* something without *losing* something. Something's going on here, Hooper. We'll ride it as far as it takes us, but when it gets to the end of the road... when it gets to the end of the road..." Broomsie stopped, reached up, and patted Danny on the side of his face, his old soft hand warm against Danny's prickly cheek. "Ah," he said, "enough talk, laddie. We'll see you Tuesday morning, son. Take a day off. Hardearned and well done, whoever you are." The old man turned to walk the lonely walk up the drive and out of the stadium to Fourteenth Avenue, outside the old ballpark's center field wall. Danny watched him go and wondered what it all looked like to him, what all of this looked like to a man who'd given decades of his life to Cloppingshire United Football Club of the English Third Division.

What must all of this look like to Graham Broome, Danny thought, now all alone in Multnomah Stadium in Portland, Oregon, in the United States of America.

The Giganticos spent that weekend in Brazil. They had a gap in the league schedule—they had *arranged* a gap in the league schedule—so they had flown down to play an exhibition in Rio de Janeiro, in front of a hundred thousand people, and they had won—of course they'd won—and the Pearl stayed on the pitch for over an hour after the match, and they threw flowers at him and sang to him. The Russians sent men to Rio too, just to make sure nothing happened to the great man, who had to play in the Bonanza Bowl that summer in New York. Nothing happened to the Pearl in Brazil. No one could be safer in Brazil than the Pearl.

EIGHTEEN

"Dad," Danny said into the telephone in the corner of the Grand Douglas lobby.

"Hello, son. Hello, Danny, my boy. How's America been, then?"

Danny thought for a moment, took a sip from his tall brown bottle of beer, and said, "Confusing, Dad."

"How's the squad?"

"The squad? The squad... well, the team's all right. Better than I'd expected."

"I see you're on top of your division. You beat Sweet Billy Robinson. Never thought you'd play against Sweet Billy Robinson, eh, son?"

"How'd you see that?"

"Other people have telephones too."

"Suppose they do."

"What's it mean to be on top of the 'Frontier Conference'?"

"If we stay there, it means we get a shot at the Giganticos in the final."

"The final, eh?"

"The Bonanza Bowl. You'll see it on TV, Dad. The whole world will."

"The Bonanza Bowl, they call it. Hmm. First Sweet Billy Robinson, and then the Pearl himself? Well, that would be something. Don't suppose you could beat the Giganticos?"

"I reckon we'd be in with a chance," Danny lied.

"Maybe so, maybe so. Are you well, son?"

Danny considered his answer, considered it carefully. "There's a lot going on here, Dad."

"All of it good I hope?"

Sharp man, Danny's dad. Good line of questioning. "Just... a lot going on."

Danny's father left that one be. He inhaled on his cigarette, breathed it out, Danny could hear it all like a picture, and then Danny's father said, "Well, then... the *Bonanza Bowl*. Make sure you get there, son."

"I'll do what I can."

Danny's father breathed in and out on his cigarette again and said, "I miss you, Danny."

"I miss you too, old man."

"Baseball? Molly, no—"

"Yes, Danny. It's time."

"What do you mean 'it's time'? Why on earth would it be time for *me* to see a baseball game?"

"Come on, big man. You want all these people to love *your* national game. You should at least find out what you think of ours—"

"But I don't care—"

"—and the Revolution and Nutria share a stadium. You're like roommates... *flatmates*."

Danny *was* curious—what *were* those dirt cutouts on the Multnomah Stadium plastic? What *was* the little hill in the penalty box at the north end of the pitch that sometimes the grounds crew left there for the Revolution and their opponents to navigate while other times they removed and replaced it with a roundish greenish patch? If Americans were so sure soccer was "boring," how electric, how positively riveting, must this American game of baseball be? And what was a nutria?

"OK then, Molly. I'll do it. I'll attend an American game of baseball. With you." Those last two words were the real reason, of course. "It would be a positive delight."

"I shall make sure it is, Danny," she said.

"Will I see a nutria?" Danny asked.

"You will see a man in a nutria suit. I think it's a man, anyway."

"Right then, Molly. I am yours."*

Danny met Molly in front of Multnomah Stadium on a cool spring evening. The atmosphere was conspicuously devoid of pregame buzz—parents and children (though not many, Danny noticed) walked toward the park's entrance with what put Danny in mind of reluctant congregants on their way to church on Sunday morning.

Molly took Danny by the hand—that itself supplied some pregame buzz—and led him through the turnstiles and into the stadium's dingy concrete concourse. Here Danny's nose reacted

---

👕 Portland's minor-league baseball club had been the center of the city's sporting interests for the first half of the century. For most of those years the team had been known by some variation of the Mudhose nickname it had acquired during the particularly soggy summer of 1896. The '36 league-champion Brown Sox had drawn overflow crowds to their championship series against Los Angeles and earned a downtown parade. Until the '50s, local ballplayers were household names in the Rose City and a day out at the ballpark was amongst Portland's greatest charms. But big-league baseball's westward expansion had chipped away at the Coast League's importance, and now the team comprised no-namers hoping for a shot in the big leagues and whiling away their careers in a town that had shifted its focus to basketball and—astonishingly for the purveyors of the National Pastime, and perhaps only temporarily—to soccer. The adoption of the nutria nickname—the rat/beaver-like creature had arrived in Oregon only in the 1930s—was just one of many attention-craving gimmicks the club had tried over the last few years, including the use of a left-handed shortstop and a gay Republican at third and the first known Druid in American baseball history, all of which had gained the team a brief flurry of Sunday morning talk-show notoriety but failed to draw Portlanders to Multnomah Stadium. The annual Pelt Night had become the club's biggest draw, though 1975's had turned into a riot when twenty-seven thousand fans showed up and the team had been able to round up only fifteen thousand skins.

to a potpourri of smells that transformed the soccer stadium into something alien to an Englishman: "It's a *ballpark*," Molly told him. "Not a football ground. Popcorn, peanuts, cotton candy, hot dogs. Hear that organ, Danny?" Molly cupped a hand to her ear and smiled; Danny could hear the carny strains of something that sounded like a combined Hammond B3/calliope emerging from the tunnels that led down to the field. "*That's* what a ballpark sounds like, Danny. *Listen* to that organ." She closed her eyes; she smiled to herself. "I need a hot dog," she said. Once again, she grabbed Danny's hand and pulled him over to the concession stand.

"Two Nutria Dogs, please," she said. "And a bag of peanuts and a couple Cokes."

The man nodded, disappeared, reappeared moments later with two sweaty sausages, the nuts, and the drinks. He put them on the counter and Molly paid him. She looked at the food, smiled, and rubbed her hands together.

Danny looked at the offering and winced. Molly laughed and said, "You don't have to love it, Danny, but you can't watch a ball game without it." She took the peanuts and the Cokes and told Danny to grab the dogs.

"I'll grab them, Molly, but I'm not eating a *Nutria Dog*. Not tonight, not ever."

She gave him a dramatized sad look and said, "Oh, I think you will. Anyway, you haven't fixed it up yet." She led the way to a condiment stand that at least confirmed Danny's suspicion that the sausage was not, in fact, yet prepared for human consumption. By means of demonstration, she buried hers in ketchup, mustard, relish, and—ye good gods—sauerkraut until the meat was an afterthought. "Now you, Danny. Fix up your dog."

The relaxed gathering of maybe a couple thousand was spread throughout the twenty thousand seats like moviegoers who didn't want to sit near each other. Every now and then one of them would belt out some mysterious incantation, like a casual prayer to the game: "Hey, batta, heyyyyyy, battabatta," "Throw him the dark one!" "Can o' corn!"

Danny—who had been gaining comfort in his new country— grasped now that he'd spent most of his time in America around Englishmen, and what comfort he felt he'd earned drifted up and off of him like hot dog steam. He vowed to just keep his mouth shut and watch: the players and the ball moved around the diamond with what looked to Danny like leisure; the man on the hill threw it to the man behind the "plate—it's called a *plate*, Danny," and the man behind the plate threw it back to the man on the hill; sometimes a man with a bat catapulted the man's toss up into the air—astonishing heights—and sometimes the man hit it along the ground; on occasion the men ran, and sometimes it seemed as if they should run, but they didn't bother, or the man who had hit the ball ran and kept running.

Once, a man hit the ball all the way to Fourteenth Street. He didn't run—he cantered around the little diamond with a slow, entitled swagger. This particular man was from the other team, so the stadium was silent as he made his slow passage around the bases. Even if he'd been a Nutria, though, the cheer wouldn't have amounted to much, Danny thought.

"Where is everyone?" he asked Molly.

"Oh, this is actually a pretty good crowd for the Nutria," she said.

"Doesn't anybody care?"

"Oh, kind of. This is the minors."

"The minors?"

"Second Division."

"Ah," Danny said. "I see, I see." But he didn't quite see, not yet. East Southwich came out to see the Royals ply their trade in the *Third* Division—passionately, desperately, the fans and players both—but...

"This is America. You're either in the *first* division—the major leagues—or you're not. You know what I mean?"

Now when Danny said, "I see, I see," he meant it.

"That's why the Giganticos matter here. And the Pearl. Without them, you're *all* minor. With him, you're *major*. It's all the difference in America, believe me."

Danny resumed his baseball viewing. He could hardly believe Americans loved this game. Men sporting hats and gloves and *pants* moved about slowly, deliberately, along the stations of the diamond. When the players allowed themselves to be covered with dirt, they asked for time while they patted down their white or gray suits. While they took their occasional breaks, the spectators sang delightful, collegial songs. It was dignified and slow to the point of Englishness, with the exception of a six-foot-tall fluffy nutria wearing the home team's kit and trying to drum up the kind of cheering you'd expect people who had paid the cost of entry might be able to supply of their own accord.

"But," Danny said, "nothing is *happening* out there."

"Oh, that's not true. There have been four walks, two steals, some loooong foul balls, two double plays, and that guy from the other team hit a homer. You just have to know what to look for." She offered to explain the game, and just as she said, "So Portland's up to bat right now," a Nutria batter slapped a looping flare over the visiting first baseman, who turned to chase as his outfield teammate charged the ball. Molly leapt to her feet—everyone in the stadium rose—and she drew in a quick breath; Danny realized that something *was* happening out there so he stood too. The visiting players collided as the ball landed just inside the line and spun sharply on the carpet toward the doorway that the Revolution used to come out onto the field. To Danny's eyes, the ball was well out of the field of play—it had crossed the line! it had made its way to a *doorway!*—but the Nutria player kept running and the other team's players ran for the ball, and Molly was screaming and everyone was screaming, and the Nutria runner rounded the last base and his helmet flew off and he sprinted toward where he had started from, and Molly put her hand around Danny's neck and jumped up and down, yelling, "Go, go, *go!*" as the ball finally made its way toward the visiting player in his pads and his mask and he was guarding the plate, and the Nutria runner extended his legs in the most spectacular slide... perpendicular from the ground, his cleats—his *spikes*—extended maliciously directly at the visiting team's man, who had the ball now and was braced for the collision, but not braced well enough, and he sprung backward on impact, his mask, his pads all flying from his body, the ball leaking away across the artificial turf as if ashamed, and the Nutria, to a cheer greater than Danny thought this gathering could offer, scrambled over to the plate and slapped it with his hand. Molly jumped off the ground, wrapped her legs around his waist, a great and good squeeze—he was now holding her up in the air, by himself, just Danny—and screamed. "Yes!" she screamed. "That was awesome!"

That was *awesome*, Danny thought. And Molly unwound herself from him, and Molly stood next to Danny, still clapping.

"That was legal?" Danny asked. He'd been exiled from his home country for something like that.

"What do you mean 'was that legal'?"

"What Portland's bloke did to that other bloke? You can *do* that?"

"Well, Danny, he has to get home."

"But what he did, you can *do* that?"

"Danny, the man has a *job* to do." She was impassioned. She demanded that he agree. "How else—"

"I got it. I think. *You gotta do what you gotta do,*" he said in a vaguely American accent.

Molly smiled. "Danny, *yes.* You *get* it." She punched him in the arm.

"I think I do. That was pretty cool," he said, feeling very American indeed. So he said it again: "That was pretty cool."

Molly scooted over a little. Danny held the bag of peanuts, and Molly picked at it, leaned herself on Danny's shoulder. Nothing much happened for the rest of the game, the Nutria won 2–1, and Danny and Molly walked out of Multnomah Stadium holding hands, and Danny thought, *A man's gotta do what a man's gotta do.*

A Giganticos game against the L.A. Glitter was called in the sixty-first minute when Sweet Billy Robinson passed out cold in the midst of an unwelcome embrace with the referee. Sweet Billy fell over on top of the poor man grumbling the word "mother" over and over again, and he could not be moved. The Giganticos led 6–0.

NINETEEN

The Revolution had arrived at their longest road trip of the season, a Thursday-Saturday-Monday expedition to Miami, Toronto, and Detroit, the kind only a league like the AASSA, in its desperation for open stadium dates and economic travel, could devise.

The trip began easily enough: the Revolution beat the Flamingos of Florida on a tropically hot and humid Thursday evening in Miami. Beat them on a narrow, overgrown high school field with goals shaped like H's, connected to gridiron football posts that had been painted red, white, and blue in acknowledgment of the bicentennial. The pitch was surrounded by a worn cinder running track; bleachers featured on only one side. Danny estimated that the game had drawn approximately seven hundred people, seven hundred people who grilled Cuban food and who smoked and danced to a live Cuban folk music band and who milled about on the track and by the grill as if the event were a family picnic and not a professional football match in a league containing World Cup veterans and men who had won medals and trophies and cups and vases in some of the best championships in the world. Danny got the idea that everyone in attendance knew or was related to a Flamingo.

The Flamingos of Florida played in all pink and were, without question, the worst professional soccer team Danny had encountered to that point in his career, and the entire event would have settled in at the bottom of Danny's footballing experiences even if he had not only recently played a full match in front of eight thousand people who wished that he had been a steer roper.

The Revolution took the match seven–nil after six first-half goals, three to Juanito, one to a Todd who had never scored in his life and did not score in this match on purpose, and two to Surley, both from Sniper Shots. Danny headed one home from a Surley cross in the waning moments. He had felt almost unsportsmanlike doing it, but no one had made any effort to stop him. So he scored, and the Flamingos could sod off for being bloody horrible. Danny was in no mood for charity.

No noticeable injuries, no noticeable Communist activity, despite all the Cubans—Danny was sure he'd missed something—and no defeats for the Rose City Revolution.

On to Toronto, where the Revolution lost to Red Star Toronto and their red stripes and their lavish, lush mustaches.

It had to happen, had to come, this loss. Almost felt good, Danny thought. It was time. Six wins, one loss for the Rose City Revolution. Six and one they called it in America. Still first place in the Frontier Conference, and comfortably: Chicago and Seattle had each beaten the other twice, Los Angeles couldn't get any sobriety or wins out of Sweet Billy Robinson, and the Romanian Cowhands were winless. The Revolution even got points out of their defeat, strange American points. Two, in fact. Red Star Toronto won, 3–2, on a Saturday afternoon—*Saturday*, didn't it feel *right* to play on a *Saturday*, in the *afternoon*—in a beautiful little stadium on a beautiful natural lawn on a beautiful little university campus in front of ten thousand beautiful Canadians on a beautiful Canadian afternoon. It felt like real football to Danny, played in front of knowledgeable people in a professional atmosphere; it felt better than winning had felt in North Beef or Miami; it felt to Danny like he was in a real league, really and truly earning his way as a real footballer in the real football world. It finally felt like something worth winning, this league, like being the champion of the AASSA was a worthwhile aim after all.

Another good thing had happened in Toronto: Kelvin returned to the team. Flew straight in from Portland. Broomsie had used him only in the last fifteen minutes, and he hadn't done much, but it was good to have him back. Kelvin was back on his right wing for the first time since being clattered into that brick wall in Chicago, since the last time the Revolution had played an away match in a beautiful stadium in front of educated fans against commendably mustachioed Slavs. Kelvin was back. *The Communists must be so happy,* Danny thought. *We're solid at right wing again.*

A wild one played out that night in Chicago between the Butchers and the Giganticos, the champions just winning by the odd goal in three.

When Chicago scored, just before the interval, their butcher mascot had swung his slice of cow carcass in the air, spattering the Giganticos with its blood as they left the pitch for their halftime break. Some of it got on the Pearl himself, leaving a little pink cloud on his shorts. The crowd bawled and howled its approval.

The great man determined to sit out the second half for fear of suffering a career-ending injury, the Ukrainians and the Poles aiming to have their names associated with his in those far-off Eastern European newspapers, aiming to hear that bawl and howl all over again, even if it was for ending the great man's career. Still, the Giganticos got a neat late finish from the Dutchman and saw off the Butchers 2–1, their closest league game in two and a half years.

TWENTY

The Detroit Demolition,* in their hazard-striped yellow-and-black jerseys, played in a vast, bleak suburb in a vast white dome that was as unlike Toronto's wonderful little venue as it could have been and virtually commanded anyone inside or even nearby to feel lonesome. Detroit's American football team owned the desolate structure and was happy to offer the owner of the Demolition, a reclusive old Olds dealer with money to burn, a bargain on rent as a means of filling the stadium's empty summer calendar and parking lot. But while the Demolition successfully occupied a few summer dates, it had been much less successful in finding Michiganders willing to occupy most of the dome's acres and acres of seats. On and on those seats went by their many, many thousands, loaning their eerie, echoed acoustics to the suburban Detroit professional soccer experience.

👕 A NOTE ON THE DETROIT DEMOLITION: The franchise had been born in 1973 as the Fort Lauderdale Beach Nuts. The Beach Nuts' logo—a pair of soccer balls hung in the place of coconuts on a cartoonish palm tree—had so offended the sensibilities of enough family-oriented organizations in South Florida that by midseason the Nuts were drawing vigorous protests to their home games. What began as a few concerned citizens carrying signs that inevitably drew additional attention to the many and wondrous ways the logo could be misconstrued metastasized into a full-blown soccer-hating horde, the area's cranks turning the occasion of a Nuts game into an opportunity to protest everything from the phallic nature of the Nuts' palm tree to soccer's non-American origins to the encroaching Red Menace. Preachers of the apocalypse stood in the midst of sign-carrying soccer-haters barking about Jesus and the Beach Nuts—"Jesus didn't die for your Nuts!" "If you can't use your hands, you can't use our palms!" "God is not your frond!"

The Olds dealer and the gridiron football team conspired to develop two rather ingenious, non-soccer-based methods for drawing warm bodies to those cold seats: 1) Hold the games on weekdays, and right in the middle of the day. That way, up until school got out, you could provide a convenient springtime field trip for public schools desperate to fill the days leading up to summer vacation, and during the summer break you could invite groups of day campers or YMCA drop-offs to hang out in the dome. You could take as many as you wanted to come as there was no danger of a sellout, no danger of that at all. And it didn't much matter whether those kids liked soccer; the team supplied the kids with an endless supply of mascots—they were everywhere, giant fuzzy beasts roaming the stands, giving kids piggyback rides, posing for photographs, doing the hokey-pokey. And the other ingenious method of luring curiosity seekers to see the Demolition was 2) . . . an actual demolition derby.

On the strip of green carpet between the bleachers and the pitch, unwanted Oldsmobiles—of which the Demolition's

---

Beach Nuts games became something of an occasion. A congregation in Coral Springs declared that the Beach Nuts were in open defiance of the Ten Commandments, the Book of Psalms, and the U.S. Constitution and that the team's owner was doomed to a life of eternal damnation. Soon, word spread in the Hell's Angels community that there were Christians to pick on at soccer games; for the Giganticos' visit, five thousand Hell's Angels from all over the Southeast (and a few from Quebec—the really mean ones) and a militia battalion paid the full price of admission to support the Beach Nuts, who defeated an intimidated New York team 6–1. For the rest of the summer, the pregame Christians vs. Hell's Angels clashes became one of the AASSA's first media sensations. In time, Hare Krishnas came out too, and antiwar folks came to argue with the Jesus freaks, and one game was visited by a mass of women lobbying for the passage of the Equal Rights Amendment. By the team's third game, only sixteen fans paid admission, nine of which happened to be from a local branch of the Hell's Angels, lured by the promise of soft, warm pretzels with hot mustard; the other seven were militia types. A rumor spread throughout the area that the Rolling Stones were going to show up and play before the game against the Butchers—thousands came, got mixed up with the growing and motley menagerie, and a full-blown riot would owner had plenty—smashed into each other over the course of a match, making ninety minutes of pro soccer a lot more fun for American grade-schoolers and summer day campers, but awfully distracting for actual soccer fans and for professional athletes engaged in what most of them were trying to pass off as something like "major-league" competition. (Also, the sort of individual who has time in the middle of a weekday to take in a demolition derby on the outskirts of town might not be exactly the kind of person you want lingering around semi-supervised throngs of ten-year-olds. Fortunately for the team, the car-sales magnate had capable legal protection, and not too many kids went missing, and the Detroit Demolition Pro Soccer Club usually managed to post attendance figures in the eight to ten thousand range, which wasn't too different from what East Southwich Albion drew. Still, it was different. Everything about it was different from East Southwich Albion Association Football Club.)

None of the members of the Rose City Revolution had ever seen anything quite like it. Not at a football ground, anyway. So

---

have broken out had not the Krishnas intervened and demanded, "Namaste, namaste." There were no Stones, there was no concert, there was no riot, and soon there was no crowd—one and all having decided that the whole affair was more trouble than it was worth... and then, there was no team. Not enough of the protesters had ever paid to see a match, and so despite being the central attraction of a generally weird summer in Fort Lauderdale, and despite being pretty good, the Beach Nuts' owner had had enough of the AASSA and sold the franchise to a surprisingly willing buyer from Wisconsin, who relocated the team to Milwaukee for the 1974 season.

The new owner, an American beer magnate of German extraction, had seen enough soccer on his trips to the Old Country to fancy himself something of an expert on the game. He revealed his ignorance, however, with his first decision as proprietor: having failed to properly tally the number of players on the field at any given time, and thinking he could attract the area's many baseball loyalists with what he believed was a fortuitous commonality between the World's Game and the National Pastime, he declared that the new team would be known as the Milwaukee Nine. For the month of the Nine's first and only training camp, no one said anything, thinking that the number had some significance to the club's rich riveted were the men of the Revolution by the metal-on-metal destruction before them—and the mix of children and disturbing adulthood in the stands—that they didn't even warm up for the game. They just stood and stared, stood and watched as Oldsmobile after Oldsmobile collided with each other, sending metal and glass into the stale, stagnant air of the giant dome. The kids squealed, the grown-ups grunted and waved their fists, the mascots flapped their arms, and Danny had a rush of fond feeling for North Beef, Colorado.

While the Revolution wasn't warming up, the Demolition wasn't showing up. As the cars smashed into each other and the kids raised a mighty ruckus into the un-air-like air of the convex enclosure, the opposite end of the pitch lay empty. The Revolution got the odd feeling—pub-league-style, in an entirely non-pub-league setting—that the other team might not show up, that someone had read the schedule incorrectly, that they were at the wrong field. But that wasn't possible, not here, not with all the cars, the mascots, the maniacal demolition and demolition-derby fans, and the kids, all those kids...

They couldn't *all* be at the wrong field, but... where was the other team?

And then Danny saw what the next ninety minutes of his life was going to be like. He saw why the Detroit Demolition was black and yellow, and it wasn't because of the hazard tape at a

and benevolent new boss, and if it was good enough for him it was good enough for them. Maybe he had nine kids? And besides that, the team was such a jumble of nationalities and languages that many of the players were unsure they knew what "Milwaukee Nine" meant. But then the local sports page ran an interview with the Beer King of Cheese Country in which he went on at some length about the strategy and tactics of the game—one goalie, three fullbacks, two halfbacks, two quarterbacks—which roused the curiosity of the immigrant community. "Is American soccer maybe not the same as European football? I thought it was..." went one letter to the editor, and when the question was put to the Beer King during a subsequent radio interview, he refused to answer the question other than to say that it was all a misunderstanding and a misspelling and that the name of the team was now the Milwaukee Nein!, exclamation point included. "You want to score in our goal? Nein!" he said. "You want to win in our stadium? Nein!

car wreck. He saw that these were no ordinary mascots, and he saw that revenge, in this particular case, was a dish best served indoors.

The mascots took off their costumes and descended from the bleachers to an ecstatic, high-pitched roar. And when they did, when they had reached the field, when their costumes were off and they were no longer mascots but the professional foot-ballers with whom the Rose City Revolution would do battle this Michigan mid-day, Danny realized that the Detroit Demolition of the Liberty Conference of the American All-Star Soccer Association was, in fact Dire Vale United of the Fourth Division of the English Football League.

Bloody Dire Vale, on summer tour, contracted to be the Detroit Demolition and fill the warm months in preparation for the English League slog. They'd been waiting for this day, waiting through the cod football of North Beef and the muggy miasma of Miami and the stark humiliation of an opening-day savaging by the Giganticos in New York, waiting through everything the AASSA had to offer so they could warm their embittered, al-most-relegated-mostly-because-of-their-missing-Welsh-winger-to-non-League football hearts to see, in Rose City red and black and not East Southwich royal blue and white, Danny, to see him these thousands of miles from home, where they could sort him out once and for all.

You wish to defeat the Milwaukee Nein?! Nein!" He claimed this is what he had meant all along, and he went to some length to establish how proud he was to have brought the only punctuation mark in American sports to the great city of Milwaukee, Wisconsin.

The confusion—it was too late to change the logo, a giant 9—and the inherently negative Teutonic nature of the new moniker proved prohibitive to fan loyalty, as did the fact that you couldn't fit a standard soccer field into Milwaukee's baseball stadium (the team played on what could most charitably have been called a trap-ezoid). The local Germans came for a game or two, scoffed at the parallelogram, and subsequently stayed away. No one else gave the Nein! a shot, and the Beer King sold the franchise to a Pontiac, Michigan, Oldsmobile dealer who had some trade-ins that had been on the lot for a long time—and an idea.

And thus did Detroit, Michigan, join the AASSA for the 1975 season.

They were there to crush Danny, *crush* him, to end his career if at all possible.

Hooper could see it in their eyes: They weren't even there to win. They were there for him. Only him.

A word Molly used a lot came to Danny: this was going to *suck*.

Danny knew he had to play. He had no choice. If he begged out, the story would make the rounds, up and down the Football League, and whatever his reputation was now, it would be worse, much worse. He had to survive, just *survive* the next hour and a half, with the sounds of cars smashing and children squealing and all of it bouncing around this awful concrete snow globe where soccer dignity knew not the depths to which it might sink.

Good thing this one's not on the telly in Portland, Danny thought. *Good thing at least for that.*

Broomsie knew who and what Dire Vale United was and were to Danny, so he asked him what he wanted to do. "You'll play as much as you want to play today, Danny. You don't have to—"

"I'm fine," Danny said. "I'm fine."

"It's down to you, lad. I'll remove you when you say the word."

"Don't plan on it, boss," Danny said, and he could see that Broomsie knew he meant it, but Danny knew that it was only the look of him—the big and the strong and the beard—that gave Broomsie that idea. In point of fact, beneath it all, Danny knew that he was in big trouble.

He recognized most of the Dire Vale boys. They had the obligatory American or two, of course—they'd found big ones too, big and ugly ones. But he knew the Dire Vale faces, last seen coming at him in masks of rage, last seen wanting him dead. But he also recognized them as types, Fourth Division types: their heavy ones five or ten pounds too heavy, their small ones too small and slight, their old ones well past too old. They had a

"Peter Surley" of their own, a decomposing, stationary midfielder they liked to play through, but their Surley had a pronounced comb-over to go with the pillow up his shirt. To look across at them made Danny think that maybe he could just outrun them long enough to diffuse their rage—

—but then it all kicked off and their anger and spite crackled about in the dome like lightning, making Danny's hair stand on end, making his heart beat faster than he needed it to.

Danny sized up the situation this way: his best and most dignified escape was a red card. But that had a downside, a major downside: he'd have to sit one out, and not just any one: the home fixture against the Giganticos. Couldn't miss that, for numerous reasons. But the longer he stayed in the game, the less the Dire Vale Demolition cared about beating the Revolution and the more they'd want to take out Rose City's number five...

Then one of Detroit's American beasts was near him, near him with revenge in his eyes, and the ball was sixty yards away, getting lost in the corner under Juanito's feet, and the referee was watching that, watching Juanito, and the linesmen were watching Juanito, but the Detroit bench was watching Danny. The Dire Vale men were pointing him out to the American—"'*e's the one, the big 'un*"—and Danny brought his shoulder up and his elbow out across the cheekbone of the Demolition man's face with a quick, merciless jab, and the big Detroit man dropped right on the spot as if he'd just had a heart attack. Danny jogged away, casually, so that by the time the referee knew there was a man down, Danny was twenty yards gone. The Demolition's bench was apoplectic, screaming and waving and pointing at Danny. *So,* Danny thought, *that's one of them done. Ten left.* He thought maybe he'd do it again.

The referee, an American who had only the most incidental knowledge of soccer and had done most of his refereeing on a gridiron football field, who was in fact wearing a zebra-striped gridiron-referee shirt, who had no patience for a *soccer* injury, and who hadn't picked up on any of the latent animosity between the two teams, waved the Detroit's medical staff onto the field and urged them to remove their player with all due haste.

Minutes later, the Demolition had the ball in the Rose City half. It looked like they might even turn the possession into an opportunity to score until the ball got near to Danny, and Danny clattered into the Demolition's striker as if to kill him. *Two,* Danny thought. *That's two.* The Detroit Demolition gathered around Danny, they screamed at him so he could feel their warm, dog's-mouth breath. They wanted to draw and quarter Hooper right there, to make him pay for everything, but this was a referee disinclined to let the anger play itself out in the *soccer* way; no, he was a *football* man, and *football* men did not let men gather around other men and bellow and bawl and bark. So he dispersed them, waved them away with a brisk "Let's play ball, men," gave Detroit a free kick they were far too angry to make any use of (over the crossbar by a good twenty-five yards and into a hectare of empty seats, where it plonked around like a Pachinko ball), and showed Danny a yellow card. "One more and you're outta here," the American said, but he didn't seem to worked up about it.

Two late-model sedans smashed into each other behind the Revolution bench, the children screamed, the adults up in the stands grunted, and Danny saw something go out of the Demolition's eyes. He could see they weren't finished quite yet, but he could also see that it was dawning on them that maybe this dome, in this far-flung suburb, in front of these American children, amid the din of smashed, twisted metal—this was not the Fifth Round of the FA Cup, this was... well, whatever *this* was, vengeance may not be as easy to come by as they'd imagined. They could see, at least, that Danny was up for the fight.

By halftime, nil–nil, Danny had ridden out a few hard tackles, endured the inconvenience of a couple pushing matches, been called things you can't put in a book like this, been booked and warned again by the referee. His right hip was bloody to halfway down his thigh from a five-yard skid along the sandpaper of Detroit's home field—he thought he might have even picked up a few flecks of formerly automotive metal for his trouble too—but he was fine, and he had started thinking that seeing out a match against bitter, vengeful Dire Vale United sounded like his idea of a good time.

Broomsie roared and screeched at his team to ignore the flying car parts and the screaming children and "stop staring at the *roof*—it's just a *roof*, lads... I know you've never played underneath one, but you've *seen* one before, haven't you? You look like *fools*, and you should be ahead by three or four against these brutes—" but Danny didn't hear any more than every third or fourth word... he was forty-five minutes away from a trip back to Portland, and he couldn't believe how much he missed Portland. *We are, we are, we are the Revs. Yes, Portland would be nice,* Danny thought. *Portland, Oregon. Home.*

The second half scarcely resembled football at all.

The Demolition played as if they knew that every passing minute was a minute less time they had to destroy the Revolution's number five—but the time did pass. The Revolution was a marginally better team than Dire Vale—Surley and his midfield cohorts dominated possession, and Kelvin put in a particularly solid match, his first full ninety since his injury in Chicago, on the left wing—and the ball stayed at Detroit's end for great stretches of the half. The Demolition's forwards circled Danny, stood near him in a menacing way, but the ball was just too far away for them to do anything without being entirely too conspicuous, and whenever it did come near Danny—who had instructed the Revolution defense not to keep the ball, not to pass it to him, but to hoof it upfield and "Away, away, *away*, boys!"— he got there first and kicked it as far into the stands as he could, and the kids whooped and hollered, and Detroit would reposition themselves for the throw-in, and... that would be that. The minutes passed, and they passed, and Juanito took a through ball from Surley that was so delicately backspun on the rubber pitch that it settled against Juanito's feet as if it had sought out his comforting touch, and Juanito had become a real profession-al by this point of the summer, and he did his part, and it was one–nil for the Revolution.

"Keep it *away* from me, boys," Danny barked, and so they did.

Detroit called for a substitution. The menacing rat-faced forwards who'd been lingering in Danny's vicinity for seventy minutes departed and two new men ran toward Danny, their heads down, and something about them—their build, their hair, their gait, their *aura*—none of it seemed at all English. Danny didn't recognize them from the Auld Moors—

—and that was because they had never played at the Auld Moors, nor were they English.

They ran right at Danny, the Russians, the Communists from the trees, and when they took their spots as the Detroit Demolition's center forwards, they smiled at Danny and Danny said, "Oh, dear me," which isn't something he usually said.

"Hello, Danny Hooooper," one of them said, smiling. "Hap-py to seeing you here."

The other one said, "It is always our pleasure, as you are knowing."

Danny, still pleased at what his forearm had done to one of Detroit's Dire Vale men in the first half, lifted his shoulder and elbow to do it again to the first man, but the second inserted himself between them and said, "You do not want to do that. We are friends now. OK, we are maybe not friends now, but we have something you want, and there is something we need you to do for us. That makes us friends of a kind, don't you think?"

The referee demanded the game proceed.

The Russians kicked off after the Rose City goal, and within minutes the Revolution had them pinned deep again. The Revo-lution's central defender stood in between the Demolition's new forwards.

"What are you doing here?" Danny asked them.

"We are always with you."

"No, I mean, *here*, on the bloody pitch," Danny huffed.

"We needed to speak with you."

"How did you get on their team?"

"We arranged it."

"Do you not understand?"

"Do I not understand what?"

"We are arrangers, Danny."

"You're what?"

"Arrangers. We arrange things so that they are how we want them to be."

"We arrange for people to be in situations so that they must do what we want them to do."

The ball flew over their heads. All three of them looked up, tracked it, watched it until it bounced all the way to Big Lou, then watched as he punted it back over their heads toward Detroit's back line, where it bounced and then got lost under a clutter of Rose City and Detroit feet.

"We are arranging, even now, for you to play in the Bonanza Bowl, Danny. Against the Giganticos."

Danny brought his shoulder up again and extended his elbow. *"You what?"*

"No, no, no, Danny—no elbows. For now, we are friends."

"No—"

"Yes, and when you are in New York, you will help us, help us do something spectacular that the whole world will see. It will be a great moment for our cause."

"I will not."

"You will. Of course you will. You have no choice."

"Also, we are playing because we are tiring of watching so much terrible football and not playing. We wanted a match. Looks so easy, this league, hmm? So much... fun! That is the word: fun."

"And to tell you: we are arranging for you to do what we need you to do."

"Oh, yeah?" Danny said. "Yeah? Is that a fact?"

"It is a fact, Hooooper."

"How do you plan on doing that?"

"We plan on paying you for it."

"I won't take your money."

"We will not pay you with money."

"Then—"

"Trust us. You will wish to do business with us."

"You will want Molly back."

"But—" Danny took a sharp short breath. His eyes widened. He could see by the look on the Russians' faces that his face showed the fear he was trying to conceal. He looked over at the Revolution's bench—Molly was there, perched on the end of it as she always was—and turned back to the Demolition's interloper forwards and said, "Fu—"

"Save it for later, Danny Hooooper. When you want Molly back, you may meet us in the tree. In Portland. We'll explain what we get when you get Molly."

"But Molly's right there." He pointed over to the Revolution bench. "Right over there—"

The ball went over their heads again, but this time the Russians chased it. Their speed caught Danny by surprise, and he realized that if they got to it first—*"Shite,"* Danny said to himself, *"shite,"* and he chased them. But one of them got there first and dribbled in on Big Lou, alone. The children screamed, Danny screamed—it was all he could do—and the man took his shot, a surprisingly skillful bent little ball around Big Lou, delicately hit at full speed—the man could play, the Russian could *play*— and the ball slithered along the unnatural surface... on grass it would've had time to come around, but not here, it just couldn't get enough purchase on the carpet, and it struck the post and pinged away for a goal kick. The children groaned, or at least their version of it.

The man—it was Lev—smiled as he jogged back, and he patted Danny's face.

"Why would I score when I want you to win, Danny Hoooooper?"

And then it was done. One–nil. Danny walked with his team through the customary post-match handshakes with the opposition, taking the leaned-in shoulders and the fleshy-faced Dire Vale glares and the withdrawn hands from the men who hated him, but he had survived. He was bloody and sore and he limped a little, and when he got through the line he jogged—he would've run, sprinted, dashed, but a jog was all he had—to the Revolution's bench, and there was Molly, she was right there, asking players how they were, how the field had treated them, doing her job. She smiled at Danny, her vast, welcoming smile.

She was fine. Just fine.

TWENTY-ONE

The team allowed itself a day of rest before commencing deep preparations for their visit from the Giganticos.

The Revolution convened in the lobby of the Grand Douglas at nine o'clock for breakfast with a loyal core of supporters—"boosters"—who had come bearing all manner of morning food and drink for the returning warriors of the Rose City. Pastries, sausage, coffee, tea—the tired and hungry players rotated themselves through a sizable buffet over and over again until it was gone. One of the boosters stood in front of them and made a short speech about how Portland was getting more and more excited about its new team. The stocky, small, elderly woman who had kicked out the first ball in the rain before the Toronto game was there and told the team they were the most important thing that had happened to the city since the man from Portland, Maine, had won the coin toss against the man from Boston. "Keep winning, boys," she said. "Keep winning." Danny didn't know what she was talking about, and he still didn't really know who she was, but he liked how she talked. In East Southwich, the club represented the town and its people, and Danny knew he was damn well one of those people, but the Royals represented the pessimism of the place, the years and years of never really being special at all. Danny loved that this new club had no history at all; the Revolution was Portland's future, and if the Revolution won, then Portland could win too, and keep winning.

But winning for the Rose City Revolution was about to get a lot more complicated. Broomsie replaced the old woman in front of the team and in front of the boosters, proffered deep and heartfelt thanks to the supporters and to the old woman, and then he said, "I know the boys are right knackered from the journey. We've traveled far and wide and we've brought back some victories for this great city, but we're up against it now—one of the very best sides in the world is coming to our humble ground in a few short days. It will be as difficult as anything we've done, but on this form, we may be able to surprise them. We may do. I wouldn't have said it when the season began, but I'll say it now: the Revolution can do anything. I believe it. I do. Anyone else believe it?"

The boosters murmured and shouted a confident flurry of yeses and of courses that only reinforced for Danny that these wonderful people didn't know a damn thing about soccer. The players were silent.

Broome said, "They're human, and we're human too. And the way the lads have put themselves about lately, I reckon we can make ninety minutes hard work for just about anyone, even the Giganticos," and then he mumbled, ". . . even the Giganticos," to himself, as if he knew it probably sounded insane to everyone else and he wanted to see if it sounded insane to himself.

"So listen, lads, you see the film projector at the back of the lobby, you see this screen here behind me. Settle in." He motioned to a booster stood next to the projector, who dimmed the lights and started the rattle and clack of the projector. It was the Giganticos against the Flamingos of Florida. Graham Broome said, "Don't think, lads. Just watch."

The ball bounced and bobbled about on the thick, uneven Miami pitch, causing even the Pearl and the Dutchman and the Giganticos' German sweeper to make poor passes and cough up the ball on the dribble. But still the Giganticos made a mockery of their opponent. The pink Flamingos were entirely unable to advance any kind of goal-scoring cause against the champions, and despite the general sloppiness of the game, the only method the home team had of relieving the pressure on their defense was to clear the ball mighty distances—to be gathered up calmly and easily by the Giganticos' back line, recommencing the slow, entrancing, inevitable process of easing it back toward the Florida goal. As Danny sat in the semi-dark of the Grand Douglas lobby, surrounded by his teammates and the locals who loved them most, the clicking and the whirring of the projector and the deliberate poetry of the Giganticos' game eased him into a sense of calm that had eluded him for months—since before he'd grown tired of East Southwich Albion's Paleolithic approach to the Beautiful Game, since before he'd ruined his FA Cup chances, since before he'd been exiled to America, since before he'd been recruited into—whatever he'd been recruited into. He nearly fell asleep.

But Broomsie leapt in front of the screen, casting a ghoulish black shadow onto another Giganticos buildup. "Did you see that?" he barked. "Did you *see* that? Stop, *stop* the projector." The projector sputtered, and the coach went on about how the Flamingos had given the Giganticos' central midfielders too much space to make their overlapping runs, "and then did you see, *did you see*, when the Brazilian and them get out wide, their defenders fill the space while Florida's forwards just look on, just look on, and just like that the Giganticos have more attackers than they've got defenders. Did you *see*? So now the Pearl or the Dutchman have the ball in space and the Giganticos have numbers in the box, and the other lads are right *fooooked* is what they are, and no one's even broken much of a sweat, have they? And no one even really noticed. Roll the film again, my boy, roll the film again." And the film rolled again, and Danny saw it play out just as Broomsie had said it would, and the great Brazilian beat his man on the wing without really trying and floated in a lazy cross that the German met at the end of what must have been a twenty-five- or thirty-yard run out of the space Broomsie had just pointed out, and the headed ball went into the goal without so much as a flinch from the Florida goalkeeper. The coach didn't stop the film this time, just hollered out from his easy chair, "We can stop them, lads, we *can* stop them." But Danny had been around football long enough to know belief when a team had it, and he didn't feel any in the lobby of the Grand Douglas apartment complex high in the lush green hills of Portland, Oregon.

The camera panned what passed for the grandstand of the Flamingos' modest ground. The crowd cheered the Giganticos' goal; the camera moved in and out of focus as it considered various groups of fans—a row of five youngish women sporting black sweaters, each with one big white letter: P, E, A, R, L; a knot of ten or fifteen nine- or ten-year-old boys in matching jerseys on a team outing; a pair of men up in the top row, standing against the railing, wearing black suits and dark sunglasses.

Danny sat up in his chair, looked around, looked at Broomsie, looked at Surley. Neither flinched at the sight of the men in their suits and sunglasses. Danny looked for Molly, found her standing just to the side of the film projector, almost hidden by the dark of the back of the room, but he could see that she was waiting for his gaze, and she met it, and she nodded.

When the game was over, the projector clacked itself to a gradual halt, the lights came on, and the team and the boosters rubbed their eyes and shifted from their seats, lulled into a stupor by the film they'd just seen—8–0 to the Giganticos—Graham Broome stood at the front of the room and said to no one in particular to remember that the Flamingos were the worst team in the league and that they made some ridiculous mistakes on five of the eight Gigantico goals, mistakes the Revolution would never make, and that with their best game, with work and graft and "a bit of luck, yes, I'll admit it, we'd need a bit of luck," the Revolution could "win by the odd goal maybe, maybe" or "get them in a Super Soccer Showdown," and then the world—"the *world*, lads"—would be asking itself who and what the Rose City Revolution was and were—"the *world*," he kept saying—"and in our stadium, in front of our people, you know it can happen, you *know* it can." But the boys were gathering their things, picking at the remaining pastries, and even the boosters had it on their faces: many of them had never seen any better football than the AASSA at its non-Gigantico very best—even some of the new Cloppingshire lads had never seen a better team than the Chicago Butchers in person, and had certainly never seen anything like the almost bored precision with which the Giganticos had just taken apart the Flamingos of Florida on their bouncy and bobbly and thick and uneven pitch. No one in the room—none of the Todds, or the Petes and Peters, or the Jimmies, or Juanito, or anyone from England—believed Graham Broome and his incantatory pleadings for the Revolution to consider the idea of defeating the mighty Giganticos. They may have believed him before seeing the film, but not now.

The lobby emptied itself like a punctured football, the air easing itself away into nothing.

Danny stood in front of the Grand Douglas, hands in his pockets, contemplating the woods, absorbing the light summer rain. He wished he smoked. A cigarette might have calmed his nerves, or at least given him something to do as his mind considered the gigantic task ahead of him, a task he knew was much more likely to make a fool of him than to make the world wonder at the surprising footballing grandeur of the Rose City Revolution.

"The Giganticos are fun to watch, aren't they?"

He turned his torso, hands still in pockets, and saw Molly, arms crossed, hugging herself against the morning cold. "I'm still learning your game, I admit, but it sure looks easy when you watch them play it. It will be so much fun to have them in Portland, won't it?" She stood herself next to him and appeared to contemplate the woods as well.

Danny said, "Well, that's one way to look at it." Molly didn't say anything, so Danny said the obvious: "I saw them."

Molly said, "Of course you did."

"Why were they there?"

"They're making plans."

"Can't you just arrest them, or something?"

She shook her head. "Well, I wish it were that simple, Danny. But it's just not how the game works. And besides, if we did...we wouldn't know who we should be watching."

Danny almost thought this made sense.

"No, Danny. They're observing. Learning the Giganticos' routines. How they handle game day, how they get to and from, what the Pearl does before and after."

"Did we have people there? Watching them watch the Giganticos?"

"Ah, very good. It's 'we' now—good to hear. Of course we were there."

Danny didn't say anything right away. He closed his eyes at the thought of the Giganticos and Molly, East Southwich Albion and the FA Cup, and the Rose City Revolution and all of it, all of it. "Funny they wore their suits to the match," he said. "Hot as balls down in Miami."

Molly laughed. "They're not so smart, Danny. Thank goodness, they're not so smart."

She waited for Danny to answer her assertion, which she had made to comfort him, but it hadn't worked, and Danny didn't answer. A few seconds passed, and he said, "I think I'll go on in and get some rest."

Molly said, "I have a better idea."

"A better idea?"

"It's a day off, Danny. You won't have many more this summer, believe me. Around here, when you get a free day and the sun shines, you go to the beach."

Danny pointed out the obvious: "There's no sun, Molly."

"Ah, this will burn off by lunchtime, Danny. Let's go to the shore." She leaned a little closer and said, "We might even drag those Russians out of town for a little while. Worth a try anyway, don't you think?" Danny wrinkled his brow and looked down at her, boring into her American eyes for confirmation that she really thought of this espionage business as a game.

"Besides, Danny, it's *time*," Molly said. "You're part of Oregon lore now. People are telling their friends and their families about you, the mighty bearded Briton who slammed a goal home *with his head* against *Seattle*. Time we dipped you in our waters, Danny."

Danny hadn't said no to Molly yet, and he wasn't going to start now.

TWENTY-TWO

The drive from Portland to the Oregon seaside, to a town called Seaside, is a miraculous ninety minutes for a first-timer; there's a tunnel—maybe thirty miles west of the city, up a steep grade, past the last gas station and under some trees—that feels like a portal to another, still greener world, after which the road winds down and up and through a forest that feels like the kind of place that was once represented on maps by demons and dragons, and in myth by hairy beasts who eluded capture for generations, for centuries, for aeons.

"We're going to the beach?" Danny asked.

"The beach!" Molly answered. But first, she explained, they had to traverse the Coast Range, a fold in Oregon's terrain that Danny had never even heard of, but whose summit was higher than any peak in all of England. Danny looked out the window and into it and saw waterfalls and burbling creeks and great husks of ancient trees that stood decomposing, feeding another round of lush life that needed nothing at all of humanity for its verdant hale and heartiness. Danny's eyes scarcely had the means to tell his brain whether he was seeing in two dimensions or three, or how many shades of one color he was seeing. Deep in those woods, high in that range that would have been the spine of every English legend but here was just another feature of a state so few even talked about, Danny wouldn't have been at all surprised to see creatures he had never seen before leaping behind trees never to be seen again. Danny would have been surprised at nothing.

Molly pulled the car over at a promontory from which you could see for... ah, Danny couldn't imagine how far. He gazed and he looked, looked and he gazed, spent a few long minutes trying to understand the wilderness that rolled itself before him. He was sure he was looking beyond Oregon, to other states, other lands, but he didn't really know. He didn't know how America's borders worked or in which direction he was looking. But he was sure he'd never cast his eyes as far as he cast them now.

He wasn't next to Molly anymore—she had stayed next to the car—but he walked toward the woods, the trees, as if he could change his view. He couldn't, but he was inexperienced in the art of stretching his eyes to this astounding degree. And besides that, he needed to relieve himself.

The light and warmth past the first row of trees changed drastically. A bright, sunny day became shady and cool in an instant, as if he'd gone from outdoors to in. The forest seemed to envelop him, and he was tempted to keep walking, to keep walking, and to disappear. And be done with it, be done with it all. He knew he could.

It was a morbid thought, though—especially with a girl like Molly right over there—and he tried to push it from his mind. Then he looked down, and the thought was gone from his mind, because...

...there at his feet was a suit of clothes, black, perfectly dry, and next to the suit of clothes, a pair of black leather shoes. A man's outfit, in its entirety, ready to go. Danny looked around him, stunned by the incongruity of it. *Could there be someone right nearby, waiting to, what, put these clothes on? No, no, no,* Danny thought, *no.* Molly and Danny had *just* pulled over, just now, and just *now,* someone, some *who?,* would need this, this... outfit. *Even here,* Danny thought. *Even in these woods, even in this place.* Danny thought he heard his name: "*Danny Hooooper.*" He spun at the sound of it, saw and heard nothing more, shivered and turned to walk back into the light, unrelieved in body and soul.

Molly saw him, smiled, and said, "Ready to go?"

He grunted.

She said, "Isn't it beautiful? Look at it one more time."

"It is," he said. "It is."

"You OK? You don't look so good."

Danny lied and said he was OK.

They drove up and up, to a sign that said they were at the summit of the Oregon Coast Range. He opened his mouth to tell Molly what he had seen, but it didn't even feel like a story yet in his mind. He wasn't sure how to even tell it. There was a suit of clothes, and... he heard his name, and *what?*

He said nothing as the car rolled down the longest hill he had ever seen.

Danny and Molly stopped at a coffee shop just a few blocks from the beach to warm up and get some eggs. They sat just inside a window, the big Briton and the American girl, brought together by football and fate, and gazed through the glass at a feverish gray-blue spring rain that fell in graceful, filmy sheets, creating a milky lunar face on the street, not so far from the edge of the continent. They laughed at its intensity, wondered at it power.

"Oh man, this is straight out of the Old Testament," Molly said.

Danny laughed at that. He wasn't accustomed to people speaking so dramatically. He'd spent most of his life around footballers, and footballers didn't talk like that. His dad hardly spoke at all, and a footballer would've said, "It's raining hard." Then Molly said, "No, man, this, this is a rain sent by a power we don't understand... a *goddess* has sent this rain." She was laughing, holding her coffee mug to her lips with two hands. "Could be," she said with a wistful little smile. "You never know, Danny."

He smiled. He still wondered whether he was Communist hunter or Communist prey, still wondered whose suit of clothes he had just seen and left alone, still wondered whether he was up to the task of saving the great Pearl of Brazil, still wondered whether it was even true that Danny Hooper of East Southwich was the man to save the greatest Gigantico of them all, still wondered if he really was on the path to winning something, winning a championship for his sins, still wondered that *he* was here, with *this* girl, thousands of miles from home, in first place and with the Giganticos next up on the schedule.

He was happy enough for now, though, for this very moment. He opened his mouth to say something in this general spirit to lovely, American Molly Hart, but she saw it coming and, probably anticipating Danny's lyrical limitations, said, "Just listen to the rain." So Danny listened. Molly and Danny listened. Then Molly said there were only two times it was worth being at the coast: in the clear blue sunshine and "in rain so thick you can drink it. Let's head down, Danny. Let's go to the beach."

Her eyes were blue or green depending on the weather and her smile was dependable and kind. The lads considered her to be one of the Revolution's greatest attributes—not out of lust, though there was that, but they all just felt that the act of being near her was accomplishment in itself. When she was with them, they got smiles at the airport and better service at restaurants. They even got taken care of just a little better when they arrived at the other stadiums—Molly would leave the bus first and say, "Hi there. We're the Rose City Revolution. Where should we dress for the game?" and whoever it was would say, "We're *so* happy to have you—bring the boys right this way..." That wouldn't happen if Graham Broome was the first one off the bus.

Some of the boys were sure they were going somewhere with her, someday, in time, if they just waited—but they were not. Danny had gotten somewhere, however. She had her reasons, he knew—but still: here he was, alone with Portland's own Molly Hart, within salty smell of the edge of America, and it felt, for the mystery of it all, *good*, like a premonition of Danny's very own championship, his very own League Vase.

As soon as they left the coffee shop, the rain having rained itself into a much-deserved break, Danny transferred that energy—all of that energy: the lingering Communists, the lurking Giganticos, the lovely Molly—into a wet sprint through the post-deluge sun to the end of the street (the end of the *country*) toward a trail that led through the dunes and down to the beach and the ocean. Why not? Danny was a footballer, and when footballers are excited they *run*, it's all they really know how to do.

An old wooden bench stood at the trailhead, and Danny, in his vigor, his escapism, his hope that every Gigantico would live through the season, and his affection for Molly, planted a foot on the bench with the thought of springing himself into the air and toward the ocean. Instead—and predictably—his foot slipped away from under him, and he thunked to the ground in a balletic pratfall as if he'd been undercut by a Dire Vale man while leaping for a header. Danny writhed on the wet sandy ground, more embarrassed than hurt (he hoped). Molly ran to him. "Oh, motherf—" he wheezed.

Molly grasped immediately what he'd done—popped his shoulder out of its socket—and rammed it back in. "American medicine, " she said.

"Oh, that hurt, Molly."

"You dislocated it, Danny. Popped it right out."

"Oh Jesus, that hurts."

"Going to hurt for a while, Danny."

He sat there in the wet sand and considered the possibility that the entire day—and maybe more, maybe the whole summer, the whole season—had just gone entirely wrong. But he hated the thought, hated it too much to let it overtake him.

He held his shoulder, looked up at Molly, and grunted, "To the ocean, Molly Hart."

She laughed a sympathetic laugh and patted Danny's other shoulder. "How English of you, Danny. You're hurt, big man. Stiff upper lip isn't much of a prescription, you know—"

"OK then—stiff upper lip and a cortisone shot?"

"Graham Broome may not be happy with us, Danny."

"Graham Broome will never know about today," Danny said, which would not turn out to be true.

They walked through the high grass, over a dune, and down toward the Pacific Ocean. They took off their shoes, rolled up their jeans, and entered the water. *Cold as f—... ah,* Danny thought, *cold as—oh Jesus.* But it took his mind off his shoulder. Just a little.

He held Molly's hand. His shoulder hurt like something far, far worse than a silly mishap at the beach should hurt. He knew he had a problem there. A real one. Actually, he knew he had a problem on the other arm too.

Danny recognized his surroundings, even though he'd never been to Oregon's coast before: Seaside wasn't so different from an English coastal resort towns, complete with dodgy aquarium, sketchy arcade, and kitschy shops. Danny and Molly had lunch at a distinctly American diner that still managed to remind him of the fish and chips shops in Whitbey or Cornwall.

The waitress called Danny "you poor dear" and "hon" and brought him a bag of ice, which Molly affixed to his shoulder with an artfully tied napkin. That, the aspirin Molly had brought along, and a tall cold beer had dulled some of the pain. Molly introduced Danny to the corn dog.

They tried to resume the trappings and habits of a nice day out at the beach. After lunch, they went to an antique shop where Danny bought a rusted bear trap. They went to an arcade, where Danny spied Skee-Ball for the first time and couldn't resist, despite having to play left-handed. They played the horse-race game, where you fire a water pistol at a target and drive your horse along to victory; they spun giant wheels for prizes. He thought what a wondrous person she was, what outrageous fortune he'd had to come all this way, borne along by football and reconnaissance, to find her. To find *her.* They held hands.

She gave him a kiss on the cheek. His shoulder hurt, but he was happy. Couldn't believe his luck. Molly. Molly and Danny.

Molly offered to go and get a couple of Cokes, and Danny said thank you and kissed her on the cheek. He sat down on a bench between a hoop-shoot and a photo booth, closed his eyes, and, despite the throbbing ache in his shoulder, pretended everything was all right.

To get his mind off the pain, he let himself ruminate on the Giganticos. He thought maybe Broomsie could crowd the midfield with the overanxious Todds, just to make life tough on the Dutchman, maybe throw Surley up front just so that if the Revolution lucked into a chance or two they'd have a veteran there to finish with some poise. Danny knew there was no way his team could match the Giganticos for anything but pace and effort, so maybe Juanito could play the wing opposite Kelvin and at least give the visitors an extra something to worry about... if the Giganticos worried about anything. *Yes, that's it,* Danny thought, *get as much speed behind the ball as possible and wear them out.* Sounded to him like it was worth a try. He made a mental note to get a few thoughts into Broomsie's ear when he and Molly got back to Portland. He and Molly, Danny and Molly. Still had a few more hours to spend with Molly Hart, at the beach, in the car—

Danny opened his eyes and looked around. He realized it had been a while. He realized Molly should've been back by now. He stood, walked over to the concessionaire. No Molly. He walked around the arcade. No Molly. Went out onto the street, up the street—it was a wet weekday afternoon; there weren't that many people. There weren't that many people—and Molly wasn't one of them.

He walked to the end of the block, looked up and down from there too, saw nothing—but then he heard a man with an accent say, "Looking for someone?"

Danny spun, winced, and saw a man in a black suit, a suit that looked as if it had been rained on that day. Maybe had been rained on in the woods. The Russian smiled a familiar smile and said, "Come inside, Danny." They were outside an ice-cream shop, and Danny followed the man inside and saw the other Russian, wrapping his tongue around a soft-serve vanilla cone.

Of course, thought Danny. He cursed himself, cursed his carelessness, cursed Molly's carelessness too. *Wasn't she supposed to know how this all worked?* Wasn't she supposed to know better than Danny? And now he knew that of the three men in the booth at this oceanside ice-cream shop, two knew where Molly Hart was, and one did not.

One of them said, "Danny Hooooper, so far you have benefitted from our presence in your country. We are the reason you won in Chicago, we are the reason Billy Robinson missed the first half in Los Angeles and played drunk in the second half. My friend here could easily have tied the match in Detroit, but he did not. You are maybe thinking we are helping you, but we are not on your side, and it is time you understood that. Hmm? Do you not think it is reasonable that we helped you understand what it is we are capable of doing?"

The other Russian nodded and said, "I am thinking so, yes," as if the question had been addressed to him.

"We are capable of great things," the first man said.

The other man went on: "Your Molly is not an innocent, Danny. I believe you understand this. She is not paid only by the Revolution. You know this, correct?"

Danny didn't answer. He didn't think it was any of the Russians' business whether he knew the answer to this question.

"You *do* know this, Danny," he said. "And now here is something else for you to know: Molly is with us now. She is in our care. You do not know when or whether you will see her again. You will drive back to Portland alone, and you will tell Mr. Graham Broome"—he said this name with scorn—"what I have told you."

Danny pulled his left arm back to strike the Russian, but the other said, "You do not want to do that."

Danny said, "I do," his arm still cocked.

The man said, "No, really. You do not. Trust me, Danny Hooooper." Then he said, "You are not even left-handed."

The other Russians said, "Our work here is done. Tomorrow the Revolution trains in preparation for the Giganticos. Molly will not be with the team."

Danny said, "When will she be with the team again? What needs to happen? What can I do?"

"I think it is time for you to return to Portland, Danny. My comrade will walk you to your car."

Hooper looked across the table at the men. He said, "If anything happens—"

"You will receive clear instructions. If you follow them, you will see Molly Hart again. If you do as we say, you will see her again."

One of the men walked Danny to his car. When he got in, the man said, "Drive until you get to the Grand Douglas Apartments. Anything else would be a terrible, terrible mistake. Tomorrow, be at the tree."

The bloody tree. In the bloody woods.

Danny was numb as he drove out of Seaside, Oregon, drove the narrow highway out of town to the road that said TO PORT-LAND. He had never felt so defeated, so lost. *Such carelessness, such hideous, grotesque carelessness,* he thought. *I lost a woman.*

He drove over that mountain, through that mysterious wood, past the viewpoint where he had seen that mysterious suit of clothes. He cried too. Mostly for Molly, but because the numbness had passed, his shoulder hurt like hell. But he cried, big and strong Danny Hooper cried, because he was confused. And scared. He had never been so confused and scared in his entire life.

"Three, I do believe we are in new territory here."

"New territory, Danny?"

"Whilst you've been having your tea and awaiting phone calls from your big and strong lad in America, Three, *I've* been doing *your* job, and not without a bit of..." He paused and switched the phone from one ear to the other so he wouldn't feel his shoulder anymore, so that Three wouldn't hear the catch in his voice.

"A bit of what, Danny?"

"Three, there's some trouble here. Some real trouble."

"Trouble?" Three's voice changed: deepened, tightened. "Explain, Danny."

"They've got Molly."

The line went silent and stayed that way for longer than Danny would have expected. "They've *what*?"

"They've got Molly, Three. The Communists. They followed us out to the seaside, they followed us around. We should've been smarter, *she* should've been smarter—she's a bloody spy... and they *took* her, Three. I've no idea where she is or how she is, but they tell me she's... she's fine, she'll be fine—"

"When did they tell you that, Danny?"

"*There*, Three. *There*. In Seaside. At the bloody beach."

Three realized—Danny could hear it in his hesitation—that they were, in fact, in new territory, and he said, "When was the last time you'd seen them, the Communists, before this?"

"In Detroit. On the pitch. They came on as substitutes. One of them nearly scored. Anyway, they came on in the second half, and—"

Three let out a chuckle, just a little one, and caught himself. "They did, did they—"

"This is not a joke, you bastard—I need you *here*, now. Right bloody now, Three. Get... on... a...plane. They told me I have something they want."

"You have something they want you *to do*, is what they mean, dear man. They have something they want you *to do*."

"Brilliant deduction, Three. Bloody brilliant. Get...on...a... plane. I need you here. I have to meet them in a tree tomorrow." Danny heard himself, heard how he sounded. *In a tree...*

"Danny—"

"Now, Three. *Now.*"

And then, when Danny was supposed to sit and wait in the tree, Danny sat and waited in the tree. *It's humiliating sitting in a tree,* Danny thought.

No big and strong man should wait in a tree for anyone. Though he couldn't say it was an awful feeling exactly: he looked up and out of the top of the decaying creature and took in the towering trees around him, admired the way they all seemed to curve to one spot in the sky, a spot they could never reach, a spot they'd been reaching toward for decades, since long before football had arrived in Portland, since long before Communism had arrived on the planet, since long before Danny's trials and tribulations mattered to anyone. They started green and went black as they rose up into the beyond, rising toward nothing at all but the sun, those trees, those magical and mighty trees—

"Danny Hooooper!" said one of the Russians. "You are here! Very good, Danny Hooooper! Good man. How is the shoulder?"

It had come as a surprise to the Giganticos' management to learn that Oregon was on the coast, so they figured that if the team was going that far west they may as well spend the week in Hawaii before returning to the mainland for weekend matches against the Revolution and the Smithereens. At the very moment Danny crested the summit and began his descent back into Portland, the Pearl of Brazil and the Belgian goalkeeper were relaxing at a bar by the beach with a couple of mai tais, having just enjoyed a surfing lesson.

TWENTY-THREE

Seven and one.

The Rose City Revolution had seven wins and one defeat, and they weren't just any seven-and-one either: the AASSA had chopped the bicentennial 1976 season down to just sixteen matches per team to help nine of its teams save money and to facilitate the Giganticos' global travels—so the Revolution was 7-1 halfway through the season and in first place in the Frontier Conference. Seattle and Chicago were 5-3, the Smithereens in second with a few more points than the Butchers; Colorado's Romanians and Tartan Ron's erratic and eccentric L.A. Glitter were well off the pace. Stay in first and the Revolution would host the conference's number two finisher in a semifinal for the opportunity to travel to New York for the Bonanza Bowl, presumably against the Giganticos. Red Star Toronto wasn't bad—they'd likely play the Giganticos in a Liberty Conference final—but if Dire Vale United/Detroit Demolition couldn't beat Cloppingshire United/Rose City Revolution, then they surely couldn't beat the Giganticos or Toronto, and the other teams in the Liberty Conference—the Flamingos of Florida and Washington, D.C.'s laughable American SuperThunder Super Soccer Team—sure as hell weren't going to trouble anyone.

When Graham Broome thought of it, he could scarcely wipe the smile off his face. He knew there was a long way to go, but he'd never dreamed, not really, that the Rose City Revolution could consider a championship. He had other things on his mind too.

"Where, Danny, where, may I ask, is our physio?"

"Boss—"

"We're in first place, Danny. The Giganticos are coming to town. A tough late-season push, games piled on top of each other. I should think we'll need our physio. Wouldn't you think so, Danny? Any idea where she might be, son?"

Danny began with the simplest, most honest answer: "I don't know," he said. "I don't know where she is." But he knew that wasn't going to do it. He was ashamed even to say it.

"I'd say we're in a spot of bother, then, aren't we?"

They were in Graham Broome's office, beneath Multnomah Stadium, each man worn out and testy. "What do you know, Danny?" He was almost whispering.

"I know she won't be with us against the Giganticos, boss," Danny said quietly, reluctantly. "And not the day after against Florida either. I don't know when we'll see her, Broomsie. I'm sorry. I wish I knew more. But that's what I know." His face flushed, his voice caught, and he backed off.

"Bloody hell," the coach said said.

"Boss—"

"Bloody *hell*," the coach said again, and ran his fingers through his thatched and thinning hair, which he shook slowly, slowly, and he lowered his eyes from Danny and hung his head. "Go," he said. "And when you do know something, tell me." He looked down at the floor. "Bloody get the hell out, big man."

Graham Broome stood in front of his team in the lobby of the Grand Douglas Apartments. Stood right next to him was a familiar face, familiar to Danny anyway, who should have been shocked to see him but was no longer surprised by much of anything.

"As you all know, Molly Hart is the best physio in the league," he said to his squad. "But we'll be without her services for a spell as she has a bit of family business in California to take care of, looking after her mum, which is the right thing for her to do and I'm hardly surprised that someone of her character has made such a decision. The club is behind her one hundred percent, and we've made it abundantly clear that she's welcome back any time she's able to refocus her energies upon the team."

Danny thought Broomsie a remarkable liar, and by the looks on the other faces in the lobby, Danny was right.

"But we need someone looking after you lads, don't we? So we are fortunate indeed to have procured the services of a similarly capable physio, an Englishman, to get us through the rest of the season—through to the Bonanza Bowl, eh, boys?—and I would like to introduce him to you now."

Three waved to the team, nodded, and said, "Pleasure, lads. A real pleasure."

"This is Terry Blackstone," said the Revolution's leader. "Physio'ed in the Northern League with Sullen Town and came over with Dickham Terriers when they played in the league as the Dallas Debacle in 1971. He's available to us for the rest of the summer, and we're happy as Larry to have him. Terry," he said, "meet the Rose City Revolution."

Three said, "Hello, lads. Just happy to be in the mix. Anything I can do, just ask." And he smiled. Three had added something of a Jack-the-Lad affect to his accent, and Danny could see that the Cloppingshire boys were happy to have another Englishman in the mix.

Danny thought, *Of course... of course.*

He walked out the front door of the Grand Douglas Apartments and stood alone in the car park in the rain. He'd never felt so confused, so lost. Life in East Southwich was frustrating and constricting, but you knew who you were and what was expected of you. If you got outside the lines, you were pushed back in. Simple. Now Danny was way outside the lines, playing a game he didn't understand at all. *Where is she?* was all he could think. *Where could she be?*

He jumped in Todd's car—he always left the keys under the seat—and drove it downtown to Surley's spot across the road from Multnomah Stadium, ordered a pitcher, and watched a couple hours of baseball with the regulars. He liked the basketball more—this game was painfully slow—but the men said Portland's team had failed to make the playoffs. He finished more beer than a man should finish before getting in a car, so he took a cab back to the Grand Douglas. Todd would understand.

Where could she be?

TWENTY-FOUR

The Saturday afternoon the Giganticos played in Multnomah Stadium, the rain had moved on and the sun shone as if the Giganticos themselves had brought it with them from Hawaii. And they might have.

The visitors strode out into the Portland sun before thirty thousand Portlanders shoehorned into that Winchester Mansion of a stadium, temporary bleachers here, added seating there, rows of kids sitting on the ground just yards from the touchlines and bylines, fire codes broken everywhere you looked. They wore sky-blue tracksuits with yellow and green trim and GIGAN-TICOS arched across the back in stark white so bright it seemed like neon. They seemed to walk in dramatized slow motion. Each man looked as if his suit had been tailored just for him by Savile Row's finest, and indeed each suit had been on the team's most recent pass through London. They were imperious in their bearing, these men who were the best in the world at what the world loved most; they sniffed the Rose City air as if to pass judgment upon it. The crowd, the Oregonians—the hippies and the stoners and the descendants of fishermen and loggers, who knew so little of the global game but could sense the Giganticos' greatness in their very stride—stood and applauded; the Giganticos blew kisses, they waved, and they bowed. Danny wanted so badly to hate them, but he had rarely seen anything so beautiful.

Before the game, Graham Broome had explained to the team that there were only two ways of managing a game against the

Giganticos: "Defend and hope, or... you can play. You can take it to them, enjoy the moment, try and create a little bit of beauty right along with them. Park the bus and you'll keep the score down," Broomsie told his team. "But you won't feel good about it. Play with them and they'll take you apart," he said. "But it'll be a good show for the people, and you'll have been taken apart by the very best."

After a pause, Broomsie said, "Today, lads, we play."

The Giganticos played close to one another, their passes brisk and fast, like a snappy conversation. Each of them seemed so grateful to receive the ball from such a debonair colleague, each of their first touches easing them into comfortable areas, exquisitely positioning their bodies at ideal angles for them to face wide-open space and never a defender. They made no particular effort in the early stages of the game to advance upon Danny's goal; instead, it was as if they were showing the Revolution how to play, how to elevate *soccer* to *football*, how to raise the game up and off today's uneven artificial baseball turf and into its universally beloved lyricism. Still, they *were* doing it on Multnomah Stadium's uneven artificial baseball turf, when it would have been so easy just to play the ball long out of the back, and though Danny was right there, literally, amidst it, for the first time in his life drawn into the human geometry of football at its highest form, he could scarcely work out how; he could almost detect the proportions, the shapes and curves being drawn upon the field, the tight parabolas being described in Portland's summer air. None of them seemed to move at any greater pace than a casual jog—and yet somehow they connected with their Brazilian centerpiece with every third or fourth pass. He seemed to emerge from another plane whenever they needed him, in just the right place, in just the right position, at just the right speed, and he always, *always*, moved the ball along to its best possible destination... and then disappeared again, only to re-emerge moments later and do the same thing—each time with simple yet surprising flair and grace, his sole placed on the ball for a still moment, the outside of his foot flicking the ball just slightly onto a new course, his hips lowering and shifting so that he didn't need any touch at all to destabilize his midlevel English defender. Danny had dreamed that he knew what self-expression meant in football, but he had never dreamed any of this.

The fans gasped with respect, awe, and confusion; rank novices unlearned enough to lack a true understanding of what it really was but were smart and humble enough to know they were gazing upon something magnificent. Danny knew how much so many would have given in so many parts of the world to be able to see what Portland, Oregon, was seeing now. He knew most of those people deserved to see it more than Portland deserved to see it, but he sensed the reverence in the stands, and his respect for the soccer neophytes of the Rose City went up a few notches.

The Giganticos made only one mistake early in the game, an odd one, the result of a back pass that probably ran a little faster on Portland's matted mat than the Colombian Gigantico defender had meant it to and it had slipped away for a Revolution corner, which came to nothing. And then the Giganticos found their rhythm again, and the magisterial display resumed. Twenty minutes in, they were still playing keep-away, and the match was still scoreless, when somehow Surley found himself with the ball.

For want of a better idea, he backspun a lob toward a corner flag, one of the only players in the entire league who could put a ball in the air with enough torque to make it consider slowing down upon the hardened Multnomah Stadium floor. As it slowed, Juanito and Kelvin chased after it, followed by the Giganticos' graceful world champion Brazilian defender, his mighty Afro and lamb-chop sideburns eased back by the Portland breeze. The Pearl's World Cup teammate eased himself in front of Juanito and Kelvin, shielded the ball on its way out for a goal kick. But it hit the corner flag, ricocheted off the Gigantico's expensive shins, and bobbled out for a corner. The crowd gasped—they had never seen that happen before and they wondered what might happen next—but the gasp morphed into a hesitant cheer as Surley jogged over to the corner to take the kick, and the Revolution's players filled the penalty box. The crowd seemed to think that maybe, maybe...

Surley curled a tight corner goalward with a little extra fizz, and the Belgian goalkeeper had no choice but to tip it over the bar for another Rose City corner. The fans' gasp became a roar. As the round veteran prepared another speculative launch into the area, a Gigantico positioned himself a little too close; Surley hit him with a low, petulant drive—just to be cheeky—and it went for yet another Revolution corner.

This time the 1963 League Vase winner Surley essayed a listless lob, and the Belgian arrogantly collected the cross as if to say, *Enough of this folderol,* and he rolled it out to the big-haired Brazilian, and so resumed the Giganticos' exhibition. Fifteen, twenty passes in a row, and soon even the loyal rooters behind the north goal were cheering the visitors, who were now prancing more than running as they worked the ball through their exquisite Pearl, who would wheel in a direction you would never have imagined he could to make the least likely pass you would have considered, and the Giganticos would have vast swaths of space you hadn't noticed before, and it would all begin again.

And yet, forty minutes in: 0–0.

In the waning moments of the first half, Kelvin, who was playing better with each passing game, becoming a real weapon for the Revolution, won a tackle from an Italian (who seemed offended at Kelvin's nerve) and sprung the ball optimistically—but to no one in particular—down the left wing. He put his head down, speedy Kelvin, got to the ball first and angled himself toward the goal, and just when it looked as if he might shoot, the Belgian clattered into him (even his clattering seemed genteel, but it was a clattering to be sure), and the referee had no choice but to point to the spot.

A penalty kick for the Rose City Revolution. Out of nothing.

The crowd knew this was good. As the men in their green-and-yellow jerseys hung their heads and cleared the box, and as Surley approached the ball, the murmur turned into a hum, and the hum into a rumble, and the rumble became a cheer, and then Surley approached ball, struck it, and...

...the Belgian leapt and balletically palmed the ball around the post. It happened in an instant—the goalkeeper had disappeared from one spot and reappeared in another in a spooky flash, and while the crowd was unpleasantly surprised by the ball not resting inside the Gigantico goal, they once again applauded a stunning moment of European athleticism.

Danny realized, a moment before anyone else, that this failure carried with it an immediate opportunity for redemption: the Revolution was on their fifth corner kick.

He imagined he might have to take it, but—

Broomsie surprised the team by hollering for Kelvin to take the Sniper Shot, he was playing so well, had earned them the opportunity, and Kelvin *converted*, right there under the watchful and eager eyes of the north end crowd, and the good Portland people erupted in confused and ecstatic Portland pride.

Halftime struck, and it was—against all logic, against any expectation—one–nil for the Revolution.

In the tunnel the teams used to disappear underneath the stadium, the Pearl of Brazil jogged by Danny and Peter en route to his halftime break. Peter and Danny stepped back, alarmed to be in his presence, but Peter recovered before Danny and spoke. "Hey, Pearl."

The great man stopped and extended a hand. "Hello," said the greatest footballer in the history of the game. He smiled, as relaxed as if he were out for a stroll. He offered a hand to Danny too.

Both men shook the Pearl's hand. Then Peter looked right into the Pearl's inviting eyes and said, "Bet you never thought you'd be down to us at the half, eh, Mr. Pearl?"

The Pearl smiled again and said, "Ah well. We don't mind. You have a full stadium, don't you? If it were five–zero at the half, the crowd might go home, never come back. Bad for league. We don't want that." He let that sink in and then said, "Now, they stay. They think it is a game, no? We thought you could get two. Gave you a penalty. Ah, you get only one goal, OK. That is not so bad." He paused, then he looked at Danny. "Not so bad, big man." He reached up and patted Danny's hairy cheek. "See you boys in second half." He turned and walked the rest of the tunnel, showing perspiration-drenched Peter Surley and Danny Hooper his dry, sweatless back. The Dutchman was holding the door for him, smoking a cigarette.

In any event, the Revolution took the field for the second half, and the Giganticos beat them 6–1. Danny had never had an experience like the second half of that game, wasn't even aware that it could be done, that one team could keep the ball for that long. The visitors' first two goals came easily, casual tap-ins at the end of long strings of passes during which the Giganticos moved almost imperceptibly closer and closer to the Revolution's goal until there was nothing left to do but walk the ball over the line. For the next two, the Giganticos seemed to have made themselves a deal that no one could shoot until each player had touched the ball and no one could shoot from inside thirty yards. They were mighty blasts, those two goals, but the Lithuanian and the German who struck them had hit the ball with such little visible effort that the Revolution's defenders—and even Big Lou—were a split second too slow to react, and the ball met the back of the Revolution's net still on the rise. And then, as if revealing a long-planned finale, two Pearl goals of shocking grace: airborne, gymnastic maneuvers that left the crowd gasping and the Revolution feeling like magician's assistants. When the referee blew for full time, the most famous man in the world ran behind Multnomah Stadium's north goal and blew kisses to the Revolution faithful. They cheered him as they would cheer any immortal, and he smiled back at them beatifically, casting upon them a blessing he had brought from football's Holy Land.

The duel between the top teams in each conference hadn't been much of a duel at all. The Giganticos had beaten the Revolution by exactly the score with which they chose to beat the Revolution, and they had managed to turn the Rose City faithful into Gigantico fans with what Danny considered the finest forty-five minutes of football he had ever seen.

Danny's dreams of winning a championship withered. It's a funny old game, football—he knew that, and he knew that anything could happen. Except for the Giganticos losing the American All-Star Soccer Association's 1976 Bonanza Bowl in New York City.

Danny had expected a visit from the Communists, but the Communists did not appear. No word on Molly's whereabouts, no word about what awaited the Brazilian or why the Communists wanted the Revolution in the Bonanza Bowl. Nothing at all. Just a football match.

The Rose City Revolution, through the magic of the AASSA's basketball-and-baseball-inspired scheduling, played again the next day, this time against the Flamingos of Florida. The Flamingos had just been battered in Seattle by the Smithereens and limped into Portland with nothing on their minds but getting out of town. Their coach, when asked by Portland's newspaper what he thought of the Pacific Northwest, said, "I hate Canada."

A rare humid Portland sun filled the subterranean bowl like hot, thick liquid that Sunday afternoon. It sat heavy on the plastic stadium floor, turning anyone more than fifteen yards away into a mirage and choking the air with the smell of slowly burning tire. Anyone in Portland who cared about soccer had gotten their fill the day before, so only a couple thousand curious souls turned out to see the Revolution and the Flamingos drag their tired bodies around the pitch on a soupy early-summer Sunday afternoon. The game played out at a desultory pace, and halfway through the first half Danny remarked to himself that he couldn't remember either team passing more than three times in a row. The ball seemed to be out of bounds more than it was in. Broome removed Surley, who looked as if his rapidly reddening head might explode, after about fifteen minutes, much to everyone's relief.

Late in the first half, a Flamingo fired a close-range shot into the roof of the goal that struck the support that held up the back netting. It should have stood as a goal—it had gone in— but the ball rebounded out of the goal so quickly that the poorly positioned referee waved play on, thinking it had gone off the crossbar. The Flamingos protested, but even their protest lacked energy, and the incident seemed to sap them of what little will to win they'd brought all this way from Miami via Seattle. With ten minutes remaining, and only a few hundred people left scattered about the stadium, Kelvin crossed from the left wing, drawing the Flamingos' keeper off his line. He collided with a retreating defender and the ball deflected off one or both of them—tough to tell—and into the goal. That was it. Crap game, crap goal. A one–nil win for the Revolution. No one hung around to sing.

Danny had lost eleven pounds over the last thirty hours of his life. And his shoulder still hurt.

Eight and two. Still first place. The good news: still in line to host the Frontier Conference playoff game for the right to go to New York for the Bonanza Bowl. The bad news: that's exactly what the Communists wanted. For some reason.

Six left to play.

Danny took inventory:

Shoulder, better;

Football, humiliated Saturday, a result Sunday, still in first place;

Molly, well... no. No Molly.

Danny had barely slept since Seaside. Danny was scared to death.

He took an evening ride on his recently acquired bicycle down to the river that split Portland in two, found a bench at the waterfront, and admired the shipyards where welders cast their monstrous shadows against the massive steel walls. Below Danny's bench, railroad tracks hugged the land above a rocky rise from the river. Danny climb down toward the water and threw rocks at the tallest of a series of pilings in the peace of the scene's white noise: a train chugged on the opposite shore, a foghorn descended from up the river, something flew by. Water slapped below; tinny crashes crossed the river from the work on the dry dock. Danny wished Molly was here, throwing stones into the river with him. He hit a piling with a slim river rock—a miraculous shot—then climbed back up the bank to his bicycle and rode up into the hills, to the Grand Douglas Apartments.

Where—and *how*—was she?

TWENTY-FIVE

The league's Washington, D.C., entry was descended from a star-crossed line of unsuccessful attempts to make pro soccer work in the nation's capital. The first Washington entry in the AASSA, 1972's Wonders, had been a run-of-the-mill hodgepodge of foreign bits and bobs who could no more play together than talk to each other. The few fans curious enough to come out for a look left disappointed, and within a short summer the Washington Wonders were no more.

Their 1973 replacement, the Capital Congressionals, covered every bus stop in town with ads featuring their tagline, TWO PARTIES MEANS TWICE THE FUN, but the team, comprising primarily hyper-defensive, Catenaccio-enthralled Italians, was exactly zero fun. Also, most of the area's few soccer fans weren't really sure what the tagline even meant, and it wasn't a good time to try to derive your cool from the federal government. Almost nothing about the Capital Congressionals worked, so that was their only summer in the league.*

👕 The Capital Congressionals achieved some footballing notoriety by presaging the basketball concept of employing unusually tall African tribesmen. A seven-six Rwandan had come to the team's attention through a Peace Corps connection; the Congressionals inserted him amid the Italians late in close matches for corner kicks and free kicks, and he headed in five goals, nearly got the otherwise terrible team into the playoffs. The Congressionals used his garish statistics to sell his contract to a club in Portugal's Second Division, where he continued his scoring ways until he struck his head on a crossbar, retired from soccer, and returned to America to finish his sporting career as a minor-league first baseman with a long reach but much too spacious strike zone.

In 1974, with the sudden collapse of the Philadelphia Phun, the Rochester Foreign Stars, and the Montreal Communards, the league found itself down to seven teams. Needing one more to provide the legitimizing cover of two divisions and the scheduling ease of an even-numbered league, and anxious for a team in the capital city, the AASSA propped up D.C.'s top amateur side, Nico's Deli Pancyprian Greeks, renaming them the USA Americans (worth a try) and paying for a summer's worth of dates at a small college's track-and-field facility and a marketing campaign that gave the illusion that Washington was serious about soccer. The campaign worked (briefly); the soccer, however, did not. Opening day drew a fair crowd to the tiny stadium, but the Bonanza Bowl champions-to-be, the Atlanta Astronauts, eased themselves by the Americans, 6–0. For the team's next home game, against Dallas, most of the opening-day fans stayed away; the hardy few who dropped by saw the Debacle's only win of the season. The Americans played in front of friends and family for the rest of the summer. Even Nico stopped showing up after the fourth game.

Prior to the '75 season, the league's few remaining owners convened a special session to seek legitimate expansion ("Has anyone here ever been to Portland?" was the first question; "The one in Maine?" was the second) and address the D.C. situation. Each owner agreed that a *good* Washington presence, a competitive, respectable team, was key to the league's growth and could generate a future rival for the Giganticos. So they conceived a plan to combine half of a strong British side with half of a reputable South American team. Seattle's owner had a friend in London whose team needed to get out of England for the summer; then all eyes turned to the Flamingos' Cuban owner, who rolled his eyes and said, "Well, you know, Cuba's *not* South America, but I'll make some calls." The league's brass thought the combination would seem semi-relevant to the local diplomatic corps, draw from the city's Anglo and Hispanic communities, and maybe, just maybe, be a pretty good team.

As it happened, the mixture of East London and working-class Buenos Aires made a mockery of the team's maladroit new name: United States United. For a club with "United" in its name twice, the team failed to cohere. This led to a tragedy considerably worse than defeat: during an August game in Los Angeles, the season's stress, the Southern California heat, and a flurry of goals and anti-English invective from Sweet Billy Robinson turned Englishman and Argentine against each other. What started as a nasty spat became a common fistfight and escalated to a pretty good melee before metastasizing into a full-fledged riot involving players, coaches, fans, even a few stray dogs. In the chaos of flying bodies and general '70s mayhem, one of the South Americans choked an Englishman to death, and United's center back, a misplaced Scouse, caved in an Argentinean forehead with a head butt that, a week later, would be given as the cause of the man's demise. The tumult subsided when United's coach, a seven-foot-tall Turk who had taken the job only because he thought USU was a basketball team, withdrew a pair of scissors from the team's medical kit and stabbed the first four players and two dogs he came upon. (Two of the players he stabbed were his own; three players and a dog died.) Most of United's players were detained by the LAPD for periods ranging from twenty-four hours to much, much longer than that, and the team's final three games were written off as forfeits. And that was it for United States United.

These were the events that led the league to conceive 1976's version of pro soccer in the capital city of the United States of America: the American SuperThunder Super Soccer Team.

The august men running U.S. soccer when America turned two hundred years old were sick of having a national team that wasn't any better than a capable ethnic squad from Chicago or New York. They were sick to death of the USA being a team of mediocre collegians and naturalized journeymen who came together only days before their matches against the Netherlands Antilles or Nicaragua, shook each other's hands, and played disjointed, unattractive soccer while failing to beat countries with populations and landmasses approximating Delaware and Rhode Island. The U.S. national team, circa 1976, was a deadly combination in a country obsessed with image: unknown and unwatchable. Americans may have been coming around to the game, slowly, slowly, but they weren't coming around to watching a team that represented their hopes and dreams play—and mostly lose—like *that*. And so soccer's grandees conceived a seemingly splendid triple whammy: get the national team ready for 1978 World Cup qualifying, create a nice media story for the '76 season, and generate some buzz in the Washington, D.C., market. In the bicentennial, even. And call it: *American SuperThunder.*

And so the decision was taken. The Washington Wonders/ Capital Congressionals/USA Americans/United States United would become the American SuperThunder Super Soccer Team, the de facto national team of the most powerful nation on earth (probably), and they would play in the biggest stadium in the capital city of said superpower. Done and dusted. Unanimous vote.

America's best players in 1976 came in three forms: 1) collegians with flashy stats who were about to find out that a league of even the AASSA's middling quality was a quantum leap from the scrappy soccer they'd been playing on the varsity circuit; 2) play-

---

👕 Todd Adams, for example, had scored four goals for Western Washington University in an NAIA league playoff game against a nearby Bible school of 150 students in a Bellingham, Washington, city park while a man threw a Frisbee to his dog and two "fans" sat on a picnic blanket behind one of the goals. Other than those three people and the dog, no one saw the game. But despite the fact that Western Washington won 14–0, and Todd Adams was not a very good player, Todd's name ended up in Soccer USA, a publication with a readership of about five hundred people (including every coach in the AASSA) as the "Offensive Player of the Week"—and so he got a call from the American SuperThunder.

ers who'd been born and raised where the United States had had servicemen at one time or another;* or 3) foreign-born AASSA veterans who'd gotten naturalized in order to benefit from the league's requirement that each team carry three North Americans and have one on the field at all times.*

The league had hoped to assemble a team comprised primarily of the first two categories: fresh-faced Yanks whose names you could pronounce and whose hometowns you could care about, relatable guys who could end up on the cover of the *Sporting Times* in a red, white, and blue jersey with lightning bolts down the sleeves. That seemed a reasonable hope. But there's a difference between a hope and a plan. And very often, especially in American soccer, there's a difference between a plan and reality.

👕 Johnny Doyle, for example, had been born in Hamburg to a German woman who had had a fling with an American soldier. Johnny's mother had never left Germany; he had never met his father and couldn't speak a word of English. But he was a fair German Second Division player and he was 50 percent American, and when offered a contract to play for the American SuperThunder Super Soccer Team in the same league as the Pearl of Brazil, the Dutchman, and Sweet Billy Robinson, he thought that sounded like a pretty good time.

👕 Wednus Maghammar, for example, had come over from the Swedish league because an old friend from Stockholm had been hired as the coach of the '73* Philadelphia Phun. Maghammar thought making a few bucks at the end of his career while touring America sounded like a nice vacation. He bounced around the league a little, met a nice American girl, got his citizenship, got an offer to play for the SuperThunder, had it written into his contract that he wouldn't have to practice on Fridays, and signed up. (*As a Footnote to the Footnote: The 1973 season was notable for the presence of Atlético Caracas, who played in the colors of the Dallas Debacle, and Racing Club Helsinki, who spent the summer as the Phun. The league was initially ecstatic at having landed the Venezuelan and Finnish clubs to represent AASSA teams for the season—until the squads arrived and it came to light that Atlético was a baseball team and Racing was a basketball team. As fortune had it, Dallas and Philadelphia played each other in the first game of the season; in a high-scoring affair, the Phun used its size advantage to keep the Debacle from scoring for most of the first half, but the dam eventually broke and the smaller, faster baseball players outscored the Helsinki hoopsters 9–4 over a poorly played ninety minutes that didn't look that much different from any other AASSA game that year.)

The kids coming right out of college wanted to play for established teams with established players, not some new outfit with a cockamamie marketing scheme, and the Americans who'd been in the league for a few years and were worth anything at all had nice gigs going with L.A., or Seattle, or Detroit, or even the Giganticos (who needed to fill the quotient too), and saw no reason to leave those teams to join up with the SuperThunder. To make matters worse, despite voting to make the team a reality, the owners and coaches who actually liked the Americans on their rosters weren't keen on letting them go. So when word got out that a few of the best Americans weren't joining the SuperThunder after all, the next few figured out that turning down the opportunity wasn't *exactly* the same thing as turning down the national team, and the enterprise started to unravel.

But it was too late. The American SuperThunder Super Soccer Team had been sold to the public as the U.S. national team and as the AASSA's contribution to the bicentennial celebration. The maestros of the U.S. federation had even assembled something called the Bicentennial SuperCup, in which the SuperThunder would represent America against the national teams of Ireland, Mexico, and Brazil (yes, Brazil) in some pretty big stadiums, in some pretty big cities.

So... *someone* needed to find some "American" soccer players, and fast.

The Johnny Doyle, Wednus Maghammar, and Todd Adams of earlier footnotes were joined by one Andrzev Dwørczyk, a Polish Georgian from Chicago who'd had a falling out with the Butchers, and by a former NFL punter named Dave something who volunteered to play in goal, and there were three friends of Todd's from Western Washington who Todd said were OK but who weren't, and a couple of guys from the Nico's Deli team whose papers checked out, and Maghammar's brother, who hurried over from Sweden and gained surprisingly quick citizenship. Graham Broome volunteered every Todd he had for the cause, but they were at a disadvantage versus the Western Washington kids because people had seen them play.

The American SuperThunder Super Soccer Team, in star -spangled Evel Knievel uniforms featuring winged collars, lightning bolts down their sleeves and shorts, and V-necks that descended nearly to their navels, played their first game in Boston against the Irish national team. A Boston visit from the Irish guaranteed a decent crowd, and the while the game had been promoted as a "New American Revolution," it was the same old same old: in front of twenty thousand mostly Irish fans, the Americans were played off the park, conceding three in each half while firing no shots on the Irish goal. The Dublin paper's headline: "Nice Kit, Though."

Their second contest was the AASSA opener at home against the Giganticos. The game had been scheduled the day the SuperThunder was conceived, when hopes for an America vs. the Rest of the World soccer extravaganza to launch the bicentennial summer were at their highest. A nice crowd came out to see the international stars of World Cup '74 play the American hopefuls of World Cup '78 on a brightly colored pitch—one penalty box had been painted red, the other blue, and the center circle featured the SuperThunder's logo—a red, white, and blue soccer ball featuring a star and a lightning bolt—and the Giganticos did their part to keep things interesting, but there's only so much the world's best can do against the fake U.S. national team, and in time the Giganticos—and everyone else—came to realize that not scoring was a greater offense than pouring it on. And so they poured it on: 7–0 was the final, and the dream of the American SuperThunder died on national TV with fifteen matches and three full internationals—including one against Brazil—still on the docket.

The league managed to substitute the Giganticos for the SuperThunder against the mighty Brazilians, with the Pearl playing a half for both teams. It was one of the brightest days of that summer's soccer calendar, drawing a worldwide TV audience in the many millions. Brazil won 2–1 on a sunny day in Miami to the delight of an overflow crowd. As for the American SuperThunder Super Soccer Team, they did win games here and there—over the Flamingos and the Cowhands, and they picked up a shock Super Soccer Showdown triumph in Seattle. But mostly they toured the country as a pale representative of the American Dream and lost a string of three– and four–nil games, disappearing from the playoff hunt before the first half of the season was over. By the time they rolled into Portland, they were 3-9 and traveling with a skeleton squad of just fourteen men, and the league had asked them to shorten their name to the American Thunder, just to make the experiment that much less embarrassing.

The American Thunder played the Revolution on a cool Wednesday night. The Portland press had sold the visitors under its guise as the U.S. national-team-in-training, so that brought a few patriotic sports fans out of the woodwork for their first soccer game, and the Revolution's rowdy crew from the back of the north goal returned after their Sunday afternoon off, all contributing to another lively crowd. Not Giganticos or Smithereens lively, but the old building hummed just a bit from the buzz of the home team taking on something as grand as a possible U.S. national team. Even Danny was excited (though he had yet to meet an American player he thought was worth anything, other than maybe Juanito, who he knew could help the Thunder—though they'd never called and Graham Broome would never have let him go). International football was well beyond the most distant of distant dreams for Danny's like, beyond even the horizon of his hope of winning a championship. Danny knew he'd never play for his national team, but at least now he was, in a manner of speaking, playing against *a* national team.

While his championship dreams were alive—he knew the Revolution could at least get to the Bonanza Bowl—the American Thunder failed to quench Danny's thirst for international football. They were pathetic. What their naturalized imports created, their native youngsters wasted: passes directly at the feet of the American boys slipped away and out of bounds; players left wide open to cross the ball floated their aimless speculations behind the goal; the Thunder's fullbacks misplayed the simplest of loose balls so that Juanito learned to wait five yards away, pick the ball up off their shins, and slide by them toward their awkward but gargantuan gridiron-football-refugee of a goalkeeper. Juanito missed a few chances through raw fear of the mammoth goalie (whose main method of keeping his team in the game was running as fast as he could toward any attacker who approached him, regularly leaving the box), and so did Kelvin and two of the Todds, but in time Surley determined to draw the beast out and then either chip him or lay the ball off for someone else to walk it in—and the Revolution cruised to a 5–1 victory, and it could've been worse.

After the match Johnny Doyle approached Danny and began miming for a jersey exchange. *A jersey exchange?* Danny thought. *After a match like that?* It seemed an offense to one of football's most gentlemanly of traditions; it seemed less than dignified to even play-act a ritual hard-earned by the greatest footballers on the planet. A photograph of the Pearl himself exchanging jerseys with England's captain at the '70 World Cup was one of the most famous images in soccer history; pictures of men carrying trophies Danny could only dream about in their opposite number's shirt became tribal talismans to entire nations—and now here was a man who wanted Danny to take a tasteless (yet dazzling) jersey that seemed better suited to *American Bandstand* than to a time-honored ceremonial rite of the football tribe in exchange for Danny's red-and-black RCR shirt. Danny didn't even know if the Revolution had another number 5 jersey.

"Me?" Danny said, pointing to himself as Johnny Doyle came near. "You want my shirt?" *Maybe the Thunder have been coached to do this after every game? Just to keep up the charade?* Danny thought.

Doyle, whose English wasn't great for someone named Johnny Doyle but was pretty good for a German, said, "Yes. I want your shirt." Doyle's shirt was already off. He held it like a dishrag. "Here. It would be an honor for you to have mine."

Danny screwed up his face and looked down on Doyle with a patronizing wince. "*An honor?* Why's that?"

Doyle reached his arm up and around Danny's neck, mimicking the way England's captain had embraced the Pearl in that 1970 photograph, and spoke into Danny's ear: "Because you are the man who will save the Pearl."

Danny pulled back—snapped back—from Doyle's half-embrace. "What did you just say?"

"We know, Danny. We know who you are and why you are here. You're here to save him."

"You don't know who I am."

"Yes, I do. *We* do. You are not from *Cloppingshire*. You're not one of these... these guys." He cast his gaze upon the rest of Danny's new team. "You're here to save the Pearl of Brazil. From the Communists. For all of us," Doyle said. "Now give me your shirt, Danny. This is now looking suspicious."

Danny complied, even though it hurt his shoulder—now that the adrenaline was gone—to do it. He even put on Doyle's American Thunder jersey, which was two sizes too small and crept up to Danny's navel. Danny said, "How do you know this?"

Johnny said, "That doesn't matter. We know, Danny, and we are behind you all the way. Save him, Danny. You must save him."

"Do you know where Molly Hart is? Do you know where Molly—"

But Doyle turned and ran away. Danny ran after him— "WHERE IS MOLL—?"—but Doyle kept running, and Doyle was too damn fast. And Danny knew he'd heard him. Bloody Johnny Doyle didn't know where Molly was. So Danny stopped and turned and found himself facing the Revolution's north end supporters, who let out a desperate yell for their giant center back in his silly new costume. Danny jogged over to them, took off Doyle's American Thunder shirt, and hurled it into the crowd. *Good riddance,* he thought. They went wild.

Danny, with considerable effort—his shoulder and his heart still aching in the worst way—clapped his hands above his head, a thank-you to Portland's emerging soccer minions. He inhaled a little of the pot smell that had drifted down to field level, then jogged into the stadium's ancient undercarriage, wiping sweat and tears from his anguished and tired eyes.

Three stood behind the training table rewrapping Danny's shoulder and gave Danny the first good news he'd gotten in days.

"We know where Molly is, Danny."

Danny sat up a little straighter and raised an eyebrow. "Really?"

"Really."

"Is she all right?"

"She's all right. For now—but they wouldn't have her if they weren't going to use her. Somehow. To get what they want." He paused. "However it comes to pass that we see Molly again, it will be because of you."

Danny breathed, then thought, then spoke. "This is your fault, Three. I hold you responsible for this, for this—"

"For this *what*, Danny?" Three walked around the table, stood in front of Danny, and spoke in a low voice. "For you becoming expendable at East Southwich Albion? For you falling for her? For you running off to a remote seaside town with a government agent who any idiot would've known was in a vulnerable position? Any of this sounding like *my* fault so far?"

One of the Todds appeared behind Three and said, "Hey, Blackstone, when you're done with Danny can I get you to look at my ankle?"

Three turned and, in a deft return to his physio persona, asked Todd for a few moments. "Tell the lads I'll be with all of them in five minutes. The big man's shoulder is a right mess, it is." Todd said, "Thank you," turned, and left, all smiles.

Danny, once again, wished to hit Three in the face. Three could see it in his eyes, so Three asked it again: "My fault?"

"Sod off" was all Danny had in response to that. "You didn't tell me Johnny Doyle, Johnny Doyle of the American bloody Thunder, is in on all this."

"Excuse me?"

"Johnny Doyle told me I'm going to save the Pearl of Brazil."

Three went silent for a moment, his face slack. "That's right, Three. It would seem as if someone"—he spoke as slowly as he could—"in Washington, D.C., or elsewhere, is aware that Danny Hooper of the Rose City Revolution has been tapped by the hand of fate to play some small role in preventing the Communists from assassinating the greatest player our game has ever known. Any of this making any sense to you?"

Three rubbed his chin. "Yes, yes... I think I see what they're going to ask of you in exchange for the fair Molly Hart."

Todd reappeared in the doorway between the changing room and the training table. "About the ankle, Blackstone—"

"*Go!*" barked Danny and Three in unprecedented unison. Todd went.

"All right then, Three. What is the quid pro quo? You mind explaining?" He took a breath.

"Of course. The Bonanza Bowl. On the telly. In front of the world. They'll take him out then. The Pearl—"

"The Pearl?"

"But they'll need help. Possibly your help."

"My help?" They were whispering now. "I'll never help them—"

"Of course not. You're a good lad. You would never *help* help them, unless..."

"Unless..." Danny and Three looked each other in the eye.

"Exactly, Danny."

Danny's shoulder spasmed, and he winced. "Oah," he said, and stepped back a little.

"Yes," Three said, still bearing a look of discovery. "They want you to help them pull off the most visible murder since, well, JFK maybe. That *was* a big one. Don't mean to be flip, lad, but this could be up there."

"But how does Johnny Doyle know?"

"That's a good question. Doyle may be here in America for reasons unknown to you and me. Might have to see if I can track the lad down. What matters is that unless we do something in the next three weeks, something I have not yet determined, you're either going to have to participate in the televised murder of the most famous man in the world, or you're never going to see Molly Hart again. One or the other. How *is* that shoulder, by the way? Todd! Get in here, Todd! Let's have a look at that bloody ankle of yours."

That afternoon in New York, the Pearl had pitched the first three innings of the Mets' shutout win over San Francisco. It was the Mets' first sellout of the season.

TWENTY-SIX

Peter and Danny sat at their new local, poring over an official AASSA match program and each team's remaining schedule. They had only five matches remaining to secure their playoff spot: at Seattle and Colorado and then a nice little home stretch to finish things off, against Los Angeles, Chicago, and, for drama, the Smithereens again.

"Won't be easy," Peter said.

"What do you want, an egg in your beer?" said their waitress. Neither man had any idea what she meant.

In any other league in the world, five matches would have meant five weekends, maybe four with the odd midweek fixture. In the AASSA, in 1976, it meant just two: the Thursday night in Seattle was followed by a Sunday trip to Colorado, then home for a Wednesday-Friday-Sunday grind against the Glitter, Butchers, and Smithereens.

"If we don't beat those Romanians in Colorado..." Danny said.

"Least of our troubles, kid," Peter offered in response.

They'd be shattered to be sure, but if the Revolution could gut it out, hold on to that top spot, they'd earn the right to host a semifinal against either Chicago or Seattle for the conference title and a trip to New York for the Bonanza Bowl. But as matters stood, the Butchers and the Smithereens were fast gaining on the Revolution—either team could yet steal the top spot, and the math made clear (Graham Broome had calculated every possible result) that a run of bad fortune (or a sudden reversion to 1975 form) could bump the Revolution all the way down to third... and out of the playoff picture altogether.

No Bonanza Bowl, no saving anyone's life, no *Molly*.

The Thursday bus to Seattle was a bullet of nervous and tired testosterone. Cloppingshire footballers were, by tradition, ill prepared for a championship stretch; other than Surley, no one in the bus had ever won anything.

Municipal Stadium was packed to the rafters. Nowhere left to sit, nowhere left to stand. It wasn't big—even "packed" meant only fourteen thousand people, give or take—but it was loud, and those fourteen thousand were right on top of you. It felt to Danny like they were *too* close: there was no track here, no baseball outfield—this was an *American* football stadium, built for battle, and Danny could *feel* these people, *feel* their *hate*. He couldn't believe these people hated the Rose City Revolution this much after only two years of rivalry, but he was starting to get it: it was Seattle-Portland, these two cities that had more in common than not, two peoples with the same trees, the same mountains, the same sky—but not the same teams.

This was derby-level madness, and Danny was impressed. People divided by their similarities. Danny loved it. He knew this was going to be hell. The Seattleites had even painted a sign in Danny's honor—he was already an enemy in this rivalry. The sign said SASQUATCH SIGHTING—he didn't know who Sasquatch was, but he got the idea: the sign featured a crude rendering of a giant gorilla-type beast wearing a red-and-black-striped number 5. *OK then*, Danny thought. *Someone will have to pay for that.* But still, he admired it.

Danny had never really understood the home-field advantage—it was still eleven-on-eleven, but somehow the home side elevated their game just that little bit, and that meant they were first to every loose ball, harder in the tackle, stuck in just that little bit more... but *why*? Why was the first ten minutes of matches like these such a nightmare? You knew you'd be peeling men off you, you knew you'd be untangling their legs from yours, you knew you'd be blindsided at least once, suffer some ridiculous foul, and the referee would play-act a *calm down*—Danny hated the whole pantomime, mostly because he played that way all the time and despised players who needed a derby, and their own home supporters, to wind them up. But Danny did respect the fans, the electricity, the anger, the emotion. If this game ever catches on in this country, Danny figured, it will be because of places like this, rivalries like this.

And then a Yorkshireman six inches shorter than Danny clattered into him with a scything knee-high tackle that might have ended Danny's career if the lad had been big enough to do anything other than just annoy him. The Yorkshireman—Yorkshire squire, really—had intended grievous harm but had only fouled Danny, not damaged him. He had ended up the one on the ground too, and had only left Danny blinded with rage and in no bloody mood. Danny leaned over the Smithereen from Leeds as the referee attempted to intervene and told the referee that if anyone in green, especially this little twat, tried that again he'd kill him.

The Smithereen lay on the turf giving Danny two fingers and telling him all sorts of terrible things, and Danny ignored him and walked away across the boy, planting one foot in the kid's groin and the other in the palm of his nonsignaling hand. The Smithereen grunted, and the referee saw it, but the Revolution took the free kick and the game went on, now well and truly kicked off.

To Danny's dismay, he found that he had only enraged the crowd, fired up the home side, and put the Revolution on the back foot. Seattle came at them in waves. Big Lou screamed behind Danny for help *here* and help *there*, but Seattle attacked with the kind of adrenaline rush that people get when they need to lift cars off babies. Danny hollered at his halfbacks to join the rearguard, thinking that if the Revolution could keep the Smithereens from scoring for another eight or ten minutes the insanity might pass and the game would settle into actual football—*They just can't keep this up,* he thought, *this is madness*—but Seattle broke through. The great Bulgarian, Petrov, collected a punched Big Lou clearance and drove it into the net from twenty-five yards. A mighty goal. The fans in their concrete bleachers bawled for more, and minutes later, the Smithereens scored off a corner, and just before half Petrov scored again. The crowd was delirious. The noise from the cement stands rose out over the field and collided in a joyous racket above the players, and Danny wondered what it was about these people's lives that they could be so happy about a 3–0 halftime lead over the Rose City Revolution for their Seattle Smithereens. He felt foreign, like there was something about northwestern American life that he would never understand, like there was something amongst those logs on the highway, something in that inscrutable soggy sky, that explained why they had fallen for this game so fast, so hard—as an American could never truly understand what it was that made East Southwich so hideously desperate.

The second half lacked the crackle of the first. The Seattle crowd and the Seattle team seemed spent by the fervor and the fever of the first forty-five—but the Smithereens were still the better team, and by a fair margin. Two Sniper Shots landed in the Rose City goal, the Smithereens tapped in a meaningless but spiteful late goal, and the affair petered out to a dismal six–nil defeat for the Revolution.

Danny's team squad was jeered off the pitch. Juanito was doused with a flying beer.

The Rose City Revolution was going the wrong way. Danny wondered whether the Russians wanted them in the Bonanza Bowl anymore. Sure didn't feel like it.

The Smithereens, the goddamned green Smithereens, were 8-4; the Revolution, 9-3. They were separated by only ten points in the twisted algorithm of the AASSA's point system. *This could all go terribly, terribly wrong,* Danny thought.

Terribly wrong.

The Revolution flew to Denver and stayed at an old downtown hotel. Graham Broome had made the executive decision that he'd had enough of North Beef in the team's first visit and had determined to spend as little time there as possible this time around. They stayed at a place called the Diplomat, a grand hotel with a lobby photo display in celebration of the bicentennial, even though the city was only about 120 years old. The photos showed Denver before modernity, is how Danny saw it: before the Italian section had become an off-ramp, and before the squat brick building at the 74-219 interchange had become a bank, instead of the clubhouse for the nine-hole course that formerly lay in the 74's eastbound lanes. He imagined someone probably still lived in the hotel who knew someone who had accomplished a hole-in-one at Smallstone East in 1937. He imagined jazz, financiers, a basement bowling alley. It all transported him, put him in mind of East Southwich's days of yore as well, the football clubs founded by miners and their churches and social clubs, their tours of Brittany, their forgotten triumphs and defeats. He loved the pictures, he loved the stories, and when he turned the corner to take in a newer era, to see what had become of Denver sportsmen during the war, he came upon men that he did not love.

"I am Lev, Danny. There is no longer reason for you not to know my name."

Danny's heart stopped. The blood left his face. He nearly fainted.

"It is OK, Danny. It is OK. I admire you very much. Everything the Revolution has done. All of your many successes. We did not think you could do what you have done. Yes, we have helped. We have helped very much, but still, Danny. All of these victories."

Danny closed his eyes, restored himself to this moment. "How about your friend here?"

Lev said, "That is not a name you need, Danny. But you should shake his hand."

Danny said, "Rather not."

"Actually, Danny, you should."

Danny rolled his eyes. *These blokes and their bloody hand-shakes.* He shook it.

"Isn't Denver remarkable, Danny?" Lev said. "The history. I really love it. We do not have anything quite like it. The cowboys. All these cowboys and their big hats."

"What do you want?" Danny said.

"Ohhhhhh, here in Denver? Not much. Everything is in order. Your Molly is safe. Your team is on target for the Bonanza Bowl. You are playing such wonderful football. So are the Giganticos. Now that everything is working so well, we thought we would come and watch one more game in rodeo ground and say hello to you. Why not, Danny? We feel like you are a friend."

"We are not friends, Lev."

"I know what you mean, but... you know what I mean too."

There was something about that last remark that hit harder than Lev probably even meant it to hit. Danny knew. He knew what Lev meant.

The Colorado Cowhands had three wins against ten defeats in their cowboy shirts, and they were anchored to the bottom of the Frontier Conference. While the Romanians who made up the team may have been good players in ideal circumstances, their mile-high rodeo adventure had been a complete failure. Most of the Romanians were no longer even around: six had defected into the Rocky Mountain hinterland, four had returned to the mother country, and one was in jail. The club had replaced them with local fill-ins, and the existing version of the Cowhands was almost inexcusably bad. As a promotion, they had even played one home game with a team comprised entirely of boys who had been raised by wolves and adopted by a local family. While the youngsters had never played soccer before, they were aggressive and seemed to want a win more than the Romanians ever had; the Flamingos of Florida managed only a 4–2 victory. The Cowhands had expressed interest in signing the boys for the rest of the summer only to learn that they too had disappeared into the wilderness.

When your season's showing signs of unraveling and you aren't sure that your team is any good at all, a trip to Colorado might well be just the thing.

The atmosphere in North Beef, Colorado, was entirely different for the Revolution's thirteenth match of the 1976 season from what it had been for the Cowhands' home opener. No parade, no marching bands or tractors or Cadillacs or rodeo clowns. The little town seemed to be over the Cowhands before the Cowhands' season was over—but the bus driver's instructions were the same: go to the parking lot of North Beef's only 7-Eleven and someone from the team will meet you there.

The man who met the Revolution at the 7-Eleven was one of the men who'd greeted the team before the parade on opening day, and he was dressed as he'd been dressed on that festive occasion: in a cowboy hat, a bolo tie, a satin Colorado Cowhands jacket, and cowboy boots. But there the similarities ended; then, the man had been a jovial civic booster—now he was all business.

The man and his hat approached the bus, climbed the stairs, and stood next to the driver. "Good to have you boys back here in North Beef," he said, rubbing his crisp, calloused hands together. "We have a real soft spot for you Oregon boys here in these parts after that parade and all—our first game at the rodeo arena. Darn it, that was fun to watch, even if we didn't win." But he did not smile.

Danny was sure most of the lads had never been called an "Oregon boy" before and it hadn't landed quite right. The man sensed the team's antipathy in its murmur of ambivalent thanks and moved on. "Anyhoooooooo," he drawled (but he still didn't smile), "the summer hasn't gone exactly as we'd hoped or planned around these parts. Don't know that North Beef has quite taken to soccer exactly, and darned if the Romanians didn't quite take to little ol' North Beef, Colorado, neither." He laughed to himself a little. "We've lost quite a few of them actually," he said, and seemed to lose himself in thought. And then, with western gusto: "In any case, boys, *welcome* back. Sorry we won't be providin' you quite the audience you had for your last visit, but we'll see if we can make it a good time all the same. Meanwhile, I wonder if I might have a word with your trainer? We've got a few injuries on our team and I understand you have someone who's been around the game just a little bit. We've got a baseball man, I'm afraid, and he seems a little bam-*boooo*zled by the bumps and bruises of your foreign game. You did bring along your trainer, didn't you?"

Three raised his hand. "Yes, sir, we did bring a trainer, and I am he." He strode forth from the fifth row of the bus, hand extended. "Blackstone's the name, good sir. Terry Blackstone. Over the moon to help."

"Good to meet you, Blackstone," the man from North Beef said. He gave Three's hand a mighty tug that almost took the spy to the ground. "Say, I wonder if you'd step off the bus for just a quick minute. Like to bend your ear some about our *ma*ny and *sun*dry maladies, and I fear it would bore the rest of the boys here just *sil*ly. Know what I mean, Blackstone?"

Three told the man that he knew exactly what he meant, and the two men left the bus. They stood with each other in the 7-Eleven parking lot and talked for longer than you'd think they might, talked solemnly and seriously. After a few minutes, Three walked back toward the bus. But the man stood right where he was, reached into the pocket of his light blue satin Colorado Cowhands jacket, pulled out a pack of cigarettes, put one in his mouth and lit it. Three walked up the first couple of steps of the bus and said, "Danny Hooper? Would you mind coming on out here for just a wee moment, please?"

Danny didn't like the sound of that—and he wished he'd been more surprised by it—but he rose, looked at Broome, who gave him a look that said, *I'm just the coach of this outfit is all...* , and walked through another light Revolutionary murmur to the front of the bus.

Danny and Three got off the bus together and walked toward the man in the satin jacket. As they walked, Three said, "So sorry to do that in front of the lads, Danny. There really just wasn't any other way. We'll manufacture some story about an injury you've got that one of theirs is dealing with too. It'll sound like a lie, but the boys will let it go. I'm quite afraid this is a conversation we have to have right here, and right now."

When Danny and Three got to the man, the man said, "Thanks, Three," and he introduced himself to Danny. "I don't understand your sport," he said. "Not one bit. Don't much care for it, truth be told. But you're good at it, Mr. Hooper. I respect that." A little of the cowboy had gone out of his accent. He blew a long stream of smoke out of the corner of his mouth and it disappeared into the thin Colorado air. "I'm good at my job too. You know what my job is?"

"No," Danny said. "I don't. What's your job?"

"Fucking with Russians," the man stated with a frontier directness.

Then he explained to Danny that when the plan started, the Butchers were in on it. Then it turned out the Ukrainians the Russians sent over met up with some distant relatives in Chicago and decided to defect. They thought they had some dirt on Ivan Petrov, and the Smithereens were already a good team so they could get Petrov to the Bonanza Bowl... but their intel on him wasn't any good and he wouldn't play ball. "Then the Russians gave us all these Romanians and told them to 'stand by for further instructions.' But our season kind of imploded, and the captain of the team had a crisis of conscience and spilled the beans. But Broomsie... Broomsie was always their plan Z. He really is a Communist, you know." Danny turned and looked at the bus, made eye contact with his coach, who smiled back, a little weakly, like he knew what they were talking about. "But he's a softie," the man from Colorado went on. "Wouldn't hurt a fly. Really wants to win that damn Bonanza Bowl." He sucked on his cigarette. Danny leaned in. "Anyway, Danny—this leaves you. You gotta save the Pearl, kid." He threw his cigarette to the ground.

The man lit up again. "See, Danny, that Petrov is a prince of a man. And the Ukrainians and the Romanians too—they're all good guys. And since they know what the Russians are planning, they want to get to the Bonanza Bowl to stop it. Save the great Pearl of Brazil themselves. The Russians didn't know what to do—and then they thought of the Revolution. No disrespect, Hooper, but nobody—and I do mean nobody—expected the Rose City Revolution to have a shot at the Bonanza Bowl. I mean... come on. When you guys tied Seattle in the preseason, we started paying attention. So did the Russians. Good dudes, when it comes down to it. Just doing their patriotic duty. Lev anyway. Nice guy. Spent a nice holiday with him and his family on the Black Sea..."

"A poet of sorts," Three agreed. "And a keen football mind. Remember that Sandpoint story? Sent those Butchers to Idaho? That was a good one."

"Always liked that kid," said the man from Colorado.

Danny looked at them in disbelief.

"This job's like any other," the man said. "We have professional regard for each other."

"I still don't understand why you just don't cancel it. Or forbid the Pearl to play. Or something."

Three tsked him and the man chuckled. "That wouldn't be fair now, would it? Would you give up in the middle of a game, or a match, or whatever it is you call it, just because things weren't going your way?"

Danny could feel the gaze of the boys on the bus. "Finish your story."

"Oh yeah. Yeah. Sorry, Danny. Anyway, then you went and beat Toronto, and when you won here, Lev and the boys set plan Z into motion. Made sure we had a three-team race in the Frontier Conference—and they made sure that if they needed any help from the Revolution, they had something you wanted back."

"So how do we get Molly back?"

"We'll figure something out. We usually do. This isn't the first stunt they've tried. But we keep crushing their dreams, Hooper, and we're going to crush this one too."

Danny looked at Three. Three nodded an approval of this man and his story. "Keep winning, son. Seattle and Chicago still want to get to New York. They don't know the plan and they can't save the Pearl. The Russians—the ones you've been talking to—have lost control of the Smithereens and the Butchers." The man flicked another cigarette to the ground and said, "You have to get to the Bonanza Bowl on your own, or we can't get Molly back, or save this Brazilian superman of yours."

The three of them looked at one another in the car park of the North Beef 7-Eleven, and Danny missed England.

"Today, Hooper, you and your friends will leave North Beef with a win, you have my guarantee of that. But you better take care of business against Chicago and Seattle, Danny, or we've got trouble. *Global* trouble, you got me, Hooper?" He sucked in some smoke and said, "Now grab your knee. Point to where it hurts." He pretended to care about Danny's knee. "Yes, yes. I think you'll be fine. Now go win those games."

Danny let go of his knee. The man laughed and pressed the pack of cigarettes into Danny's hand and said, "Now get on the bus and offer some of those limey friends of yours a cancer stick."

It was an easy game for the Revolution at the North Beef Stampede Days Arena. The Cowhands played as if they'd thrown matches before—they even led for a while just before halftime—but they got out of the way when they needed to get out of the way, and none of the alleged 1,785 in attendance left with the idea that they'd seen anything other than a fairly competitive 8–3 victory for the Rose City Revolution over the Colorado Cowhands that featured Danny's first hat trick.

The Giganticos won that day too. Actually, they won twice: once in an exhibition over the champions of Austria and then in a league game against Detroit. The Pearl had played the first half against the Viennese visitors and the second half against the Demolition, contributing six goals and four assists to the Giganticos' thirteen-goal total haul. Fifty thousand people had turned out in New York for the festivities, including the secretary of state of the United States of America, who had embraced the Pearl and the Dutchman between games.

TWENTY-SEVEN

AMERICAN ALL-STAR SOCCER ASSOCIATION STANDINGS

Frontier Conference

	W	L	GF	GA	P
Rose City Revolution	10	3	42	30	69
Chicago Butchers	9	4	34	18	60
Seattle Smithereens	8	5	50	19	59
L.A. Glitter	4	9	32	33	35
Colorado Cowhands	2	11	40	66	27

Liberty Conference

	W	L	GF	GA	P
x-Giganticos	13	0	58	13	104
x-Red Star Toronto	9	4	39	22	58
Detroit Demolition					*Doesn't matter*
Flamingos of Florida					*Irrelevant*
American SuperThunder			*A national embarrassment*		

x-guaranteed playoffs

The Liberty Conference's playoff was already set, had been for weeks: the Giganticos would host Red Star in New York.

In the Frontier Conference, however, things were a little tighter.

The day before the Glitter game, a reporter asked Big Lou if Portland could ever really "fall in love with soccer."

"As far as we're concerned, it already has, mate," Big Lou said. "Compared to most places we go, this is bloody Soccer City, USA." The headline in the paper the next day read "Soccer City, USA, Ready for L.A. Visitors." It stuck.

When the Los Angeles Glitter came to Soccer City, USA, on a balmy evening, the stadium was almost full, jittery, and loud. The smell of hops and barley wafted into the stadium from the downtown breweries, and the sweet smell of whatever the boys were smoking high up in the north end drifted down to the field from the ancient wooden rafters. Danny could feel the lads soaking in Portland's new soccer love and buzz; they stood in their end watching Los Angeles warm up by the south goal, their sequined jerseys nearly blinding to look upon in the bright glare of the setting Oregon sun. "What a pack of poofters," one of the Trevors said. It was the first time Danny had heard him speak in a month.

The home team had an advantage beyond their more dignified kit: Sweet Billy had called Graham Broome ahead of the match and demanded he be allowed to score or he wasn't making the trip.

Broomsie knew Sweet Billy well enough not to be surprised, so he gave Sweet Billy a simple "no" and prepared to hang up the phone.

"*Think on it now,* Broomsie," Billy barked. "I'm here to bring in the crowds, ain't I? It's why I'm in America, Graham, innit? No Billy, no crowds, mate. No crowds, no money for ol' Cloppingshire Graham Broooome."

Broomsie said, "Billy, you're pissed as a newt, and you can well bugger off. We don't need your help to fill the place, and we're not letting anyone score on us tomorrow. Not you, not anyone."

Billy said, "Don't need me help? Of course you do, Broomsie. Final offer. I'll nae play unless you let me stick it in. Don't ask much, do I—just need the one."

Graham Broome said, "We'll fill the ground on our own, Billy. Portland's Soccer City, USA, or hadn't you heard? That's you and me done. Cheers." And he hung up the phone. Broomsie had been right, and Broomsie had been wrong: the Revolution would indeed fill the stadium on their own, but he and Sweet Billy were not done.

After telling Danny about Sweet Billy's attempted shake-down, the coach said, "Are you ever going to tell me what happened in that car park in Colorado?"

Danny felt something shift in his stomach, but he kept the flicker of surprise from reaching his face and said, "Probably not, boss."

"'Probably not,' hmm? *'Probably,'* is it? That's a good word, Danny, a mysterious word. A mysterious word for a mysterious man."

Danny did not respond.

"So," Broomsie said, "what probabilities *would* lead to you telling me about that conversation in the car park in Colorado?"

"If I had to tell you, I'd tell you, I reckon. I'd tell you if I had to."

"If you had to, then."

"That's right, boss."

Broomsie put his hand on Danny's shoulder. "My boy..." and then he just walked away.

So the Los Angeles Glitter came to Portland without one of the greatest British footballers of the 1960s and early '70s, and the good people of the Rose City still filled Multnomah Stadium, and the Revolution rolled over the despondent, bored, and besequined Glitter 3–1.

Multnomah Stadium was starting to feel downright English. The Portlanders clapped politely when a Revolution player made a nice pass into space or controlled a difficult ball with a deft touch. They no longer chanted, "De*fense*, de*fense*, de*fense*," when the opposition crossed the half-way line, and they even seemed to have gained a decent understanding of the offsides rule—at least enough to boo every time it was called on their team. And the booing—Danny loved the booing. He loved the maniacs behind the north goal, and the eruptions from the crowd after each goal took Danny back home. Danny wanted a playoff game for these people. He wanted a playoff game for other reasons too, but he thought these new and hungry soccer fans deserved a winner almost as much as the good people of East bloody Southwich. "We are, we are the Revs," they chanted, and it washed over the team and brought smiles to the faces of men whose careers had not prepared them to smile at the sweaty ends of football matches, had not prepared them to be thinking about a championship this late in a season, had not prepared them to be happy.

The Revolution's record was now 11-3, sitting on 77 points, and ready for the Butchers and the Smithereens to come to town.

Lev put the envelope in Danny's hand. "You played well against Los Angeles, Danny. They are good team. Better than people think."

"We can be better."

"Of course you can. Of course. But for America, that was good football, Danny."

"Thanks, I suppose. Anyway, nice to be out of the woods, innit?" Danny said, looking at the Grand Douglas Apartments from the building's parking lot.

Lev said, "You are not out of the woooods yet. Oh no." He threw his cigarette at Danny's feet and turned to walk toward his car. "Keep playing good football, Danny!" he shouted. "It is pleasure to watch."

"Hey," Danny shouted after him.

Lev turned around. "Yes?" he said.

"What if we don't win?"

The man walked back toward Danny. "Then someone else will," the man said.

"But... if we don't win, and Molly—"

"I thought we were understanding each other, Danny Hoo-oooper. *You* do what *we* want, *you* get what *you* want. It is not complicated."

"But if Chicago or Seattle—"

"Then you do not get anything." The man patted Danny's cheek and smiled. "It is so simple." He spun, and he walked away in a manner that made it quite clear to Danny that he wasn't coming back this time.

Danny opened the envelope. It was a picture of Molly holding a copy of yesterday's paper. She looked safe, healthy, unhappy, shoulders a little slumped, still strikingly American. She looked... all right. She was all right. It was Portland's paper.

Danny put the picture back into the envelope, put the envelope into his jacket pocket, and walked toward the Grand Douglas and into a lobby full of Cloppingshire men playing cards, smoking cigarettes, drinking free beer, and developing a collective suspicion that one of the Rose City Revolution's non-Cloppingshire men knew that Molly Hart was probably not in California taking care of her mum.

The version of the Chicago Butchers that stood opposite the Revolution waiting for kickoff in Portland was not the version Danny had seen in their previous meeting. In Chicago, they had been soldiers without their commanders: they had looked solid enough at first inspection, but you could sense that they knew their leaders were gone. These Butchers looked like statues of supermen you'd unearth from the tomb of a Slavic warlord from the Middle Ages, and not a one of them looked the slightest bit nerve-racked by the bowl of Rose City noise, by the haze of red and black smoke left over from the pregame festivities and the sweet, weedy smell. The smoke swirled around them, but they all stared straight ahead.

From the start, the Butchers owned the match. The singing, screaming, bellowing Portland fans quieted by the minute as the visitors played monkey-in-the-middle with the first-place hosts. Chicago's dominance took Danny back to the dispiriting early-season days of the Revolution chasing games like dogs chasing cars. The Butchers seemed to be running a version of a basketball weave: every passer left his space and opened a new one up behind him; every pass revealed a new opportunity; and every third or fourth exchange seemed to bring the Butchers five yards closer to the Revolution's goal. It all had the inevitability of waves easing their way toward the beach.

Then Todd—the halfback Todd, the one who almost never played and who wasn't any good, but was a broad, strapping American athlete and had been an American football player—did something truly unexpected. He took one of them out. Football-style. *American*-football-style.

For all of Danny's years applying vicious English tackles in the viscous English mud, he'd never seen anything like it. The crowd, however, recognized it immediately, in a way that an English crowd simply could not have—the Americans *had* seen its like before, just in a different kind of football—and responded with a distinctly American roar, a sound Danny hadn't heard yet, a combination gasp of surprise and scream of approval, and it could only have been produced by people who knew and loved a game in which it was permitted, in which a hit like this was a fundamentally sound component of winning.

It was *bonkers*, is what Danny thought. Even *Danny* thought it was bonkers.

They didn't even run to their man, the Chicago Butchers. They seemed worried that the Todd might do to them what he had done to the Slav (who lay motionless on the unforgiving Portland turf), as if maybe Todd had a gun and you couldn't go near him.

Their man did not roll around and he did not writhe—he didn't move at all. He had been flattened, quite literally, and he was, as anyone in the entire stadium could tell, done for the day. The referee, as shocked as everyone else on the field, offered only a yellow card and asked Todd to *please* never, ever do that again.

Only a week before the Butchers had tied the Polish national team in front of forty thousand in Chicago, and then two days later had eased by the Cowhands 4–1 in Colorado, and they had arrived in Portland fully prepared to bring their version of world-class football to bear upon the upstart Revolution—and that's exactly what they'd been doing until Todd had crushed one of their own, inspiring his teammates to finally go toe-to-toe with the imperious Chicago Butchers Professional Soccer Club, American All-Star Soccer Association champions in 1972 and '73. For the rest of the half, the Butchers seemed almost paralyzed, sapped of even a will to carry on.

It was nil–nil after forty-five minutes. "It had to stop," Todd told the team in the changing room. "That's why I did it. It had to stop, so I stopped it."

Broomsie barked and slobbered into the moist, hot summer air about the win his side needed, about how badly they needed these points, about how Peter Surley had won the League Vase in 1963 and "how many more cups and trophies did you think you'd win, Peter, when you were young? You probably thought you'd bloody win one every bloody year, didn't you, Peter? Now here you are, here you bloody are, Peter, in the basement of this bloody baseball stadium in Oregon—in *Oregon*, Peter—hoping with everything you've got that maybe you can win just one more. But not if we don't win today, and not if we don't win on bloody Sunday. C'mon, lads," he spat. "C'mon, lads..." and his voice gave out.

Hooper thought Broomsie might shed a tear. *The 1963 League Vase*, Danny thought. *Still talking about that one trophy, the one single trophy anyone in this room had ever won.* Danny wondered if Peter even thought it was a trophy anymore, or just baggage weighing down a career that had never really met its promise. Baggage he wished he could lose.

Nineteen-sixty-bloody-three.

It never stops following you, football. It never bloody stops.

But the game, in the second half, did. At least for the Revolution. Stopped cold. The Butchers won the Super Soccer Showdown, got their revenge, and took four points in the standings to none for the Revolution. For Danny and his teammates, just getting to the Showdown kept Chicago from gaining much in the standings, and the way things stood, if the Revolution could

is you don't, men"—and Three had the dubious task of giving each man a rose, and the men went into the stands and passed them out, and the elderly councilwoman kicked out a ceremonial ball, and the teams stood for the national anthem and Danny took the field for what he realized now, just now, could be the last game he ever played in the United States of America.

Seattle kicked off, the place still alive with anticipation, the good people of Portland salivating for the Revolution to beat their rivals, to reach the semi-final, and then for the Revolution to play against the Pearl himself and the Giganticos in the Bonanza Bowl on TV, and the ball went to a Seattle midfielder and then back, slowly, as it does, to a green-shirted defender. But he misplayed it, and Kelvin was upon him. Kelvin had raced down his wing, low to the ground, hair back, as if he had known that this was where the ball was going, and he forced the defender into a bad pass, which went right at a slow-moving Peter Surley, who had eased into Seattle's half, just barely, but there he was with the ball, forty yards from Seattle's goal, and he looked up, and Seattle's keeper was off his line, of course he was off his line, the game had just begun, and Peter thought—you could see it in his face—*Why not?* and he lobbed the ball goalward, high in the air, maybe too much of an arc it appeared at first, but then the ball descended, fell from space just under the bar, and Portland erupted. The Revolution mobbed Surley—who only looked pleasantly surprised—and a tsunami of noise fell from the stands and Danny yelled, he just yelled, and he couldn't even hear himself.

The sun shone, the smell was good—natural, clean, herbal and beery—and the Revolution were ahead one-nil in the biggest game of Danny's life. They had not yet played a minute.

But the Smithereens chose not to cower but to fight back, and within fifteen minutes they had quieted the crowd—twice—and were ahead 2–1. Danny couldn't stop them, no one could stop them. They were the better team, they just were, and Danny felt it slipping away, but...

...Kelvin—Danny had never seen anyone play as Kelvin was playing today, like a terrier that had never been off its leash—fought his way down the wing and instead of crossing he cut inside and found himself just fifteen yards from the goal and he lashed the ball into the far side netting and it was 2–2. He had scored at the south goal but he ran the length of the pitch and basked in the love of the crazies behind the north goal. Danny had never seen him bask in anything, had hardly seen him smile, but he loved this new Kelvin, comfortable in the adulation no English crowd would have ever given him, comfortable in this new, unconditional, unexpected American love.

By halftime Seattle had gotten their fifth corner and Petrov had netted a Sniper Shot. 3–2 at the interval. To American eyes and English minds, a scoring explosion. Danny and Big Lou stropped off the field in a mood, embarrassed at having let in three, and with Seattle now positioned to take maximum points from a win. Even if Chicago stumbled in L.A., the Revolution would have to return to bloody Seattle Municipal Stadium for a semi-final if they wanted to get to the Bonanza Bowl. Danny let loose a string of the most vile epithets at no one in particular; he looked at Big Lou and he could see that his goalkeeper agreed entirely.

But the Revolution were on their fourth corner and within the first ten minutes of the second half they reached five and Surley was true from the center spot. 3–3. The crowd's response was more relieved than ecstatic, but the stadium returned to nervous when a Trevor brought Petrov down in the box just four minutes later and the Smithereens converted the penalty. 4–3 now and just a half hour remaining. Danny started yelling at his teammates, pushing, cajoling, begging them to be better. Juanito—where had *he* been the whole game?—let a Surley pass slip beneath his feet and out of bounds; one of the Todds took a shot from ten yards out that struck a hippy behind the north goal who wasn't even paying attention to the game—Danny thought it must have gone thirty rows into the stands—and Danny bellowed at them: *"Better, boys, better!"* He leaned forward as he yelled, the bellowing contracting his stomach, he could feel the muscles in there doing everything they could to make him louder, to make his voice heard over the din, he clapped his big hands as desperately as he could. He ran over to Peter Surley and yelled, "We *need* one, Peter. *Now, Peter, now.*" He thought tears might come—he didn't think he would cry exactly, but he thought tears might come.

And then a Todd scored. Of all people. The Todd who had run around up front next to Juanito all summer long to almost no effect other than to keep the Revolution at its minimum threshold for North American players, had latched onto a loose ball near the top of the box and had struck it with power and precision and it looked to almost everyone there—not everyone, but almost everyone—as if he had meant to do what he had done, and the ball caromed off the crossbar and down into the goal and it was 4–4. The stadium had almost lifted itself off its moorings at that one. Danny imagined the old place might actually elevate if the Revolution could score again, imagined that the raucous burst of these frenzied, frantic former baseball fans might place enough thrust under the roof and who new where the ballpark would land if that happened.

4–4. Surely the winner would finish first in the Frontier Conference, and surely—surely—the loser would finish third. All to play for, six thousand miles from home, in a place he had never known to exist, with all these Cloppingshire men around him, more to play for than he had ever know you could have to play for.

Fifteen more minutes. For Molly. For these people. Against Seattle. And the Communists. For a championship. Maybe, maybe. All to play for. For Molly. For fifteen minutes.

But...

Seattle took the game over again. They weren't rattled, they weren't concerned. They'd had the better of the game, they were the better team, they knew it, Danny knew it, he'd always known it, and with Petrov and his band of green-clad and capable Englishmen they looked much more likely than the Revolution to be hosting the Frontier Conference championship match in a week's time.

With ten minutes remaining, one of the Trevors committed a foul twenty-five yards from the goal, just on top of the semi-circle, and Big Lou bossed the Revolution's midfielders into a wall and Petrov stood over the kick, and the Portland thousands had the feeling, Danny could feel it, that the Bulgarian was about to ruin the Rose City's bicentennial summer, and Petrov took the free kick, took it sublimely, and without emotion, and it curled toward the upper V, and Danny thought *He's done it, the bloody Bulgarian, he's done us in.*

But Big Lou, a cast-off of Cloppingshire United Football Club of the Football League's Third Division, a big hulk of a man who didn't always look like an athlete exactly, but he *was* big, and his reflexes were there, and his instincts were right, and he took a step back, almost inside the goal, and he contorted himself so that his left arm was outstretched toward the very corner of the goal, and he leapt in the strangest way, the way only a goalkeeper can, and he reached, and Petrov's lovely bent ball bent slowly, and Big Lou became the most important person in all of Portland, Oregon, and surely more important than he knew. He tipped the ball—just grazed it—against the post, and it popped back out into the box where no Seattle players stood. They had already decided it was a goal—they'd seen Petrov do this before, they knew it was supposed to be 5–4 now, they had watched, admired, gawked and gazed. But the score was still 4–4, and Danny half-volleyed the ball seventy yards upfield—*Louuuuuuuuuuuu*—it was possibly the single longest single kick of Danny's life—and there were eight minutes left, eight minutes, and for the first time in the previous eighty two minutes, the Seattle Smithereens—it was in their faces, in their gaits even—looked like they were not destined to host this year's version of the Frontier Conference championship.

Louuuuuuuuuuuuuuuuuuuuuuuuuuuuuuuuuuuuuuuu.

When you've given up a penalty, no matter how little choice the referee had in the decision, you always have a feeling, especially when you're at home, that he owes you one too. It's unfair to the man in the middle, whose job is so thankless anyway, but you do think, if we can just get in there, and get a bump, a nudge, and whoever it is that gets that bump or that nudge might have stayed on his feet and tried to score, but in the back of his mind he remembers that the referee gave them one so he's got to give us one now. It's only right, and it's only fair, and you've been reminding him of it all match long.

The poor man. There was Peter Surley, just across the eighteen-yard line, Peter Surley who was as rare a sight in either box as he would've been in a health club, but he was in the box now, he knew that all he had to do was cross that line, and he did, and he faked left—wasn't much of a fake, he really just shifted his prodigious weight—and the Seattle defender dove in, hung his foot out to dry, hung his team out to dry, and Surley shifted his weight the other way, and...

...when a man of Peter Surley's weight hits the deck, a referee has to do *something*. Surley's body collapsed to the Multnomah Stadium floor with a sound that gave Danny to think he might not get back up. He'd barely been fouled, but his fall was real enough. And the referee bit, he had too: Surley had sold what he had to sell so completely that even the Smithereens accepted their fate, knew that this was the natural course of things.

Kelvin was having the game of his life, so he took it, and he made it. The sweat burned at Danny's eyes, and it seemed to him as if maybe there was something else in there, tears maybe, but he couldn't be bothered either way. It was 5–4, and it stayed 5–4, and the Rose City Revolution was 11-5, and they were the regular season champions of the Frontier Conference.

Graham Broome hugged each of them. He hugged Danny, Danny hugged old Peter Surley, and Danny squeezed Kelvin and Juanito until he thought they might break. They ran their victory lap, stood in front of the north end and the north end screamed and yelled down at the Revolution and the Revolution screamed and yelled back at the north end and then someone started singing, "We are the Revs, we are the Revs, we are, we are, we are the Revs."

Danny thought he might never go back to East Southwich. Never again.

The Russian was alone in the Grand Douglas parking lot. Danny thought that was unusual.

"Good game, Danny Hooooper. You are good team now. Congratulations to the Revolution. It is good news, good news for everyone."

"Good news for everyone, is it? How's that?"

"The *plan*, Danny Hooooper."

"We aren't through to the Bonanza Bowl yet though, are we?"

"You are not, Danny, but you will be. You will be. I am confident of that."

"Seattle not easy to beat twice in a week. Dare I even inquire what makes you so confident?"

"You boys are playing well. The public is behind you. I like your chances very much, Danny Hooooper."

"Where's your friend been, then?"

"My friend? Oh, of course, of course, Danny Hooooper. My friend. Already in New York. Preparing. The Bonanza Bowl is almost here, Danny Hooooper. The planning must be perfect, as you know. We must be careful. We must take care."

"Yes, you must take care. I can only imagine." The men looked at each other, until Danny said the obvious: "Where's Molly?"

The Russian sucked on his cigarette and blew its smoke out the side of his mouth. "Molly. Of course. You would like to know where Molly is. So rude of me." He took another drag. "She is in New York too."

Danny stepped back. "Excuse me?" he said.

"That is where we need her, so that is where she is."

"So I'll see her there, will I?"

"The way you boys are playing, Danny Hooooper, yes, you will."

"And if I we suddenly don't play so well? If I'm not there?"

"You mean if Seattle qualifies for the Bonanza Bowl and you do not?"

"Yes. If we lose."

"And you have nothing to offer in exchange for Molly Hart?"

"Well," Danny said, "yes. Yes. If I have nothing to trade for Molly Hart."

"This is what I do not understand about capitalists, Danny Hooooper. Why am I having to explain to you that you cannot get something for nothing? I am a Communist, Danny. You should be explaining such a thing to me."

Danny rubbed his beard; he didn't feel big and strong, didn't feel big and strong at all next to this small, smoking Communist. Danny looked down at the man, but he couldn't figure out what to say.

The Russian let his cigarette fall to the ground. "Why am I always having to explain this to you Western people? Such a surprise it is to me. Such a surprise." He walked away, got in his little car, left the Grand Douglas parking lot, and drove up into the woods of Portland, Oregon, back to wherever it was that he hid himself when Danny Hooper was doing everything he could to get the Rose City Revolution to the 1976 American All-Star Soccer Association Bicentennial Bonanza Bowl.

TWENTY-NINE

Danny rode his new American bicycle from the Grand Douglas down to Multnomah Stadium for training on the Thursday before Saturday's Frontier Conference championship game against the Seattle Smithereens.

When he got to the Fourteenth Street entrance, to the ramp that descended behind the south goal, the same ramp he'd driven down with Molly in that enormous Lincoln those many weeks ago, the first time he'd been to Multnomah Stadium, he saw a mass of Portlanders stood next to the old park's exterior wall, a great queue of Americans waiting patiently, shuffling quietly, moving toward what he did not know. He determined to keep riding, following the line. No one had recognized him, not yet, so he kept going, kept following as the queue turned the corner and stretched up the street. Danny kept riding, and Danny found the end of the line—or, rather, its front—at the stadium's box office, underneath a banner that read: SATURDAY NIGHT, SOCCER PLAYOFFS, REVOLUTION VS. SEATTLE. Danny stopped his bike next to a policeman and asked what this all was for.

"What's this all *for*?" the policeman said.

"Yes," Danny said, "this queue. What's it *for*?"

"You're one of them, aren't you?" The policeman didn't say this in a nice way.

"I am one of what?"

"One of these... *soccer* people. Commie sport, if you ask me. And it's not a queue. It's a line. They're in line."

"All right then," Danny said. "What's this great *line* about? And please don't call football a Commie sport."

"It's not *football*," said the policeman.

"I'm sorry?"

"I won't let my son play it."

"But these people... what are they here for?"

"They're here for *you*, limey."

"Me?"

"You and your Commie sport."

"Excuse me?"

"You got a game on Saturday night?"

"Erm, yes," Danny said. "We do."

"Well, these idiots are standing in line because they want to see it."

"All of these?"

"All of these. Beginning of the end, if you ask me."

Danny looked at the queue—the *line*—and smiled. "Cor blimey," he said.

"Exactly," said the policeman, shaking his head. "Whatever that means."

You could see the roofs on the row houses across Fourteenth Street from the pitch. And today, Saturday, as the Rose City Revolution warmed up for the 1976 Frontier Conference championship game, the men of Cloppingshire, and Danny, and the Americans, could see people on those roofs. *People.* People who couldn't get a ticket for a *soccer* game, sitting on roofs across the street.

And you could see light posts along Fourteenth Street hugged by young American boys as if those posts were their very parents, young American boys whose parents had allowed them to climb a light post in downtown Portland to see a soccer game. Danny had not seen any boys on any light posts at the baseball game. No one had sat on the roofs across the street for the baseball game.

Danny looked at the other end of the field and there they were, the Smithereens in their grotesque green warm-ups, a shade of unripened avocado that disgusted Danny, and Danny knew what that meant: it meant he was a Portlander now, a Rose City citizen who could no more stomach Seattle's green than he could tolerate Bumfleet's claret, Bloat's deathly black, or Hibble's sky-blue stripes, teams and colors that were repulsive to the East Southwich constitution. *That green*, Danny thought. *That color.*

Everywhere there could possibly be an extra wooden bench or bleacher, there was an extra wooden bench or bleacher. They were too close to the touchline, Danny thought. Someone, likely Kelvin or a Todd, was going into the third row, and was probably going to hurt one of the kids who sat right on the floor, right on the turf, in front of the first row. Danny thought maybe the Communists had kidnapped the fire marshal too.

Danny thought of the chairman of East Southwich Albion AFC, trapped forever in his subterranean office, trapped forever on top of a forever middling football club, dreaming of a Fifth Round FA Cup tie, dreaming of the top half of the Second Division maybe, dreaming through a cigar-smoke haze of things that were never going to happen and if they did wouldn't even matter. Not really. The top half of the Second Division? The Fifth Round of the FA Cup? None of that mattered; it was all just another year, another gray season destined to slip into the gray, middling past. But this—this American season in this American place... it *mattered*, even more than these people knew, and to them it mattered as much as it needed to, more than they'd expected it could.

The East Southwich Albion refugee basked in the love of thirty-two thousand people who had never had a championship, bathed in the affections of thirty-two thousand Americans who just wanted ninety minutes from the Revolution to prove that they could *be better than the bastards from Seattle*. Danny never wanted to play for East Southwich Albion Association Football Club again. He wanted to play for these people. Until something awful happened—and he knew it might, knew it probably would. He wanted to play for these people for the rest of his life.

At halftime Seattle led 1–0. Good goal too. Nice passing at the top of the box. Seattle had a giant holding center forward, the kind who could keep the ball, and if you were behind him you wouldn't even know he had it, he was so big, and he laid it off to Ivan Petrov, and Petrov knuckled it home from twenty-five yards. Danny had raised his arms and clapped. "Fair play to you, Commie," he said as Petrov jogged back to his half, and Petrov winked.

Danny felt the fear in the stadium as he departed the pitch at the interval. Seattle had owned the park for the first half as thoroughly as they had in that preseason game in the rain at their place. Danny looked up at the light posts along Fourteenth; a couple were empty now. *Shite,* he thought. *Shite, shite, shite.* There were so many reasons it couldn't end this way. And Molly was already in New York.

The first ten minutes of the second half was more of the same, and Danny started wondering if the thirty-two thousand were ready for the disappointment that was second nature to supporters of East Southwich Albion, Cloppingshire United, Dire Vale, Wolves & Wolves, and all those clubs in all those towns that exist just to exist, that have no greater grasp of optimism than a prisoner serving a life sentence, that have none of the Americanness that all these Americans whose sense of drama and entitlement and the very theater of life suggest to them, "Why not? Why not us? Why should Seattle have something we can't have, we, us, Portland—why not?"

The Smithereens passed the ball back to their Canadian national team goalkeeper, who, despite his Canadian-ness, was easily the best non-Gigantico keeper in the league, a trapeze artist, a tightrope walker, a fearless freak of nature—there was nothing like him. Even the Pearl and the Dutchman and the Butchers and Sweet Billy Robinson steered clear of the Smithereens' goalkeeper, his long hair, bushy sideburns, and ambitious eyebrows not to be trifled with, at risk of grave injury, and Kelvin and Juanito gave him a wide berth, running all the way past him, their momentum taking them over the end line, as he left his goal to collect a back pass from the Seattle Londoner who had played it to him with supreme confidence.

The Canadian laid the ball upon the turf, rolled it ahead a few steps, picked it up, and set it back down again, rolled it again, and by now Kelvin and Juanito were back on the pitch now, behind the Canadian, in his blind spot, and one looked at the other, and Kelvin nipped in behind the Canadian, just off his shoulder, just off his outside shoulder, and got a toe to the ball and poked it into Juanito's path, and there in front of Juanito was an open goal. The Canadian reacted, ran back instinctively toward his goal, but it was too late, and Juanito rolled in an easy one, and it was 1–1, and the Portlanders screamed as if they were at a Beatles concert, and three ten-year-old boys ran out onto the field and hugged Juanito and then ran back to their seats.

It had been the Revolution's first shot of the game.

From there it was a struggle. The game had no rhythm, nothing in it. Petrov was easily the best player on the pitch, but he was only one man, and he couldn't settle his jumpy, now-nervous English teammates. Big Loooooooooouuuuuu made a big save or two, and the Smithereens hit the post twice. Broome made a few time-consuming substitutions, and one of the Todds rolled around on the turf while the clock ran from ten to twelve minutes. And then the clock got under five minutes, and Danny thought, *Anything can happen now...*

Still Seattle pressed, still Looooooooooouuuuuu came up big, and with just a couple of minutes left, Kelvin had the ball thirty yards up the line and tried to push it past his man. The fullback had defended Kelvin well, but Kelvin's touch had been so heavy—and the turf so slick—that the ball rolled over the Smithereen's foot and all the way over the byline for the Revolution's first corner kick.

Danny went into the box by the north goal. In fact, every-one except Big Lou went into the box by the north goal—twen-ty-one men in there, twenty-two with the referee—and Peter Surley lobbed the ball into the cool Oregon summer air, into the sound of thirty-two thousand nervous fans, the sound like the crackle of an untuned radio, the *bzzzzz* of electricity with nowhere to go, and a Smithereen met it first, but his header cleared the ball only as far as Juanito, in his usual corner-kick position at the top of the box, and Juanito took a shot, not a good one, that ricocheted back to Peter, still in the corner. Peter played the ball back into Seattle's six-yard box, just over the outstretched arms of Seattle's Canadian goalkeeper, and into the path of one Danny Hooper, who headed the ball home as if nothing could have been easier.

The sound. That's what it sounded like, Danny thought. *That's the sound I've been waiting to hear.*

The sound continued until time had ticked away, and it con-tinued as the good people of Portland rushed onto the field and amongst and around Danny and his teammates. The sound con-tinued when Danny was deep inside the stadium, in the chang-ing room, with only four or five of his teammates, and then with five or six, and then with six or seven—one by one they burst through the door, missing a shirt, or a *sleeve*, or a shoe or a sock, looking as if they'd been chased for miles by wild beasts. They looked frightened when they came through the door, but then they sat down, on a bench or on the floor, opened a bottle of Henry's, and they just listened, listened to that sound, a sound none of them had ever heard before.

Meanwhile, the Giganticos had barely beaten Red Star To-ronto. They'd battered away at the Serbs' goal for ninety min-utes, but the ball kept hitting the post, and the linesman's flag kept going up, and Red Star's goalkeeper had one of those days... and the amassed New Yorkers who weren't even entirely sure other teams were *allowed* to beat theirs grew in their ner-vousness and the low hum of fear seeped from the stands to the pitch and the players tightened up and Red Star started thinking maybe, maybe...

But the Giganticos survived the Super Soccer Showdown—the Dutchman saved them after even the Brazilian had missed—and the stage was set: the Pearl would play one last time, in the sun, for a trophy, on worldwide television. He would give of himself these ninety more minutes, grace the world with his magic, and his team would once again be what they had been so often:

They would be champions.

THIRTY

Danny stood at the pay phone at the tavern across the road.

"Dad."

"Hello, son. Hello, Danny."

"We're in the Bonanza Bowl, Dad."

"So I've read. You've made the papers here."

"I have, eh? American soccer in the English press? I'd be surprised if I could be surprised anymore."

"Why's that, then? Too worldly in your travels? A bit flash now you've a date with the great Pearl of Brazil?"

"Long story, old man. Long story."

"More to it than meets the eye, my son?"

"—"

"Danny? You there?"

"I'm here. I can barely hear you, Dad. Bit of a party here, I'm afraid."

"Give it to me, son. What's going on over there?"

"—"

"Danny?"

"I gave them my youth, Dad, I gave it to them, and they sent me over here, sent me over here to... to..."

"To America."

"No, Dad. Not to *where*, to *what*."

"To *what*, then?"

"They didn't send me over here just to play, Dad. There's something I have to do. Something I have to do in the Bonanza Bowl."

"What's that?"

"Watch the match, Dad."

"I wouldn't miss it."

"You won't forget it."

"Of course not."

"I miss you, Dad."

"—"

"Dad?"

"I miss you too, son."

New York City, in the summer of 1976, was red, white, and blue. Old Glory hung from every lamppost, from apartment windows, and from the antennas of taxicabs. Street hawkers wore and sold Uncle Sam hats and all manner of USA bits and bobs.

The Rose City Revolution team that arrived in New York City for the Bonanza Bowl, still shocked at their bounty and surprised at having survived two straight games against the Smithereens, was still coming to terms with what they were and what awaited them: they were the Giganticos' opponents for a Bicentennial Bonanza Bowl party. The match itself was a virtual testimonial, a celebration of America's ability to build the best team in the world's most beloved game out of thin air with America's greatest resource: cash. The trophy was probably already engraved with the Giganticos' name.

None of the European and South American journalists enjoying a paid vacation in New York City was wondering how the Dutchman was going to deal with Peter Surley in the Revolution's midfield. None of the many pundits arrived from Great Britain was analyzing the difficulty Juanito and Kelvin might pose to a back line that had three World Cup finals under its belt. None of the game's wandering intellectuals was wondering whether perhaps Big Lou might keep a clean sheet. Some of them weren't even getting it right: Danny read an article in a New York paper that previewed the championship as a matchup between the Giganticos and the Seattle Smithereens.

Another featured the logo of Portland's basketball team in its match preview.

The Russians were there in the lobby, as Danny knew they would be, sitting by a fire, reading their newspapers, just as they had done in Chicago. Communists in midtown Manhattan.

Danny walked over and sat down.

"Well, here we are," Danny said. "After all of that. The Rose City Revolution is in the Bonanza Bowl. You must be so relieved. Pigs in your slop, you must be."

They put their newspapers down and smiled. "You could say that," Lev said. "We left as little as we could to chance, but sport is... unpredictable, is it not? You can only control so much."

The other Russian said, "You were good against Seattle. You deserved your victory. We are so happy that you are here."

"Thank you," Danny said, and laughed a dark little laugh. "I expected to see you there."

"We were there. But we left you alone to enjoy your triumph. Why not? You have played hard this summer. It is maybe your last victory. We thought you should have a little bit of fun with the Portland people—"

"How's Molly?" Danny cut them off.

The Russians looked back at Danny as if he had not said a word.

So Danny said, "Well, then?"

Lev told Danny that Molly was in great condition. "She's a wonderful girl, Danny. You are fortunate she cares so much for you."

"Yeah," Danny said. "I feel fortunate."

Lev's friend said, "We are very excited for the match. It will be a marvelous contest, I am sure. We brought Ivan Petrov with us from Seattle. Did you know that? We added him to your team."

Danny bristled. "You *what*?"

"Yes. Why not? Make a better game of it."

"Listen, stop messing with our side. We have a good thing going right now—"

"And Sweet Billy Robinson too. He will make the match much more interesting—"

"You can't just add players to teams like that. And Billy Robinson's not playing for the Revolution. Not now, not ever—"

"Please—please stop acting as if you have control over these matters. You do not. *We* do. Do you understand? And no one will notice. No one knows who Petrov or Billy played for in the season. No one who matters."

Danny did not respond. Petrov? And Sweet Billy?

"It is in our interest for the Bonanza Bowl to be a good match. And your team—your team is lucky, but it is not so good. We have arranged help. For this you should be thanking us, not making such an angry face."

This was not the conversation he wished to have with these Communists. He had no interest in giving them even the passing impression that he had anything but hate for them and what they had done with or to Molly, and for whatever they planned to execute here in New York. "Let's cut the bull," he said, feeling awfully American to have said such a thing in a Manhattan hotel lobby. "Tell me what I have to do, and I'll do it, and then tell me how I get Molly back."

"All right, Danny. We have good news for your: your job is simpler than we were once thinking." He nodded at his compatriot.

"Sometime between the eighty-fifth minute and the end of the match—the result will be settled, of course—you will play the ball out for a corner. You will make certain that it is the Giganticos' fifth. Are you understanding, Danny Hooooper? This should not be difficult, but it may take some planning ahead. Hmm? Some *planning*, Danny Hooo—"

"I got it, I got it," Danny said.

And then, the Russians explained, the Pearl of Brazil would stride to the center spot for his Sniper Shot, for one last swing of his enchanted right leg, for one last goal, awash in the love of the tens of thousands in the stadium and the millions watching on

TV, where he would end the greatest sporting career of all time, *of all time*, alone, exposed, defenseless, vulnerable, helpless—Danny would cause this to happen. The movie playing in Danny's head was now, for the first time, the same as the movie playing in the Russians' heads. He could see what they could see, as clearly as if it had already been filmed and shown on *every evening news program on the planet, which is what was surely going to happen.*

"You need only do this," the man said, "and you will leave New York with your friend Molly Hart. Nothing will happen to her. Nothing. We assure you."

"And what will happen to the Pearl?" Danny asked, just to see if they would say it.

The men did not answer Danny, and Danny knew that they never would. One of them looked down. So Danny asked another question. "Do *you* know what will happen to him?"

The Russians leaned in toward Danny and raised their eyebrows. The one who hadn't been speaking said, "Danny, are... you... understanding?"

Danny tilted away from the inward-leaning Communists and said, "That's it, then? I give the Giganticos a Sniper Shot in the dying minutes of the game... and I get Molly back? That simple? So, how *exactly* do I get Molly back?"

"As the Giganticos are preparing for the Sniper Shot, you tell Broome you are hurt, you need a substitute. You go into the tunnel behind your bench with the team physio and we will be there—"

"You? You will be there?"

The Russians looked surprised, as if pulling something like this off were somehow complicated for them. "One of us will be there."

"And?"

"And Molly Hart will be with us. We will transfer her to your care at that time, Danny," said one.

"You will want to be in the tunnel before the Sniper Shot," said the other. "If you are, Molly is yours."

"And if not? If I don't get there in time?"

"We are making this simple, are we not? Just get there before the shot."

Danny entered the elevator, and Three was there.

"Saw you talking to them," Three said. "Very good. What did they say?"

"They said—"

"Never mind, Danny. We know the plan."

"You know the plan?"

"We know their plan."

"This is my floor, Three."

"Hit 'Lobby.'"

Danny hit L. The elevator changed direction.

"We'll take a little walk. I'll explain."

"They'll see you."

Three put on a baseball hat and sunglasses. With his Rose City Revolution jacket and white tennis shoes, it was a decent disguise. He didn't look like a secret agent of the Queen; he didn't look English at all, actually. "Follow me," he said.

The New York summer sunshine hit them like a solid object. The men adjusted their eyes and took a right. "We'll walk around the block," Three said. Then he told Danny that Molly was in no danger. "Not really, or not yet, anyway," he said. "Well and truly frightened, I should think, but if you do what the Russians want you to do, Danny, we'll get her back in one piece."

"But—"

"Exactly, Danny. You're right, of course."

"All they want me to do is make sure the Giganticos get a Sniper Shot at the end of the game."

"Let me help you think this through, big man. By the time you give them their fifth corner kick, the Giganticos will be ahead, comfortably ahead. This whole thing—the worldwide TV audience, the pomp and circumstance—it's all for the Pearl—"

"And I will be in the tunnel, with Molly."

"You probably will. If they're true to their word, you will be with Molly, underneath the stadium, in our care."

"But, Three—"

"But, Danny."

They stopped, stopped and looked at each other, on a street corner in Manhattan, New York City, USA. Danny looked at the ground. "But—"

"If you put the Pearl on the center spot tomorrow afternoon, alone—"

"I understand," Danny said.

"And do you understand that if you don't, you will never see Molly ever again? Do you understand that?"

"And all they want... all they want is a Sniper Shot."

"I think you understand, Danny. You've always had the nous, my boy. Always had the nous. That's why we picked you, Danny."

Danny looked at Three as hard as he knew to look at a man. *Even now, Three, you bastard, you make it seem like I had something to do with this.*

Three stopped him.

"Listen, my boy, that's *their* plan. We have a plan too. You're going to give them their shot, but you're going to give the Pearl something else too. Something to really remember you by."

Danny had a hand on his forehead and a vexed look in his eyes, on that Manhattan sidewalk in New York City, USA. Three said, "Something the world will remember you by, just as Dire Vale has."

Danny shook his head in disbelief. "This is your solution?"

Three said nothing.

"Just so you can play your silly game?"

Again, Three said nothing.

"Say it out loud. Tell me what you want me to do."

And so Three did.

THIRTY-ONE

New York's stadium was like a bullring. High, round, and steep it rose, the masses on top of the players like those bloodthirsty Spaniards dying for a dignified killing. The New Yorkers breathed down on the players, exhaling their Gotham confidence into the hot, heavy air that settled down upon the pitch.

During the warm-up, Danny stared up into the stands, into that muggy breath, losing himself in the Americanness of it, the sheer scope of a cup final in the most important city in the world on international television. The close, clogged air coursed with electricity and menace, and Danny wondered that all of these people imagined that the highest prize available today was a mere championship. *Can't they feel it?* Danny wondered. *The danger—don't they know?*

At the other end: the great Brazilian, and the Dutchman, and all of them, playing keepie uppie with one another, clearly comfortable in the knowledge that in two hours the world would see them parading a trophy the size of a refrigerator around this perfectly manicured field. Deep inside the stadium, another game took place, a game no one was watching, a game no one could see.

Lev, in nothing more complicated than a blue workman's jump suit and a Giganticos baseball cap, had slipped behind a flimsy wooden barricade with nothing but a tip of his cap to a bored security guard who couldn't quite believe that New York's monument to America's National Pastime was being co-opted for a soccer game. Simple as it was, it had been a good trick and well planned: the Russians had sent a man in the same outfit to each Giganticos home game, and the man (it had been Lev on three previous occasions) had passed into the ballpark's innards in the same way each time: a purposeful walk, a businesslike nod, and then a silent slip behind the scenes. Lev had used his visits to wander and seek and search and probe amongst the hallways and the stairways and the back ways and the rafters; by the Bonanza Bowl he knew where to hide and when and where and how to emerge upon what perch for the game's exciting conclusion, which he would provide.

The other Russian had entered the ballpark's bowels in his own blue jumpsuit and ball cap. His job was to stay on the ground level, in the general area where the teams entered the pitch, as near to the head of Bonanza Bowl security as he could remain without seeming terribly conspicuous, and make certain that no one ever had an idea that someone unaccounted for had occupied a perch high over the first base line, above the press box.

A great swarm of red and black balloons drifted toward the milky sky to mingle with an equal mass of green and yellow balloons as the teams emerged from the tunnel. Danny watch them ascend, watch them reach toward the blimp that hung in the heat above the stadium. He had an idea that it might be too hot for real football; his shirt was already soaked through, and he felt every stitch holding every rose and every star and every letter and every number onto his jersey. His eyes already stung from the sweat.

Each player received an escort to the center circle from a cheerleader wearing a decidedly minimalistic version of his team's kit. When the sides were assembled in a row at the center of the pitch, a man rode a motorcycle out to meet them, sang the national anthem, shook the Pearl's hand (no one else's), got back on his motorcycle, and rode away.

And then the Rose City Revolution was arrayed on its side of the field, no longer Cloppingshire United and a few guests, but a more typical AASSA conglomeration, featuring English-

men, the newly Portlandized Bulgarian, the energetic and optimistic Todds and Trevors, Juanito, and Sweet Billy Robinson
(drunk, but oddly calm... he may have known he was in over his
head if he knew where he was). Opposite were the Giganticos,
who looked as comfortable on their home field, in front of this
massive crowd, in the field of view of all of these cameras, as if
they had just come over for a kick-around after breakfast. The
Pearl of Brazil was like a pure beam of light hovering above the
ground, radiating a beatific glow. He knew everyone was looking at him, and he smiled and waved up into the bowl of New
Yorkers and to the world's soccer audience beyond. The fans
roared their love in response. The Dutchman looked bored; his
eyelids dropped down as if he might doze off where he stood. It
didn't look to Danny as if the Dutchman would sweat today at all.

Danny and Peter Surley locked eyes. Peter had been transformed by a long, hot summer from looking like a slightly oval
headmaster into something more like a never-that-famous rock-
and-roller past his prime. The alcohol his body hadn't processed
yet was stowed away in the bags underneath his eyes. He didn't
look at all like he could run for ninety minutes in the sun—on
TV—with the best footballers money could buy, or as if he wanted to. He hadn't come to America to win anything. He had come
to *retire*. Juanito hopped on his spot where the center circle met
the halfway line like he wished he'd gone to the toilet before taking the pitch. Kelvin looked as if he wanted to crawl inside himself. Sweet Billy Robinson stood opposite Juanito on the other
side of the circle, chatting absentmindedly with the nearby Argentine Gigantico, and Petrov waited with no facial expression
at all. Everyone else with RCR on his shirt looked scared to death.
Danny thought of all the televisions in England dialed into the
1976 American All-Star Soccer Association Bonanza Bowl, and
he knew how bad this all could be.

In those first forty-five minutes, the Giganticos had becalmed
the Revolution with their gentle grace and precision. It was like

petting a dog's belly. An Italian used the outside of his foot to bend a perfect pass around Surley as if he were a pylon, and the crowd gasped and hmmmmmed. So close were the first few rows of fans that Danny could hear fathers saying to their children, "Did you see that?"

For most of the half, the Giganticos weren't playing real Cup final football; they had applied no killer instinct—not yet. They were merely putting on a show. The seventy thousand, treated pregame to scantily clad women and motorcycles and fireworks and an air force flyover, had been transformed into polite congregants. Of all the emotions Danny had ever felt tumble pitchward from a packed grandstand, he had never been conscious of humility. The Americans celebrating their bicentennial at a football match had been humbled by foreign men playing a foreign game.

"Focus, Danny, focus." It was Three, yelling from the bench. "You have a job—"

Three was right. Danny was embarrassed, realizing that his trance was visible even from the bench—and maybe even from England, through all those televisions. He did have a job to do, so he snapped out of it, left his place atop the Revolution's eighteen-yard box, and chased until he found the ball, and when he did he kicked it toward the Giganticos' goal sixty yards away, where their goalkeeper, the one who'd played for Belgium when they came third in the '72 European championships, collected it and bounced it a few times, and Danny thought of Broomsie saying, What's the score? What's the score? What's the score? and the score was 0–0 and Danny barked at his men: "Kelvin, well in! YES, KELVIN! Juanito, cover back, BACK, we need you. Todd, yes, you. C'mon, Peter, c'mon, Peter, c'mon, Peter, dig in." The Giganticos felt his energy, seemed surprised and a little hurried by it, as if his response was their cue to go ahead and play now.

The Giganticos pressed and passed and passed and pressed, and the Revolution chased and chased, and the crowd recovered a little from their stupor and the bowl filled with heat as if it were water and the stadium a bucket. An Argentine lobbed a sublime cross in from of the right wing and Big Lou came out and Danny heard the Giganticos' prolific Italian center forward call for it; Danny knew that Big Lou would get there first, but for some reason Danny leapt in between the two men and headed the ball away for a corner.

Big Lou screamed at Danny. "That was *mine*, Danny! *Mine!*" Big Lou pointed at his ears. *"Listen*, Danny. *Listen.*" It was the first time Danny had ever not listened to Big Lou, and the goalkeeper looked like his feelings were hurt. But Danny felt good. One corner. That's one down.

The crowd stood as the Dutchman prepared to take the kick. *"Gi-gan-ti-cos! Gi-gan-ti-cos!"* they yelled, ready for a goal, anxious for a lead. The Dutchman's strike hugged the end line in a head-high parabola that somehow gained speed as it entered the six-yard box, where it was met by the Italian, who redirected it into the goal with astonishing ease.

Danny looked at Big Lou. Big Lou looked at Danny. Danny wasn't sure Big Lou would ever forgive him. That was the look.

The bowl filled itself with joy. The people were so happy that Danny almost felt it too. Danny was still surprised by it, the way people cheered here in America, *for* their team, not *against* yours. These people *loved* their Giganticos and they were now *happy*, reassured that today was going to be a party after all, an affirmation of their superiority, because the Giganticos had scored a goal.

But the linesman who had been standing on the corner by the Dutchman stood with his flag in the air. He didn't wave it, didn't leave his spot; he just stood there with his flag in the air. The referee jogged over to him, the crowd quieted itself some, the referee and the linesman spoke, and the linesman motioned with his arm that the parabola had taken the ball over the end line before it came back in and the referee waved off the goal and indicated for a Revolution goal kick.

Now the crowd booed lustily and the referee was encircled by men from every continent, but the referee waved his arms as if he were surrounded by bees and he moved them all away, and Danny thought, *It's nil–nil.*

That was the good news. The bad news was: Now it was most definitely a game. Now the Giganticos wanted it. Also: One corner. One corner for the Giganticos.

Just before the end of the half they scored one that stood. It was the Pearl who scored it, but half the team had been involved and the finish itself had been a simple pass into an empty net. The seventy thousand rained their love down upon the great man and his teammates as they made a near lap of the field in celebration of their inevitable Bonanza Bowl lead. It took forever, but Danny didn't mind—the clock ran, and he knew that the tight TV time constraints meant not much would be added on. The Giganticos could celebrate all they wanted as far as Danny was concerned—the clock kept ticking toward halftime, and the Giganticos weren't scoring any more goals. By the time Juanito kicked off, there was less than a minute remaining before the interval. Still, the Giganticos mounted one last attack, Big Lou saved for a corner, Danny headed the corner away, and...

... halftime came, and the score stood at Giganticos 1, Revolution 0.

The Dutchman looked at Danny in the tunnel and smiled. "Bravo, Hooper!"

When the team had gathered in the spacious, well-appointed locker room, Broomsie clapped his hands, leaned toward the team, and pleaded for one last half, one last push at the championship that would provide him with free beer and a great story at Cloppingshire's many pubs for the rest of his days: "Well *done*, lads, well *done*. We're *in* it, boys, we're playing the game of our lives and we're *in* it, in with a *chance*. We really are." But no one believed him. Danny felt it in the room. The Revolution knew who'd be champions in forty-five minutes. Dear old Broomsie went through the tired exercise of asking a few men the score, got a few despondent "One–nothings" and

"One–nils," but no one answered with any enthusiasm and no one said, "We just need one more, boss."

Graham Broome leaned back against the chalkboard, exhausted. With no particular enthusiasm, he said, "Boys, no one's unbeatable. I'd just like you to know that." He looked at the floor, seemed to realize that his coaching for the 1976 season was pretty well done, and said, "Hooper, the physio would like to see you. Blackstone. Training room with you then, through there."

Danny went into the training room. Three was there, said, "How are we feeling? Hamstring all right?"

Danny sat on the training table, looked at Three, and said, "Now what?"

Three explained to Danny that he could give the Giganticos their Sniper Shot, protect the Pearl from the Communists, and get Molly back. The plan was still in place. Everything was a go. "What began in your flat in East Southwich, Danny... all that time ago... seems like forever now... but it's on, my boy. It's not going to be easy to pull this off, but—"

"I can do it, Three. If I'm not going to win a championship, I can do this."

For a time in the first half, the other Russian, who by now had scooped up a discarded lanyard with a press credential, walked out onto the grass and enjoyed a few moments of the match mere yards from the teams' benches. He was just testing his own mobility, assuring that he could get in and out of the entrance at will and as necessary. He had spent an inordinate amount of time practicing the American manner of cap-tipping, a detail he realized was probably not exactly material to the mission, but had the potential of smoothing out an interaction that could be foiled by his not-entirely-concealable accent. He found now that it worked magnificently. Between the lanyard and the cap, he was free to go wherever he pleased. Short of Lev missing his shot, he could not imagine anything going awry. Danny would do what he needed to do to get the girl back. The Russian knew that for sure. The deed was as good as done, he told himself. He had the soldier's customary tang of exultant regret—the Pearl was a good and beloved man who meant everything to Brazil and to football, but the Union of Soviet Socialist Republics had to do what the Union of Soviet Socialist Republics had to do.

Lev, half a mile up, it seemed, in the sky, enjoyed the waning minutes of the first half from behind a floodlight support. He knew his chances of being found out were as good as zero, but he was proficient enough at his job to remain exactly the right kind of inconspicuous. Still, he watched in the belief that he was about to transform the history of a game he loved like he loved his family and his country. He watched in the belief that in an hour, football would be shrouded in deepest tragedy, an anguish from which Lev believed it might take decades to recover. He allowed himself to watch the first half as a humble acolyte, and his heart swelled when six Giganticos combined for a particularly elegant goal in the half's waning moments. He knew it might be the last goal he ever really enjoyed. The Brazilian, the Dutchman, the Haitian, and a pair of Italians embraced by the near corner flag, smiling their smiles and bathing themselves in the love of the New York faithful. Lev applauded and chewed his lip and disappeared behind the pennant hanging from the floodlight. When the referee blew for halftime, he sat down, leaned his back against the metal latticework, and allowed himself one final cigarette before his ability to enjoy world-class football disappeared forever.

THIRTY-TWO

Early in the second half, the Giganticos earned a free kick just outside the Revolution's box. Big Lou assembled his men into a wall, with Danny on the near post side. The Dutchman stood over the free kick and stared straight at Danny. Something in his bearing communicated to Danny that ancient boast, *Watch this*, and he curled his shot within a hiss of Danny's ear, and as Danny spun he saw it carom off the post-crossbar joint and back toward the wall. Danny played it out over the end line when he could have played it out for a throw, and positioned himself to defend the third Giganticos corner. The Dutchman allowed the Haitian to take this one, stood himself next to Danny, and said, "Like to see me do it again?" He was almost laughing, the Dutchman, but Danny wasn't amused. The Pearl was there too, waiting for the corner, and he smiled and patted Danny's cheek, just as he had done in Portland.

Danny smiled back at the Pearl, because he had no choice, and then he zeroed in on the Dutchman. "I've news for you, old man," Danny said. "It's only one-nil. You've won nothing." And Danny vowed to himself that he'd had enough of the Giganticos' festive antics. He remembered (he really had just about forgotten) that he wasn't so far from the championship he'd wanted so badly for so long, and it gelled in his brain that this was the championship to win: beating the Giganticos in front of the entire world. That was no bloody 1963 League Vase, was it? *That* would be expressing himself on a football pitch, big and strong Danny Hooper.

It didn't make any sense, what Danny was thinking. It wasn't going to get Molly back—he thought maybe he'd solve that later, some other way—but the adrenaline had kicked in, muddling the logic circuits within Danny's giant head, just as adrenaline had done not so long ago at the Auld Moors. He was suddenly sure he could get everything out of this magical day, everything he wanted.

Big Lou collected the corner kick and motioned for the Revolution to move upfield. Danny ran toward Ivan Petrov and barked, "Let's win it, Ivan—c'mon, man." He yelled over at Sweet Billy Robinson: "Just need one from you, Billy. Just one. Show them who you are!" Danny elevated and won the header. He thought, *Maybe... maybe. Maybe I can get everything.*

Lev saw it. So did Three. They both shuddered, but in different ways and for different reasons.

With thirty minutes remaining, the Pearl of Brazil was galloping as freely as you like from one touchline to the other, threading himself in and out of the Giganticos' sophisticated passing patterns as if engaging in a lighthearted drill. But it was all happening thirty or forty harmless yards from the Revolution's goal, and the Revolution was loading in numbers behind the ball.

Danny shouted at his men to at least put *some* pressure on the Giganticos, at least make them work harder for them to do what they were going to do anyway. His men complied. Petrov applied a scissor tackle to one of the Giganticos' Argentineans that looked like something you could learn only in the Bulgarian army—he was carded for it—and Kelvin initiated a few collisions that clearly annoyed the supercilious Spaniard on the Giganticos' left wing. But the Revolution's aggression only contributed to the Giganticos' free-kick count; nothing could disrupt their custody of the ball. Still, the fouls, and the subsequent squawking at the referee, and the restarts—especially the free kicks lobbed into the box, which Big Lou collected with calm authority—took time, and Danny thought,

If this thing is still one–nil with a quarter hour to play, then we've got a chance.

Big Lou regularly punted the ball a good eighty yards downfield, and Danny knew all it would take would be for Juanito or a Todd to get his head on one of those and then all it would take, just once, would be for one of those to spin its fluky way toward Sweet Billy, and then all it would take would be for Sweet Billy to see through the angry hoppy haze in his mind of everything that hadn't gone his way—the fluke of birth that had made him a Scotsman and not a World Cup–winning Englishman, the bitterness of his addiction, the shame of his unrealized potential—and if he could see his way through all that, and settle the ball, and work a flicker of sober magic and then find himself in front of the goal, and if he put the ball past the Belgian, if—if all of that happened, and it was 1–1, *one–one*, with the entire world watching... in the Super Soccer Showdown maybe, *maybe*, Portland, the Rose City, and Danny too could get their championship. Then the summer of 1976 wouldn't be the summer of the Pearl and the Giganticos and the bicentennial... then maybe 1976 would be the summer of the Revolution, the Rose City Revolution. Then they would see the big and strong Danny Hooper express himself.

He hadn't forgotten about Molly, of course he hadn't, but...

...maybe there was a way. Maybe Danny could have his way.

Then one of Big Lou's really did make its way to Sweet Billy, and Billy really did beat the Brazilian center back who'd been Brazil's center back in the 1970 World Cup, and because he was Sweet Billy Robinson, he waited while the Brazilian recovered—"C'mon back, big fella," Billy said—and then Billy beat him again. And then he was in the box with just the Belgian to beat, and he feinted left, almost imperceptibly, and down the goalkeeper went, and up went Billy's shot, a soft, cheeky little chip that landed between the goal line and the net and stopped right there, just stopped right there in the grass.

Lev stood up. He applauded. Couldn't help himself. What Sweet Billy Robinson had done was beautiful. Three sat on the Revolution's bench as everyone around him leapt into the air. He shook his head and whispered, looking up nervously into the stands, "Danny. What have you done?" The man from Colorado, deep inside the stadium, heard the sound, the strange sound, and wondered what had just happened.

The Americans, the seventy thousand, weren't even sure it was a goal. They made a sound like turning off a vacuum cleaner, a quick smothering of noise. Billy stood on the six-yard line in front of the fallen Belgian and blew the great crowd a kiss.

Then he pulled down his shorts and mooned the seventy thousand and the world.

Billy turned toward the onrush of his new teammates—just getting his shorts back up in time—and he blew them all a kiss too. Danny picked him up and spun him around, as if Billy were a drunken little figure skater, and when Danny set Billy down, Billy fell over. The Revolution screamed and cheered and you could hear them everywhere, everywhere in that stadium.

It was 1–1.

Danny locked eyes with the Pearl of Brazil and gave him a look that made one thing perfectly clear: no one—not on that pitch, not in that stadium, not in the world—knew who was going to win that game.

But that wasn't exactly true.

Danny had never really truly pictured winning the FA Cup, never even imagined that East Southwich Albion could win something as modest as the Third Division. And winning the Frontier Conference of the AASSA—that was nice, but it wasn't a *championship*, not really; the league didn't have a trophy for it. And when he'd gotten on the plane to New York City, to play in the Bonanza Bowl, he hadn't bothered himself with the thought of the Rose City Revolution defeating the greatest collection of talent in the long and glorious history of the world's most beloved game. He had flown to New York to get Molly back and to protect his good name from grave embarrassment in a game that had the potential to make him look shamefully overmatched.

But nine minutes... eight... seven... is a long time to hold off players like these, and the best amongst them had the ball. The Pearl coasted by Surley with almost unsportsmanlike ease and had more space than you'd like him to have just twenty-five yards from the goal. The crowd rose—Danny could feel them rise—and the Pearl wound up to shoot. One of the Trevors was there, and he lunged to stop it, but the Brazilian—split seconds later than Danny had ever seen anyone do it, impossibly late—pulled the ball back and slid a pass by Danny's left foot—frustratingly close to Danny's left foot—that played the big Italian into the box, right in front of Big Lou, but Big Lou was not just Big Lou of Cloppingshire today: he was the best goalkeeper on the pitch in the biggest match on the planet in the summer of 1976, and the big Italian had nowhere to put the ball, and the big Italian slid his shot wide, just off Big Lou's fingertips, for a fourth corner, a corner that came to nothing.

But the Giganticos kept coming. The Pearl, the Dutchman, the arrogant Spaniard, the giant Italian, all of them... they ran and they ran and they didn't sweat, and Surley, Juanito, Ivan, Kelvin, and Danny, they had all soaked the RCR on the fronts of their jerseys and the roses and the stars down their sleeves, and they were very nearly spent in the late going of the Bicentennial Bonanza Bowl on international television—but they were not behind.

The gray men of East Southwich would be watching—Danny knew they'd be watching—and noticing that he was a real footballer, more than just big and strong, and they'd be wondering why they had never invited him to express himself for East Southwich Albion Association Football Club.

As grotesque as the requirements of Lev's regrettable, yet necessary, American job were, he had at first focused on the silver lining of spending a summer observing these Giganticos up close, the opportunity of seeing the Pearl and his collaborators tested by the likes of Toronto, Chicago, and Seattle. And yet that's not exactly how it had worked out. He had been forced, instead, to follow the fortunes of humble Rose City Revolution, an afterthought in an afterthought league. Early on, even as they won a game or two, they had been so clumsy and disjointed, so awful to watch. Lev and his comrade had despaired at the far-fetched idea of conspiring to shoehorn them into the Bonanza Bowl without it appearing preposterously stage-managed. But something had come over the Revolution—gradually—as the summer had passed. Yes, their confidence had grown with wins they had not earned, but they had become a real football team. The addition of the giant and surprisingly handy Hooper had been a catalyst for sure—he played so hard, he was so frightening, so dangerous in so many ways. But it hadn't only been Hooper: the team had grown in its belief, finally thought itself capable of winning, and maybe even winning today—it was obvious. Lev admired the Revolution. He hadn't meant to—he'd thought himself too much a connoisseur to possibly take interest in itinerant island plodders like Cloppingshire United and their sundry hangers-on. But he saw something in them that earned his respect.

And now, in the late going, they pushed the great Giganticos. The Revolution ran and tackled a little harder, seemed to be a step closer to every loose ball. All the huffing and puffing and graft and grit were unlikely to produce another real threat upon the Belgian's goal, but it also looked unlikely that the Giganticos could create something of their own against a team as energized as the visitors. *Could be there's a future for the game here,* Lev thought. It was a real cup final. One last title worthy of the Pearl's illustrious career. Lev had not foreseen admitting to himself that America's championship was a legitimate companion to the other trophies the Pearl had earned during his magical travels, but Lev knew what his eyes told him. Today, in New

York City, the Giganticos and the Revolution were showing the world a real American soccer game. And it was good.

He wished he could watch it to its natural conclusion. He wished he didn't already know how it was going to end, and he wished he could finish the day feeling the way about his beloved game of football that he felt about it right now.

The Brazilian received the ball in the corner, on the dust surrounding home plate, just inside the corner flag and a yard or two up the third base line, right around where a catcher would stand to block the plate. He had to beat only Danny, who was moving toward him on the line, right about where a base runner would be, sprinting toward the plate.

Just about everyone who cared about football in America and England and Brazil and Europe and anywhere else was watching on their televisions, and everyone who knew Danny Hooper in East Southwich was watching, and everyone in Moscow who knew there was a plan was watching, and everyone in that stadium stood and leaned forward. And the 1976 American All-Star Soccer Association season, with its rodeo grounds and amusement-park stadiums and demolition derbies and cows on spits and glittery uniforms and all of it—all of it—existed between the divinity of the great Brazilian and the brute force of a big and strong Englishman in the kicked-up dust of the third base line at the biggest baseball stadium in New York.

Danny ran as if he were a base runner charging a catcher on a cool spring night in front of a couple thousand baseball die-hards at Multnomah Stadium; he ran at the Brazilian like an American. The master looked up, had a flash of fear in his eyes—no one had ever run at him like that—and before he crossed into the penalty area Danny launched himself parallel to the ground, his studs flying at those famous knees as if they belonged to a wee Welshman trying to beat East Southwich Albion at the Auld Moors, or as if they belonged to a catcher from Tucson. And as he clipped the ball away for the Giganticos' fifth corner kick, Danny Hooper also caved in those Brazilian knees—both of them, in the same split second, folded them back on themselves, demolished them, vaporized them.

Danny could feel it, the air being sucked up into seventy thousand mouths. The Dutchman ran to where Danny stood and held his arms out wide, a *how could you?* for the world to see. Even Danny's teammates looked at him as if he had changed, had become an animal, a savage. The referee didn't even hold a red card up for Danny; he just waved it in the direction of the tunnel, waved Danny away as if he couldn't even stand to look at him.

The reaction was entirely unlike the reaction at the Auld Moors when Danny had snuffed out the little Welshman. No one attacked Danny, no fight or scuffle or brawl ensued. Everyone just went silent. Even the Americans knew to be quiet.

The greatest story in football history, which had started in the fifties, was over. Someone else, for the first time in decades, was now the best footballer on the planet. Danny commenced the long walk toward the tunnel looking up at the stands, where somebody, somewhere, must have been taking apart a rifle.

He wanted more than anything to yell, "I *had* to do it! I saved him! I saved his life! I SAVED the Pearl of Brazil!" but he knew he couldn't yell. He knew he had done the right thing, but he also knew that many, many millions, and everyone in East Southwich—everyone, everywhere—thought he was nothing but a big and strong sociopath, a beast. After a summer of playing the football he had always wanted to play, a summer of scoring goals, a summer of leading his team on a journey from mediocrity to New York City, he had reverted to what they knew him to be all along. As the world watched, Danny was nothing more than a big, bearded brute. As he left the pitch, Peter Surley looked at Danny as if he wished he had never met him, and Danny saw that Juanito was crying.

I had to, Danny thought. *For the game, for the good of the game.* He wanted everyone, everyone everywhere, to know. *I had to, I had to, I had to.*

Lev knew what Danny had done, and he respected it, but Lev did not know what to do next.

THIRTY-THREE

Danny had only to deliver that man to that spot. And then Lev would shoot the patron saint of the Beautiful Game.

Lev watched as the Giganticos' medical staff hovered over the fallen hero. Danny had done one part of his job—deliver a Sniper Shot to the home team—but had botched the second part: the Pearl of Brazil had been rendered unable to take the kick. A shadow crossed the sun, as if a heavenly force had turned a dimmer down over the Bonanza Bowl. Lev smiled—just for a moment—at the realization that the crowd thought it had just seen something awful, which of course was noth-ing in comparison... but then he went through his options. His first thought was that he could take Hooper out, put a bullet through his chest. Lev thought it might have the desired effect: it would sufficiently amplify the trauma of the afternoon, and it would be a gruesome spectacle, a man shot down in his prime like that, right after doing something so awful, and on TV for the world to see. But it wasn't what Lev had been instructed to do, and he wasn't sure the morality of it fit with the mission of Soviet terror. And besides that, he couldn't find Danny on the pitch. Lev scanned the field, checked each of Rose City's play-ers for the big man, for number 5... but no Danny.

Danny had left the sunlight and the world's accusing eyes and entered the deep dark of the stadium's core. At first he couldn't see a thing, and he had a moment of real fear as a se-curity guard appeared from the shadows and grabbed him by his shoulders—but Danny relaxed when he heard the whispered words, "Good job, Danny. Now come with me."

When Danny's eyes adjusted, he saw that the guard was the man from Colorado, last seen wearing a cowboy hat and a satin jacket. "Hey," Danny said. "I know you."

"You sure do, kid. And I know what you're thinking." He pointed to his head. "You thought this was just a hat rack." Then he pushed Danny through an open door into a small changing room. "Put that on," he said, pointing to another security uniform. "Quick."

Danny got out of his soaked Revolution kit and into the security uniform. The man gave him a pair of scissors and a razor and told him to get rid of his beard. "Fast," he said. Danny did, faster than he thought he could. Felt like a new man. Just took five or six minutes to expose a face no one had seen for years.

"Gotta hurry, kid. Follow me."

Molly had spent the entire match alone in a small room deep inside the stadium. She heard the muffled murmurs of the PA, the great cheers, groans, oohs and aahs of the throng. She thought she might even know the score, though it was tough to tell the difference between the sustained exultation of a goal and the staccato excitement of a sudden great play. They hadn't left her in the dark, but they had left her alone, alone to wait and see if everyone would do what everyone had promised to do.

When news of the fifth Gigantico corner kick reached Lev's comrade deep within the stadium, he was with Three. The Russian opened a door and out walked Molly. It had been a simple plan, and both parties had upheld their end of the bargain.

Then Three shook the Russian's hand, and the Communist smiled and said, "I would like to go watch the end of the match. Good-bye."

Three resisted smiling, put his head down, took Molly by the elbow and guided her in the opposite direction. Toward Danny Hooper.

Danny heard it. Seventy thousand people above him, seventy thousand people who hated him, really truly hated him, let out a cheer, a relieved, aggrieved roar, and he knew it was 2–1 now. Someone other than the Pearl had converted the Sniper Shot, and that meant the Russians' plan was foiled, thoroughly and completely foiled, but it also meant that the Giganticos would be champions. Of course they would.

Danny and Molly's reunion was short. "No time, kids," said the man from Colorado. "There are some angry Soviets in this building. They find us, they'll kill us. Me for sure—they thought I'd turned. They thought I was their big American catch."

Danny looked at the man from Colorado.

"I told you, son. I like fucking with Russians." The man pointed toward the field. "Go," he said.

"Really?" Danny said.

"Really," the man answered.

They ran—Danny and Molly and Three and the man from Colorado—down the hall toward the pitch, passing an excited and worried medical crew carrying a small, broken man on a stretcher, and when they got there, it looked like a festival had broken out. A stage had been rolled onto the infield where second base would have been, and Tartan Ron was upon it singing something about being the Kings of America, and red, white, and blue balloons were everywhere, flying up in the air and bouncing along the grass. The Giganticos—looking like champions, because they always did, but also looking lost, reluctant, and confused without their leader—and their cheerleaders were up on the stage too, and the fans had been invited down onto the field, and Sweet Billy was onstage with Tartan Ron and the Giganticos.

The field was packed with people trying to convince themselves that everything was all right, that New York was the deserving center of the soccer universe, and beardless Danny—he kept touching his face, thinking, *Where did I go?*—and the man from Colorado and Molly and Three forced themselves through

the crowd. "There!" yelled the man from Colorado, his bravado gone now. "There they are!" A pair of workmen sprinted in
from the outfield, sprinted toward them, and the way they held
their right arms straight down at their sides showed they meant
trouble and weren't terribly concerned about collateral damage.
Three pointed toward the opposite dugout—"There, Danny, we
have to get *there*"—and Danny grabbed Molly by the hand and
pushed people aside.

The Russians closed fast. Danny took a sharp left, pulled
Molly harder than he had meant to, Three and the man from
Colorado trailing behind, and Danny knocked over a couple of
oblivious teenagers in the thralls of Tartan Ron's performance.
They lost the Russians for a moment as they found themselves
close to the stage, tangled in the swirl of kids dancing to Ron's
madcap shouting. Danny and Sweet Billy caught eyes, and Billy
yelled, "Danny *Hooper*!" and Danny looked askance and scam-
pered away.

Toward the dugout they ran now, harder, faster, past knots
of clamoring fans, and they knew that if the Russians escaped
the crowd in time they'd have a shot, and Three knew that Lev
could take any of them out from his lonely avian perch, if he
chose to, and in the madness of it all there was an even chance
no one would notice.

Lev observed the chaos unfolding below him. He knew people
in Moscow were cursing his name at that very moment and cursing a lot more than that. The Pearl of Brazil was alive, broken but
alive, and nothing more frightening than his gruesome injury
had happened at the Bicentennial Bonanza Bowl. The people of
New York were still celebrating their championship, maybe with
less joy than they might have had things ended the way they
should have, but still: there they were, down on the pitch, enjoying their decadent American party. And for all the planning—
the summer in the Oregon woods, the chasing of the Revolution

to Chicago, and to Detroit, and to New York—the worldwide television audience was left with a greater fear of Danny Hooper than of the Soviet Union.

Lev saw four people, three men and a woman, scampering across the field, and though he struggled to pick them out through the balloons' herky-jerky skyward flight, he knew that he could line up a few shots and more than likely take out two or three of the plot-foilers and get away with it, and at least have that to report back to Moscow. Within the madness, it would be so easy. He had been ready to kill today, ready enough that even though he had never wanted the Pearl dead he had gotten himself to the point of actually wanting to pull the trigger. He had wanted to be useful, to do a job. It would at least demonstrate Lev's loyalty, his hunger to injure the West, to do some small damage to the bicentennial, to show Russia's reach.

But he watched the runners run, watched the balloons rise, watched it all play out beneath him, and he prepared to leave his perch and disappear into the bedlam below.

And in an English pub, a man named Hooper sat stunned, stunned next to an empty pint glass, as men he had known for decades shuffled slowly by and clapped him silently upon his hunched-over back.

They reached the dugout, the runners, all four of them, and the tunnel, and they ran, ran again through the recesses of the great stadium, and when they passed an empty office the man from Colorado stopped Danny and Molly and said, "Go into there. There's an outfit for the two of you. Wait an hour. Then go to the Braniff terminal. Newark. Three will be there," and closed the door, and he and Three disappeared.

They held each other for a while, silently, shaking at first, then still. They spoke not a word, and no one came for them.

When they could no longer hear Tartan Ron, and the dull whisper of a dispersing crowd gave way to the low hum of the old stadium's electricity, Danny opened the door and looked around. They walked down a long passageway and saw a sign that said EXIT, and they went out that door and left.

Just left.

They got into a cab, and Danny said, "The airport, please."

Molly looked at Danny and said, "No championship, Danny."

Danny said, "No championship, Molly." He leaned against the back of his seat and let out a great breath. Danny closed his eyes for a moment, felt himself still sweating, still sweating through his strange new clothes. He patted his face where his beard used to be, and he said, "But we won."

THIRTY-FOUR

A week after the Bonanza Bowl, Three called Danny in Portland.

"Well, lad, how *are* we, then?"

"I got the girl, Three. Other than that... the world hates me, and I'm sure there isn't a football club on the planet that would have me. But I reckon things could be much, much worse."

"That's the spirit, my boy. There's someone here I'd like you to meet. Can you be at the Benson Hotel, the lobby, in half an hour?"

"Three, no more, please—"

"This is quite worth your while, Danny. I can assure you of that."

So Danny said, "Yes, OK then," hung up the phone, and got on his bicycle.

An older man, a very proper older man, sporting a high collar, a dramatic tie, and cuff links you could see across the lobby, sat next to Three in a darkened corner of the lobby sipping a cup of tea. Danny felt underdressed in a gray T-shirt and blue jeans, but he did feel cleaned up with his nice new beardless face. He strode toward the men, and as he did the men rose.

The gentleman in his collar and cuff links extended a hand. He introduced himself and said, "Pleased to meet you, Mr. Hooper. Pleased indeed," in an English accent entirely unlike Danny's.

Danny stepped back and said, "Haven't heard those words in a while, sir."

"It was brave what you did, son. What you did for your country. I admire you for it. Don't know as I would have risen to meet the moment."

Three told Danny that the man was from the FA. He had come from London to Portland to thank Danny for saving the Pearl's life. "Sit, sit," Three said to both men, and they did.

"You will understand if we are not yet able to make the details of your heroism public," the man from London said. "But we have arranged for you to visit the great man in hospital—he would like to meet you—and he has agreed to make his forgiveness known to the press and to the world. You and he will appear at a press conference together next week in New York, and the FA will make clear that we understand that you were just playing for a championship like any footballer would and you were merely doing everything in your power to win."

Danny said, "No one will buy it."

The man said, "Some will, some won't. But you're already in the good books of every chairman in the Football League. They all know the truth. Every coach in America will too. The story will make its way through our game, my boy. It will become the stuff of legend. But the public must never know how close the Russians came to doing the job. Must never know, lad."

"You came all the way to Portland to tell me this? Could've rung me."

"You deserved far more than that, Mr. Hooper. It is a most unusual circumstance, and it is my honor. I know a little bit about your career, young man. I know Aldy Taylor and Mumbles McCray. I know dear old Broomsie and I know Peter Surley. They all say the most flattering things. You're a *survivor*, Mr. Hooper. A survivor is what you are. I admire you."

Danny looked at the man, then at Three. Danny said, "You know, survivors of plane crashes eat people. Ever heard that one? It's a little something players say to each other. Surviving ain't everything, you know."

The gentleman laughed a plummy laugh, and Three grinned the sneaky grin that made him sneaky Three. The gentleman said, "A certain gallows humor must help..."

Danny said, "When it's down to the likes of the chairman of East Southwich Albion to tell you when you're past your sell-by..." Danny felt the blood in his face, felt the anger that had gotten him excused from the FA Cup, felt the rush of emotion he'd last felt when the circumstances of an otherwise well-lived life had forced him to end the Pearl's career, and he stopped himself, took a sip of lukewarm tea.

He looked at Three, then looked back at the gentleman, then said, "You'll tell me dad?"

The man nodded.

"Not ring him. Not write him. Go to East Southwich and tell him everything. I can't talk to him until you do."

The man from the Football Association said, "Mr. Hooper, I will travel as directly from here to there as I am allowed. You have my solemn word." He extended a hand, and Danny shook it, and the three of them sat and bantered about the greatest game the world had ever known until the greatest game the world had ever known turned the tea into beer and the beer into whiskey and today into tomorrow.

EPILOGUE

When the fallout from the '76 Bonanza Bowl settled, and everyone from the Pearl of Brazil himself to England's Football Association to the mad scientists who ran the American All-Star Soccer Association had offered Danny Hooper their welcomes of reentry into the global football community, Danny had a decision to make.

Despite an offer from Aldershot Taylor and the chairman of East Southwich Albion to rejoin his former club on a considerably higher salary, and despite a solicitous call or two from clubs in the higher leagues of England and Scotland, Danny determined to stay in America and see how he got on with Molly when Communists weren't lurking about. He took Peter Surley out for a pint to explain everything, and he found Juanito playing in a fall men's league game at Delta Park, watched him score five on a bunch of burly, hopeless longshoremen, and waited for him to come off the pitch, and when he did, Danny looked him in the eye and said, "I'm so sorry, Juanito." Juanito said, "It's OK, Hooper. I know you had to. I know you're a good man, number five."

Danny took a coaching job at one of the local schools that had decided to ride the wave of Portland's soccer euphoria and create a team. He regrew his beard, and he settled in to see what Oregon was like when the rains really came and the ground turned to sodden mush and the local sporting attention turned to basketball. What he found out was that Oregon looked and felt a lot like East Southwich, but with cleaner air. He felt quite at home.

Which is exactly what he was thinking when Portland's October-to-March cloud lifted, the star that warmed the planet revealed itself again, and Graham Broome started making the telephone calls that would reconvene the Rose City Revolution for the 1977 season.

The global buzz generated by the spectacle of the Bicentennial Bonanza Bowl and the sellout crowds in Portland, Seattle, Chicago, and New York had made the American All-Star Soccer Association look like a tempting investment for a motley array of business interests and civic boosters across the continent, and the league blossomed from ten teams to sixteen for the summer of '77.

Two teams joined from north of the border: La Poutine de Montreal and a version of the American SuperThunder that played in Vancouver and went by the mouthwatering name of Canadian Bacon, even though Canadians don't call it that. Just as the ersatz national team idea took hold north of the border, the SuperThunder scrapped the plan, loaded up on distinctly un-fun Englishmen, and rebranded as DCFC (the District of Columbia Fun Crew). The Cowhands moved to Anaheim to play as the Californians in a parking lot outside of Disneyland. Atlanta resuscitated the Astronauts (again), St. Louis brought back the Apple Pie, a team in Houston received the sponsorship of a space-inspired soft drink and called itself the Tang, and the new San Jose team went by "Moon Weasels" at the behest of the owner's six-year-old daughter.

The Revolution had Sweet Billy Robinson under contract, and after a Portland winter in detox he pronounced himself ready to keep his shirt on for the first few games of the season. Ivan Petrov decided to stick with the Revolution too; he and Broomsie conspired to add three more Bulgarians, and Broomsie managed to persuade a few more of the Cloppingshire boys— the good ones—to come over and give America a try. They added a spry, speedy striker named Lev—just the one name—and told their fans he was from Montenegro.

The Rose City Revolution entered the 1977 season as Pioneer Division favorites and the smart choice to represent the Frontier Conference in the Bonanza Bowl for the second straight year. Danny had the season of his life, nearly leading the team in scoring on headed-in corners alone. He was named Most Valuable Player of the Conference and the team rewarded him with a VW microbus painted in red and black stripes.

The Revolution cruised to a division title, beat the San Jose Moon Weasels and the Houston Tang in the playoffs, and hosted Red Star Toronto in the Bonanza Bowl (the Serbs had finally found their way past a less Brazilian version of the Giganticos in the Liberty Conference final).

The Revolution won 3–0. Danny nutmegged the keeper for the last goal. Nearly everyone in the sold-out Multnomah Stadium descended to the field after the game to celebrate. Someone stole Danny's shirt. Someone stole Sweet Billy Robinson too—he was never heard from again. Graham Broome cried like a baby, and Peter Surley had a massive coronary and died a splendid champion's death right there in the center circle.

The city threw a parade. The biggest street in downtown Portland, Oregon, USA, overflowed with well-wishers, and ticker tape floated through the clear, balmy summer air. Danny rode his bike. When a reporter asked him if he thought soccer would ever catch on in the United States, really catch on, Danny said, "Maybe, maybe..."

He had his championship. He had his girl. He had a home.

Meantime, Three foiled a Soviet plot to arrange for a Russian woman to win Wimbledon. Wasn't that hard—the idea was far too ridiculous be taken seriously. A Russian woman winning Wimbledon...

Danny and Molly rented a small house up in the hills, in the woods, not too far from the Grand Douglas and the hollowed-out tree where Danny had first come across Lev and his friend. There they hunkered down, parked the red-and-black-striped bus, breathed the fresh air of Soccer City, USA, and awaited their next Revolutionary adventure.

AFTERWORD

**Thoughts on Trevor Hockey (the Man on the Cover),
and Men Like Him.**

There's a Trevor Hockey goal on YouTube that, from everything
I have read, is representative of him as a player. It's from a World
Cup qualifier in 1973 between Wales and Poland. From the looks
of it, it's a soggy March evening in Cardiff; Hockey, then of Norwich City, wins a tackle in the midfield, executes a quick one-
two with a teammate, outworks an opponent for the loose ball
in the box, and fires home. He raises his arms and beams out a
massive smile before being swallowed by a mob by players and
fans. (Poland was no slouch, either—they were on their way to a
third-place finish at the '74 World Cup.) It's a moment of football
magic, the kind you live for, whether you're a player or a fan.
Three years later, after spells at Aston Villa and Bradford City
(and not quite making the World Cup), Trevor Hockey was in
bright and sunny southern California, wearing the bright and
sunny colors of the brand-new San Diego Jaws of the fairly new
North American Soccer League.

Any consideration of the NASL these days focuses on its
many peculiarities: the uniforms (no article fails to note the leather fringes of the one-year Caribous of Colorado), the Astroturf,
the shootouts, the fading superstars. But to a young soccer fan in
those days, it was less a cavalcade of soccer curiosities than our
major league; its Cosmos, Sting, Whitecaps and Rowdies were
our Steelers, Cowboys, Dodgers and Yankees. Seriously—I was
born in 1968; I didn't know the difference. Now, thanks to You-
Tube, I can watch NASL games with 2017 eyes, and while there's
plenty to laugh at—the announcers in particular—the soccer, all

things considered, is pretty good. The players manage the difficult surfaces admirably, the mix of playing styles from around the world adds spice that you didn't see in the English and German league games shown public television back then; the passing is sharp, and no one plays for a draw. And now that we're accustomed to numbers on the fronts of shirts and names on the backs, the kits aren't all bad. Especially compared to the '90s.

While Pele, Johann Cruyff, Franz Beckenbauer, Carlos Alberto, George Best and luminaries like them drew big crowds and offered the league what credibility it had, the real reason an average mid-season NASL game from the late '70s stands the test of time is because of men like Trevor Hockey. The Portland Timbers, the team I followed back then, were loaded with them: men from Villa and Wolves mostly who weren't looking for a quick buck or a vacation (though they were happy for both) but who were anxious to prove themselves to anyone who would give them a chance. I've spoken with a few of them in the planning of this story: Willie Anderson, Brian Joy, John Napier—thoughtful and generous men all—to name three, and while they laugh at some of their adventures over here, they're quick to point out that the standard was high, that players played hard, and that playing in America was a high point in their careers.

The player I had in mind when I wrote this book was Graham Day, a big and strong player from Bristol with a serious beard who came to play for the Portland Timbers in 1975 and became something of a local folk hero. Until not so long ago, I had never heard of Trevor Hockey. But then I came across the picture of him that graces the cover of this book, and thought "That's an impressive beard." After some research, I discovered that he had an impressive career too, in England and in the United States.

On April 23, 1976, Hockey, of Keighley, in West Riding of Yorkshire, England, who had played for Bradford City, Nottingham Forest, Newcastle United, Brimgham City, Villa and Norwich, made his North American Soccer League debut for the San Diego Jaws against the Rochester Lancers in front of 3,400 people at a stadium called the Aztec Bowl. A few weeks later, he played for the Jaws in Portland, against the Timbers. Over 18,000 showed up for the game, and I may have been one of them. I was seven years old. The Jaws beat the Timbers that 1976 summer day, 2-1. Hockey played in Portland the next year too, for the Las Vegas Quicksilvers, with Eusebio. That season, Hockey and the Quicksilvers beat Pele and the New York Cosmos 1-0 in Las Vegas.

Over a career that lasted from 1960 to 1978, he played in 587 senior matches, including nine for Wales. I may have used his smiling face on this cover had he not come to America—so remarkable is that beard—but it's the 42 games he played in the NASL that told me he was the right man to stand in for Danny Hooper. By all accounts, he was always the funniest and toughest man on his team—quite possibly the ideal combination in a teammate. (He was selected as San Diego's '76 player of the year.) He was known as "The Werewolf" and was known to play in rugby boots to correspond with his physical style. Trevor Hockey and all of those men who were so far from home enjoying the American summer sun and proving they belonged on the pitch with Bobby Moore (San Antonio Thunder, 1976) and Geoff Hurst (Seattle Sounders, '76) came also to help us understand what was so great about their sporting religion, and they succeeded.

When the league ran itself out of gas through bad business and poor planning in 1984, many millions of us were, nonetheless, hooked. We had lost an entire league, but we had gained a global game, and now we had our own American moments of soccer magic and nostalgia, as if we were English or Mexican, or as if we were basketball fans. The 1977 Soccer Bowl between the Cosmos and the Sounders at a sold-out Portland Civic Stadium is as watchable as any sporting event of the decade. The '79 Cosmos-Whitecaps semi-final at Giants Stadium (a game, a mini-game, two shootouts) in front of 44,000 holds its own for excitement with any Super Bowl of the era. We had our own soccer heroes, beaming out their own massive smiles from a near and friendly past populated by Roughnecks and Rogues, Diplomats and Drillers, and once you've got those no one can take them away.

Trevor Hockey died of a heart attack in 1987 after playing in a 5-a-side tournament in Keighley, in West Yorkshire, almost exactly thirty years before the publication of this book. He was 43, younger than I am as I write. (The goalscorer from that Quicksilvers-Cosmos game, Victor Arbelaez, also died on the field, collapsing while coaching a high school team at the age of 54.) Hockey remains beloved in the Keighley area; after his professional playing days, he remained a servant of the game, passing on his love of football to kids in Keighley through Trevor Hockey Soccer Camps, and he helped revive Keighley Town FC. In my successful effort to locate his family, I contacted a journalist named Clive White of the Bradford Telegraph & Argus. White gave me what help he could, and let me know that Hockey had been "one of the 'old school,' hard tackling, give-no-quarter footballers," which is what Graham Day had been too, and which is what had endeared Day to Portland's fans. "Just don't see 'em today," White said.

In time, I did find the Hockey family, who still live in the area. I first located Meltyn, Trevor's nephew. He put me in touch with Amanda and Tracy, his daughters, and then with his wife, Eileen. They have been gracious and kind, especially considering the surprising nature of my inquiry from the many thousands of miles away.

I have his family to thank for allowing me to use his picture for this book, and I have him, and the hundreds like him from all over the world, to thank for converting me to the greatest game on the planet.

Dennie Wendt
Portland, Oregon
2017

ABOUT THE AUTHOR

Dennie Wendt is a veteran storyteller from the shoe and soccer business. He has been a copywriter, creative director and marketer, mostly for Nike and Converse, and was the public address announcer for the Portland Pride of the Continental Indoor Soccer League. He spent a year in the '80s on the junior team at FK Proleter Zrenjanin, when that was still Yugoslavia. He has written for *Portland Magazine* and *Howler*, among others, and he is a graduate of the University of Portland. *Hooper's Revolution* is his first novel.